Jayci Lee writes po[...] romance every free s[...] in sunny California [...] husband, two amazin[...] a fluffy rescue whose cuteness is a major distraction. At times, she cannot accommodate reality because her brain is full of drool-worthy heroes and badass heroines clamouring to come to life. Because of all the books demanding to be written, Jayci writes full-time now and is semi-retired from her fifteen-year career as a defence lawyer. She loves food, wine and travelling, and, incidentally, so do her characters. Books have always helped her grow, dream and heal, and she hopes her books will do the same for you.

Reese Ryan writes sexy, contemporary romance featuring a diverse cast of complex characters. She presents her characters with family and career drama, challenging love interests and life-changing secrets while treating readers to emotional love stories with unexpected twists. Past president of her local RWA chapter and a panellist at the 2017 *Los Angeles Times* Festival of Books, Reese is an advocate of the romance genre and diversity in fiction. Visit her online at ReeseRyan.com

Besides writing, **Ann Major** enjoys her husband, kids, grandchildren, cats, hobbies, and travels. A Texan, Ann holds a BA from UT, and an MA from Texas A & M. A former teacher on both the secondary and college levels, Ann is an experienced speaker. She's written over sixty books for Mills & Boon and frequently makes bestseller lists.

Indecent Proposals

Indecent Proposals
The Rival

JAYCI LEE

REESE RYAN

ANN MAJOR

MILLS & BOON

All rights reserved including the right of reproduction in whole or in part in any form. This edition is published by arrangement with Harlequin Enterprises ULC.

This is a work of fiction. Names, characters, places, locations and incidents are purely fictional and bear no relationship to any real life individuals, living or dead, or to any actual places, business establishments, locations, events or incidents. Any resemblance is entirely coincidental.

This book is sold subject to the condition that it shall not, by way of trade or otherwise, be lent, resold, hired out or otherwise circulated without the prior consent of the publisher in any form of binding or cover other than that in which it is published and without a similar condition including this condition being imposed on the subsequent purchaser.

® and TM are trademarks owned and used by the trademark owner and/or its licensee. Trademarks marked with ® are registered with the United Kingdom Patent Office and/or the Office for Harmonisation in the Internal Market and in other countries.

First Published in Great Britain 2022
By Mills & Boon, an imprint of HarperCollins*Publishers,* Ltd
1 London Bridge Street, London, SE1 9GF

www.harpercollins.co.uk

HarperCollins*Publishers*
1st Floor, Watermarque Building,
Ringsend Road, Dublin 4, Ireland

INDECENT PROPOSALS: THE RIVAL © 2022 Harlequin Enterprises ULC.

Temporary Wife Temptation © 2020 Judith J. Yi
A Reunion of Rivals © 2020 Roxanne Ravenel
Terms of Engagement © 2012 Ann Major

ISBN: 978-0-263-31784-8

MIX
Paper | Supporting
responsible forestry
FSC™ C007454

This book is produced from independently certified FSC™ paper
to ensure responsible forest management.

For more information visit: www.harpercollins.co.uk/green

Printed and Bound in Spain using 100% Renewable electricity at
CPI Black Print, Barcelona

TEMPORARY WIFE TEMPTATION

JAYCI LEE

To my tall, dark and handsome husband.
You'll always be my favorite hero.

One

In reality, Garrett Song, Hansol Incorporated's VP of Business and Development, was just a man. A creature of flesh and blood. Yet from everyone's awe and fascination, he might as well have been the Dark Knight.

His grandparents had founded Hansol Incorporated, and it was now one of the top fashion retailers in the country. It was the Song family's hard work and dedication that accounted for its success, and Garrett was a Song through and through. His workaholism was renowned in the industry, and Natalie Sobol had witnessed it firsthand. Well, not in person, but through emails and phone calls.

Prior to transferring to Los Angeles a month ago, he'd worked out of the New York office. When the VP of Human Resources there had gone on medical leave last year, Natalie was appointed the interim VP to manage her key duties. She'd worked remotely from the LA office, and reported to Garrett Song for eight weeks. He was exacting but unerringly fair, and she respected his keen intelligence and dedication to the company. And she could swear there was a wicked sense of humor beneath his curt, dry words.

Now that he was in LA, Natalie couldn't fathom why he couldn't find half an hour to review and sign the HR documents to finalize his transfer. A pang of disappointment and anger jarred her equilibrium. Did he think his royal status put him above ordinary employees? Had she misjudged him so abysmally?

"Well, tough," she muttered, tapping her pen against his empty personnel file. Everyone had to abide by the company's policies and procedures. Even the company's heir apparent.

It was a good thing she was skilled at putting arrogant executives in their places. She hadn't become the youngest HR director at Hansol by cowering from her responsibilities. *Hell, no.* She would lay down the law this minute. After placing a neat stack of unsigned documents into his folder and tucking it under her arm, Natalie headed for his corner office. No matter how entitled he felt, he should be able to sign documents placed right under his nose.

After the briefest of knocks, she stepped into his office and shut the door behind her with an audible click. From the slim metal-and-glass desk to the single abstract painting on the otherwise bare wall, it was a great deal more stylish and far less pretentious than his counterparts' offices.

His head was bent over the desk, dark hair glinting in the sunlight from the window. Her heart stuttered with the sudden awareness; she was finally meeting Garrett Song in person. *This isn't a social visit, Nat.* She marched up to his desk, her sensible pumps clacking on the floor like the beat of a battle drum, but he didn't bother looking up. *Ugh. Is he waiting for a formal announcement of my arrival?* She raised a fist to her mouth, but the "ahem" never made it past her throat.

"Yes?" Garrett Song raised his head and his dark brown

eyes locked on hers. She felt hot and cold at once, her heart tripping over itself. The grapevine had been on fire due to his renowned good looks, but she hadn't been prepared for his magnetic presence. The man was breathtaking and she was reminded, with shocking intensity, that she was very much a woman.

You didn't come to drool over him. You came to reprimand him.

"Mr. Song, I'm Natalie Sobol." She stuck out her hand, relieved to see how steady it was. "It's a pleasure to finally meet you in person."

"Ms. Sobol." He nodded, accepting her proffered hand. "The pleasure's all mine. I haven't forgotten your invaluable work as the interim VP of HR. You're truly an asset to our company."

His compliment brought color to her cheeks, and sparks skipped along her skin as her body responded to the warmth of his hand. She noticed how his broad shoulders and muscular arms strained against the confines of his dress shirt. His upper-class polish barely contained his raw strength and sexuality. Did he ever let his control slip? Let his powerful sensuality burst through? Natalie suddenly wanted to be the one to shatter his control.

"What can I do for you?" he asked.

Startled out of her reverie, she tugged on her hand to break contact. For a second, it felt as though he tightened his grip, but then she was free. With her expression restored to polite indifference, she placed the folder on his desk. It didn't matter that he made her blood rush; he was an executive of Hansol and she was its HR director. It would be unprofessional of her to so much as smile too warmly at him.

"What's this?" His eyebrows drew together and his gaze turned glacial as he scanned the papers inside.

"Your personnel file." Natalie cleared her throat and

drew her shoulders back. "And a written warning for violating company policies."

"I can see what it is, Ms. Sobol. What is it *for*?" He enunciated each word with care.

"All employees are required to sign their employment documents within two weeks of hiring, or in your case, transfer. You've been here over a month, but you still haven't signed them. As the HR director, I have a duty to write you up for violating a company policy."

He stared at Natalie as though she'd sprouted a third eye on her forehead. Then, he leaned back in his seat and crossed his arms over his chest, making everything bulge and strain against his shirt. *Gah.* It was so much easier to work with him when she didn't have to look at him.

"Of course, if you sign the documents here and now, I won't put the written warning in your personnel file." Her words tripped over each other. She'd taken on many executives as part of her daily dose of kick ass, but none of them had melted her bones before. She stomped down on the lust raging low in her stomach.

"Correct me if I'm wrong," Garrett drawled, "but that sounds curiously like a threat."

"I don't see how doing my job comes across as a threat to you." Her words were laced with iron. "It's imperative I enforce company policies consistently across the board."

"If you want to insist on going strictly by the book, you're violating a company policy right now. Employees are entitled to a verbal warning prior to a written warning. Isn't that correct, Ms. Sobol?"

She already knew he was well versed in the company policies, but she was impressed nonetheless. Unfortunately for him, she knew them better.

"HR gave you countless reminders. Those were more than adequate preliminary warnings. But if you prefer the process to be more official, I'll be sure to invite you to my office for your next verbal warning."

"I appreciate your dedication to Hansol." His full lips quirked into a sexy grin in an abrupt shift in mood. *Or tactic.* "Why don't I sign the documents now? Please have a seat."

Damn it. She was dying to get out of his office—she didn't understand her reaction to him and she didn't like it—but he'd effectively trapped her. Gritting her teeth, she sat down and clasped her hands on her lap.

Virility radiated from him. She'd seen good-looking men before, but she hadn't been so attracted to a man since... well, since forever.

He worked his way through the short stack of papers. His shirtsleeves were rolled past his elbows, exposing solid forearms that looked smooth and tanned, as if he spent his days in the sun rather than in an office building. She bit her lip, unable to stop imagining the rest of him. He had a light smattering of hair on his muscular chest that tapered off above his smooth, sculpted abs only to resurface below his navel as it darkened toward his...

Stop! Natalie couldn't lust after Garrett Song. She would be a hypocrite to even think about an office romance. She was the HR director, for heaven's sake.

"That wasn't too hard." He gave her a rueful smile. "I apologize for the delay."

"Apology accepted."

Natalie jumped to her feet, eager to escape him, but he proceeded to tap the papers on his desk, straightening them with exaggerated care. Then he placed the neat stack in the folder in slow motion before holding it out to her. The man was immensely irritating.

Not trusting what she might say, Natalie snatched the folder from him and speed walked out of his office. Her unannounced arrival and abrupt departure might've con-

vinced him she was strange and rude, but better that than
throwing herself across his desk and begging him to rav-
ish her. *I bet he's an excellent ravisher.*

Besides, he could have his pick of beautiful women out
there. He'd never be interested in someone ordinary like
her. Even if he got bonked in the head and became interested in her, she had Sophie to think of.

Sophie.

Her hormone-frenzied thoughts ground to a halt. The air
rushed out of her lungs as grief rushed in, raw and real. It
hit her out of nowhere, as it often did since that fateful car
crash over a month ago.

Traci was gone.

Natalie rushed the last few feet to her office and shut
the door as a ragged sob escaped her lips. Traci's husband,
Parker, the older brother Natalie had always wished for,
had died on impact. Her older sister had hung on until she
reached her side in the hospital.

"Promise me," Traci had said as she gripped her hand.

"Anything." The last member of Natalie's family had
been slipping away. "Just don't leave me."

"Raise Sophie as your daughter." Her eyes bore into
Natalie's, frantic and terrified. "Promise. Me."

"I promise," she had pledged.

Her sister's dying wish meant little to the law. Lily and
Steve Davis, Sophie's paternal grandparents and next of
kin, would become her legal guardians by default. The
chances of the court granting Natalie's adoption application were abysmal, especially with the Davises opposing
the adoption. They were good people, but Sophie was their
last link to Parker, and they intended to take her to New
York with them even if it meant a drawn-out custody battle.

Meanwhile, a social worker had told Natalie that two-
parent families in a high-income bracket had better chances

of adopting. Too bad she couldn't pull a wealthy husband out of a hat like a fluffy, white bunny.

Natalie would do anything to give her niece a happy, carefree childhood. She and Traci knew what it meant to grow up without a mom.

With a forlorn sigh, she reached for her mouse and clicked through the forty-seven emails she'd received while she was in Garrett Song's office. One in particular caught her attention.

"What?" She rubbed her eyes and read the email again. She had to be hallucinating from her desperation. "No. Freaking. Way."

The current VP of Human Resources was retiring at the end of the year, and the company wanted to promote internally. The position had a six-figure salary with generous benefits—*Sophie, I could send you to a Montessori preschool!*—and the opening was in *New York.* Surely, the Davises would be open to negotiating custody if they could remain a large part of their granddaughter's life.

It was about time Fate threw her a bone.

If she could get the promotion, then all she needed was a husband to seal the deal. Without warning, an image of Garrett Song filled her head. His strength. His raw masculinity. Her breath caught at the visceral intrusion and heat gathered at her center before she shook it off.

What did Garrett have to do with anything?

For the first time in his nearly two months at the LA office, Garrett left work early. His grandmother had summoned him, saying she wanted to see his face before she forgot what he looked like. It was his grandmother's passive-aggressive way of telling him she wasn't happy with his biweekly visits.

She lived with his father and his younger sister at their family home in Pacific Palisades. The fact that he didn't move back in when he returned to Los Angeles was still a touchy subject with her. Customarily, Korean folks lived with their parents and grandparents until they got married. Garrett planned on dying a bachelor, and getting his own place now was a good way to start acclimating his elders to the idea.

He navigated the surface roads to avoid rush-hour traffic but eventually got on the freeway and joined the other cars crawling five miles per hour. Stuck in the mind-numbing commute, Garrett's thoughts wandered to Natalie Sobol as it had done numerous times in the last several weeks.

Hell.

He dragged in a deep breath, his shirt stretching across his chest.

When she first walked in, he'd thought—with a flash of annoyance—that she was one of their Korean-American models, tall and beautiful. He was too busy to listen to her lie about getting lost on her way to the design department, a classic but unimaginative ploy used by women to get intimate with his wallet. But as she drew closer, he'd noticed her startling whiskey eyes, creamy skin and hourglass curves, and forgot his irritation and suspicions. She was stunning, and desire pumped through him.

Then she'd introduced herself.

For the briefest moment, he'd lusted after Hansol's HR director. Someone he enjoyed working with and valued as an employee. He and the VP of HR had even discussed Natalie Sobol as her potential successor.

Restless, he changed lanes and advanced a half-car's length. She wasn't even his type. He preferred the sophisticated women from his own circle who understood no-strings-attached affairs. Everyone knew the rules and no one got hurt.

He cringed and shoved his fingers through his hair. From her button-up shirt to her knee-length skirt, she'd been the picture of professionalism. Oddly, rather than turning him off, something about her meticulous demeanor had made him want to…dishevel her. Undo her buttons and hike up her skirt—

He slapped his cheeks like a drowsy driver fighting the sweet temptation of sleep. Having the sudden hots for an employee was inconvenient and messy. Their HR director, at that. As a rule, Garrett never dated anyone in the company.

And the timing was diabolical. A scandal so close to his CEO appointment could have consequences more dire than mere personal humiliation. It could destabilize the entire corporation, and sabotage his plan for a partnership with Vivotex, the largest fashion group in the world. His family had worked too hard and sacrificed too much for him to risk the company's reputation and the livelihood of thousands of employees over his libido.

And his grandmother. The eighty-year-old was still as sharp as a surgical knife but she was growing frailer than she let on. If she lost face because of him, she would give herself a heart attack by sheer force of will. A small one, just enough to cram a healthy dose of guilt down his throat.

Damn it.

His self-control had shifted as he held Natalie's eyes. He'd wanted to kiss the woman with a white-hot lust he couldn't comprehend. As far as he was concerned, Natalie Sobol was the devil incarnate sent to toy with him, and he planned to avoid her at all costs.

He arrived at his family home with fifty minutes left until his meeting with a potential business partner, Clark Nobu. He was the backbone of Vivotex's board of directors, and earning his trust would boost Hansol's chances for a partnership.

"Hey, Gare. Colin's taking me to one of his new clubs." His sister, decked out in a black sequined dress that was six inches too short, skipped down the staircase and pecked him on the cheek. "Bye, Gare."

"Good seeing you, too, Adelaide," he said dryly. Their cousin Colin ran several successful nightclubs in Koreatown and Hollywood. A self-made man. Garrett respected that, but the family branded him as the black sheep. "I'm rooting for Colin but he can't avoid Grandmother forever."

"I know." A somber shadow clouded Adelaide's eyes. "And I'm rooting for you, *oppa*. Good luck with Grandmother."

"Yeah, thanks. Have fun, kiddo." He frowned at her back as she hurried out of the house.

After their mom died, Garrett had done his best for his baby sister, but there was only so much a fifteen-year-old boy could do for a seven-year-old girl. By the time their dad emerged from years of grief, Adelaide was a petulant high-school kid who switched boyfriends like pairs of old shoes, seeking affection and comfort from superficial relationships.

Adelaide was smarter than him, though. Watching his father fall apart after his mom's death hadn't been enough to teach him the destructive force of love. It had taken Samantha to nail home the lesson and bleed him dry of sentimental delusions. Even years after their breakup, the mere thought of her singed him with a flash of betrayal and humiliation.

Garrett knocked and entered his grandmother's room. It didn't contain any Western furniture, such as a bed or chairs. Rather, she sat with her back ramrod straight on a thick floor mattress with her Samsung laptop set up on a low table beside her in a fusion of the old and the new.

"Hal-muh-nee." He bowed at his waist, then kneeled in front of her on a *bang-suk*, taking his usual position on the comfortable floor cushion. "How was your day?"

"The usual. Incompetent idiots running around like their asses were on fire." She was fluent in English but she spoke to him in Korean. An outsider would be thrown by the conversation conducted in two different languages—as though there was an invisible translator between them translating English into Korean and Korean into English at lightning speed. "Did you eat?"

"I had dinner at the office."

"Good. Sit down more comfortably."

That was code for him to settle down for a long conversation. Garrett shifted to sit with his legs crossed in front of him and waited for her to speak.

"We have half a year until you're appointed CEO. I trust you're diligently preparing for your new duties."

"Of course, Grandmother." They both knew he was ready to run the company. He'd been trained for the job since he was a child.

She nodded and breathed deeply. If he didn't know better, Garrett would've thought she was hesitating, but that was preposterous. She wielded her authority with unwavering confidence.

"When we announce you as Hansol's new CEO at the press conference, we will also announce your engagement."

"My what?" His heart lurched as he studied his grandmother's face. *Did she have a stroke without anyone noticing?* "Are you feeling all right?"

"Of course I'm all right." She waved aside his question with an impatient shake of her head. "As I was saying, we will announce your engagement to Jihae Park of the Rotelle Corporation in Korea."

His blood chilled as disbelief turned to outrage. Every minute of his life had been micromanaged to mold him into the perfect heir. Edges that didn't fit into that box were sliced off without mercy. Skateboarding was for hooligans. Golf was more appropriate. Basketball could get too rough. Tennis reflected higher culture. *Now she wants to decide who I marry?*

His parents' marriage had been a union of two wealthy Korean-American families and their businesses. They had found love and happiness in their arranged marriage, but when his mother succumbed to cancer, the warmth and laughter in their home had faded away. Garrett and his sister's childhood had been dominated by the sterile, suffocating demands of upholding their family name.

"Am I being married off to the woman or the corporation?" He forced his voice to remain calm.

"You…" Her eyes widened to reveal an unnatural amount of white around her irises. "You dare talk back to me?"

A stab of guilt pierced his heart, but Garrett clenched his fists and pressed them onto the hard floor in front of him. His grandparents had built Hansol from the ground up, working sixteen-hour days in front of sewing machines, their eyes going blind and their fingers deteriorating with arthritis. After a decade of single-minded determination, Hansol opened its first retail store and took its place as an up-and-coming fashion retailer in mainstream America, but his grandfather passed away too soon to see his dream realized. To Grandmother, Hansol was more than a company. It was her late husband's soul.

"I've obeyed you without question my entire life because I know of the sacrifices you've made for our family, but an arranged marriage is out of the question." He'd rather crawl across sizzling lava than become a bartered stud for the Song family. "Please reconsider, *hal-muh-nee*."

"Min-*ah*." As his grandmother addressed him by his Korean name, her stern features softened imperceptibly. "I arranged the match with your best interest at heart. Jihae is a lovely, accomplished child from a well-respected *jae-bul* family. She will make a good wife and mother."

"My best interest? And it has nothing to do with having a *jae-bul* granddaughter-in-law who will bear you *jae-*

bul grandchildren?" The only way to obtain the power and authority of a *jae-bul*—the rich, pseudoroyal families in Korea—was through birth or marriage. No matter how successful, the Songs were still part of the nouveaux riches, not a *jae-bul* family. "Grandmother, I respect our heritage and want the best for Hansol, but I could uphold our family name without a *jae-bul* wife."

"Such insolence. Defying your elders." She bowed her head and shook it slowly as though she was too ashamed to hold it up. "This is my fault. After your mother died, I did my best to raise you and your sister right, but it's obvious I failed you."

Garrett swallowed a roar of frustration. Reasoning and pleading wouldn't get him anywhere with his grandmother. She was ruthless and obstinate, and she would hold her ground until it crumbled beneath her. It was time to reclaim his life.

"You haven't failed. You raised us to stand up for ourselves and to fight for what we believe in." His voice shook with colliding emotions. Taking a deep breath, he straightened his back. He wasn't the scared young boy who'd lost his mom. He was a grown man and it was time his grandmother accepted it—even if he had to lie to get it across to her. "I'm already engaged to another woman, and I will fight for her."

For the second time that evening, she was at a loss for words, but only for a moment. "Well, you need to tell the *other woman* the engagement is off. There is no harm done, yet. The press is unaware of either engagement."

"No harm done? I was taught that honor should be upheld at all costs. Casting aside the woman I love to marry another with wealth and power is not honorable."

"I am your grandmother. Do not presume to lecture me about honor." Her slight figure trembled with outrage. "If you do not marry Jihae, I will stop you from ascending to the CEO position. Don't forget I am the majority share-holder."

"And I'm the most qualified CEO candidate, and the only one who could deliver the Vivotex partnership. If you vote against me, you'll be voting against the company." Garrett stood and bowed to her. "I'm keeping my promise to my fiancée. I trust you to act with Hansol's best interest in mind."

With those last words, he left the house with long, fast strides. There was rebelling and there was *rebelling*. He was surprised his grandmother hadn't passed out. Then again, she wouldn't be Grace Song if she showed weakness in the face of adversity.

Garrett planted his hands on the hood of his car as vertigo blurred his vision. Not only did he now have to find a fiancée, but he also had to marry her. If not executed flawlessly, his plan could split his family apart, and Hansol could take a blow. There was no room for error.

Once he secured the partnership with Vivotex, his grandmother wouldn't oppose his CEO appointment. She would never put her personal agenda ahead of the good of the company. Hansol meant too much to her. But Garrett wasn't safe from her interference with his personal life until he married his imaginary fiancée.

Where can I find the perfect bride? He slid into the driver's seat with a mirthless laugh. *Now there's one question I never thought I'd ask myself.* His brief dalliance with self-pity and panic ceased as he focused on how to pull this off. His partner in crime had to be someone discreet, practical and desperate enough to agree to a fake marriage. Simple. Raking his hand through his hair, he stepped on the accelerator and made a sharp left, heading toward Melrose.

A real marriage was the last thing Garrett wanted to inflict on himself. It made little difference whether it was an arranged union or a love match. Marriage was a senseless gamble. He would never risk the kind of love that could break a man and his family.

When Garrett drove onto Melrose, the traffic stopped, killing any breeze he was able to enjoy. As soon as he saw the club's valet sign, he shot out of his car and tossed the key to the parking attendant.

He grimaced as he stepped into the meat market known as Le Rêve, and headed for the private VIP room. Garrett usually steered clear of places like this, but Nobu was a widower who thrived on the kind of excitement Le Rêve had to offer.

Garrett was relieved the VIP room was empty. But the civil war he'd instigated with his grandmother wrapped him in a fog of anger. How had it to come to this? He pinched the bridge of his nose as tension built in his temples. When his phone buzzed in his back pocket, he sighed with resignation, knowing it was Nobu canceling.

I'm tied up in a work emergency. Not getting out of here until past midnight. My apologies. I owe you one.

Garrett was officially off the clock. He huffed a humorless laugh. If he married that Korean heiress, he would never be off the clock. Even the most intimate aspects of his life would be intertwined with Hansol. He was tempted to grab a stiff drink, but he didn't get drunk in public and rarely did so in private. Control was much too valuable, but tonight, his was dangerously close to shattering.

Where the hell would he find his convenient bride?

Two

The cool silk of the dress caressed Natalie's bare skin as she inched forward in line. She winced at the reminder that a slip of fabric was all that stood between the world and her rear end. Sighing, she crossed "going commando" off her bucket list.

"You. Lady in red."

When no one stepped up, she craned her neck to peer behind her. Maybe the bouncer meant the blonde in hot pink? After three seconds, Natalie realized he meant her.

"Come on through, gorgeous." His smirk was a tooth short of a leer.

According to her internet research, Le Rêve's Hulk look-alike bouncers upheld the less-is-more philosophy. Her dress was definitely less. The strap of her scarlet mini flowed into a bodice that exposed a third of her right breast, and the back of her dress... Well, there wasn't one. Natalie didn't recognize herself in the mirror, especially with her dramatic eye makeup, but she couldn't afford to be modest. Getting in mattered too much, especially as it was a Friday night and everyone was dressed to kill.

Forcing a smile, she sashayed past Hulk Number One and ascended the steep staircase in her four-inch stilettos. Natalie reached the top without falling on her face or mooning the crowd. *Yes-s-s.* She pulled back her elbow in a discreet fist pump.

Lily Davis had called at 4:00 a.m., sobbing and hiccupping a jumble of words, including "Sophie," "high fever" and "vomiting." Natalie had instructed Sophie's grandparents to take the baby to the nearest emergency room from their hotel and rushed over to meet them. By the time the doctor explained that it was a twenty-four-hour virus a lukewarm bath would've eased, she'd missed her interview for the VP position.

Stupid rookie mistake. She should've researched the symptoms online instead of panicking like that. But the damage was done. Natalie had no luck rescheduling her interview. The hiring committee had decided staying with her sick niece in the ER rather than showing up for the interview proved she lacked the commitment for an executive position. They'd waved aside her explanation as though she was making a my-dog-ate-my-homework excuse. She gritted her teeth at the unfairness.

What had happened this morning could ruin the one chance she had at adopting Sophie. But it wasn't over yet. It couldn't be over. Garrett Song was the future CEO of Hansol. Surely, he could convince the hiring committee to give her a second chance. Ambushing him at a nightclub wasn't the most professional move, but she had run out of options.

According to his calendar, he was having a business meeting at the club, which also meant there was a good chance of his leaving for a business trip the next day. This might be the last chance she had to talk to him face-to-face for a few weeks. There was no time to waste, so Natalie had resorted to desperate measures.

Squaring her shoulders, she ventured deeper into foreign territory. Her lips parted at the sight of beautiful people writhing and rocking to the DJ's mixes. They made sweaty, drunk and horny look attractive. The blinking strobe lights and reverberating bass pulsed in rhythm with her jackhammering heart. Natalie unclenched her clammy fists. *Just find him, ask him and leave.*

But first, she needed liquid courage.

Icy blue accent lights slashed artfully across the circular bar, its central column of spirits reaching high to the distant ceiling. *How in the world could they get those bottles down?*

Natalie shook her head to rein in her wandering thoughts, then froze. She'd spent an hour taming her black curls, but they were already straining against the five hundred bobby pins holding them down. She had half an hour, tops, before she turned into Medusa. At the hottest club on Melrose. *That's just swell.*

Hustling through a tiny space between revelers, she managed to snag a stool, then waved for a bartender. A boyish mixologist with tattoos hugging his biceps gave her a nod and a wink, as he performed a hair-raising cocktail stunt involving two jiggers and a tumbler for another customer. After all the juggling and shaking, the pink liquid he finally poured into the martini glass was underwhelming. Even the fresh mint and cucumber garnish—added with a flourish—couldn't save it.

When Biceps made his way over to her, she took a deep breath and broke his heart. "Double Scotch. Neat."

"Any particular brand?" he asked, pouting at the sheer uncoolness of her order.

"Bowmore. Twenty-five years old."

"Nice." His eyebrows drew up and he flashed a grin. "A beautiful woman who knows her whiskey."

She smiled back, glad she'd dodged the showman's bullet, but her relief was short-lived.

"Power up!" he hollered.

"Power up!" his compatriots echoed.

A few customers clapped excitedly as a small skateboard-like contraption with handlebars zoomed around the liquor column on hidden tracks and stopped where Biceps waited. He stepped on and secured a harness around his waist, becoming the center of attention as he spiraled upward. Grasping the bottle of Bowmore from the top of the column, he descended like a rock star.

By the time he handed her the Scotch, her cheeks were burning and she seriously considered hiding under the bar. It was bad enough being at a club, not wearing much at all, without a bunch of strangers staring at her.

Forcing herself to relax, she took a long sip. The whiskey caressed her throat and kindled a fire in her stomach. She closed her eyes and smiled at the simple pleasure. When she opened them again, Biceps was standing in front of her, sporting an odd gape-mouthed look. Then, sudden realization flamed her cheeks.

"Oh, jeez. I'm so sorry." She hurriedly grabbed her credit card from her clutch and handed it to him. "Here you go. Thank you."

Looking a little embarrassed, he enveloped her outstretched hand in his. "The drink's on me, beautiful."

"That won't be—"

"My name's Kenny and I get off in three hours. Can you stick around?" His lips curled into a boyish smile. It was only when his gaze lingered on her cleavage she realized he was hitting on her.

"I can't, um... I..." Natalie had no idea what to do. She wasn't used to getting hit on at a bar.

"Thanks, Kenny," a deep voice rumbled behind her. "I got this."

Natalie stiffened in her seat as the hair on her arms stood on tiptoe and a shiver ran down her spine. The deep, rich voice did strange things to her body, but she wasn't sure she approved of the stranger's high-handedness. Either way, she couldn't face him until she reined in her galloping pulse, so she downed the Scotch in a single tilt.

"As a matter of fact, why don't you put her drink on my tab?" A strong, long-fingered hand passed a hundred-dollar bill to Kenny, who dropped her hand and accepted the tip with a grudging shrug, bowing out to the alpha.

Okay. She definitely did not like that. Natalie spun around to give the arrogant stranger a verbal ass kicking, but the sharp challenge froze and died a quiet death on her lips.

The stranger with the sexy voice was none other than Garrett Song, and he was even more magnificent outside of the office. He was closer than she'd thought—only a few inches separated them when their gazes collided. The amusement flickered out of his eyes and a charged silence tightened around them.

Natalie vaguely heard Kenny's curt "two double Scotch, neat," but she remained fixated on Garrett's jet-black hair, strong jawline and full lips. *And my, oh, my, those fiery eyes.* Her gaze flitted down to his broad shoulders, chest and long, muscular legs. The conservative dress shirt and slacks couldn't hide the power of his body.

Her heart fluttered like a dragonfly taking flight under his insolent perusal. His face didn't register a hint of recognition, which wasn't surprising. Natalie didn't resemble the woman he'd seen at work.

Natalie drained her second drink without breaking eye contact. She uncrossed her legs and slid off her seat, her calf accidentally grazing the side of his body. She was about his height in her four-inch heels, so they faced each other squarely. His heat embraced her, and his masculine scent, like an autumn wind, beckoned her closer.

She couldn't follow her instincts to climb her boss like a tree even if her inner thighs were slick with desire. She would act professionally. Natalie would state her business and not take no for an answer. She opened her mouth but promptly closed it shut.

Apparently, she'd forgotten how to speak.

Garrett was lost from the moment she swiveled in her seat.

She had glided into the club as he was leaving. Then his legs had brought him to her without his permission. Her sculpted body was meant to bring men to their knees. And her dress seemed like it had been painted onto her lush curves.

The sight of her made him weak with lust, but her air of vulnerability made him want to shield her from other hungry eyes. His fervent urge to possess and protect the woman tripped all kinds of alarms in his head, but his brain had decided to take an inopportune hiatus.

"Dance with me," he said.

Her eyes widened and his pulse quickened in anticipation. She looked familiar but he wouldn't forget a woman like her if he'd met her before. He held out his hand and she stared at it, her head cocked like a curious bird. After a pause, she placed her hand in his. It was warm, smooth and delicate. The thrill of their connection gripped him by the shoulders and shook him alert.

As their feet touched the dance floor, Garrett wrapped his arm around her waist, cradling her right hand against his chest. They swayed softly to the music while the crowd gyrated around them. He brushed his fingertips against her bare back. Her skin was like warm silk. As a gnawing hunger filled him to the brim, Garrett laid his palm on her lower back and pressed her body flush against his. A tremor ran through her.

God, she feels so good. He struggled to make sense of her—the stark contrast between innocent wide eyes and a body that radiated raw sensuality.

"Who are you?" he rasped.

Her eyelids fluttered at his question as though he had awakened her from a dream. She shook her head briskly and a veil shifted across her face. Suddenly, he recognized her and his arms fell to his sides.

"You…you really don't know who I am?" she said, unease crossing her lovely features.

That thrill. He'd only felt it once before, and he belatedly realized this was the same woman who'd made him feel it the first time.

Was her voice this velvety when she barged into my office?

"Should I know you?" He stalled to figure out what her game was.

Samantha had been his first lesson in gold diggers, but she certainly hadn't been his last. Naturally, Garrett considered himself something of an expert on the issue, and Natalie Sobol didn't fit the profile. He trusted and respected her. She had backbone and integrity, which made her damn good at her job. Even so, she must've orchestrated their run-in to get something out of him.

"I'm…" She cleared her throat and drew back her shoulders. Regrettably for him, the small adjustment managed to thrust her glorious breasts forward, nearly derailing his focus. "It's Natalie Sobol, Mr. Song."

"Call me Garrett," he said, leading her by the arm to the relative privacy of the outdoor balcony. "While we're getting familiar, care to tell me what you're up to?"

He couldn't make out her expression in the moonlight,

but he heard a sharp intake of breath. To his surprise, she didn't pretend their run-in was a coincidence.

"I came here to ask you for a second chance." She spoke quietly, but her words carried the weight of determination.

"A second chance at what?"

"VP of Human Resources. I missed my interview because of a family emergency, but I'm confident I could do the job better than anyone else."

So that was her game. His lips twisted. "How do you suppose I fit into that?"

"Please. All I ask for is a chance to get my interview. You'll soon be our new CEO. The hiring committee would listen to your request." She swallowed, hesitating for a second. "Please believe me when I say I would never dream of imposing on you like this if I had any other choice. I need that job."

She was good. He'd long outgrown any disappointment at being used for his money or connections. But he almost believed this woman. Sympathized with her. Garrett hadn't allowed anyone to manipulate his emotions since Samantha, and his brief slip infuriated him. It made him want to test her.

"And are you offering something in return?" He didn't bother disguising his disdain.

She gasped and her hands clenched into fists. He watched through hooded lids as pride, anger and mortification splashed across her features. Then, she breathed slowly through her nose before replying in measured tones.

"I'm offering to be the best VP of Human Resources Hansol has ever had." She arched an eyebrow in cold challenge. "Do I need to offer anything beyond that?"

When he didn't respond right away, Natalie turned her back on him and strode toward the door with the poise and dignity of a queen. *Damn it*. He caught up with her and grasped her arm, trying not to notice her warmth.

"Wait."

It was true. She was a perfect fit for the position, especially with her experience as the interim VP. She wouldn't have needed his help if she hadn't missed her interview. Maybe he'd misread her. It was difficult to think with so much of his blood pumping away from his brain.

"Are you willing to consider my request?" Her tone was clipped, but at least she was talking to him.

He understood the hiring committee's refusal to reschedule her interview—reliability was the bare minimum requirement for an executive position—but Garrett respected her decision to put her family before her promotion. He was only too familiar with putting his family ahead of his own needs.

Garrett froze. It couldn't have been more than a few hours since his declaration of independence. What if the key to his freedom stood in front of him? Natalie's appearance was timely enough to be eerie. She was intelligent, pragmatic and *desperate*—maybe even desperate enough to accept his unconventional proposal.

"Yes, and you can help me in return."

"You need my help?" Her eyes widened in surprise, but not alarm. He was gratified she didn't jump to an unsavory conclusion despite his earlier brutishness.

Garrett scanned their surroundings. They had some privacy in their corner of the patio, but a popular nightclub wasn't the place for a lengthy discussion of his plans.

"I need a wife."

"You want me to find you a wife?" Her eyebrows scrunched together as though she was struggling to untangle an intricate knot.

"No. I want *you* to be my wife."

Her eyes grew impossibly wide, and he was struck once more by her alluring beauty. Her contrasting layers—demure and sizzling, uptight and witty—intrigued him. She was intoxicating. But for this arrangement to work, he couldn't go there. Something told him sex would mean more than an enjoyable pastime to Natalie Sobol, and messy emotional entanglements could make even the most rational people reckless. No matter how tempting, she was off-limits.

"In exchange for getting me an interview?" she asked.

"You won't need one. The job is yours if you accept my offer."

"I don't need you to hand me the position." She lifted her chin, narrowing her eyes at him. "I could get it on my own if I get my interview."

"I wouldn't hand you the job if you weren't qualified. Why don't we say your performance as the interim VP was your interview and you passed?"

"I could have the job? Just like that?" She arched an elegant brow, communicating both her skepticism and distaste.

"If you marry me as soon as the wedding can be arranged, I'll promote you to the position at the end of the year." She did a poor job of hiding her eye roll, and Garrett rushed to clarify. "The marriage obviously won't be permanent."

"Obviously." Her expression told him none of it was obvious. "Just out of curiosity, how long is not permanent?"

"Good question." Garrett hadn't thought through the details, but it had to last long enough to convince his grandmother that the marriage was real. But, most importantly, it had to last until he closed the Vivotex partnership and was appointed as the new CEO. *It will happen. It has to.* His grandmother had been grooming him for the position since the day he was born. It was her greatest wish to see him become Hansol's CEO. Once he sealed the Vivotex deal, she could give in without losing face. "About seven to eight months until your new position opens up. Perhaps a few months longer. But definitely no more than a year."

Natalie sighed deeply, and raised her eyes to the night sky. "Why?"

"It involves a sensitive and complicated family issue." She deserved to know everything about his unorthodox proposal, but not here. "I trust you'll keep this conversation confidential until we can discuss the details somewhere more private."

"Anything else?" She met his gaze, but her voice sounded distant and tired.

"You have the key facts," he said, tension edging into his words. "Will you marry me?"

She stared back at him for a few seconds then shook her head. "That's probably *the* worst proposal ever made. Like catastrophically bad."

A bark of surprised laughter escaped him. "You're probably right, but this is the most efficient and effective solution to both of our problems. If—"

She held up her hand to stop his words, and he obeyed her silent command out of shock. He was accustomed to deference from executives twice his age. He long admired her strength and confidence but being on the receiving end of her imperious attitude was startling.

"This scheme of yours is beyond ludicrous." She heaved a ponderous sigh, making the milky mounds of her breasts rise and fall. It took Herculean effort to keep his eyes focused on her face. "But I'm desperate enough to consider it."

"Good call," he said with equal parts irritation and relief. To his chagrin, her reluctant not-quite-assent stung his ego, but his rational side was relieved she would even consider his preposterous proposal. Natalie Sobol was practical to a fault, but this time it worked in his favor.

"I highly doubt that," she said with a quirk of her red lips.

Of course she did. The more she thought about it, the

more dubious everything would seem. He couldn't give her too much time to think things through. "Given this is a time-sensitive situation, you have until tomorrow at midnight to give me an answer."

"Tomorrow? You're impossible." With an exasperated glare, she spun away and stalked toward the staircase inside. His mouth curved into a grin. He'd spiked the ball into her court and she wasn't the kind of person who would back down from a challenge. He was looking forward to her next move. Before he could turn away, the sight of her softly swaying hips recaptured his attention and his smirk morphed into slack-mouthed admiration.

When she disappeared from sight, Garrett leaned against the railing and frowned at the starless sky. *Why is she so desperate that she'd consider giving up a year of her life for a second chance at a promotion?*

Three

Natalie shut down her computer after a long day and stretched her back with a groan. She was determined to catch up on the projects that had fallen behind while she was on bereavement leave. Challenging work kept her mind sharp and focused, and made a great excuse for avoiding Garrett. Her heart leaped at the mere thought of him, as though it was startled awake by his magnetic pull. *Gah.*

After tidying up her desk, she left the office and drove home on autopilot with tension tightening her shoulders and pain drilling into her temples. A bubble bath and a glass of wine should take care of that. But as soon as she sank into the fragrant bath, Garrett invaded her thoughts. The way his hand had trailed down her naked back and how her softness had molded to fit his hard lines. She sighed as she ran the washcloth down her legs, her oversensitized skin trembling with pleasure. Her body begged for release, and the warm water and her slippery skin tempted her hands to slide up her thighs.

"No, no, *no*." Natalie scrambled out of the tub. She would not pleasure herself daydreaming about her boss.

Why the heck did he want a temporary wife anyway? His proposal was pure, unadulterated madness. They would have to live a lie for the duration of the contract. And how could she weather the vicious rumors that were sure to come? There had to be another way to secure Sophie's adoption.

With Tin Man–stiff shoulders and a migraine, Natalie sprawled out on the living-room couch and glared at her ceiling. There was no other way. If she agreed to Garrett's crazy scheme, she and Sophie could move to New York in seven months. *Maybe a few months longer if her and Garrett's objectives weren't met by the end of the year.* But still, Natalie could start a new life in no more than a year. The custody battle alone could last longer than that and would likely bankrupt her.

With Garrett's help, Natalie could convince the Davises to reconsider contesting her adoption application. They couldn't want a drawn-out custody battle any more than she did. Even if they continued to contest the adoption, having a wealthy husband with a recognizable name would support her position that Sophie would have a secure, stable home. And with her promotion, Natalie could afford a nice place and excellent childcare for the baby even without a rich husband.

More importantly, something about Garrett Song centered her. True, he made her hormones streak naked across her mind, but on a deeper level she trusted him. He was too arrogant to say something he didn't mean and he valued his word too much to go back on it.

As for the anticipated gossip, Natalie could handle the ugliness for a few weeks. The wedding bells would soon soothe her coworkers' ruffled feathers. An office fling was fodder for gossip, but love and marriage wrought oohs, ahhs and well wishes.

With a long, frustrated growl, Natalie sat up on the couch. She needed to handle some time-sensitive work before making a decision about Garrett's proposal. She reached into her bag to retrieve her laptop, but her hand came out empty. In her rush to leave the office—and Garrett Song—she'd forgotten it. *Grr.* She exhaled with enough force to collapse the third pig's house.

Reining in her temper, Natalie left for the office. From her Koreatown apartment, it took only fifteen minutes to reach downtown Los Angeles.

When she got there, Natalie tapped her toes as the elevator crawled up to the fifty-fifth level. Once she arrived on her floor, she sidestepped through a six-inch gap in the elevator doors, while rummaging around her purse for her office keys. Half of her head was crammed into her tote when she walked straight into something big and solid. She wobbled and a pair of strong hands reached out to steady her.

She didn't need to see whom she'd run into. Her body already recognized Garrett Song. Fire kindled where he held her and blazed across her skin. Keeping her head bent, she focused on slowing down her pulse.

"I'm sorry. I didn't know anyone was here." Natalie tried to back away, but his hands stayed firm on her arms. She raised puzzled eyes toward his face and her voice caught in her throat—his gaze was boring into her with unsettling intensity.

"Are you all right?" Garrett's voice sounded husky.

When she nodded, he stepped back and folded his arms across his chest.

"I forgot to bring my laptop home." Nerves on hyperdrive, Natalie babbled on with her explanation. "I need to finish up some work tonight. A good HR director never rests."

He didn't respond and continued staring at her, as if trying to decide whether he was amused or bored. She couldn't help noticing how well he filled out his jeans and T-shirt. He looked younger, more approachable, in his casual outfit. Without her consent, her eyes traveled down to the sculpted pecs pushing against his white shirt. He could've been used as the mold for one of those anatomically correct Batman suits. Dual forces fought inside her—part of her wanted to run as far from him as possible, but a troubling and foreign part of her wanted to run straight into his arms.

"Okay." Natalie willed her lips into a polite smile, making sure no hint of her inner war showed through. "Have a good night."

"I was on my way out to see you." His expression was unreadable but his eyes looked predatory. "I believe we have unfinished business to discuss."

Her drumming heart bruised her ribs, and her mouth opened and closed in her best goldfish imitation before she could form her next words.

"Tell me why."

"Why what?"

"Why do you need a temporary wife?"

She might think he was overreacting or being a coward for taking such drastic steps to escape his grandmother's control. Some people had a difficult time grasping how sacred family, duty and respect were in his culture. Perhaps Natalie had raised similarly and would understand. He was accustomed to derision for what others perceived as weakness, but he didn't want her to see him as some stunted man-child.

"My grandmother arranged for me to marry a woman I've never met based on her family's wealth and connections."

"She did what?" Natalie's voice rose an octave, her expression a mixture of shock and indignation. "There are so many things wrong with that sentence. Your grandmother chose someone for you to marry? Based on the woman's *family* assets, not the woman herself?"

Garrett smiled at the protective edge that had crept into Natalie's voice. "Yes to both, but Grandmother insists the woman herself is also satisfactory."

Natalie's eyes flashed. "Satisfactory to *her* standards. You haven't even met your *betrothed*."

"She isn't my anything. Have you forgotten that I've asked *you* to be my wife?"

"But… I still don't understand why you want to marry me."

"Are you familiar with Korean culture?"

She sighed with a sheepish shrug. "I'm half-Korean, but all I know about our culture comes from K-drama."

He cocked his head and stowed away that information to explore at another time.

"As the eldest member of our family, my grandmother commands absolute respect and obedience from her children and grandchildren. I couldn't flat-out refuse to marry the heiress she chose. That would be like spitting in her face. So I told her I was secretly engaged to someone else and I couldn't go back on my word to my fiancée."

"Hmm." Natalie's eyebrows drew together as she digested his explanation. "And your grandma's okay with that?"

"Of course not. She threatened to stop my CEO appointment if I don't break off the engagement."

"I need to sit down." She looked dazed. "What are you going to do?"

"First, we're moving this conversation away from any prying ears." With his hand on the small of her back, Garrett led her to the privacy of his office, and settled her onto a sofa. Once the door was shut behind him, he continued,

"Then I'm going to get married as soon as possible because my grandmother will meddle with my personal life until I do."

"But what about the CEO job?"

"You could help with that, too. I'm working on a partnership with Vivotex. It's nearly done but I still need to convince some key executives over there. Presenting myself as a family man could strengthen my credibility, and help me win their trust. Once I get the partnership sealed, the board wouldn't dream of electing another CEO. They need to do what's best for Hansol, as does my grandmother."

"That all makes sense in an upside-down kind of way."

"I'm glad you think so," he said quietly, relieved she didn't think less of him.

"If I marry you…" A burst of triumph spread through his chest, and the caveman possessiveness reared its head again. He opened his mouth to speak but Natalie cut him off. "If I do, I have some conditions."

"Conditions?" He wasn't fond of conditions being placed on him, but he didn't have a line of contract brides waiting to marry him. "Name them."

"I won't share your bed," she blurted. "My professional life and my personal life never cross."

"Agreed," he said, but his eyes raked hotly over her body against his will. With effort, he focused his gaze on her face. Consummating the marriage would complicate an already complicated situation. "It'll simplify the dissolution of our marriage. An annulment is more efficient than a divorce."

"Good. And I also want to ask you to not have…relationships while this lasts." She flushed a bright shade of pink.

"What kind of relationships?" It both surprised and amused him to watch her squirm and blush.

"The extramarital kind involving sex with people who

aren't your wife." She jutted out her chin in a show of defiance that was becoming familiar to him.

"Ah, that kind."

"Yes." Natalie rolled her eyes. "That kind."

"Agreed." Unable to resist, he teased her with a grin. "I presume you will do me the same courtesy?"

"Of course. It's important we convince the world our marriage is real. Not only for you, but for me, as well." Her expression grew fierce. "I'm fighting to adopt my niece. She was orphaned when my sister and her husband died in a car crash."

"Your niece?"

"In my heart, she's already my daughter, but her grandparents are contesting the adoption. It's already difficult for a single woman to adopt, but if the child's next of kin contests it, it becomes nearly impossible. The Davises aren't heartless people, but they want Sophie with them in New York." Natalie gritted her teeth, near tears for a brief, heartbreaking moment before she regained control. "I thought if I became the new VP of HR and transferred to New York in December, I might be able to convince Sophie's grandparents to withdraw their opposition to the adoption."

"That's why you agreed to do this." His gut lurched at the realization.

Her desperation to get the promotion and her agreeing to consider this marriage—it was all for her niece. It would complicate everything. He couldn't let Natalie get under his skin, especially with a little girl in the picture. But he couldn't turn his back on her. It went against his very core to abandon a mother fighting for her child. Also, on a logical level, his time to search for a contract bride was up, and he wouldn't find anyone more invested in pulling off their fake marriage than Natalie.

"Yes, so if we do this, I'm going all in. Marrying you will boost my chances of becoming Sophie's mom, but if anyone finds out our marriage isn't real, then I could lose her."

"I understand." He understood only too well how important a mother was to a child. He couldn't let Natalie bet her future on the promotion and the goodwill of Sophie's grandparents. His name, wealth and influence could help her adopt her niece. "I'll do everything in my power to help you get custody of Sophie."

"Thank you." A tremulous smile lit her face.

She was so beautiful. Dangerously so. Heat unfurled low in his stomach, and resisting the need to touch her made him dizzy.

"Anything else?"

"Just one thing. Is it absolutely necessary for us to be seen in public together?" Her words picked up speed, tripping over each other. "I was hoping to avoid situations where I'd have to come up with spur-of-the-moment lies. I'm the worst at lying."

"I need you to attend functions with me. There's no way around that."

"Couldn't you tell them I have a headache or something?"

"For months on end?" He raised an eyebrow at her.

"Fine." Her shoulders drooped and she narrowed her eyes. "I could smile and play along, but you're in charge of making stuff up on the spot."

"Deal."

"Okay." Her sigh was tremulous but her beautiful features hardened with determination. "I'll marry you."

The silence stretched and Natalie shifted on her feet. *Damn.* He couldn't tear his eyes off her, and awareness shrouded them like moist, tropical heat. *What is it about this woman that drives me crazy with desire?* Whatever it was, he couldn't have her. Maintaining distance was crucial to avoiding complications when they annulled the marriage.

Even so, his gaze dropped to her lips and his breath hitched to find them wet and softly parted. Garrett swayed toward her without conscious thought, and Natalie tilted her head, leaning in. The evidence that she wasn't immune to the dizzying attraction chipped away at his willpower. He couldn't have sex with her, but there was no harm in kissing her.

Like hell there wasn't. She was a good woman and he wasn't a complete bastard. She'd agreed to the contract marriage, but her decision was an emotional one, a sacrifice for her niece. She was probably more vulnerable than she let on. Their lips were only a breath apart when he pulled back and shoved his hands into his pockets.

As he drew in a steadying breath, Natalie closed the distance between them and pressed her lips against his. Surprise held him immobile but she was warm and intoxicating. When a sound that was somewhere between a moan and a whimper escaped her, he lost the fight for control. He deepened the kiss with a low growl, and Natalie pushed her body against him. Burying his fingers roughly in her hair, he tilted back her head to better taste her.

Something cold and alarming seeped through his mind even as he leaned back on the wall and nestled her between his legs. Her skin smelled like vanilla and sweet musk, and felt like silk beneath his hands as they slid down her bare arms before settling on her hips. Her cool fingers skimmed his stomach just under his shirt and he hissed at the intense pleasure.

His reaction to the simple touch shocked him out of the moment. Garrett broke off their kiss. Natalie stumbled back from him with her fingers pressed against her lips. Their gazes crashed and held, their panting breaths filling the silence.

Natalie didn't seem aware that her fingertips were brushing back and forth across her lips, pink and swollen from their kiss. The movement was hypnotic—a seductive lure that could capsize his meticulously planned life. He couldn't give his body the chance to win the battle.

"I'll make some arrangements and contact you soon."

"Okay," she said in a husky whisper, her hand finally dropping to her side. She gave her head a vigorous shake and inhaled deeply. "Um… That was good practice. Some public displays of affection will be necessary. I'm glad we got the initial awkwardness over with."

"Initial awkwardness?"

In all fairness, he had brushed aside their kiss, but to hear her call it "awkward" pricked his pride.

"Yeah, well…" she said. "Our first kiss shouldn't be in front of an audience, so I'm glad we got that over with."

"I approve of your strategy. Good night." With a curt nod, he spun around.

When he reached the parking structure, he made for his car with long, impatient strides, intent on leaving the building as soon as possible.

He slid into his Aston Martin and sped through downtown LA with the windows down, putting much-needed distance between himself and whatever the hell had happened back there.

When he was certain he could speak in a normal voice, he called Michael Reynolds, his oldest and closest friend, as well as Hansol's PR specialist. Garrett needed to think things through, and Mike was his most trustworthy sounding board.

His friend picked up on the second ring, sounding winded. "This better be important, Song. You interrupted my dinner with two of your senior executives. I'm missing the good parts of their prostate exam stories."

"So you ditched them?" Garrett smirked.

"I don't know what you're talking about."

"You owe me one, Reynolds."

"I know. Thanks."

"By the way, this *is* important." He pulled up to the Ritz-Carlton. "I'm getting married."

"What?" Mike's voice rang across the lines. "To who? And why haven't I met her?"

"You know my grandmother. We kept our relationship under the radar so she wouldn't worry." Garrett left his explanation vague to avoid lying to his friend. "I'm marrying Natalie Sobol."

"*The* Natalie Sobol?" Mike said after a lengthy pause.

"I didn't realize she was famous." As the valet drove away with his car, Garrett walked into the hotel lobby. "You know her well?"

"I've met her a few times at Hansol's functions, but her reputation precedes her."

"And what reputation is that?" He stepped into the elevator and pressed the button to his penthouse.

"How do you think a twenty-eight-year-old became a regional HR director? Actually, she was twenty-six when she was promoted."

"Well, she's exceptionally bright and competent."

"She certainly is, but that's not all." Mike's voice held a note of awe. "That woman's got nerves of steel."

"I believe that." Garrett chuckled under his breath.

"She's known as the Ball Buster."

"The what?" He tugged his tie loose. "What the hell did she do to earn that title?"

"About a year ago, someone in middle management wasn't playing by the rules." By the sound of it, his friend was cupping his hand over his cell to whisper. "Natalie investigated the allegations and found evidence he'd been giving preferential treatment to male employees. She fired his ass and convinced him to sign a release stating he won't sue the company. She laid down the law."

"That's my woman." Garrett grinned as he got off the

elevator. The city lights greeted him through the panoramic windows of his penthouse.

"So how should we handle this from the PR side of things?"

"We need to release a statement announcing your engagement."

"That's a given." Garrett dropped onto his leather lounger and kicked off his shoes.

"But first, you should 'sneak around' with your fiancée and make sure to get caught. Invite the public into your 'clandestine' romance."

"The public might dig that, but Hansol employees will be out for blood. We need to announce the engagement as soon as possible. The venom will leach out and everything will become rosy and romantic as soon as marriage enters the picture. How long do we have to sneak around?"

"Two weeks."

"Fine, but she's moving in with me within the week." Two weeks would give his grandmother time to wreak havoc on his plans. He had to make the first move.

"Impatient, are you?" Mike chuckled. "Luckily, that's a good PR move. A fast-paced, secret romance is even more popular."

"Perfect. Let me know what else you need from my end." Garrett pinched the bridge of his nose, running through the list of things to get done the next day. "You can go back to your little party now."

"What?" Mike sounded panicked. "Don't you want to have a long conversation about your bachelor party?"

"Not happening."

"I was worried Samantha ruined you for love and happiness. Now that you have Natalie, I'm sure you're thankful for the narrow escape," Mike said without a hint of levity. "I'm happy for you."

"Thank you."

Garrett ended the call and leaned back on his seat. Love and whatever happiness it might bring weren't worth the risk of heartbreak. The last time he'd let his guard down—worn thin by buried grief and loneliness—Samantha had happened.

Trust and sentimentality inevitably led to pain and loss. Logic and reason, however, had never let him down. He could almost understand why his grandmother devoted her every waking moment to Hansol after his grandfather died.

His engagement to Natalie had nothing to do with love and happiness, or out-of-control attraction. She was his partner in a project to change their lives. He would get his CEO position and a personal life that belonged to him, and she would adopt her niece and start a new life in New York. They would both get what they wanted and walk away content.

This might *actually* work.

Four

Natalie smacked her palm against her forehead. She was so dazed from their kiss she'd returned home without her laptop. Color flooded her cheeks and her heartbeat kicked up a notch. *Would kissing him always make her want to rip off his clothes?*

Miserable and mortified, she shuffled down the hall and knocked on her neighbor's door. Mrs. Kim was her friend and confidante. Natalie wouldn't have made it through her sister's death without the older woman's kindness and wisdom. If anyone could help sort out this mess, it was her.

Mrs. Kim cracked open the door then swung it wide with a welcoming smile, but Natalie's smile wobbled at the corners. Her neighbor's only reaction was the slightest tilt of an immaculately shaped eyebrow. Then she nodded her head as though she'd reached a decision.

"Soju."

Natalie had been accepted as part of Mrs. Kim's exclusive "in" crowd by fearlessly tilting back the potent liquor, matching the older woman shot for shot.

She didn't know a whole lot about her neighbor except that she lived a quiet and solitary life. When Natalie had first met her, she'd guessed her to be in her midthirties, with her trim figure and smooth skin, but she soon learned that Mrs. Kim was well into her fifties. Natalie was beginning to think that *soju* was the secret to her youth.

The two women settled in at the kitchen table and Mrs. Kim poured them each a drink. She hissed in appreciation of the soju's kick, and lifted her shot glass for Natalie to refill. Once her glass was filled to the brim, she took the bottle from Natalie and refilled hers. "You know *Forrest Gump*?"

Natalie blinked several times. That was random. Nineties cinema was not a frequent topic of their conversations. "Do you mean that Tom Hanks movie?"

Mrs. Kim nodded.

"Yeah, I've watched it on TV before."

"Well, he was wrong." Mrs. Kim poked the air with her index finger. "Life is *not* like a box of chocolates. You'd never find a piece of crap in a chocolate box."

Natalie nodded somberly, then they downed their shots. She would've found the observation hilarious if it hadn't made so much sense. Life could bury you in a mountain of crap, but the worst you could do with a box of chocolates was bite into a piece with nasty pink goo inside.

"Still no headway on Sophie's adoption?" Her neighbor's eyes were soft with understanding.

"No," Natalie whispered, desperation clogging her throat. "The odds are stacked against me, but I can't let her go."

"And now, you have a man," she said matter-of-factly. Sometimes she could swear Mrs. Kim was a psychic. "That complicates things even more."

Complicates things? That's such a genteel way of describing the mess I'm in.

"I don't exactly *have* him." There was no use denying there was a man. Mrs. Kim jutted her chin at Natalie to continue, then poured more shots into their glasses. "I'm just engaged to him."

To her credit, Mrs. Kim swallowed her *soju* before she coughed and sputtered, "You're what?"

"I got engaged to Hansol's VP of Business and Development."

"Fancy."

"He's also the heir apparent to the entire freaking company."

"Holy crap."

"Exactly. And you know what else? He's melt-your-clothes-off hot, and for some reason that really pisses me off!" Natalie slammed her palms on the table. *Shoot.* Mrs. Kim was twice her age. She shouldn't be disrespectful. "Sorry. I mean he's very handsome."

"Don't be a prude. I'm not that old. He's sex on a stick. I got it," she said. "And you're not *pissed off.* You're just *turned on.*"

Natalie emptied her glass and glowered mutely at her.

"How did all this come about?" Mrs. Kim studied her face with concern.

"Suddenly." Natalie couldn't lie to her but couldn't tell the truth, either. She inhaled a fortifying breath. "We...understand each other, and marrying him will help me adopt Sophie. I think it'll be a mutually beneficial arrangement."

"And that's enough for you? Sometimes doing what we think is best for our children comes at a cost, Natalie."

Mrs. Kim sighed and opened up another bottle of *soju.* She raised it and glanced at Natalie, but she shook her head. She had urgent matters to deal with first thing in the morning, thanks to *twice* losing her wits over Garrett Song.

"There was someone…after my husband died, but I ended things with him to focus on my kids. Overcompensating for being a single mom, I guess. But now…" Her unflappable neighbor sighed, a small, forlorn sound. "My children have grown and left—as they should—and I'm a lonely old woman with only bygone memories to warm my bed."

"Mrs. Kim… I…"

Natalie didn't continue. She was in no place to comfort Mrs. Kim. She was too afraid to give her heart to anyone, knowing she didn't stand a chance of keeping him. The one guy who'd wanted to stick around was a narcissistic jerk from college. No man worth having seemed to want her. Natalie poured Mrs. Kim another shot and lifted her glass for a refill. They raised their glasses in solemn silence and drank to bygone memories.

Unlike Mrs. Kim, who had loved and lost, Natalie didn't even have memories to keep her warm. She only had a sexless marriage to an unfairly hot husband to look forward to.

Natalie didn't hate giving presentations *too* much. She just had a hard time breathing and got a wicked headache. Even so, it beat "hanging out" and "socializing." The actual event was never as bad as expected. She had to focus on that. Today it was just a quick office-etiquette seminar.

"You look bulletproof," Garrett said, close to her ear. "Why the power suit?"

She squeaked, nearly jumping out of said suit. Immersed in her mental pep talk, she hadn't heard him approaching in the hall. Her hand on her chest, she scanned their surroundings and didn't see any prying eyes on them.

Even when her mind grasped she wasn't in mortal danger, her fight-or-flight instinct raged inside her. The man next to her was dangerous. Seeing him, and in such close proximity, made her heart play hopscotch in her chest.

Natalie reined in her hormone-induced reaction. She lived in the real world with real problems, like bills to pay and a daughter to adopt. She didn't have the luxury of lusting after her future husband.

"Good morning," she said as she continued swiftly down the hallway. "Did you need something?"

"Not at all." He fell in step beside her, his face a careful blank. "I'm just stretching my legs."

She couldn't help stealing a peek at his long, muscular legs, and heat rose to her face. Her gaze roamed over him, lingering on his strong jawline and full lips. When her eyes met his, amusement glinted in them. He was well aware of her perusal, and quite enjoying himself.

"Go stretch them somewhere else," she said through clenched teeth.

He chuckled, the corners of his eyes crinkling. Rather than casually parting ways, as she'd hoped, he took her by the elbow and led her toward the landing of the emergency stairway. Too startled to react, she allowed the door to click shut behind them. She huffed an exasperated sigh and slumped against the wall.

"Why did you bring me out here, Garrett?"

"We need to discuss our sleeping arrangements."

"What—what do you mean?" Awareness stormed through her, making her knees weak. After their kiss, she'd imagined sharing a bed with him. It involved very little sleeping.

"I want you to move into my place as soon as possible."

"No," she blurted in a panic, her heart jumping and stuttering.

Garrett shrugged. "If you'd rather buy a new place, I'll have my Realtor call you."

"It's not that." She pressed her palm against her forehead. "Why do we have to move in together already?"

He arrogantly raised an eyebrow. "Our engagement will be announced soon."

"I haven't forgotten, but I don't know what the rush is. I could move in after the wedding."

Garrett raked his fingers through his full, dark hair, tousling it into a sexy mess. "My grandmother isn't going to give up on the arranged marriage easily."

"And that's why we're getting married. I haven't forgotten."

"Knowing her, she's going to use all her influence to stop our wedding. Maybe even leak my 'engagement' to Jihae Park to the press."

"Why would she do something like that?"

"Then it won't be just the CEO seat on the line for me. I'd be responsible for burning bridges with Rotelle Corporation and publicly humiliating a young woman." Garrett squeezed the back of his neck. "But it'd be a risky move on my grandmother's part since Hansol will receive negative press if you and I still went ahead with our wedding. Neither Grandmother nor I would do anything to harm Hansol, but I don't know how far she'll go. We've never been on opposite sides of a conflict before."

"When are we announcing the engagement?" she asked, her teeth tugging at her bottom lip. Their conversation sounded more dramatic than a scene from a soap opera. She'd be sitting on the edge of the couch stuffing popcorn in her mouth except this was actually happening to her. Cue the *Twilight Zone* music.

"In two weeks." Garrett rubbed a hand down his face.

"Couldn't we move it up?"

"We have less than two weeks to warm up the public to the idea of us. When we announce our engagement, we need people to feel like they're part of the romance. If we blindside them with it, they'll feel duped. That won't win us any fans."

She nodded as his words lit up a dark corner of her heart. *He's protecting me.* He lived in the limelight and could charm the press with a grin and a witty remark, but Natalie would be vulnerable to the public's scorn. She soaked up the warmth of the knowledge.

Wait, no. This way lies trouble. Natalie couldn't let her loneliness fool her that his kind gesture meant anything more than what it was. She and Garrett had a purely business arrangement and she shouldn't forget that.

"You'll be an open target to your grandmother's manipulations. Are you sure about waiting?"

"No." Garrett shrugged and pinned her with his gaze. "That's why I need you to ruin me for the Korean heiress."

"Ruin you?" Natalie was horrified at how far his grandmother would go to control his life. It had to be suffocating to bear so much pressure. Yet, he was risking so much to protect her reputation. "I don't know... I've never ruined a hotshot billionaire before."

"It's simple." His lips quirked in amusement. "Move in with me."

"But how does moving in together ruin you?"

"Jihae Park's family, as well as my grandmother, will be scandalized if we moved in together before our wedding. At least superficially, propriety and virtue are still important in Korean culture, especially to those *jae-bul* families. If I'm lucky, her family will call off the wedding first. At the very least, my grandmother won't be able to make any engagement announcements of her own."

"Virtue?" She blinked and searched her mind for the right words. "My moving in with you will compromise your virtue?"

"And yours." He grinned mischievously.

She gulped. *Yes, he would definitely be a good ravisher.*

"Fine. I'll think about ruining you." She rolled her eyes to hide how much the thought of tainting his virtue aroused her. "If we're done here, I have a presentation to give. You can leave in fifteen minutes."

"What?"

"I don't want anyone seeing us come out of the stairwell together." She could do without adding "stairwell quickie" to the gossip fodder.

"You want me to waste fifteen minutes of my time out here?"

"Not at all." She wished she could snap a picture of his expression. She could look at it for a good laugh whenever she was having a bad day. "You can sit on the stairs and productively check your emails if you'd like. Just don't come out for fifteen minutes."

Natalie scanned the hallway before slipping out and shutting the door in Garrett's stunned face.

His fiancée had locked him out of his own company.

Garrett glanced at his watch, feeling ridiculous hiding in the dimly lit stairwell. He waited exactly five minutes; that was all she was getting. Even so, he made certain the hallway was empty before he left his confinement.

After shutting his office door behind him, Garrett sank into his desk chair and sifted through a pile of documents, then tossed them back down. They were getting married in a few weeks and would be living under the same roof for months. What was there to think about?

Growling with frustration, he pushed back from his desk and stood, making his chair skid drunkenly. Enough nonsense. She was moving into the penthouse by the end of the week. Coming to a decision, he placed several calls to make the arrangements, then strode out of his office with determined steps.

Natalie was back from her meeting and was sitting with her nose nearly pressed against her monitor, as though she wanted to fall into the computer. And she was singing softly under her breath. He leaned a shoulder against the door frame and listened for a few seconds. Then, he recognized the song.

"Are you singing 'YMCA'?"

Her bottom shot an inch off her seat and her cheeks turned red.

"What now?" She studied him with wary eyes.

"I need you," he said, deepening his voice. Her mouth rounded into a plush O and he allowed himself a satisfied smile. If flirting was what it took to get her attention, then he wasn't opposed to engaging in some harmless fun. "Have lunch with me."

"Lunch?" Her eyes darted around her office, as though she was searching for an escape route. He watched her, wondering what excuse she'd come up with to wiggle out of it. She took a deep breath and squared her shoulders. "Sure. Let me just log off."

"You will?" Garrett's eyebrows shot up. He didn't think she'd give in so easily. "Great."

Recovering from his surprise, he walked beside her through the cubicles. Natalie kept a respectable distance between them and lengthened her strides as though trying to escape the surreptitious glances of curious employees.

"See you in the lobby," she said in a terse whisper and made a sharp right.

Her barely audible words and sudden change of direction caught him by surprise and he almost turned to follow her. Catching himself at the last moment, he made an awkward pivot to continue down the hall.

It'd been inconsiderate of him to just show up at her office. They needed to be seen together in public, but they didn't need to give the employees an exclusive sneak peek. Natalie still had a day or two before the rumors flew at work.

By the time they reunited in the building lobby, her

cheeks were back to their creamy white, and her features were as serene as a placid lake. Away from prying eyes in the elevator, something perverse in him wanted to disturb the calm surface of that lake. He would press her up against the back wall and slide her prim blouse off her shoulders. He would finally discover the exact shade of the tips of her lovely breasts… *Are they pale pink like a soft blush against her translucent skin? Or creamy brown like sweet caramel?*

Garrett shifted on his feet, his trousers growing uncomfortably tight. *Hell.* If he didn't stop his adolescent fantasizing, he was going to have to walk to his car with the swagger of a cowboy after a long day on the saddle.

"This way." He led her toward the parking elevator.

"We're driving?" she asked, meeting his gaze for the first time since they'd left her office.

"Yes. I'm taking you to my place."

"Oh." Natalie swung around to gape at him, then nodded slowly. "Is it far?"

"No." He wondered what she'd think about his choice of residence. "I live at the Ritz-Carlton on Olympic Boulevard."

Other than a slight tilt of her eyebrows, she didn't reveal her thoughts. "People know who you are over there, right?"

"Right."

She nodded absently and was quiet on their walk to his car.

As soon as they pulled out of the parking structure, Natalie freed her hair from her customary bun and shook her head to make the curls bounce around her shoulders. Garrett forgot to watch the road as he stared at her undoing the top three buttons of her blouse. When she bent to rummage through her purse, he caught a glimpse of her lacy white bra and his blood rushed south again. He was ogling her, his jaw slack. *Damn it.* He snapped his mouth closed, and returned his attention to the road.

"Is this better?" She scrutinized herself in the car mirror after painting her lips a deep pink rose.

"Better how?" He wouldn't have been able to pull off the cool-guy act even if his voice hadn't cracked. There was no use denying it. He was going to spend the entire afternoon obsessing over her perfect pink lips and wondering what other parts of her matched that shade.

"I figured you were taking me to your place so we could be seen together before our engagement announcement. You mentioned it was important I look the part, but this is the best I could do on a moment's notice."

"Don't worry about it. You look nice." *Nice? What am I? In sixth grade?*

Garrett drove the car into the hotel's circular driveway, and opened Natalie's door himself. When he helped her out of her seat, she stood on tiptoes and brushed her lips against his cheek. She seemed to have thrown herself into the role. While he stood in shock, she wrapped her arm around his waist and glanced up at him. Snapping back to attention, he pulled her to his side and kissed her hard, letting his hand slide up to rest an inch beneath her breast. It was all for show, of course.

He lifted his head before his control slipped again. Natalie stood and blinked her wide eyes, and he felt a surge of pride. Grinning broadly, he wrapped his arm around her shoulders and they strolled into the lobby. Seeming to emerge from a fog, she smiled prettily at him, back in character.

As soon as the elevator doors closed behind them, she dropped her smile and he dropped his arm from her shoulders. Natalie was so pumped from the performance she was practically shuffling her feet, reminding him of a scene from *Rocky*. An image of her in silky red boxing shorts and a tight black tank top flitted through his mind. *Goddamn it. Is there anything this woman does that I don't find sexy?*

They reached his penthouse before he did anything foolish, and were met by the spectacular views of downtown that stretched all the way to the Hollywood sign. The gusty spring winds had carried away much of the smog, and all of Los Angeles stood clear and arresting before them.

"Come on." He beckoned her with a tilt of his head. "I'll give you the five-cent tour."

Natalie followed him with her bright eyes scanning the condo, but her attention kept drifting back to the city view. The condo itself wasn't much. Three bedrooms, three and a half bathrooms, a couple dens, a kitchen and dining room, two libraries and an exercise room. The two of them should have enough space without feeling too cramped.

"Um... Is this where we're going to live after we get married?"

He hadn't given much thought to what Natalie would need or want. He was, without a doubt, an insensitive tool. "I don't have a particular attachment to the place. We can move if you'd like."

"No. I wouldn't dream of imposing on you like that. I'll only be here a while." Natalie waved her hands.

"You don't need to feel like a guest while you live here. It'll be as much your home as mine." If Mike or Adelaide heard him, they'd be shocked. Garrett valued his privacy as though his life depended on it.

"That's very kind of you." Her lashes fluttered shyly. "Thank you."

"You're welcome," he whispered. Her sincere words touched and humbled him. "Thank you for rescuing me from an unwanted marriage."

"Don't thank me, yet. You won't be safe until I ruin you for good." Her mischievous smile made him hold his breath. "I'll pack over the weekend and move in by Sunday."

His breath left him in a hoot of laughter, and he enveloped her in a bear hug and swung her off her feet. She squealed and held on to his shoulders.

"Garrett, put me down," she said in a voice breathless with laughter.

After another spin, he steadied her onto the floor, keeping his arms loosely wrapped around her. He couldn't stop grinning. To his surprise, he very much looked forward to playing house with Natalie.

Five

Garrett was picking her up in fifteen minutes and she was still in her bra and panties. Natalie enjoyed big shindigs as much as she liked rolling around in a patch of poison ivy. She was agonizing over her attire for the dinner party—her bed was littered with half a dozen dresses. Garrett had sent them to her, and they were all beautiful, fashionable and—no doubt—expensive. She had to look the part, but he'd gone overboard.

It was their official "first date" and Natalie's insides were tangled into knots. They had gone out to lunch almost every day to strategize about their next moves, and let the paparazzi take pictures of their "secret romance." But this evening, she was accompanying Garrett to Michael Reynolds's birthday get-together to convince his friends what a happy couple they were.

Five minutes late, she eeny-meeny-miny-moed a black, strapless dress from the pile and slipped into it. She wore her hair in a loose updo, away from her bare shoulders.

As a finishing touch, she sprayed her favorite scent on her wrist and behind her ears. After a pause, she spritzed her cleavage.

With a last look in the mirror, Natalie rushed down the stairs and out of the building. Garrett had parked his car close to the entrance and stood outside, leaning back against the passenger-side door. He looked sinful in a tailored gray suit with a navy shirt, unbuttoned at his throat.

"Sorry I'm late." She sounded breathless. It had to be from running down the stairs, not because of how handsome he looked.

Garrett glanced up from his phone and froze as something hot and predatory flared in his eyes. He opened his mouth then closed it to clear his throat. "You look beautiful."

"So do you." The words popped out of her mouth before she could stop them, and blood rushed to her cheeks.

The corners of his eyes crinkled as his lips tugged to the side in a sexy grin. "Thank you."

"You're welcome," she mumbled, sliding into her seat while he held the door for her.

Natalie was surprised that Michael Reynolds was Garrett's oldest, closest friend. She knew Michael as a laid-back man with an easygoing smile, always cracking jokes. He was so different from the reserved, intense person Garrett was… It was difficult to imagine them as friends. But then, she didn't really know her soon-to-be husband all that well.

Forty-five minutes later, Garrett pulled up to a South Pasadena estate with a huge front lawn. The circular driveway was packed with luxury vehicles. Valets in bow ties and black jackets rushed around to take the guests' keys.

"This is his house?" Her voice rose at the end. She'd expected a casual get-together. Sure, she figured rich people would have fancy hors d'oeuvres and a Dom-Pérignon fountain or something, but not *this*.

"Yes," Garrett said, then switched off the ignition and stepped out of the car.

Natalie followed suit when one of the valets opened her door. Smiling her thanks at the man, she took Garrett's arm and whispered, "You said it was a 'small gathering.' This is a freaking wedding reception."

He furrowed his brow. "He's a publicist so he invited some influential acquaintances, but it's hardly a huge party. There can't be more than a hundred people here."

"Good Lord. What have I gotten myself into?" She dug her fingers into Garrett's forearm, which was muscular as hell. *Big party. Hot man.* She wanted to run off into the night.

The other guests were in their element, drinking and laughing, taking all the opulence for granted. Natalie was grateful to be wearing her new designer dress. Even so, she felt like she was on the wrong planet.

She rubbed shoulders with rich, powerful people at work and held her own, but that was her job and she knew what she was doing. This was a completely different beast. Small talk and mingling were not her forte. Garrett led her through the throng, stopping frequently to greet people he knew. As promised, she smiled and nodded in the right places, relieved she wasn't expected to talk.

"Mike." Garrett clapped the host on the shoulder. "Are you old enough to drink yet?"

"No, but I shaved for the first time today," Michael Reynolds said with an easy smirk. His smile broadened when he turned to her. "I'm glad you could make it, Natalie."

"Happy birthday, Michael." She dropped her voice to a conspiratorial whisper. "And let me know if you need a fake ID. I know someone who knows someone."

"I see you speak my language." Michael chuckled. "And call me Mike."

Natalie laughed with him and the knot in her chest loosened a notch. She didn't know their host well, but he had an openness to him that she liked.

She glanced up at Garrett when his arm snaked around her waist and he drew her close, but he addressed his friend without meeting her eyes. "You're a bad influence on my fiancée."

"I think it's the other way around." Mike lowered his voice and winked at her. "Congratulations, by the way. As his oldest friend, I thank you in advance for putting up with the grumpy son of a bitch."

Natalie snorted. "You're very welcome."

When Mike walked away to mingle with the rest of his guests, Garrett dropped his hand from her waist. She shivered at the sudden loss of heat.

"Are you cold?" A small frown marred his smooth forehead.

"No. I'm fine, but I could use a drink."

"Bowmore?" he said, one side of his lips tipping up.

"Just a glass of champagne." Her stomach fluttered—she was surprised he remembered her drink from Le Rêve. "I need to stay sharp for our audience."

Garrett resisted the urge to glance over his shoulder to check on her. Natalie was a grown woman and he didn't need to protect her from being swarmed by admirers. Besides, she was the one who had proposed they refrain from *other* relationships, so she wouldn't do anything to hurt his reputation or hers.

Earlier, at her apartment, he'd caught fire at the sight of her in her little black dress. It was demure compared to the one she'd worn at Le Rêve, but it hugged her hourglass figure and highlighted the curves underneath just enough to tease his imagination.

He walked to the bar for his Scotch and grabbed a flute

of champagne from a server on his way back. As he'd anticipated, Natalie was now surrounded by a group of men and he lengthened his strides to reach her.

"Sorry to keep you waiting, sweetheart." He pressed a light kiss on her lips and handed her the champagne.

"Thank you." She leaned her head against his shoulder when he pulled her to his side, playing her part like a pro.

"Natalie was just taking us to task about USC's new head coach. It seems neither he nor I truly understand college football," said one of Mike's college friends.

"Is that so?" Garrett raised an eyebrow at her and she shrugged.

"Taking you to task is a bit harsh." She hid her grin against the rim of her champagne flute as she took a long sip. "It's just that I have a *better* understanding than you guys."

The audience winced and guffawed at her cheekiness. As Natalie continued with her lecture, all the men listened intently, as did Garrett. She was funny and down-to-earth, and her mind was quicker than lightning. Lost in her words, Garrett belatedly noticed the crowd had grown. Her champagne glass was depleted and her smile was becoming strained.

He leaned down close to her ear. "Tired?"

"And hungry."

"All right, gentlemen. I'm whisking away my date now. I'm tired of sharing her."

When the crowd finally dispersed, Natalie slumped against him with a groan. "I need food, champagne and somewhere to sit."

A server walked over with a tray of bacon-wrapped shrimp and Natalie snatched a couple of them. She popped one in her mouth and mumbled around her food, "Not necessarily in that order."

Garrett laughed and guided her toward the French doors

leading out to the garden. Natalie ate every single hors d'oeuvre she met along the way and finished another glass of champagne.

"Holy cow. Is everything really, really delicious, or am I just famished? I would totally go back for that crab cake if my feet weren't screaming at me to get my butt on a chair."

He glanced down at her zebra-print high heels. They did amazing things for her legs but didn't look remotely comfortable. "There's a bench around the corner."

"Oh, thank God." She kicked off her shoes as soon as she plopped onto the seat.

Garrett shrugged out of his jacket and draped it around her shoulders before sitting next to her.

"Thank you," she murmured, gazing at the garden. "It's so beautiful out here."

"Is it?" He and Mike had grown up tearing apart that very garden, but Garrett had never sat still and taken it all in, like they were doing now. "I guess you're right."

"Mmm-hmm."

He studied her profile, her high, regal cheekbone and the graceful curve of her neck. Half of her hair had escaped the loose knot behind her head and fell down her back and shoulders. He wanted to sweep aside her hair and feel the softness of her skin, which he absolutely should not do.

"So how do you know so much about college football?" He tore his gaze away from her and stared at an old maple tree ahead of him, hard enough to make his eyes water.

"Long story."

"We've got time." He made a show of checking his watch. "I'll give you ten minutes."

Her laughter filled the garden, then ended on a wistful sigh. "My dad and I, we weren't very close. The only time he didn't mind my company was when we watched college football together. He was a huge fan. I don't think he even noticed I was sitting there half the time."

Garrett understood what that felt like. As soon as he finished graduate school, he'd thrown himself into his work. It was satisfying in its predictability and it created a common ground for him and his father. His dad had stepped down from the CEO position when his mom died, but returned to Hansol a few years later as an executive VP.

"I thought if I learned enough about the sport, he'd like me a little better." Her shrug told him it hadn't worked, but Natalie told her story without an ounce of self-pity— like she owned her past, hurt and all. His respect for her deepened. "But soon I noticed I wasn't faking my enthusiasm anymore. I'd grown to love the sport. Who knew it'd come in handy at an intimate birthday party for a hundred people?"

"You certainly won over quite a few of them."

"I did?" Her eyebrows shot up in genuine surprise.

He huffed out a laugh. "Why did you think that crowd was hanging on to your every word?"

"Watch yourself, Garrett Song." Natalie narrowed her eyes and pointed a finger at him. "I know where you live."

He snatched her hand and tugged her to her feet. "Yes, and you'll be living there with me starting Sunday."

"Ugh." She hooked an index finger in each of her shoes, not bothering to put them back on. "Do you ever stop thinking about work?"

"Yes." He cocked his head and pretended to consider her question. "But only when I'm thoroughly distracted."

Her lashes fluttered and color saturated her cheeks, and his gut clenched with heat. She could definitely become his most dangerous distraction.

Six

Still groggy from sleep, Natalie stepped out of the shower and wrapped herself in a warm woolly bathrobe, yawning until her eyes watered. Garrett hadn't brought her home until past one last night, and she hadn't fallen asleep until close to three. She yawned again.

It took a while for her brain to piece together that someone was knocking at the door. *It's not even eight, for God's sake.* Natalie cracked open the door a sliver and peered into the hallway. All traces of the sandman's influence evaporated at the sight of Garrett standing outside with two steaming cups and a brown paper bag.

He looked damn gorgeous and relaxed in his black T-shirt and jeans. He'd obviously had a good night's sleep. She'd had a fitful slumber only to wake up at the crack of dawn. Not fair.

"I bring strong coffee and warm croissants." He held up his offerings. "May I come in?"

Her stomach rumbled on cue, and Natalie opened the door wider. "My stomach welcomes you."

As Garrett closed the door behind him, Natalie remembered she was naked underneath her robe. *Stay calm.* She smoothed out her face in an expression of serenity. At least she hoped she looked serene. She could be bright pink *and* calm, right?

She waved for him to follow and led him into her small kitchen. "You can put those over there."

After setting his burden on her kitchen table, Garrett leaned a shoulder against the wall and focused his attention on her. His gaze drifted down her throat to the deep V of her robe, and her body warmed and softened in response. He might as well have been drawing a line of fire down her skin.

Could they really keep their hands off each other living under the same roof?

Things would get so much more complicated if she succumbed to the temptation. What if she got needy and clung to a man she could never keep? *God, no.* She was a grown woman and her brain dictated her actions, not the hot, aching center of her body.

"Have a seat." *Damn it.* She sounded breathless. "I'll be right back."

Her blush deepened and she licked her lips. *Crap.* There was something erotic about him seeing her fresh out of the shower with her wet curls sticking to her cheeks. Natalie scurried into her bedroom and leaned against her closed door. After stuffing her screaming hormones in a deep, dark corner of her mind, she threw on some tights and a soft tunic and went out to meet her fiancé.

Garrett had pulled out two small plates from her meager collection and set out their breakfast on the table.

"Plain or chocolate?" he asked when she sat down across from him.

"I'm not a crazy woman." She snorted and rolled her eyes. "Why would I pass up on chocolate?"

He chuckled and passed her the chocolate croissant, then took the plain one for himself.

Her croissant was still warm and melted chocolate oozed out when she took a bite. Her eyes fluttered closed.

"Mmm…"

She used her fingertip to dab the excess chocolate from the corners of her mouth and licked it off. No napkin was getting a single smudge of her chocolate. She was half-way through her breakfast before she noticed how quiet Garrett was.

When Natalie glanced at him, he was glaring at her with his croissant untouched. She squinted at him. "Are you regretting not taking the chocolate one?"

"No. I don't like sweets," he said in an oddly husky voice.

They enjoyed the rest of their breakfast and coffee in companionable silence. He offered to clear the table, but she waved him aside and put their plates in the sink, which was only two steps behind her.

"Okay. What brings you by so bright and early?" Natalie beckoned him to walk with her to the living room and plopped down on the couch. He followed suit, taking up her ancient sofa with his muscular thighs and broad back. The heat radiating off him made her breath hitch.

"We can't announce our engagement without an engagement ring." Garrett lifted Natalie's hand from her side and retrieved a ring from his pocket. "It was my mother's."

"Your mother's?" she gasped. It was absolutely stunning. The ring consisted of an antique emerald surrounded by small diamonds set in a rich gold band. "Are you sure you're okay with me wearing it? Shouldn't you save it for when you propose to someone you actually want to marry?"

"Unless you've forgotten, I asked you to marry me,"

he said. "I wouldn't have done that if I didn't want you to agree."

"You know what I mean. I think you should save your mother's ring for someone you love. Someone you want forever."

"Then the ring will never see the light of day." He let out a short, humorless laugh. "I don't intend to marry for love and forever. Not everyone buys into that fairy tale. Certainly not me."

A chill ran down her spine at the finality of his words. "Well, this is lovely. Thank you. I'll return it to you when this is all over."

"Don't worry about it," he said tersely. "We'll deal with it when the time comes."

"Okay," she said slowly. A solid wall had fallen across his expression at the mention of love and forever. Someone really must have done a number on him. "You know I'm moving in with you today. You could've waited until tonight."

"Call me old-fashioned. I wanted to put a ring on your finger before you ruined me."

Garrett left Natalie's place after loading his car with the few boxes she'd managed to pack. Even though she was leaving behind her furniture to sublet the apartment, they would need to make several trips to move her belongings over. She'd shooed him out of her apartment so she could pack her stuff *her way*.

It actually freed up some much-needed time for him to visit his family. He wanted to tell his father about his engagement in person, even if he'd already heard his grandmother's version of the story. Garrett and his father's relationship had improved over the past few years, but he wasn't sure where his old man would stand on the issue of his only son's marriage.

As he anticipated, the Song family's housekeeper, Liliana, informed him that his grandmother was "indisposed"—she smiled sympathetically at him—so he was free to search out his father. He found him in the study, nursing a glass of Scotch. When Garrett raised his eyebrows as he took a seat across from him, his father lifted the glass in mock salute and took a healthy sip.

"It's past noon. That means it's not too early for Scotch."

"Does Dr. Ananth know about your minute-past-noon Scotch rule?"

His dad was on a medical leave at the behest of his cardiologist. Garrett doubted whiskey was part of the doctor's treatment program.

"Don't you start on me, too. I have enough trouble keeping Adelaide off my back."

"You should be glad she cares enough to nag."

Regret and vulnerability passed over his father's face, but they were gone too quickly for Garrett to be certain. "I have a feeling you're not here for father-son bonding time." His dad leaned back in his leather chair and steepled his fingers in front of him. "What's going on?"

Well, Dad. A hell storm is brewing, and I'm in the eye of it. "I'm getting married."

"To which fiancée?"

"I only have one." Garrett's fists clenched on his knees. *Dad did know about the arrangement with Jihae Park. He just didn't bother standing up for me.*

"Not according to your grandmother. Are you sure you want to defy her?"

"No, but I'm sure I want to marry my fiancée, not a complete stranger."

"Your mother and I…" His voice grew thick and he couldn't continue. There was no need. Garrett knew his parents were strangers when they married.

"It's not about whether or not Jihae Park is a good match

for me. Or whether she and I might find happiness in an arranged marriage." Garrett breathed deeply through his nose. "The point is I already chose my wife, and it is my decision alone. I will not be a pawn for the Song dynasty."

"So be it." His father's voice rang with a note of determination, and he straightened in his seat, drawing back his shoulders. Garrett couldn't tell whether his dad was determined to stop the wedding, or would help him stand up to Grandmother. "Well, tell me about your young lady."

"She…" Garrett cleared his throat, caught off guard by his dad's sudden interest. "Her name is Natalie Sobol. She's Hansol's HR director in the LA office."

"Ah, yes. I've met her on a few occasions. She's an intelligent and competent young woman. Isn't she Korean-American?"

"Yes, on her mother's side."

"Good, good." He nodded absently, then added, "But you took an unnecessary risk dating a subordinate."

"She's not a *subordinate*," Garrett said with tight control, fighting against the resentment churning in his stomach. "She's my fiancée and your future daughter-in-law, not some second-class citizen."

"I never implied that she was. The fact is you're an executive and she's your subordinate employee. It all worked out but that doesn't mean it wasn't risky."

"Isn't it a bit late for doling out fatherly advice?" *What the hell is wrong with me?* Garrett's emotions were too close to the surface. He dragged his fingers through his hair, and tried again. "I wanted you to hear this from me. Her sister passed away recently, and Natalie's fighting for custody of her niece, so she may have an adopted baby soon."

"A baby?" The initial shock on his father's face gave way to comical excitement, as though his birthday wish had come true. "You're going to be a father."

"Natalie needs to win custody first."

Garrett shied away from the thought of becoming Sophie's *fake* stepfather. The deal was between him and Natalie, but his father's unexpected response made him wary about how his family would react when they dissolved the marriage.

"How old is the baby?" An odd little smile tugged at his dad's lips.

"About six months."

"Well, when do I get to meet them? Dinner tomorrow evening?"

"If Natalie's free." It was Garrett's turn to be shocked. He'd gotten a lecture when he said he was marrying an *employee*, but when he added a baby into the picture, his old man turned to mush. "But Sophie's with her grandparents, so I can't guarantee you'll see her tomorrow."

"I see." His dad's shoulders drooped half an inch. "Did you already tell Adelaide the news?"

Garrett nearly groaned. "Not yet."

He and his father exchanged a rare look of understanding. Adelaide was going to flay him for keeping Natalie and Sophie a secret. Unfortunately, he couldn't tell her it was new to him as well. He would have to appreciate the irony on his own while his baby sister put him in his place.

Seven

The weeks leading up to their wedding had spun past her in a tornado of improbable events. Now Natalie found herself standing in the Song family's garden. It had been transformed into the most enchanting wedding venue she'd ever seen. The shimmering Pacific Ocean, the mild spring breeze and the deep orange sunset held an otherworldly beauty that stilled her breath.

And Natalie wanted to sob her heart out. She shouldn't be here. She didn't belong in this world of riches and luxuries. She didn't belong with Garrett.

Traci, I miss you so much. If her big sister had been here, she would shake Natalie by the shoulders and tell her to run the hell away. From the lies. *But then, if she was alive, I wouldn't have thrown myself into this ridiculous scheme just so I could adopt Sophie.*

The sudden surge of resentment knocked the wind out of her. None of this was Traci's fault. No one had twisted Natalie's arm to marry Garrett. Even the man himself hadn't unduly pressured her. She couldn't deny that his arrogant certainty swayed her, but in the end, the choice had been entirely hers. *God, I wish I could go back a month and slap some sense into myself.* Well, she didn't have a time machine, and she had a part to play.

Adelaide and the wedding coordinator had pulled off a miracle in a few short weeks. But finding a suitable venue on such short notice had proven impossible until Adelaide convinced her grandmother to allow the wedding to proceed in their home. For the sake of privacy.

Natalie sighed wistfully at the dusty pink and cream calla lilies—the color of her bouquet—and the rest of the flowers in fresh spring colors that were in full bloom throughout the garden. If she ever got married after this madness ended, her real wedding would pale in comparison to her fake one.

"Natalie!" Adelaide linked an arm through hers and tugged her back inside. "Garrett just got here. What if he saw you?"

"I'd say hi," Natalie mumbled under her breath.

Adelaide had had her locked up in a guest bedroom all afternoon while a makeup artist, a hairstylist and a seamstress poked and prodded Natalie. As exhausting as it had been, her reflection convinced her the hours were well spent. More than anything, she truly loved her wedding dress. It could've been a French heirloom from the 1920s. The silk inner dress hugged her figure, but the shimmery lace overlay shifted and swirled around her like Salome's seven veils.

"You know it's bad luck for the groom to see the bride before the wedding." Her soon-to-be sister-in-law huffed and threw her an exasperated frown.

"Sorry."

Adelaide and their father, James, were probably shocked by Garrett's sudden news, but they welcomed her with open arms. His grandmother, however, had refused to meet Natalie, much less attend the wedding.

She wasn't vain enough to expect everyone to like her, but Garrett's grandmother had decided she didn't like her without bothering to meet her. *I guess a middle-class woman without a family could never be worthy of her grandson.* Her absence stung even more since she'd chosen to stay in her room, mere steps away from the ceremony. Natalie couldn't imagine how hard his grandmother's rebuff might be for Garrett. Sure, their marriage was a ruse, but Madame Song didn't know that.

"People have heard of bridezilla, but I bet they've never heard of sister-in-law-zilla." Adelaide said, ushering Natalie back inside. The joke brought her out of her sullen thoughts.

Alone in her bridal suite, Natalie paced in circles, too nervous to sit. She stopped in front of a settee where her bridal *hanbok* sat, wrapped in a box. The traditional Korean dress was worn on special occasions like weddings and New Year's Day.

Natalie never had one of her own, but had always wanted one. Her mom had eschewed all things Korean when she moved to the States with Dad, a soldier who'd been stationed in Seoul. But Korea was once her mom's home, and learning about its culture made Natalie feel connected to her.

She opened the box and ran her fingers over the dress. It had a deep yellow cropped top and a crimson empire-waist skirt with hand-embroidered flowers and butterflies fluttering across the bottom of the voluminous skirt and on parts of the sleeves.

Her sister-in-law had hired a well-known seamstress to make the *hanbok*, hoping her grandmother would come around and attend the wedding. If she did, Garrett and Natalie were to change into their *hanbok* after the wedding ceremony to observe a short tradition where the eldest members of the groom's family bless the newlyweds by throwing dried jujubes for the bride to catch in her skirt.

Natalie had thought Adelaide was messing with her with the whole jujube thing, but online research verified the tradition. Plus, she learned that the jujubes symbolized children. The more jujubes the bride caught, the more children the couple would have. Natalie had laughed herself to tears imagining Garrett and her batting the jujubes away.

Lost in her musings, Natalie nearly jumped out of her skin when Adelaide knocked softly and poked her head in. "Hey, sis. They're ready for you."

Adelaide was quiet for once as they walked to the garden. She held Natalie's icy hand in her warm one. Before they reached the guests, she leaned in and carefully hugged Natalie so she wouldn't disturb her makeup and intricate updo.

"Thank you for marrying my brother. He seems cold and aloof, but he's a really good guy and I can see glimpses of his old self when you're with him. And I'm so happy I finally get an older sister."

"You're going to make me cry before my grand entrance." She breathed in a shuddering breath. "I'm happy to have a sister again."

Too soon, Natalie stood at the start of the silken road, but her feet refused to budge. She hadn't been close enough to her father to miss him at this moment, but she wished she had a strong arm to hang on to. There were too many eyes on her, making her want to run in the opposite direction.

She searched the crowd. For what, she didn't know. Not until she found him.

Garrett's heated gaze bore into her and the knot in her chest broke, allowing her to breathe again. The ringing in her ears faded as he came into focus. He was breathtaking. His unruly hair was swept back, accentuating the hard angles of his face. The fitted tuxedo made his shoulders look impossibly broad. He exuded power and certainty, and for this moment, lie or not, he stood waiting for *her*. His eyes didn't leave hers for a second, and she held on to his gaze to guide her to his side. She didn't remember taking a single step until she reached him at the altar and he enfolded her icy hands in his.

"You look beautiful." His whisper caressed her ear and she shivered with awareness.

Natalie focused on the heat of his body and her skin prickling in response. Anything but the dread that threatened to consume her if she acknowledged it.

The ceremony washed over her like a flitting dream and she made the oldest, most sacred of vows with no hope of keeping them. For someone who was allergic to lying, she sure was getting good at it.

Garrett wrapped Natalie in his arms and they swayed to the music. Like the night at Le Rêve, his blood sang as their bodies touched, but this time, it was more than desire. Temporary or not, she was his wife—his alone.

"We're finishing our dance at last," he said before his possessiveness overwhelmed him. She gave him a ghost of a smile, but fatigue lined her features. He tucked her head under her chin to hide his frown. After their dance, he led Natalie back to their table and reached for her hand. "Are you all right?"

"Of course." He studied her face, his thumb drawing slow circles on her wrist. She was pale under her makeup with dark blue half circles under her wide eyes. Seeming to notice his concern, she forced a smile. "I'm fine, Garrett."

He grunted, unconvinced by her reassurance, but the stubborn jut of her chin said there was no whisking her away for an early night. With a resigned sigh, he turned his attention to the crowd and sucked in a quick breath.

"Sophie has my father wrapped around her little pinkie."

She looked adorable in her cream-colored dress with pink and white flowers dotting the skirt, and his dad held her like a precious treasure. When he lifted the baby high in the air, she rewarded him with a squeal and an infectious giggle, peppered with wet raspberries. His father laughed out loud for the first time in what seemed like years. *How will Dad take it when Sophie and Natalie leave for New York in the winter?* Something close to dread stabbed at his gut.

"She's a charmer." Natalie watched them with a soft, sweet smile, then met his gaze and held it. "And, Garrett, it'll be okay. Sophie and your family won't have a chance to get too attached. She's with her grandparents, and what little time I have with her I'll be guarding greedily."

Her voice trembled slightly. She obviously didn't want anyone to get hurt, either, especially their family. She continued to search his face, worry and vulnerability in her expression. He nodded, unable to trust his voice, but his heart twisted when she gave him a tremulous smile.

This was their wedding day—alluding to the end of their marriage left a bad taste in his mouth. Capturing his bride's hand, he planted a kiss on her palm, wanting to distract her from her thoughts. He flashed a wolfish grin when she gasped and turned a lovely pink. For good measure, he brushed his lips against the sensitive skin of her wrist, and a shiver ran through her.

"Garrett," she breathed.

Her voice was low and husky, and reckless lust flared in him again. He'd made sure their first kiss as husband and wife was short and chaste. But sitting so close to her, her soft fragrance entangling his senses, he wanted to claim her—to have a real wedding night. *Damn it.* He dropped her hand and sat back in his seat. When he saw Mike waving him over, Garrett rushed to his feet. "Duty calls."

"Does your duty entail joining that group over there with

everyone holding a bottle of champagne?" Natalie said with a wry smile. "I think there's a bottle with your name on it."

His best man held a bottle in each fist and lifted them over his head, confirming her suspicion. "It's not easy, but someone has to do it," Garrett said.

She laughed and gave him a gentle push toward them. "Well, go then."

"I'll be back." Without thinking, he dropped a kiss on the tip of her nose, the easy affection startling him. That bottle of champagne was sounding better by the minute.

When Garrett reached his friends, he grabbed a bottle out of Mike's hand and tipped down a good quarter of it.

"Thirsty?" His friend quirked an eyebrow at him.

"Very."

"Oh, what the hell." Mike shrugged and followed suit. "Gentlemen, Garrett beat us to it and drank half his bottle already. Let's drink to our unexpected groom. May you not be an ass to your stunning new bride so she will tolerate you till the end of days."

"Thank you for that touching speech." Garrett lifted his bottle to his friends and drank.

Shouts of laughter and cheers rang through the crowd, and much imbibing ensued. His emotions back in check, he risked a glance at Natalie. Her chair was empty and a flash of irritation hit him. He'd run from her a moment ago and now he wanted her where he'd left her. He conceded he was being an ass. Still, his gaze sought her out in the crowd.

He found her on the dance floor, being twirled by his father. He was smiling down at Natalie and she was biting her lip as though she was on the verge of tears. Garrett's stomach lurched in alarm. After shoving his champagne bottle at Mike, he rushed to her side.

When he reached the dance floor, her smile was still a bit watery but she didn't seem upset and his dad was chuckling.

"May I cut in?" Garrett said.

"Of course. She's all yours." After kissing Natalie on the cheek, his father strolled off.

"What happened?" He watched his dad join Sophie and Mrs. Kim—Natalie's firecracker neighbor. He'd met her during the move, and survived her intense grilling.

"What do you mean?"

"Why were you about to cry?"

Her mouth opened, then closed. "How did you know?"

"I saw you." He brushed aside her question impatiently. "Tell me."

"Your father just welcomed me to the family. He said... I was his daughter now." Her voice broke, and tears sprang to her eyes. "I don't even remember my mom, and my dad couldn't stand me. Even with Traci gone and Sophie's adoption in the air, your dad made me feel like I was part of a family. Like I wasn't alone. What he said was a gift—a gift I don't deserve—but I'll cherish it forever."

Garrett didn't know what to say, so he pulled her close and held her against his chest. *What can I say? Enjoy it while it lasts?* Things were getting a hell of a lot more complicated than he'd anticipated, and he had a sick feeling in his stomach that hearts would be broken before this was over.

And he hated himself for praying his heart wouldn't be one of them.

Eight

Garrett pressed her against him, and Natalie forgot everything—the lies, the uncertainty, the guilt. The warmth of his embrace and the sweet strains of the ballad gradually eased the tension from her shoulders.

"Kiss, kiss, kiss!"

Natalie jolted back to reality at the thundering chant of the tipsy wedding guests and the sharp chiming of forks striking wineglasses. She peeked over Garrett's shoulder to see they were surrounded by his champagne-chugging buddies. She buried her face into his chest again and groaned.

"Let's give them the kiss, then we can leave," he said, lifting her chin with the crook of his finger.

Natalie looked up at him with an exasperated sigh. By the grim line of Garrett's mouth, he wasn't too thrilled about it, either. He lowered his head slowly, brushed her lips with the softest of touches and began to draw away, but the gentleness of his kiss knocked down her defenses. Too tired to fight, she pressed herself against him and pulled his mouth back with greedy fingers tangled in his hair.

Garrett stilled for a moment, but with a moan, he took control of the kiss. Nipping and tasting her bottom lip, he sought entry with the tip of his tongue. She complied and he deepened the kiss, his fingers digging into her hips. The slick slide of his tongue against hers as they tangled and danced made her light-headed, and she slid her hands down his arms and spread her fingers across the shifting muscles of his back.

Garrett's breath caught sharply in his throat, then he pressed his hand against her back and pulled her flush against his body. Catcalls, shouts and applause rang far off in the distance, but Natalie was too busy to acknowledge the sound. An unmistakable hardness pressed against her stomach through the soft material of her dress, and she whimpered, rising on tiptoes to get closer to him.

Then she was rudely torn from him and held at arm's length. Garrett stared at her with an unreadable expression on his face, his hands gripping her shoulders. They stood silently, both breathing hard.

She'd forgotten where they were and why they were kissing in the first place. She might not have stopped if Garrett hadn't pushed her away.

Natalie wanted to become a little rodent so she could scurry into the nearest mouse hole. Not only was the situation mortifying, but she also couldn't let this happen again if she wanted an easy-peasy annulment.

Tonight had to be a fluke. They'd kissed plenty of times since their engagement. Yet she'd successfully resisted the temptation to tangle tongues with him. The wedding wasn't *real*—at least not for the bride and groom—but she was only human. How could she help but notice how beautiful and romantic everything was and get a little carried away?

"Let's go." Garrett's voice was gruff but his expression was impassive.

He had put their kiss behind him. And why not? It was just another kiss to him. Not just that, but it was a fake kiss. He couldn't help that he was an excellent kisser and his fake bride couldn't take the heat.

In a blur of smiling faces and well wishes, they bid their guests and family a hasty goodbye and headed for the Ritz-Carlton. Since it was only a marriage of convenience, they'd agreed a honeymoon was unnecessary. Besides, she had a baby to adopt and he had a partnership and a CEO seat to secure. It was time they focused on the important goals.

"Here we are." Garrett waved away the valet as they arrived and opened her car door for her.

He put his hand on the small of her back and led her into the hotel lobby. Once the elevator door closed behind them, he dropped his hand and stepped aside, putting some space between them. Natalie annoyed herself by missing the heat of his body next to hers. As soon as they reached the penthouse, Garrett headed to the foot of the stairs.

"You did well today," he said, loosening his tie and the top buttons of his shirt. Her eyes were riveted to the hollow at the base of his throat, which had been revealed by his unintentional striptease.

"Thanks?" Natalie said, bemused by his review of her wedding performance. "Good night."

Garrett stalked off without a backward glance. She blinked. *What the heck just happened?* She stood alone in the vast emptiness of the living room and looked around. The city lights twinkled, taunting her that the people out there were actually living their lives, while she was putting hers on hold for months.

Natalie sighed, bone-deep tired from being lonely. This had to be the most *un*romantic wedding night in the history of contract marriages. In the romance novels she read, the fake couples at least played chess or watched *Die Hard* together.

Her husband watched her descend the staircase with hooded eyes. Natalie was wearing a floor-length column dress in emerald silk with a sweetheart neckline that lovingly cradled her breasts. Her hair fell down her back with a single barrette sweeping to keep the curls out of her eyes. Gold shadow dusted her lids and her lips were painted Old-Hollywood red. She looked damn good and hoped to find at least a spark of appreciation in Garrett's gaze.

"Hey," she said, joining him at the foot of the stairs.

He wore a tailored tuxedo that emphasized his broad shoulders, narrow hips and long, muscular legs. Pure female appreciation fluttered in her chest, then died at his next words.

"We're late."

Right. There was no time to waste on complimenting his wife.

"Of course," she said with sweet sarcasm. She was exactly four minutes late. "Sorry for holding you up."

Garrett raised his eyebrows in response, and Natalie fumed inside. They'd been married for thirteen days and twenty-one hours, and she was beyond tired of her husband's cool apathy toward her. They were going to a charity ball that Clark Nobu and Sebastian Diaz were attending, and she wanted to help Garrett make a good impression.

Maybe she should come down with a sudden, blinding migraine. Natalie suppressed the childish impulse. A deal was a deal. She would do her best to help Garrett. No matter how infuriating he was.

Silence had been a staple during their short marriage, and it followed them on their drive to the ball. Most days, Garrett left for work before she woke up and came home after she went to bed. She hardly even ran into him at the office. Being busy was one thing, but she didn't understand why their conversations had become so stilted. Couldn't they be business partners who talked to each other?

"What's our plan?" She hoped strategizing would break some of the tension between them. "You said Sebastian's attending with his wife, but what about Clark? Is he married?"

"No, he's a widower."

"Oh, no. That poor man."

"Life goes on."

Something in Garrett's tone sent chills down her spine. *Is it because James is a widower, too?* She could let it go and enjoy the stifling silence again. Or not. She sensed an old hurt there and found herself wanting to ease it.

"How did your mom die?" she asked softly.

Every muscle in Garrett's body tensed, and Natalie thought she might have crossed the line he'd drawn between them.

"Cancer."

"I'm so sorry." She knew the pain of having someone she loved being stolen from her too soon. "I didn't know."

"Not many people do." Garrett kept his gaze on the road. "It wasn't a long battle, though. She went quickly."

"How old were you?"

"Fifteen."

"Oh, Garrett." Natalie reached out and put her hand on his arm.

"My parents were crazy about each other," he continued in a voice so low she almost didn't hear him. "My father... he broke down, as though someone cut off his life source."

"You had to grieve for both your parents."

His eyes snapped to her, and in that moment, the vulnerability and loneliness of the fifteen-year-old Garrett stared out at her. Natalie's heart bled for that boy.

"I want you to introduce yourself to Sebastian Diaz and his wife. They're visiting from Spain. Sebastian is a substantial shareholder and the COO of Vivotex. His opinion carries tremendous weight," Garrett said, regaining his composure and severing the brief connection they'd shared. Natalie pulled her hand from his arm, knowing her touch was no longer welcome. "I know everything about him on paper, but I don't know what really makes the man tick. Meeting him socially might show you something I haven't learned."

"What about you?"

"I'm going to chat with Clark Nobu, the head of Vivotex's US headquarters."

"Sounds like a plan," she said with false bravado.

Her emotions collided with each other hard enough to give her whiplash. Empathy, anger and hurt churned in a primordial soup in her stomach, but she focused on the most pressing emotion at the moment. Nervousness. Major panic-inducing nervousness.

Natalie clenched her teeth, determined not to let Garrett see through her calm facade. She'd never been to a ball before and he planned on leaving her on her own. Before it could take form, she stomped down on the twinge of resentment prickling inside her. He had no reason to know she felt like Cinderella five minutes before midnight. Even if he did, she didn't need him to protect her. If her designer gown turned into rags when the clock struck twelve, she'd rock it as the grunge-chic look and rescue her own behind.

They arrived at the famed Music Center, the venue for the charity event, and maneuvered through the glamorous mob to enter the grand hall. The modern building emanated subdued opulence through deep, dark wood and rich royal blues.

Garrett scanned the crowd from the elevated entryway, then guided them down the steps. He placed his big hand over her cold fingers curved on his tuxedo sleeve. The night air brushing her bare shoulders had chilled her, but his touch warmed her up—far too efficiently. When he lowered his head and nuzzled her ear, a shiver ran down her spine and her toes curled.

"I'll come find you in an hour." Unlike the intimacy of his touch, his voice was cold and businesslike.

Her body's response to his proximity and his apparent immunity to hers made her temper flare. Before she knew what she was doing, she snaked her hand around the back of his neck and tugged so she could capture his startled mouth in a hot, demanding kiss, daring him to respond.

Garrett didn't back away from the challenge. He crushed her body against his and cupped her face as he deepened the kiss, his tongue plundering her mouth with frantic, deep plunges. Even as her body softened and opened in response, her mind retained a strand of reason. She'd made her point and she needed to end the kiss before her self-restraint broke.

Natalie managed to maneuver her hands against his chest, which proved challenging since there was no room between them from chest to thigh. *God, he has magnificent pectorals.* She leaned back at the waist at the same time she pushed against his chest with all her strength.

Garrett barely budged but lifted his head an inch away from hers. His eyes were molten onyx, filled with undisguised longing, and her blood pumped in triumph. But she couldn't fall back into his arms if she wanted to retain her pride.

"Okay," she said, her voice husky but functioning. "I'll see you in an hour."

After a featherlight kiss on his cheek, his wife sashayed away, her perfect round ass taunting him. He was able to swallow after three attempts, but it was only when she was out of sight that his lungs expanded to capacity. Her warm, vanilla fragrance had clouded his mind the moment she stepped into his car earlier. But standing with his arm around her had given him a whiff of the warm musk that could only be called pure, delicious Natalie. Combined with her dress and red, pouty lips, the woman was lethal to his sanity.

Garrett had been avoiding Natalie since their wedding, unwilling to gamble on his self-control holding out if he got too close. But there was an unexpected side effect to depriving himself of his wife's company. The suppressed desire slammed into him ten times stronger the moment he laid eyes on her.

He scowled with frustration at the ridiculous predicament that he couldn't make love to his own wife. A server passing by gasped and hurried past him, mistaking herself as the target of his displeasure. He released a deep breath and rearranged his expression to one more suitable for the event, then strode in the opposite direction from Natalie. He had a partnership deal to secure.

Clark's formidable intellect and shrewd instincts were unmatched in the industry. He also happened to be a decent human being by all accounts. Both of them being in the fashion industry, they'd exchanged pleasantries in the past. Even without an official partnership between their companies, Nobu would be a valuable ally.

Garrett found him leaning against the bar nursing a drink. "Just the man I was looking for."

"Song." Clark assessed him with a shadow of a smile. "Eager to claim that drink I owe you?"

"We're on the same wavelength." He saw no point in playing games when the other man would see right through them. "The partnership already looks promising."

"It's always looked promising. The problem is the timing and the execution."

"The shared vision is the crucial factor." Garrett grinned. "The rest is technicalities."

"I would like a preview of your plans for the *technicalities*. People say your genius is in the details."

"That's quite a reputation to live up to, but I appreciate your vote of confidence." He raised his glass in salute.

His conversation with Clark flowed easily and soon they were on their second glass of Scotch. Garrett scanned the throng of partygoers, hoping to catch a glimpse of his wife, but she was nowhere to be seen.

"I know you're new at this so I'm going to give you some unsolicited advice," Clark said. "Does your wife know anyone at this party?"

"Not to my knowledge."

"And you left your brand-new bride to fend for herself amid all this massive hoopla? I hope you're looking forward to sleeping in the guest room tonight."

Garrett chuckled at the irony, pushing aside his prickling unease. He recalled her brief panic over the size of Mike's party, but she'd single-handedly won over that crowd. He had no doubt she was charming her way through this ballroom full of guests. Even so, anxiety tugged at him.

"Natalie is far too independent to need me hanging around her all night."

"You poor, clueless bastard."

They went in search of Natalie and found her a few steps outside the ballroom with Sebastian Diaz and his wife. From the booming sound of Mr. Diaz's belly laugh, she was having a successful night.

"Maybe I misspoke," Clark whispered, and walked ahead to greet the Diazes.

"Sorry to keep you waiting, sweetheart." Garrett slipped his arm around Natalie's waist and dropped a chaste kiss on her red lips, unwilling to torture himself with anything more.

"I missed you, darling, but your lovely friends have kept me from wilting away." She smiled sweetly at him and leaned her head against his shoulder.

Even though her affectionate greeting was for the benefit of their audience, he couldn't help pulling her tighter against him, drawn by her warmth. "Sebastian. Camilia. It's good to see you."

"Good to see you as well," Sebastian said. "I'm glad I got to meet your beautiful bride."

"I hope you were behaving yourself," Garrett replied, and the older man burst into another guffaw. "Natalie, I want you to meet Clark Nobu. Clark, this is my better half."

Clark smiled and lifted her hand to his lips. "It's a pleasure to meet you."

"Nice to meet you, too." Natalie blushed, lowering her lashes.

Garrett frowned and tightened his fingers around her waist. Widower or not, Clark had a reputation with women.

"Please forgive me for detaining your husband. He was eager to come back to you."

"That doesn't sound like him. He knows I don't need a chaperone." She arched an eyebrow at Clark and glanced at Garrett. "Don't you, my love?"

Clark's eyes widened and Garrett grinned. "Of course I do."

"Well, I still say your husband's a madman for leaving your side." Clark winked at Natalie, drawing a bright smile from her.

Breaking the man's jaw wouldn't help Garrett win his support, but refraining from the satisfaction wasn't an easy call. *Where the hell did that come from?* He forced himself to breathe and unclench his fist.

"I have a prior engagement but I hope to see you again soon, Natalie." Clark turned to Garrett and said in an undertone, "And, Song, please have your secretary call mine to schedule our meeting."

"Absolutely. Looking forward to it," said Garrett with a firm handshake.

After bidding everyone good-night, Clark disappeared into the crowd. With a surge of protectiveness, Garrett stepped behind Natalie and wrapped his hands around her waist. Her proximity and warmth eased the brief unease that had seeped into his veins. He'd never been much for public displays of affection. But it was different with Natalie. He had difficulty controlling his urge to be close to her. To touch her.

At that moment, Natalie glanced over her shoulder at him, her amber eyes wide and beguiling. He had to kiss her—to taste those sinful crimson lips. Garrett dipped his head to do just that when Camilia's voice jolted him back to the present.

"Natalie is such a charming young lady, Garrett. And I'm so excited we share a common passion," said Camilia. "Tennis!"

"Tennis?" He smiled vaguely and arched an eyebrow at his wife. Their faces were mere inches apart and he couldn't bear to pull away from her.

"Yes. Well…" She tensed against him and her eyes grew wide and plaintive. "I'm better at talking about the sport than playing it. Camilia is much more active in the game than I am."

"I'm not the one who played on the varsity team." The older woman wagged a finger at Natalie.

"In high school."

Undeterred, Camilia clapped her hands in front of her chest. "I have a wonderful idea. Sebastian was invited to Hansol's retreat next month. We just *have* to play doubles."

"I haven't held a racquet in a decade," Garrett said. "It

wouldn't be fair for us to go up against pros like you and Sebastian."

"Nonsense." Sebastian waved aside his objections. "It'll be a friendly game. Nothing brings people closer than enjoying a sport together."

"How could we refuse if you put it that way?" Natalie said before he could think of a judicious refusal. He narrowed his eyes at her too-innocent air.

"You can't unless you want to break an old man's heart."

"Sebastian, I would never do that in a million years," Natalie said, her eyes twinkling. "You have yourselves a doubles match."

Garrett felt a stunned grin spread across his face. His wife had hustled the Diazes into a tennis match.

Nine

"Garrett… *Garrett!*"

What the hell? Garrett ran down the stairs, bolting over the last half flight to reach Natalie. She was standing in the middle of their kitchen, pale as virgin snow.

"Are you hurt? What's going on?" He grabbed her by the shoulders and scanned her from head to toe for injuries.

"Norma is going to blacklist me after tonight. I'm sure of it. And it's all my fault." Her voice broke on the last word and tears filled her amber eyes.

Satisfied that she wasn't physically hurt, Garrett shoved his hand through his hair and swallowed a frustrated growl. Norma Rice, Sophie's social worker, was coming over for dinner tonight, and Natalie had been a nervous wreck all day.

"Breathe, Natalie. Whatever happened, I'm sure it's not that bad."

"I burned the main course. She's coming for dinner but all she's going to get is a salad."

"Didn't you say you were making shrimp scampi? How do you burn...?" Garrett coughed to cover his laugh. "I mean, I'm sure it's fine. A little char adds flavor."

She slammed the pan on the counter and Garrett winced. The contents of the pan were burned beyond recognition. They wouldn't even be able to salvage the pan, much less their dinner.

Natalie would've been the first one to laugh at herself under normal circumstances. Not tonight. She was wound so tight, Garrett was afraid she'd snap before the social worker got there. With a sigh, he unbuttoned the sleeves of his shirt and rolled them above his elbows.

"What are you doing?" Her eyes widened as she watched him.

"Helping."

Opening the fridge, he checked its contents. Garlic, parsley, lemon and white wine. She'd only bought ingredients called for by the shrimp-scampi recipe, but now the shrimp was history.

"I can manage," she said, straightening her shoulders. "I know you have work to do before Norma gets here."

"You also yelled bloody murder, calling me down here. I'm cooking and you're demoted to being my assistant."

"You can cook?" Her stubborn refusal to accept help gave way to a hopeful lift of her voice.

"Like angels can sing." He shot her a wide grin before laying out the ingredients on the counter and setting a big pot of water to boil. "We'll have spaghetti *aglio e olio*. Do we have crushed pepper flakes?"

"Crushed pepper?" Despite her protest seconds ago, Natalie smiled, unable to hide her relief. "Let me check."

"And the salad, did you already make it?"

"Make the salad?" She snorted. "Even I can dump out a salad kit and squeeze dressing over it."

"You bought a salad kit?" He grimaced. "Get out a

lemon and grate off some lemon rind. We'll try to salvage the salad the best we can."

He chopped a handful of garlic cloves and the Italian parsley. When the olive oil was warm in the pan, he added the garlic, then turned off the heat after two minutes. The simple pasta needed to be served immediately after it was prepared.

Natalie had gained some color back in her cheeks and seemed calmer after having a task to focus on. She had grated the skin off a dozen lemons but Garrett let her carry on.

"Are we serving dessert?" he asked.

"What? You bake, too?" Her expression was an amalgam of admiration and envy.

"Hell, no. I don't do measuring cups or tiny spoons."

"Okay." Natalie's smile was small but genuine. She had her panic under control. "Then we'll just go with the ice cream and berries I bought."

Garrett was suddenly struck by the domesticity of the moment—the two of them making dinner together, waiting for their guest. The odd twist in his heart was accompanied by a jab of fear. Before he could analyze his feelings, Sophie cooed through the baby monitor.

"Sophie's up," he said. Their attorney was a skilled negotiator, and the Davises agreed to allow the baby to spend two days a week with him and Natalie soon after their wedding. "I'll get her ready."

"Would you?" Natalie pressed a shy kiss on his cheek. "Thank you so much. Her outfit's on the nursing chair."

"No problem." His voice was gruff as he fought the urge to pull Natalie into his arms.

When Garrett reached the nursery, Sophie stood waiting, holding on to the railing of her crib like a prisoner doing time behind bars. But her chubby face split into a huge grin when she spotted him.

"Gah-gah!" He wasn't too thrilled about sharing the famous singer's name, but he was getting used to being called Gah-gah. With that sweet smile, anything she said was fine by him.

"Hello, sweetheart." Garrett lifted her out of the crib and over his head until the sound of her giggles filled his heart. "We're counting on you to charm Ms. Rice tonight. You can handle her, right?"

"Gah-gah."

"Okay." He took that as a yes and stared at the pink dress set out for her. "You're going to have to help me here. Does this ruffly thing go on your head or your bottom?"

Sophie tried to stuff it in her mouth, where it definitely didn't belong. He contemplated shouting for Natalie but he refused to admit he was an idiot who didn't know how to put a dress on a tot.

By the time they came back downstairs, Natalie had set the table with a centerpiece of trimmed daisies and a yellow table cover he'd never seen. It looked warm and charming, like someplace a real family would eat. It filled Garrett with a yearning he thought was dead. *No. None of this is real.* It was an illusion that a soft breeze could extinguish. Something that would end in less than a year.

But all thoughts fled when a glowing smile lit Natalie's face, and a thread of inevitability tugged him toward her. She leaned in and kissed the baby, and he wrapped his free arm around her waist. When her startled eyes met his, Garrett slowly lowered his head to kiss her, and she rose onto her tiptoes to meet him halfway.

Before their lips could meet, the elevator buzzer rang to announce the arrival of their guest. With a gasp, Natalie took a step back then another, and he stalked her, step by step, until he caught himself. He ran his fingers through his hair as the clacking of his wife's shoes rang down the hallway. After a deep breath, he joined her to welcome their guest.

"Norma, I'm so happy you could make it," Natalie said, her nervousness so subtle that he could barely detect it.

"I'm Garrett Song. It's a pleasure to finally meet you." He shifted Sophie into his other arm, and extended his hand with a broad smile. "My wife has told me so much about you and how hard you're working on behalf of Sophie."

"Oh, well…" The social worker's round, ruddy face turned blotchy with a fierce blush. "It *is* all about the little ones. I just do the best I can for them."

"Of course, and I thank you for it." He nuzzled the little girl's soft cheeks and enlisted her charms. "Sophie, say hi to Ms. Rice."

"Puuuu," she said, not skimping on the spittle. Natalie's eyes widened in alarm when Norma harrumphed and proceeded to dry her face with a lacy handkerchief.

"Well, then." He cleared his throat. "Would you like a glass of wine, Norma?"

He led them into the dining room and settled Sophie in her high chair. Then he poured two generous glasses, offering one to the social worker and the other to his wife. Natalie gazed longingly at the crisp, chilled chardonnay, but she hesitated. He sighed and thrust the glass into her hand.

"I'm the designated parent tonight, so no wine for me," he said. "Sophie's a good sleeper but she's teething right now, so she might wake up at night."

Norma nodded enthusiastically, making some of her wine slosh over the rim of her glass. Garrett caught Natalie's eye and winked, and his wife mouthed, *thank you*. As she breathed in the crisp, chilled chardonnay and smiled, warming the entire room with her light, he stared at her, slack jawed.

Hell.

"I'll bring out the salad," he said in a rush.

When the kitchen door swung shut, Garrett ran cold water in the sink and splashed some on his face. His body hadn't stopped burning since the gala. Every time he reined in his desire, her scent would waft past him or her smile would capture his attention, and he had to start all over. He breathed deeply through his nose until he had his body under control. Natalie had been amazing at the gala even though he'd abandoned her like a jerk. The least he could do was win over the social worker.

He served the first course, with cubes of tofu for the baby, and refilled the wineglasses. There was a lull in the conversation as the adults watched Sophie smash some tofu in her fists before transferring it to her mouth. She beamed proudly even though most of it ended up on her face.

"When did she start finger foods?" asked Norma.

"A few weeks ago," Natalie said, cleaning Sophie's face and hands with a baby wipe.

"She certainly is an enthusiastic eater." The social worker smiled fondly at the baby. Garrett caught Natalie's eyes and laughed at the understatement, while Sophie stuffed more tofu into her mouth.

Once the adults were finished with their salad, he cleared off the plates, waving aside Natalie's offer to help.

"I just need to toss together the pasta with the sauce. Keep Norma company." He dropped a kiss on the top of Natalie's head and heard Norma sigh from across the table. "Honey, is Sophie having her star pasta tonight?"

"Mmm-hmm." She hid her smile on the rim of her wineglass.

"We still have your homemade marinara sauce for the baby in the freezer, right?"

Natalie choked on the chardonnay but pulled herself together. "Right."

"I still rely on Natalie for most of the parenting duties," he said with a rueful look aimed at Norma. "I'm completely dumbfounded and humbled by what an amazing mom she is."

Garrett was laying on the loving husband act a bit thick, but Norma seemed to be gobbling it up. And he found himself enjoying his role for the night.

He brought out the main course and they all dug in to the meal.

"Everything is so delicious." Norma dabbed her mouth with the cloth napkin. "This pasta looks simple but it's so flavorful."

"Thank you. We're so glad you like it," Natalie said.

"Yes, my wife is a fantastic cook." *I wonder if I went too far with that one.* Natalie stared at him like he was crazy, and he decided he'd done just fine.

"Darling, would you help me put these dishes away before I bring out the dessert?" Her eyes shot daggers at him and she jerked her head for him to follow.

"Of course, my love."

The kitchen door shut behind them and she rounded on him. "What are you doing?"

"Helping you win custody of Sophie," he said mildly, fighting back a smile.

"I really appreciate your help—I do—but do you have to ham it up so much? She's going to see right through us."

"Did you see the woman's face? We have her completely charmed."

"You mean *you* have her charmed." Natalie sighed, inexplicable sadness flitting across her face.

"What's wrong?" He frowned, bewildered by her sudden mood change.

"Nothing's wrong. The day must be catching up with me." She gathered the ice cream and berries on a platter. "Let's go back out before Norma wonders where her dessert is."

Once dessert and coffee were served, Natalie lifted her

drowsy daughter from her high chair. "Norma, would you excuse me while I put Sophie down?"

"Of course," said Norma, smiling from ear to ear. "Please, don't rush on my account."

"Don't worry, honey. I won't let our guest become bored," Garrett said and earned himself a warning glance from his wife.

"So, Garrett," Norma said, her voice suddenly firm, after Natalie left the room with the baby.

His gaze shot back to the social worker. He'd been staring after the swing of Natalie's hips, and he had to clear his throat before answering. "Yes, Norma. Could I offer you anything else?"

"No, I couldn't eat another bite," she said. "I have a couple of questions for you."

His shoulders tensed. Had she saved the hardest part for last? Without Natalie there, she could easily catch him in a lie when it came to Sophie. "Go right ahead."

"You must be very busy with work. Are you gone from home often?" Norma's gaze became laser sharp and she leaned in for his answer.

Garrett had to improvise fast. "I do work long hours, but I try to be home for dinner at least twice a week. I can't avoid business trips but delegate when I can."

"Don't you think it'll be hard for Natalie to bear the brunt of the child rearing?"

"My father and sister adore little Sophie, and will help out often while we're in LA. Once the adoption is finalized and Natalie's ready to transition to New York, the Davises will want to spend as much time as possible with their granddaughter. If we get custody, that is."

Norma stared at him with narrowed eyes. A lesser man would've broken out in a cold sweat, but Garrett held her gaze with the most congenial expression he could muster. *Does the woman even blink?*

"How about the rest of the time? Both of you will be working."

"Natalie is leaning toward a Montessori nursery. Sophie is impatient to learn how to do things on her own, and a Montessori program would foster her independent spirit." Garrett paused to study the social worker's reaction. She wore an unfaltering poker face so he decided to hedge his bets. "However, I feel a bit overprotective, and would like to hire a nanny for the baby until she's around two. We're still figuring things out."

"Will you be moving to New York at the end of the year as well? Or will you be a weekend dad?"

"I'm absolutely moving to New York with my family." It was a bald-faced lie but a part of him was thrilled by the idea.

This isn't real, Song.

"Hmm," she said, releasing him from her scrutiny. He had no idea if he'd passed or failed the test.

"Sorry to keep you waiting." Natalie hurried down the stairs, the front of her blouse wet and crumpled. "Sophie decided I needed a bath, too."

"You're doing a wonderful job with her." Norma smiled and patted his wife's shoulder. "I hope you and your family are happy together. You deserve it after everything you and that sweet child have gone through."

"Thank you." The corners of Natalie's answering smile wobbled. "That means a lot."

"Well, then. It's time for me to head home to my family," Norma said, rising from the table.

"It was a pleasure having you over," Garrett said as he and Natalie led Norma down the corridor.

Natalie fidgeted beside him as they made small talk waiting for the elevator. As soon as the elevator doors closed, her excitement burst free.

"Did you hear her?" She jumped up and down with her hands clasped in front of her chest. "She called us a family."

Her amber eyes sparkled in her flushed face and happiness radiated from her. Garrett stared at the beautiful woman in front of him with overwhelming pride, and a familiar grip of possessiveness strummed through his veins. Steeped in her joy and relief, Natalie didn't seem to notice anything odd about his silent appraisal. Then, with a suddenness that surprised an "oof" out of him, she threw herself at him, winding her arms tightly around his neck. His arms instinctively wrapped around her as he chuckled into the wild tumble of her curls.

"Easy, there."

"Garrett, I…" Her words were muffled against his chest so he leaned back, loosening her death grip from his neck. He sought her eyes but she lowered her thick lashes with endearing shyness. "Thank you for tonight. You were wonderful."

"It was nothing." Her genuine gratitude felt undeserved. Considering what was at stake, Garrett only wished he could've done more. Even so… "Wonderful, huh?"

"Don't let it go to your head." Her attempt at a stern expression failed miserably. "But, yeah. You kind of were."

He wouldn't have been able to hold back his ridiculous grin even if he'd wanted to, and her answering smile was blinding. It took a moment for him to remember he still held her in his arms. The soft swell of her full breasts pressed against his chest, and her warm vanilla fragrance assailed his senses. He dropped his hands from her waist and took a hasty step back.

"Do you have an extra one of those?" he said, pointing at the baby monitor. "I should keep one in my room tonight in case Sophie wakes up."

"Why would you…" Natalie's eyes widened and she

waved her hands in front of her. "No. Really, there's no need. I…"

"I wasn't asking for permission. I wouldn't have offered you wine if I hadn't intended to keep my word." He strode to the counter and picked up the baby monitor. "You're exhausted. Go to bed and don't get up. I'm on baby duty tonight."

Garrett Song was a good man. A kind and wonderful man. He'd won over Norma and secured them an ally. And her husband's calm, rational arguments had convinced the Davises to consider supporting her adoption application in exchange for moving to New York after her promotion.

They didn't discuss any specifics about Garrett moving to New York since their marriage would probably be annulled before then. Besides, the Davises' main concern was having Sophie near them.

The very competent—and expensive—lawyer Garrett had hired was managing the legal angles in court. Against the odds, Natalie might really become Sophie's mom in every sense of the word.

With everything proceeding smoothly, Natalie was ready to tackle whatever the day hurled at her.

But not this.

Madame Song had invited her to her home at seven o'clock. Sharp. The woman hadn't even shown up for their wedding, which was literally in her backyard. What could she possibly want with Natalie now?

There was no time for introspection. Besides, Grace Song would tell Natalie exactly why she was summoned with unapologetic frankness. She vacillated about calling Garrett. Perhaps he had some insight about his grandmother's unexpected invitation, but he had a hectic schedule and she didn't want to bother him. In the end, she settled on sending him a quick text.

Meeting your grandmother. Will call you later.

She had less than two hours to get herself ready to meet the infamous Song matriarch, and she had no idea what to do. Mrs. Kim would know. Throwing everything she could grab into two giant shopping bags, she drove straight to her old apartment building.

"Mrs. Kim." Natalie was close to tears when her friend opened the door. "I need your help."

"Oh, for heaven's sake. Come inside." Her friend stepped back from the entrance and pointed to her sofa. "Put those bags down there and have a seat."

"Garrett's grandmother wants to meet me but I don't know what I'm supposed to say or do when I see her. I don't even know what I'm supposed to wear."

Mrs. Kim sifted through the bags Natalie had brought and gasped as she held up her bridal *hanbok*. "Oh, it's beautiful. A new bride should wear her *hanbok* to visit her husband's family for the first time."

"I need to wear all that fabric and present myself to her without falling flat on my face?" She'd packed it just in case, but was hoping she wouldn't have to wear it for her first audience with Garrett's grandmother.

"Breathe, girl." The older woman appraised Natalie with her head tilted to the side. "Now let's get this *hanbok* on you."

Once Mrs. Kim tugged, spun and muscled her into the skirt, Natalie gasped, "Is it supposed to be this tight?"

"Well, yes." Her friend pulled the ties another half inch tighter around her bust. "Your girls are lovely but not really ideal for a *hanbok*. If I don't bind you snugly enough, the cropped top is going to flap up in the front, and it'll look all wrong."

"Great." One of the few things she remembered about her mom was her telling everyone about how *big boned*

Natalie was. It took her years to accept her body, big bones and all. Even though the *hanbok* gaped and stuck out in places, she refused to feel bad about her figure. "I guess I'll have to forego breathing to make a good impression on Grandma Grace."

Mrs. Kim snorted. "I dare you to call her that to her face."

"Why not? Her name is Grace and she's Garrett's grandma," Natalie said with false bravado. *Yeah, I could never call her that. Your Supreme Highness is more fitting.* They'd never actually met, but she'd seen Grace Song from a distance a handful of times at the office. "What am I supposed to do with all this fabric?"

"The edge of the skirt winds around you to the left, so you could gather it in your left hand. Don't get confused and grab the right side. Women of ill repute used to wrap their skirt to the right. But don't quote me on that. It might be an urban legend, but let's just play it safe and go with the left side."

"Women of ill repute? What the literal hell?" Tears stung the back of her eyes. "How am I supposed to remember all this? I should just wear my skirt suit."

"Want to give her a nice view of your thighs and maybe flash her a little?" Mrs. Kim huffed. "You're going to have to kneel on the floor, so a pencil skirt is out of the question. I don't want you to hyperventilate so I won't even tell you about the formal bowing, where you have to cross your ankles and lower yourself to the ground and sit gracefully without falling on your ass—"

"Stop! You. Are. Not. Helping." Natalie immediately regretted her outburst. "Actually, you're a lifesaver. Thank you."

"You didn't need me. Well, maybe for the *hanbok*." Mrs. Kim clasped her hand. "Just be yourself, sweetie. She'll love you."

* * *

"Hi, I'm Natalie," she said to the kind-faced woman who answered the door at the Song family's mansion.

"I'm Liliana. She is waiting for you."

Natalie followed the housekeeper down the corridor, holding her skirt up to her *left*, grateful that they weren't going upstairs. When they reached a door near the back of the house, Liliana smiled warmly. "Good luck."

"Thank you. I really need it."

She knocked hesitantly on the door, wondering if she'd be judged by the tone of her knock. Maybe she should have knocked more confidently.

"Come in."

Natalie took a shuddering breath and drew back her shoulders. *You got this.* She opened the door, marched in and promptly tripped on her skirt. She saw herself falling in slow motion before she landed on her hands and knees with a thump.

Mrs. Song was by her side with lightning speed and ran her hands over Natalie. "Are you all right, child?"

The wind was knocked out of her and the throbbing in her knees told her she'd be black and blue the next day, but she wasn't broken or bleeding anywhere. It took her a few seconds to get her bearings.

"I'm fine, Mrs. Song. I'm so sorry."

"Grandmother." The older woman leveled Natalie with a stern gaze, settling herself back into her seat. "You are married to my grandson. You will address me as 'Grandmother.'"

"Yes, Grandmother." She might have hit her head on the floor. *Is Her Supreme Highness really asking me to call her 'Grandmother'?* Natalie worried her bottom lip, having no idea what to say or do next.

"I have not forgiven Garrett for his impudence. He dishonored me by asking for your hand without my approval."

"I—"

"You do not interrupt when an elder is speaking. I see you have much to learn about our family's ways and traditions."

Natalie opened and closed her mouth. She was a bit peeved at the scolding, but she was more interested in learning about Garrett's grandmother than smart mouthing her. Grace Song seemed nothing like the cold, calculating woman she'd imagined her to be.

"Ever since his mother died, Garrett never once disobeyed my wishes. But an iron curtain fell across his heart, and I couldn't reach him. As the eldest son of the Song family, it is his duty to bring honor to the family name, and I used his sense of duty to motivate and propel him. I could find no other way to keep him from disappearing entirely. I thought an arranged marriage was his only chance to find warmth and companionship." Grace Song met Natalie's eyes and clicked her tongue. Probably because Natalie was pressing both hands over her mouth to stop herself from blurting, *What?* "Did you have something to say?"

"No, ma'am. Please continue."

"Marrying you was the first choice he made for himself in over a decade. An important, life-altering choice. Even though he chose the wrong way to do it, I hope it means he is finding his way back to us." The older woman's eyes glistened but Natalie didn't dare believe that it was from tears.

"Thank you, Grandmother. I know he misses you and hated opposing you—"

"Well, he did oppose me and he will not be easily forgiven."

"I… But…" Her gut told her Mrs. Song missed Garrett as much as he missed her.

"I want my grandson to become the man he was meant to be, but he should never have turned his back on his elders.

He should not have kept you a secret from me. He will make penance and win the CEO position without my support."

He'd hurt her. She thought Garrett hadn't trusted her enough to ask for her support, but he couldn't have told her about Natalie since there was no whirlwind romance or secret engagement. Lies and more lies had created a rift between Garrett and his family, but telling his grandmother the truth might destroy all chances of reconciliation.

Ugh. The cell phone she'd stuck inside her calf-high stocking—traditional Korean elf-toed things—had been vibrating for the last half hour, and she was getting nervous that it might be an emergency.

"I'm so sorry, but I need to check my phone. Someone has been calling me nonstop since I got here."

Natalie spun on her bottom to face away from Grandmother's sour expression and dug out her phone from under her skirt. She heard the older woman tsk again, and blushed with embarrassment. At least she hadn't stuck it inside her bra.

It was Garrett. He'd called eight times and texted a dozen increasingly urgent messages. Basically, he wanted to know if she was okay, and demanded she call him. Natalie sighed and shook her head. Did he think she was going to slip and reveal their secret? She peeked over her shoulder and hurriedly sent her husband a text.

I'm still with your grandmother. Everything is fine.

Liliana entered with a serving tray, and as they shared a lovely cup of tea, Natalie decided she felt eight percent less intimidated by Garrett's grandmother than she had half an hour ago.

"Will you be staying home now that you're married, *ah-ga*?" the older woman asked, setting down her teacup.

Grandmother had started calling her *ah-ga*, which was

how an elder addressed a new bride in their family. She said the literal translation meant "baby," and it made Natalie feel warm every time she called her that. It was silly to be touched by such a small thing, but learning about her heritage from her *grandmother* was more than she'd ever dreamed of.

"What? Oh, no. I've worked too hard to get where I am, and I plan to go even farther. I hope I can be one of those supermoms who do everything and a half."

Grandmother's lips tightened into a straight line. "Wouldn't Garrett benefit from you staying home?"

"You of all people should understand that a woman's place isn't necessarily at home." It wasn't easy to say, but it had to be said.

"Such audacity," the older woman said, but a faint smile softened her face. "But yes. I know very well that at times it takes a woman to build an empire."

Natalie wanted to be just like Grandma Grace when she grew up. They were still smiling at each other, both a little shy and surprised by their unexpected connection, when Garrett flung open the door without knocking and skidded into his grandmother's room.

It was as though he was expecting to face a raging battle. Instead, he found two sets of shocked female eyes focused on him. His heroic stance faltered and confusion took its place. "What's going on?"

Grandmother's expression turned stoic and hard, and Natalie wanted to whack Garrett on the back of his head. *What is wrong with him? Did he think his grandmother was roasting me over a pit?*

"Grandmother invited me to tea, honey. You should greet her properly and join us."

Garrett's mouth dropped open and his head swiveled back and forth between the two women before his gaze settled on his grandmother.

"*Hal-muh-nee*, have you been well?" His tone was endearingly hesitant.

"You know that I've been anything but," she said with artful hauteur. "I see you're practically glowing with health. Marriage must agree with you."

"Yes. It does," he said, his lips pressing into a stubborn line.

Mrs. Song didn't give him permission to sit, and a tense silence filled the room.

"Please rest, *hal-muh-nee*. We'll be on our way." Garrett lifted Natalie to her feet. "Let's go."

Afraid to stumble and fall again, Natalie allowed herself to be tugged out the door. It was only when they were on the freeway heading home that she realized she hadn't said goodbye to Grandmother.

She stole a peek at her husband's profile. A muscle jumped in his jaw and his knuckles were white on the steering wheel.

"What were you doing there?" His voice was a low growl, and there was more than a small amount of anger in his words.

"She asked me to visit, and I've been wanting to meet her. Grandmother and I were getting along just fine until you barged in."

"Grandmother?" He shot a surprised glance at her.

"Yes." Natalie couldn't hold back her smug smile. "I'm to address her as Grandmother, and she calls me *ah-ga*."

"You…she…what?" Garrett's head snapped toward her; he looked dumbstruck.

"Grandmother asked me to visit her once a week from now on, and she wants to meet Sophie as soon as possible."

Her husband opened his mouth to speak, but changed his mind and turned his gaze back to the road. But not before Natalie saw the pride and admiration in his eyes.

Ten

Hansol was famous for pampering their employees with an annual retreat at a luxury resort. This year the two-night retreat was being held at Ojai, a small town reminiscent of Provence that improbably flourished in California's desert climate.

Ojai was one of Natalie's favorite places in California. It was so serene and beautiful, and the richly scented air provided continuous aromatherapy. The hacienda-style villa she'd be sharing with Garrett was gorgeous, but it only had one bedroom. Natalie's mouth went dry at the sight of the prominent king-size bed in the center of the room. She averted her eyes and made quick work of changing into her swimsuit.

Garrett had a meeting at the office, so he'd arranged for one of the Song family drivers to bring her to the retreat. A part of her had been relieved he couldn't drive with her. Something had shifted between them after her visit with his grandmother. They somehow ended up having dinner together almost every night of the week, and talked for hours, laughing like old friends until they…weren't. Their attraction would combust without warning and they would find each other mere inches apart, breathing heavily. Starving for a kiss. But one of them—Garrett more often than not—would come to their senses in the nick of time.

She was afraid that someday soon she wouldn't be able to pull away. Wouldn't want to. Natalie wanted her husband with such urgency that she was on the verge of exploding. She'd never desired anyone like this before. Not even Peter Klapper, the college boyfriend she'd fancied herself in love with. But he'd soon lost his appeal when she discovered his selfish, narcissistic nature.

The problem with Garrett was the more time they spent together, the more she liked and admired him, and her attraction only grew. Natalie released a long breath. Everything was going to be fine. As long as they didn't get within four feet of each other, she should be able to suppress her lust for her hot-as-hell husband. But they were sharing a suite for the next two nights. Tight quarters in romantic Ojai meant trouble. Horny, sizzling trouble. *Crap.*

She headed to the pool using the map she got from the front desk. She got a bit turned around and wound up taking the long way there, but she fortunately didn't run into any Hansol employees to witness her directional challenges.

She scanned the pool area and spotted a secluded corner that was perfect for her. After spreading out her towel on a lounger, she perched on the edge, ready for some sun worship. The soft melody she was humming under her breath sputtered and died as her jaw dropped.

Garrett was in the pool, swimming toward her with powerful, fluid strokes. When he reached the end by her chaise, he rested his forearms on the edge and grinned at her.

"When did you get here?" The husky tenor of his voice made the innocent question sound like a caress.

Only his glistening hair and muscled torso were visible to her, but Natalie couldn't drag in a full breath. Garrett was here and he was wet. The light sprinkling of hair on his forearms clung to his skin, and his jet-black hair rained drops of water. Mesmerized, Natalie followed the water sliding down the slopes of his broad shoulders, and wished her fingers could trail after it.

She'd never understood why people thought *wet* was sexy. Now she could write a thesis on it. The amusement sparkling in his eyes made her realize she was staring at him with her mouth open. *Kill me now.* She should be thankful she wasn't drooling.

"Less than an hour ago." To stop herself from staring at him, she focused on unbuttoning the linen shirt she'd thrown over her swimsuit and shrugged out of it. "What are you doing here? I thought you couldn't make it till later tonight."

The silence stretched on between them as his gaze bore into hers with an intensity that stole her breath. His cocky grin was nowhere in sight; instead, he looked at her with the thirst of a man lost in the desert. Confusion clouded her brain and she hid her face by digging in her tote for her sunscreen.

"Did you just get here, too?" Natalie asked to break the tension.

"Yes." Garrett cleared his throat. "Just."

"We must've crossed paths at the villa."

"Right. I saw your luggage in our room when I arrived."

Silence settled around them again as Natalie smoothed white lotion down her legs. It smelled like an orange Creamsicle. She succeeded in avoiding Garrett's eyes for as long as she could.

But she finished all too soon, leaving only her back undone. *Would it look odd if I dislocate my shoulder trying to get sunscreen on my back?*

"Here." Garrett pushed himself out of the pool. "Allow me."

Despite the hot sun, a chill tripped down her spine like tumbling dominoes.

"Th-thank you."

Natalie handed him the tube as he settled his glorious wet body next to hers. She gasped and hunched forward. She wasn't sure what startled her more—the coolness of his hands or the electric shock his touch set off.

"Sorry. The water was pretty cold." He tugged her back toward him. "Now, hold still."

He started at the curve of her neck then slid his hands down to the top of her shoulders. Cupping one, he circled his other palm down her back. His touch grew hot against her skin, and it was all she could do to keep from leaning back and purring.

"Your skin's so fair. Almost as transparent as fine china." His breath warmed the back of her neck. He leaned in closer, putting his lips at her ear. "Would you break if you're not handled gently?"

"I'm stronger than I look," she said. And right now, she wanted to test her strength with something hard and fast.

Natalie twisted around to face him, her breathing uneven. He perused her body, an arrogant tilt to his lips, and a flush of arousal spread across her bare skin. He wanted her. That much was certain. Emboldened, she met his gaze and held it before she lowered her eyes to stare appreciatively at his chest, so smooth and strong.

She'd wondered countless times what he would look like under his dress shirts, and her imagination had not done him justice. The dips and grooves of his well-defined abs begged to be touched. He allowed her to study his body, sitting so still that she wondered if he was breathing. Her hand reached out of its own accord and she pulled it back with a sharp gasp.

She was treading a dangerous path and needed to retreat several paces. It could only lead to heartbreak. He'd made it clear their marriage would be short-lived. If Natalie followed her instincts and gave herself to him, she would be the only one to blame for her regrets.

"I'm going in for a swim," she said, hoping the water was very, very cold because she was burning inside and out.

He stared at her for a few seconds, letting the electrified air float around them. Her cheeks turned an adorable shade of coral, which told him that she wasn't immune to the desire raging between them.

For a moment, he thought she was going to touch him. The image of her delicate hands on his naked torso almost made him groan.

"I'll see you later," he said, his voice curt. "I need to take care of a couple matters before dinner tonight."

"Okay, bye."

She dipped her toes in the pool, testing the water. He needed to get the hell away before she got wet. Garrett hurried toward the pool gate as quickly as he could, which wasn't very fast because the mindless part of his body refused to stand down. He hoped he was being inconspicuous as he placed his T-shirt in front of his tented board shorts and concentrated on deflating the tent.

Aunt Margo's sadistic cheek pinches. My old mangy mutt with his perpetual drooling. The food poisoning I had last summer. Just. Don't. Think. About. Her.

Natalie had cast a dangerous spell over him. He saw nothing else when she was near. Years of hard work, his family's legacy and the responsibility of ensuring the livelihood of thousands of employees were the foundation on which he'd built his adult life, but he forgot everything. He became a being of want and need. He had no control over it.

He had to devise a hands-off strategy for this weekend.

Making certain he hardly spent a moment alone with Natalie had worked so far, but his desire howled in his veins even when they were apart. *If I have this much trouble not touching her out in public, how the hell am I going to keep my hands off her tonight?* Resisting her allure would be torture—exquisite but agonizing torture. He needed a chastity belt for men.

By the time he reached the hotel lobby, Garrett had himself under control and pulled on his T-shirt. Hansol's employees crowded the air-conditioned sanctuaries of the indoor bars and restaurants, and their objective was loud and clear—consume vast amounts of alcohol and make public spectacles of themselves.

People were convinced what happened at company retreats didn't count in real life. For Garrett, who had been in the public eye his entire life, every second counted.

"Mr. Song, sir! Come join us!"

A few of the more inebriated employees tried to wave him over. These were the same employees who practically clicked their heels and scuttled away when he passed them in the office.

Garrett gave a curt nod and walked on, but he envied them with sudden intensity. He longed to forget about family expectations, and honoring your elders over your own desires. He wanted to burn away the scars of his childhood, his cynicism and his self-preservation instinct. He wished he could forget everything and be *reckless*. Get drunk in public, and make love to his wife...

A humorless laugh escaped from him. He was Garrett Song. Control was everything.

The moment he stepped into their villa and saw Natalie—lovelier in her shorts and T-shirt than any other woman he'd ever seen—he forgot all about work, plans or legacy. When he'd run into Natalie at the pool, the walls he'd meticulously constructed to shield his desire collapsed like a fortress made of smoke. His mind had been congested with yearning and hunger, and he couldn't turn to his work for refuge. Instead, he'd gone to the hotel gym to work out until his muscles screamed and he forgot how much he wanted to take his wife to bed. Unfortunately, his dick didn't care how tired the rest of his body was. One look at her and it was all too alert and ready for its own brand of workout. There was no denying he wanted her more than his next breath.

"Hi." She took a few uncertain steps toward him, eyeing him warily. "I was just about to make some tea. Would you like a cup?"

"No, thank you." He stalked her until she backed into the edge of the sofa.

He let his eyes roam her face, then down her body, soaking in every curve and flare. By the time his gaze returned to her face, all he heard was the thunder of his pounding heart. He raised his hand and smoothed his thumb across her cheek. Her lashes fluttered and her lips parted on an indrawn breath. He froze, his mind and heart battling.

In halting movements, he buried his fingers in her hair and drew her to him. With a shaky exhale, he brushed his lips against hers in a fleeting, reverent touch. He withdrew just enough to meet her eyes and waited. His whole body shook with longing and fear—of what, he didn't know.

Natalie held his gaze, peering steadily at him before leaning in. She kissed one corner of his mouth, then the other, each fleeting touch sending tremors down his spine. With a whispered sigh, she fully claimed his lips, pressing her body against his. He stood still, his hands hovering near her shoulders—to push her away or to hold on to her, he didn't know.

When she squirmed against him, demanding a response, Garrett caved with a guttural groan. His mouth sought hers while his hands skimmed her sides and hips before reaching back to cup her round ass. She mewled in approval as her fingers dug into his back. Natalie caught fire in his arms and he couldn't get enough. His tongue flicked, teased and plunged into her warmth, desperate to possess her.

Garrett growled, picked her up by the waist and braced her against the wall. He rolled his hips against her until they both moaned. Another minute of this and he was going to lose it in his pants like a goddamn sixteen-year-old. He drew back an inch and cursed under his breath.

Natalie took advantage of the brief pause to step out of his reach. He blinked at the sudden loss of heat and lifted his hands to bring her back to him.

"We shouldn't have done that," she said in a husky whisper. Her breathing was shallow and uneven, but her expression was cool and detached. "We're both sexually frustrated from our forced celibacy, but we can't lose sight of our agreement."

She was absolutely right, but it gutted him to hear the words—the same words he repeated to himself whenever she was near. Well, no more.

"I'm beyond frustrated," he said. *And damn the agreement.*

Her eyes widened, as if she'd heard the unsaid words. It was time to stop hiding from the inevitable. He was going to make love to his wife tonight, and to hell with the consequences.

Eleven

Natalie couldn't quite put her finger on it. Garrett wasn't acting any differently than usual, but she got goose bumps every time he glanced at her. He exuded the air of a panther who was leisurely circling his cornered prey.

She was probably imagining things after the heated episode earlier. The need to touch and be touched had risen like a primal instinct, and her body had screamed to take him inside her. Breaking away from his arms was harder than she could've imagined, but she'd been certain he would've done the same thing once his cool logic pierced through the fog of lust. She'd withdrawn from his embrace in the nick of time, self-preservation coming to the rescue.

Natalie sat on the couch and tied her shoes with excessive care. She heard Garrett moving behind the closed doors of the bedroom, and willed herself not to imagine him changing. She grabbed the remote and flipped through the channels. Every time she peeked at the clock, it seemed to be standing still, as though its hands were bound by invisible string. It was almost time for their tennis match with the Diazes. She wanted out of the oddly charged villa before she jumped her husband.

"Are you ready?" he asked as he strode into the living room. He wore a black polo shirt and shorts, looking thoroughly fit and masculine.

"Yes." She bolted to her feet and shot out the door, her heart beating erratically at the sight of him.

The sun was making its leisurely descent and the cool breeze felt lovely on her warm cheeks. They rumbled toward the tennis court in a golf cart, and some of the tension left her shoulders. It had just been a kiss—a long kiss with some heavy petting, but just a kiss nonetheless. She would put it past her. A glance at her husband's calm, easy expression said he already had.

When they arrived, Garrett tipped the driver while Natalie glanced toward the court. The Diazes were already there, stretching. These people meant business.

"I see them over there," she said, waving.

They had to be well into their fifties but looked as lithe and athletic as people half their age. They were decked out in matching white outfits as though tennis was their second career. Natalie's pulse leaped with excitement. *Worthy opponents.*

Garrett grimaced by her side, not half as excited as she. But she didn't buy his claims of being rusty at the game. Her husband's every movement spoke of strength and agility. If he'd forgotten how to swing a racquet, he was going to pick it right back up during the warm-up sets.

"What's your plan?" His eyes danced with mischief. "Should we throw the game to stoke Sebastian's ego? That should help me gain his support."

Natalie gasped. "Don't even joke about something like that. The only way to seal the partnership is to annihilate them and earn their respect."

"Annihilate them?" Her husband arched an eyebrow.

She shrugged, fighting a blush. "Or just kick their butts a little."

"I don't know how we got talked into this."

"Here are the newlyweds," Sebastian said as he and Camilia approached.

"You'll go easy on us, right?" Garrett smiled and shook his hand.

"Not a chance," the older man said.

Camilia hugged Natalie, squealing like a young girl. "I'm so glad we could do this."

"Me, too," Natalie said. Traci used to tell her she got too competitive sometimes, but it was all good, harmless fun. She just really liked to win, and there was nothing wrong with that. "Should we hit some warm-up balls?"

To her disappointment, Garrett actually was a bit rusty. His serves were poetic, but his backhand needed work. And Camilia and Sebastian were even better than Natalie had assumed.

"Damn it, Garrett." Natalie tried to keep the impatience out of her voice but he gave the Diazes an easy point. "That was your ball."

"Sorry, honey." His lips twitched. "I got distracted. Your skirt is way too short for me to be on my game."

What has gotten into him?

"Thank you, Natalie," Sebastian guffawed from across the net.

It was a close second set. Her limbs ached and her lungs burned. They could still win if they took the next set. Garrett hadn't made any more careless mistakes, but she had a feeling he wasn't putting in his full effort.

She glanced over her shoulder and saw him spinning his racquet in his hand, looking damn fine in his fitted polo and shorts. The man had seriously muscular thighs and his biceps flexed and bulged with every movement.

He caught her checking him out and his face split into a slow, sexy grin.

Everything happened in a split second, but she saw it in slow motion. They were all tired, which was probably why Camilia's next serve veered to the wrong side and came straight toward Natalie. She just had to lift her racquet and shield herself, but she was too focused on her husband to react in time. The ball caught Natalie squarely on the forehead. She fell onto her bottom and sat dazed with a hand over her injury.

"Natalie." Garrett was by her side in an instant and peeled her hand off her forehead. "Are you okay?"

"Oh, my goodness." Camilia had reached her side. "Are you all right, Natalie? I'm so sorry."

"Don't worry. It startled me more than anything," Natalie said, but her voice sounded faint.

Sebastian, who'd disappeared from the court when it happened, now sprinted to them with a bag of ice. "Here you are. Put this on."

"Thank you, but I'm fine."

Garrett grabbed the ice and placed it gently on her forehead, ignoring her protests. Natalie got her bearings back in a few minutes. The mild throbbing told her she was going to have some bruising the next day, but she was otherwise perfectly fine.

"That's all, folks," she said, waving her hands to dispel their worried expressions. "The show's over."

Natalie wanted to get off the cold ground, but before she could stand, Garrett reached under her and lifted her as though she didn't weigh much more than Sophie. She squeaked but reflexively grabbed onto him.

"Oh, my," Camilia said, fanning her face. "Maybe I should get hit in the head with a ball so Sebastian would carry me like that."

"There's no need for such extremes." Sebastian reached

out to grab her and Camilia slapped his hands away, laughing.

Garrett met Natalie's eyes with a smile that made her heart vibrate like a windup alarm clock. "Feeling okay?"

"Yes, I'm fine. You can put me down."

He shifted her in his arms but ignored her request. "Okay, you kids. I need to take my wife back to our villa."

"Of course," Sebastian said, pausing from their horse-play. "Please call us if you need anything. And let's play a round of golf next week to talk about your proposal in detail."

"Thank you. That sounds great. I'll call you Monday," Garrett said, and turned to leave.

"I'm sorry about knocking you down." Camilia waved, her smile bright and affectionate. "Good night."

"Wait." Natalie remembered something very important. "We didn't finish the game. We don't have a winner yet."

"Why don't we call it a tie?" Garrett said.

"A tie? But that's so…not winning." Natalie deflated in her husband's arms.

"Well, why don't we say we won?" Garrett's warm breath tickled her ear. She sighed and a shiver ran through her, awareness simmering between them. "We won Sebastian's support."

"I guess you're right." They'd not only secured their business goal, but also gained the Diazes' friendship. It was a double win.

Garrett looked down at her with a perplexed frown, but his eyes twinkled with humor. "When am I not?"

When the golf cart stopped in front of their villa, Garrett reached for his wife.

"I'm really okay," Natalie protested.

He ignored her and carried her through the door. The significance of the act hit him a moment later. How appropriate to carry his bride over the threshold on their long-overdue honeymoon.

Natalie gazed at him with wide, vulnerable eyes. He was hit again with how alluring she was—so innocent yet sensual. In an instant, his blood turned molten with raw desire. Once inside, he lowered her to the floor, letting her body slide slowly down his.

All his reasons for not touching her were still valid, but he couldn't fight what they had anymore. Their kiss earlier had proven that. Whenever he was near her, she came into sharp focus and everything else ceased to exist. Call it a cruel twist of fate, but their attraction was beyond their control. And they were caught in its vortex again.

"I'm going to collapse in bed after a nice bath." Her soft voice trembled and she hastily turned away from him.

Garrett followed her into the master suite, and she spun around with wide eyes.

"Did you need something?"

Her jaw went slack as he lifted her up again and carried her into the bathroom. He set her down by the tub and stared into her eyes before reaching around her to turn on the faucet.

"I, uh…" Her words trailed off as she bit her lip. He added some bath salt to the steaming water, making lavender and citrus steam rise around them. "What are you doing?"

"Drawing you a bath."

"I can manage," she said.

"I know."

"This isn't a good idea, Garrett."

"I know." He did, but he didn't give a damn anymore.

She stared at him with wide eyes, a pulse fluttering under the translucent skin of her neck. His gaze not leaving hers, he reached around her and carefully lifted her top off over her head. Natalie moved pliantly beneath his hands as though she was in a trance. Her shirt on the floor, he linked his fingers into the waistband of her skirt and smoothed it down her thighs, letting it pool around her ankles. His breath caught at the sight of her curves dipping and flaring in a way that could drive a man crazy. Her eyelids fluttered as though she was waking from a dream, and she lifted her arms to cover herself.

"Don't," he said, his voice gruff. "Let me look at you."

He reached out and lowered her arms back to her sides, and Natalie didn't stop him. With a shuddering sigh, he unhooked her bra and slipped it off, his hands skimming the soft skin of her arms. She trembled against his touch, and his gut tightened with desire. He stared at her bare torso. He'd never seen anything more beautiful.

When his thumbs brushed across her breasts, she groaned and arched toward him. He stilled for a second, relishing her response, before he kneeled to tug off her panties. He reverently ran his hands down the sides of her hips and her outer thighs.

"You're so perfect," he whispered, rising to his feet.

She blushed and lowered her lashes. His heart was pounding with need as he lifted her into the tub, his sleeves getting drenched in the process. He shrugged out of his dripping shirt, and Natalie's lips parted as her eyes roamed his chest approvingly.

Then she sighed, tilting her head back into the water, her eyes closing in wordless invitation. Garrett struggled to swallow, his mouth as dry as the sand dunes. He lathered the soap in his hands and lifted her arm, so soft and smooth, then moved onto her other arm. Her chest rose and fell more quickly underneath the water, but she didn't open her eyes. He washed her legs, then moved down to her feet, awed by the masterpiece that was Natalie.

By the time he reached her torso, he was trembling. He groaned as he smoothed his palms over her breasts, and

Natalie pushed against his hands, her hips lifting under the water. He wanted to heed her silent plea, to reach between her thighs and watch her fall apart for him.

For a moment, he wanted to be the man who burned for her, and she the woman who caught fire at his touch. No past, no future. No fear, no heartache.

Gritting his teeth, Garrett hooked his arms under her shoulders and knees, and lifted her out of the water. Her eyes were wide with confusion but he said nothing. With shaking hands, he dried her off, wrapped her in a towel and stepped back from her.

He wasn't going to seduce her. She needed to know what he was offering, and if she declined, he had to walk away. She should refuse him for both their sakes, but his body begged her to accept him.

Twelve

"I want you." His voice was a whispered caress, and the intensity of his onyx gaze speared through her defenses. "But this marriage, it still ends once our objectives are reached. If I make love to you tonight, I'm taking your body and giving you mine, nothing more."

Garrett stood before her, his hands in his shorts, his ruined shirt discarded on the bathroom floor. What would he look like if his shorts fell next to his shirt? She had a feeling he would be as magnificent as he was everywhere else.

If I make love to you tonight...

Natalie knew herself. She wouldn't be able to sleep with him and not become emotionally attached. The line he'd drawn was the only thing protecting her from... *What exactly do I need protection from?* It wasn't until Traci had died that she understood the agony of loss. She hardly remembered her mom, and her father was as distant as a stranger. But Natalie hadn't minded. Not really. Because she'd had Traci.

A chunk of her heart had been torn from her and buried with her sister. If the pain of losing her sister didn't kill her, then she could survive anything. Like the end of a fake marriage. Everyone left one way or another. In this case, at least she'd see it coming. She could prepare herself.

And no matter what happened between them, Garrett wouldn't end their marriage before Sophie's adoption and Natalie's promotion. He was a man of his word.

Don't I deserve to experience true passion?

She had never felt this way about anyone before and probably never would again.

Isn't it better than living the rest of my life wondering what it would've been like to make love to him?

"I understand." Natalie's heart skipped like a stone thrown across calm waters. "And I want you, too."

A predatory light flared in his eyes, but he didn't lean down for the kiss she was expecting. She could see him holding back, fighting for control. Then she understood. He was as helpless as she was against their crazy attraction, and that vulnerability tipped her over the precipice.

Natalie closed the distance between them and kissed him. Garrett stood as still as a sun-warmed boulder, but his lips parted against hers, inviting her to explore him.

So she did.

She kissed his hot, smooth lips, and she wanted to venture further—to taste more of him. When she eagerly sucked his bottom lip into her mouth, Garrett moved. With a low groan vibrating in his chest, he pushed her up against the wall and flicked his tongue across her lips. He took advantage of her startled gasp to deepen the kiss. His heat, his smell and the carnal pleasure of his touch invaded her. His lips and tongue teased and danced with hers. So wet. So hot.

An onslaught of sensations blanketed her and instinct took over. She plunged her fingers into his thick, dark hair and pushed herself up into his kiss. She hummed with satisfaction as the evidence of his desire pressed against her stomach. He moaned and slid his hand down the back of her thigh, then hitched her leg around his waist.

Lust burned through her veins. Pure, basic and animal. The hunger to touch and be touched threatened to consume her. The tepid kisses she'd experienced in the past hadn't prepared her for this man.

He ravished her lips as his hands explored her body. She braced her hands on his chest and a decadent sigh escaped her as her fingertips met his hot, bare skin. Desperate to feel him against her, Natalie dropped her towel to the floor. With an impatient growl, Garrett cupped her breasts and dipped his head to run kisses across the sensitive skin.

Instinct was a funny thing. She'd never been touched like this—the few men she'd been with were clumsy and awkward in comparison—but she knew exactly what she wanted. Gripping handfuls of Garrett's hair in her fists, she held his head against her chest and arched her back, demanding more. She whimpered when his tongue licked one taut peak. When she scraped her fingernails across his scalp, he groaned and took her fully in his mouth.

At first, she didn't even hear her phone ringing. It was coming from the bedroom.

Then she heard his phone ringing from his pants on the floor.

"Don't answer it," she breathed.

When the hotel phone rang in chorus with their cell phones, panic sliced through her lust-addled brain.

"Oh, God."

The last time every phone near her started ringing had been the night Traci died. Cold fear replaced the heat of desire. She recognized this dread. She'd felt it that night, too. Natalie ran to her phone and picked it up.

"Yes, this is Natalie." She was shivering so violently her teeth were clacking against each other.

"You need to put this on." Garrett wrapped her in a bathrobe and stood behind her with his hands on her shoulders.

"What happened?" she asked in a hoarse whisper.

"Natalie…" Steve Davis's voice broke on the other end of the line. "It's Sophie… Lily was carrying her down the stairs and her hip gave out. She managed to break her fall but she lost her hold on the baby…"

"How badly is Sophie hurt?" Natalie's mind went bright white. Garrett cursed then wrapped his arms tightly around her waist, his chest solid behind her back. She leaned back, grateful for the support.

"Mostly scrapes and bruises." The poor man choked back a sob. "But Lily's worried Sophie might have bumped her head. They're running more tests on her to rule out a concussion."

Natalie didn't recall the rest of their conversation. Once she hung up the phone, Garrett turned her around to face him and wiped the tears spilling down her cheeks with the pad of his thumb.

"Sophie fell down the stairs." Her voice sounded distant and foreign. "She might have a concussion."

"God…" Garrett didn't try to comfort her with empty words. He pulled her into his arms and held her until her trembling subsided.

Then he snapped into action, punching numbers into his phone and barking out orders. Natalie heard him mention a helicopter. They needed to go to Sophie—the sooner, the better.

As she stood rooted to the spot, Garrett pulled on his clothes then proceeded to dress her, maneuvering her limp limbs into compliance. "Sophie needs you."

The helicopter ride took less than half an hour, but it felt like a lifetime. As they landed on the hospital roof, Garrett kept his eyes on Natalie. She'd stopped crying but she was too still and quiet. Tugging her head into his chest against the rush of the propeller's wind, he ushered her downstairs.

When they got to the waiting room on the pediatric floor, they found Lily weeping silently into Steve's shoulder. Adelaide and James sat close together. When Lily spotted Natalie, she walked toward her, limping slightly, and hugged her tightly.

"I'm so sorry. It's all my fault. I'm so sorry."

"It was an accident. It's not your fault." Natalie stepped back from the older woman and scanned her. "Are you okay? Did you hurt your hip again?"

"No. I'm fine." Lily didn't sound too happy about that. "I should've protected the baby, but I couldn't hang on. I'm sorry, Natalie. I was so selfish to keep her with me…"

"Not now. She's going to be okay," Natalie said, blindly stretching her hand behind her. Garrett knew she was looking for his hand, so he took hers and squeezed. "She has to be."

There was so little he could do for her. Natalie usually acted as though her spine was made of steel, but when the phones started ringing in Ojai, she'd crumbled like ancient clay. He'd never be able to forget the horror in her eyes.

Garrett wished he could've done something to spare her from the pain. He'd never felt more helpless in his life. Over the next couple hours, he stayed by Natalie's side and held her whenever he could, but she seemed leagues away. She sat motionless, as though she was an empty husk of herself, all the blood gone from her face. Only the sporadic fluttering of her lashes indicated she was alive.

Garrett dragged his hands down his face and shot to his feet. He stepped out of the waiting room and stood uncertainly. He didn't want to leave her, but she didn't seem to notice when he walked out.

Just ten minutes. He'd stretch his legs and come back.

After no more than five minutes, he hurried back to Natalie with a cup of hot tea in his hand, hoping it would warm her up. As he neared the waiting room, he heard loud sobbing. Pain shot through his heart. It was Natalie. He ran the rest of the way and came to an abrupt halt at the entrance.

Natalie and Adelaide were hugging, laughing and crying, while a doctor in blue scrubs stood nearby. His dad stared at the ceiling with red-rimmed eyes, his lips pressed tight. When Natalie spotted Garrett at the door, she launched herself at him, barely leaving him time to move the hot tea out of the way. Leaning against the door frame to balance himself, he held her tightly against him.

"She's okay. All the tests were normal." Her voice was muffled against his shoulder, but her relief was palpable.

He squeezed his eyes shut. *Thank God.* They stood wrapped around each other until he heard a small cough. He opened his eyes to find the mild-mannered doctor smiling at them.

"Mrs. Song, you can come in and see Sophie for ten minutes," he said. "She needs rest but I'm sure she misses you."

"Thank you." Natalie's hand flew to her mouth as her eyes filled with fresh tears. Then she hesitated and turned around to face the Davises. "Would you like to see her first?"

Lily had her face buried in her hands, and Steve mutely shook his head. They needed more time to pull themselves together. Natalie bit her lip, concern for the older couple clouding her exhausted face. Garrett was standing behind her with his hands on her arms. Small tremors shook her frame and he wanted to pull her back into his embrace.

"Will you come with me?" She looked over her shoulder at him.

"Of course." His voice caught in his throat.

When they entered the room, the baby looked so pale and small in her hospital bed that Garrett wasn't surprised to hear Natalie's choked sob. She ran to Sophie's side, cooing soft words he couldn't make out, but the little girl smiled in her sleep. Garrett stood back as long as he could, but when Natalie's body shook with the force of her sobbing, he went to her and placed his hand on her shoulder.

"Let Sophie sleep. Come with me." He helped Natalie to her feet and tucked her to his side, then quickly glanced back at Sophie. "Sleep tight, baby girl. We'll be back soon."

Garrett had to twist their arms to make the rest of the family go home. In fact, they wouldn't cooperate until Adelaide put her foot down.

"Sophie's okay. We're not helping anyone by becoming sleep-deprived zombies," she said, packing up her things. "Natalie, you have my number. I'm here if you need me."

"Thank you."

Adelaide hugged Natalie then kissed Garrett on the cheek. His father followed Adelaide's example. He squeezed his shoulder on the way out and Garrett nodded his understanding. His father was there for him, too.

With a sigh of relief, Garrett turned to Natalie and helpless anger surged inside him. She hugged herself tight but her teeth were still chattering. *Damn it.* He dragged his fingers through his hair.

"She's okay, Natalie. She's going home tomorrow." With her grandparents... The Davises seemed stricken and unsure of themselves, and frustration filled him. Sophie should be with Natalie. They should see that now.

"I... I know..." she stuttered through the tremors. "But I keep thinking...what if I'd lost her?"

"Hush," he said. He sat down beside her and tucked her close to his side. She snuggled her face against his chest. "But you didn't lose her. Focus on that."

Natalie didn't answer but her shivering eased. Then her soft deep breaths told him she'd fallen asleep in his arms. He kissed the top of her head and let his eyes drift shut, holding on tight.

Thirteen

"Sophie!"

Natalie bolted upright, blood pounding in her ears. She gradually registered her surroundings, and her heartbeat regained its normal rhythm. Sophie had been discharged midmorning, and went back with the Davises to their extended-stay hotel. And Garrett had marched Natalie straight to bed as soon as they got home.

What time is it?

The room was pitch-black, but she didn't know whether it was because of the blackout blinds or because it was the middle of the night. She could've been asleep for two hours or fourteen.

Swinging her legs off the bed, Natalie waited until her eyes adjusted to the dark. A spill of light leaked under the door, and she made her way toward it. She twisted the handle and poked her head out, conscious that all she wore was an oversize T-shirt.

The light was coming from Garrett's room. Soft murmurs drifted through the open door, so she tiptoed over, holding her breath. He was on the phone. Suddenly aware she was creeping around the house, eavesdropping on her husband, she rolled her eyes and turned to head back to her room.

Natalie stopped short when she heard Garrett say Sophie's name.

"Good. Sophie has a mighty spirit inside that little body, Steve," he said, his voice deep and warm. There was a pause as he listened to the other end. "Yes, she's okay. Just exhausted. She slept through the afternoon. And how's Lily holding up? It wasn't her fault. Natalie doesn't blame her. No one does."

He was checking up on the baby and comforting the older man. Warmth spread through her body and every locked door in her heart burst open with her love for her husband. Natalie almost gave herself away with a sob.

Pressing herself against the hallway wall, she clapped her hand over her mouth. Willing her shaky legs to function, she made her way back to the master bedroom and sank onto the bed. She swiped at the hot tears trailing down her cheeks. It wasn't easy accepting she was probably the stupidest woman in the world.

She'd loved him all along—from that first heart-pounding moment in his office. She'd just been too naive and scared to see it. When she heard soft steps in the hall, she wiped her face with the back of her hand and went out to meet him. At least she knew what she wanted now.

"Natalie." Her name left his lips in a rush of breath. He scanned her T-shirt-clad body before he jerked his gaze to her face. A muscle jumped in his jaw, but he rubbed the back of his neck and gave her a strained smile. "You slept through the day. Why don't you go back to bed till the morning? Or are you hungry? Do you want to eat something?"

But his grin faltered as he walked up to her. He cupped her damp cheek with his hand and tilted her face toward the light.

"What's wrong?"

Without answering his question, Natalie turned her head to brush a kiss on his palm and smiled at him.

"Natalie, you're not…" She silenced him with a finger on his lips.

"Oh, Garrett, but I am." He thought she was too vulnerable so soon after the accident, but Natalie had never been more certain of anything in her entire life.

When she tugged him into her room, he followed with hesitant steps. She reached behind him and clicked the door shut. His Adam's apple jumped in his throat and he watched her with something akin to panic in his eyes.

"We don't have to do this tonight." His voice was strangled and his eyes greedily roamed her body.

Arching an eyebrow, she drew her T-shirt over her head. Garrett's breath left him in a whoosh and she smiled in triumph. She did that to him.

Right now. In this room. There is no one but him and me. A man and a woman. Husband and wife. I'll make him mine.

She didn't know who took the first step and didn't care. Somehow, they were on each other like a whirlwind, mouths and hands moving frantically. Natalie tugged impatiently on Garrett's clothes, desperate to feel his skin pressed against hers, his hard contours against her soft curves without any barriers. He made quick work of tearing off his clothes, then pressed her against his naked body.

God, he feels so good.

But she pushed back from him, wanting to touch him. She spread her palms flat on his chest and caressed his smooth heat, relishing the wall of muscle beneath her hands. Curious to see if she could do what he'd done to her, she ran her thumbs over the small peaks of his chest and he tilted back his head with a guttural moan. She snatched her hands away, worried she'd done something wrong.

"Don't stop," he said, putting her hands back on his chest. "Touch me."

She swallowed but did as he demanded. Slowly, she ran her fingers down to the ridges of his stomach, and his body jerked in response. He was clearly holding himself in check; she could feel his body humming with suppressed desire. But when she pressed her breasts against him and ran her hands down his broad back, his control snapped.

Garrett wanted to take things slowly so they could enjoy each other, but the longing he'd been holding back swept in like storm waters breaching a dam. Natalie seemed to be overtaken by the same storm, and she was fierce and demanding in his arms.

He explored her mouth with burning thoroughness, entangling his tongue with hers. Drinking deeply from her, he lifted her up and carried her to the bed. Her fingers dug into his shoulders as he eased her onto the mattress. Her magnificent breasts rising and falling fast, she beckoned him with the crook of her finger, a seductive smile curving her swollen lips.

Garrett reached for her, his hands roaming up the sides of her thighs and around to her back. With one swift motion, he positioned himself over her, and her softness cushioned the hard planes of his body. The contact made him catch fire. He kissed the side of her neck and ran his tongue along her heated skin, enjoying the way his name escaped her parted lips in a breathless rush.

"Garrett...please," she whispered.

He grabbed a condom from the nightstand and sheathed himself with shaky hands.

"Look at me," he commanded, positioning himself at

her entry. Her eyes widened as he touched his hardness against her. She was so lovely in her passion that his heart throbbed and he ached with the need to claim her.

She held his gaze. "I want you, Garrett."

Unable to hold back any longer, he crushed his lips against hers and swept his tongue inside her sweet mouth.

"I fought this so hard," he said, pulling his mouth from hers. "And waited much too long. I want you so much it hurts."

"Then take me."

With a moan torn from deep within, he buried his face in her neck and plunged into her in one swift thrust. Garrett froze when a sharp gasp escaped from her. He glanced down and saw Natalie had her eyes closed tight, her bottom lip between her teeth. *What the hell?*

"Sorry. I'm okay," she gasped. "It's been a long time."

Her moist, tight warmth drove him mad but he didn't move a single muscle as he bore his weight on his forearms. When he continued to hold still, her eyebrows drew together and she shyly swerved her hips.

God. He groaned, searching for his precious control. "Do. Not. Move. Give me a second. I want to go slow for you."

"But I don't want you to go slow."

"Damn it, Natalie." He'd plowed into her like a beast when he should've coaxed her body into accepting him with more ease. "I hurt you…"

"Not hurt. Just startled." She cupped his cheek in her palm and stared up at him. "Please."

His blood thundered so hard in his veins that Garrett could hardly hear her. His mind battled with his body as he searched her face.

"Please," she said again, then rocked her hips against him.

Garrett shuddered in her arms, and began to move

slowly, looking intently into her face. Gripping his shoulders, Natalie moved with him and set a faster rhythm until he broke. With a groan, he planted his hands by her head, rising onto his arms, and drove into her to the hilt.

He thrust faster and she matched him stroke for stroke. It was almost too much. She was close but he didn't know if he could hold back. Then, Natalie cried out his name and arched her pelvis off the bed. Seconds later, he collapsed on top of her with a hoarse cry.

As their panting eased, Garrett rolled onto his back, taking her with him. He held her head against his chest and ran his hand down her hair.

"Natalie?"

"Mmm?"

"Are you all right?"

"Mmm-hmm."

"Good."

He tilted her chin up with his finger and studied her face, struck by her beauty inside and out. The delicate skin underneath her eyes was pale and bruised. She was still exhausted from yesterday's ordeal, and he held her tighter, the need to protect her surging in his blood. With a sigh, she molded her body against his and her breaths grew long and steady.

He absently drew circles on her naked back. It was surreal how right all of it felt. *Mine.* Nothing in his no-strings-attached sexual philosophy explained his possessiveness. The mere thought of her having another lover scraped him raw. At least for now, she was his and his alone.

But this hunger… He had to believe it would pass. Natalie had no place in the life he meant to lead. He'd been content to pour himself into Hansol, and to find satisfaction in his professional accomplishments within the confines of his duties. Garrett had never wanted a real marriage. He couldn't change who he was. He couldn't offer Natalie anything more than what they had. *She understands that. Doesn't she?*

And yet, the future he'd accepted as written in stone now seemed like a flimsy note on the back of a cocktail napkin—crumbled and blowing across the sidewalk.

Fourteen

The last few times Adelaide had seen her brother and sister-in-law, Garrett couldn't stop touching Natalie—tucking a strand of hair behind her ear, entwining his fingers through hers, pulling her close to his side with an arm wrapped around her shoulders. Since their mom died, he'd held himself cold and aloof, becoming unreachable. Untouchable.

With Natalie by his side, her brother had finally shed his iron armor, and exuded warmth from his pores. And he became a puddle of goo when Sophie was around. The little girl had recovered from the fall scare faster than the grown-ups and was back to her energetic, rascally self.

Adelaide's heart burst with joy to see him so happy, but a small, lonely part of her shivered with fear. Garrett was her constant. His love unconditional. No matter how much she screwed up, he would have her back. *Have I lost him?* Adelaide cringed with shame. She wasn't the spoiled princess people made her out to be. She should stop acting like one.

She hadn't lost a brother—she'd gained a sister. A wide smile spread across her face—Natalie was the best big sister imaginable.

Humming under her breath, she stepped out of the elevator at Hansol headquarters and strode past the reception desk.

"Hi, Cindy," she said, waving goodbye at the same time.

"Hello, Ms. Song," said the receptionist with a grin. "Bye, Ms. Song."

Natalie was a sushi fiend. It was a surprise visit but she'd never turn down sushi no matter how busy she was.

"Adelaide." When she entered Natalie's office, her sister-in-law jumped up from her chair and rushed over for a hug. "What a wonderful surprise."

"Are you talking about me or the *nigiri* plate I brought you?" She lifted the bag holding three paper boxes from a hole-in-the-wall restaurant in Little Tokyo.

Natalie's eyes glazed over. "I love you."

Adelaide laughed shyly, pleased by her warm reception. "I got some for Garrett, too."

"Oh, no. He's in a meeting for the next few hours."

"That's fine. He's always in a meeting." She sat at a small, round table by the window and waved over Natalie. "Eat up. We have to finish his portion, too."

"Not a problem." Natalie sighed happily, her chopsticks poised over the box.

Full and happy, they sipped green tea in comfortable silence until Adelaide saw her sister-in-law frown. "What is it?"

"Garrett has been looking tense and haggard lately," Natalie said, her hands wrapping around her mug. "Do you know if he's worried about something? Is anything wrong at work?"

"You don't know?" Adelaide stared at her, shocked by her question. Her brother hadn't told his own wife about the whole mess. Keeping his baby sister in the dark was one thing, but his wife? *That idiot.* Why did he insist on bearing all the responsibilities alone?

"What don't I know?" Natalie sat up in her chair. "Garrett hasn't said anything to me."

"He's my brother but he's so stubborn sometimes." Adelaide threw up her hands. "He didn't tell me anything, either. I doubt he even told our dad. He thinks he's 'protecting' us."

"Adelaide, just tell me."

"I did some digging around. Everyone thinks I'm a spoiled little princess with an unimpressive IQ, so it's easy for me to go under the radar and gather intel." Everyone underestimated her, including her own family. Michael was the only one… She shut down the thought, annoyed she'd let him slip in again. He had nothing to do with this. Nothing to do with her. "It's Vivotex. They're considering a partnership with Yami Corporation, a small-time fashion manufacturing company. They don't have the brand recognition or the manufacturing capacity for any kind of partnership with Vivotex. Yami must have a powerful backer to catch Vivotex's attention, but we don't know who that is. My gut tells me this mystery powerhouse is using Yami as a pawn for its own plans."

"What if Garrett can't close the deal?" Natalie paled, her brow knitting with concern. "Will your grandmother really block his CEO appointment?"

"I hope not." When she was a kid, Adelaide used to fight her grandmother like a hellcat over everything—big and small. But somewhere along the way, they reached an unspoken truce. They were too much alike—strong willed, opinionated…and breakable. *Anything that doesn't bend inevitably breaks.* "I can't tell what she's thinking sometimes, but she has never let me down."

"Do you think it'll help if I beg her?" Her sister-in-law grinned but she wasn't entirely joking.

Tenderness flooded Adelaide's heart at how dearly Natalie loved her brother. It was no wonder Garrett followed her around like a puppy with hearts in his eyes. They were so perfect together. Adelaide could only hope she too would someday find that kind of love. Before she could turn wistful, she smiled brightly to reassure her big sis.

"My big brother is meant to be the next CEO." She squeezed Natalie's hand. "Try not to worry."

Natalie worried until Garrett came home that night.

"Hello, Mrs. Song." He walked up behind her and wrapped his arms around her waist. "What are you up to?"

"Making dinner."

She gave the cherry tomatoes one last rinse and reached out to turn off the faucet. Garrett had been nuzzling the sensitive spot behind her ear, but went still at her answer.

"Dinner?" He sounded more than a little alarmed. "Are you sure? Remember last week…"

Her face flamed. She remembered all too well. Filled with a sudden urge to test her domestic talents, Natalie had tried making lasagna and nearly set the kitchen on fire. Oddly enough, the lasagna had come out unscathed from the fire—as in completely raw.

His apprehension was warranted, but that didn't mean she'd let him get away with it. Natalie elbowed Garrett in his side. He grunted under his breath and she turned around to face him. He was gingerly rubbing his stomach, but his eyes were sparkling with laughter.

Her elbow had met rock-hard obliques. She doubted he'd even felt the jab. Still, contrite for her violence, she kissed the side of his neck then buried her face against him. He smelled so yummy, musk warmed against male skin.

"I'm only tossing a bag of salad." She straightened to

finish the job. "I ordered pizza for the main course, so you can stop worrying."

Garrett pulled her back into his arms and kissed her. She hadn't seen him all day and she'd missed him. She parted her lips and pressed herself to him, making him groan and slide his hands up the back of her shirt. Familiar heat spread through her and she had a second before losing all rational thought.

"Um, Garrett?"

He grunted and lifted her up onto the counter.

"Garrett." Natalie laughed and squirmed in his arms. They needed to talk about the Yami Corporation situation. It was ridiculous for him to carry all that weight by himself. "We need to talk. I want…"

He didn't seem to hear her and continued trailing kisses down the side of her neck. By the time he reached her collarbone, she couldn't remember what she'd wanted to talk about. She wrapped her legs around him and whispered the only words she could form. "I want you."

"Good." His voice rang with arrogant satisfaction. He cupped her breast with a possessive hand and something fierce burned in his eyes before he kissed her with heat and desperation. When he filled her, she cried out, marveling at how whole she felt, and never wanted to let go.

After the storm passed, Garrett lifted her down from the counter. He was bare chested and she wore nothing under her oversize T-shirt. She plucked her panties off the floor, not bothering with her jeans. When her husband reached down for his shirt, she kicked it away with her foot. "You're fine. It's casual Friday at the Song penthouse."

"Is that so?" A wolfish grin spread across his handsome face as he folded his arms across his naked chest.

Her eyes glazed over as she ogled his bulging biceps. *Gah*. Natalie hurried to the opposite side of the kitchen counter so she wouldn't jump him. Her stomach growled loudly, reminding her she'd been putting together dinner. *Yes, a woman cannot live by sex alone.* She needed pizza.

Garrett chuckled under his breath as though he knew her inner struggle of pizza versus sex. "Have a seat. I'll finish the salad."

She sat on the counter stool and made herself comfortable. Natalie decided there was nothing better than watching her shirtless husband cook for her. They chatted comfortably, warm laughter punctuating their conversation.

This was happiness. Unshed tears pricked her eyes and her lips curved into a tremulous smile. *So this is what it feels like to be whole.* Love swelled to the brim and lapped perilously at the edge of her heart. Unable to hold back any longer, she opened the dam and let it spill over.

"I love you."

"Could you pass the salad?" Natalie asked in a small voice.

"Sure." Garrett passed her the salad bowl, careful not to let their fingers touch.

"Thank you."

The conversation at the dinner table was scintillating. It might've had something to do with him all but ignoring her declaration of love. Her words had brought something fierce and hungry to life inside him, but he'd smothered it ruthlessly. *What else can I do?* He could never give her what she wanted. What she deserved. He shut his eyes and mind against the torrent of emotions threatening to breach the walls of his heart.

"Garrett." His eyes flew open at Natalie's whisper. "You don't need to worry. I haven't forgotten our agreement. I'm not asking anything of you."

"Hush." Garrett shut out what her words implied. She deserved more but he was going to hold on to her—letting her go would wreck him. He brought her hand to his mouth, kissing each knuckle before placing a lingering kiss on her palm. Her lashes fluttered and her lips parted in response. Without warning, he scooped his wife off her chair and headed upstairs, taking two steps at a time.

"What are you—"

"Hush." Blood pounded in his ears. His panic fueled his desperation. *Mine.* He laid her down on the bed, then ripped his pants off with rough impatience. She watched him with sad, wide eyes, and his heart slammed against his ribs. "Your turn."

He reached around her and pulled off her T-shirt with shaking hands. When he reached her hips, he linked his fingers into her lacy underwear and tugged it down. Then she was naked before him, and she was perfection.

Garrett lowered himself, covering her body with his. Molten heat flared at the contact. He claimed her mouth, sucking and nipping, drinking in her intoxicating taste like a man starved. She writhed under him, and everywhere her body touched his, a fire started. As he explored her, she made those small sounds of passion that never failed to drive him mad. He slid one hand down her silken curves. A guttural groan tore from his chest when he found the hot, moist warmth of her center.

"Look at me." When her eyes focused on him, he gave himself to her the only way he knew how. "Do you see what you do to me?"

"Yes." She whimpered and grasped his buttocks as he pulled his fingers from her.

"I can't get enough of you." Unable to hold back any longer, he surged into her. "I've never wanted anyone like this before. Only you."

"Please, Garrett."

"You're mine." Wanting to prolong her release, he slowed his rhythm even more. "Tell me you're mine."

"I'm yours."

Her words slashed the last of his control. He raised himself on his arms and drove into her again and again until she screamed his name, her internal muscles clenching around him. His hips bucked once, twice, then he shouted his own release and collapsed over her.

After a long while, Garrett lay with his forearm over his eyes, listening to the steady rhythm of Natalie's breathing. He'd made love to her with a desperation that should have alarmed him, but he had no space for any thought other than her words. *I love you.*

They made love every night, giving and receiving pleasure he had never experienced before. It wasn't love but it was real and tangible. Was it enough for her?

In the last few months, having Natalie by his side had grown into an unwavering need. Subconsciously, he'd been pushing aside the fact that their marriage would end soon. Thinking about it made his stomach twist and churn. His soul rebelled, screaming, "She's mine." Did he want to hold on to Natalie?

He had no answers. At least, none he could face head-on.

Garrett watched Natalie get dressed for work. She twisted around in front of the mirror examining the fourth outfit she'd shimmied into this morning. Not that he was complaining. Watching her dress—and undress—was hotter than a striptease.

"Are you sure?" she asked him for the tenth time that morning. "Adelaide talked me into buying it but I just don't know."

"Yes." Garrett twirled his wife in a pirouette. "And my answer will still be yes when you've asked me for the twentieth time."

Natalie finally settled on a black wrap dress rather than one of her severe business suits. It highlighted her curves instead of hiding them, but the tight fit had her fidgeting like it was crawling with somersaulting circus fleas.

"You look beautiful." Garrett kissed the tip of her nose. "And professional. You'll be great today." Presentations never ceased to frazzle her even though she was fantastic at them.

When she drew in a breath, he pressed a finger to her mouth to stop the objections he knew were coming. But the feel of her parted lips and her intoxicating scent threatened to derail him from the point he was trying to make.

"Our wedding pictures were featured in *Focus* magazine. Everyone has already seen your lovely figure. I assure you the employees won't treat you differently because you decided to let your hair down a little."

"You really think so?" Natalie raised hopeful eyes to his.

"Yes, I know so." Garrett paused for a beat. "They'll treat you differently because you're married to me."

"You're terrible." She punched him in the arm as surprised laughter burst from her.

He loved the sound of her laughter. Garrett pulled Natalie into his arms. "Stop being so nervous. Your presentation will be great, and short, and you'll be back to your daily routine, whipping people into submission."

She narrowed her eyes at him. "I don't whip anyone into anything. I just make sure that company policies are carried out with uniformity and consistency."

"Of course, Mrs. Song. You better move your butt, or you're going to be late," Garrett said, checking the clock.

"Oh, shoot. Okay." Natalie hopped around putting her heels on, then rushed to the door. Garrett picked Sophie up and trailed her hurried steps. "Bye. See you tonight!" Natalie called over her shoulder.

He cleared his throat loudly and held Sophie out in front of him. Natalie had almost left without giving her a kiss.

"Oops. Sorry, sweetie."

She turned to go after brushing her lips on the crown of the baby's head. But Garrett wasn't going to let her get away that easily. He shot out his free arm and crushed her to him. Shifting Sophie to one side, he kissed Natalie deeply, sipping in her soft moan. He stepped back before he tore off her carefully selected outfit, and she stood looking slightly dazed.

He reached out and patted his wife's perfect bottom. "Go!"

Natalie blinked then scowled at him again before rushing out the door.

"Didn't Mama look pretty today?"

"Yup!" That was Sophie's it word these days. It actually sounded more like "yah-pu" and involved some spit spewing on the "pu."

"Mama will do great today, right?"

"Yup!"

He'd volunteered to take Sophie back to the Davises' since he didn't have any meetings lined up till ten o'clock. This was the first reprieve he'd had in weeks.

Yami Corporation's interference in the Vivotex deal was an unexpected nuisance, but Clark and Sebastian were the loyal allies Garrett hoped they'd be. They'd successfully convinced the majority at Vivotex that Yami's overtures were merely distracting them from closing a profitable partnership, and that Yami couldn't offer what Hansol promised.

Garrett had worked night and day to finalize the details of the contract. It was grueling work but the deal was within reach, and he thrived on the knowledge. Once the deal closed, the CEO position and everything he'd worked for—including his independence from his grandmother—would finally be his.

The real headache in the fiasco was that there was someone inside Hansol leaking confidential information regarding the Vivotex deal. Every leak had given Yami Corporation an edge in the bid for the partnership. But corporate espionage was a dangerous game to play, and a small-timer like Yami wouldn't have the guts to start a war with Hansol. It meant there was someone else behind it all, and the unknown puppet master knew how to play the game well. Garrett had to catch the spy to find out who the real threat was.

Fifteen

Soon Natalie was going to look like the bride of Frankenstein. Her curls were beginning to stand from the static Garrett was generating.

"Garrett." He glanced at her, but continued to pace around his office. "I know you're nervous, but please stop pacing."

"I am not nervous."

"Of course not. You're just trying to create alternative energy with your feet." He scowled, but she just grinned from her perch on his desk. "Oh, look. It worked. I see smoke coming from your shoes."

He strode menacingly toward her, arms outstretched to catch her. Laughing at him, she let herself be caught and pressed up against him.

With a forlorn sigh, Garrett buried his head in her neck. "Okay. Fine. I'm feeling some nervous excitement. But mostly excitement. Hardly any nervousness."

"*Of course* you are. Well, there's no need for any nervousness because Vivotex is here to sign that contract. It's going to happen."

"Damn right, it's going to happen."

Garrett straightened up. Natalie wanted to pull him back to her and hang on for dear life. The grains of sand were falling in the hourglass. She cherished every moment she got to spend with him, but her heart bled knowing every second that passed meant she was that much closer to losing him.

But she couldn't think about that now. Natalie glanced at the wall clock and hurried toward his chair to retrieve his suit jacket. "Settle down, cowboy. You only have five minutes until the meeting."

She held the jacket open for him and he put it on. After running her hands over the nonexistent wrinkles on the suit, she straightened his tie and smoothed back his hair. With everything in place, she stared at her beautiful husband, taking in every inch of him, memorizing him.

All hints of his nervousness were gone, and he stood before her strong and confident. He was ready and she had to be, too.

"Are you satisfied with what you see, ma'am?" Garrett's lips tilted into an arrogant grin. Without fail, Natalie's heart sped up and desire sparked to life.

"There's no time for flirting, Mr. Song."

She made an effort to be stern, but she probably sounded breathless and flustered. With a low, husky laugh, Garrett pulled her into his arms and held her tight.

"You're right. That'll have to wait until tonight."

She walked with him to the door but stopped uncertainly. "Garrett."

I love you. I love you. I love you.

The words burned her throat, but she held her silence, knowing he wouldn't want to hear them. So she forced a cheeky grin and gave him two thumbs up.

"Go get 'em, tiger."

* * *

The Song family home rang with laughter and celebration, but the endless pop of champagne corks sounded hollow to Natalie's ears. She was so proud of Garrett, but emotion still choked her as she scanned the scene of the party celebrating the Hansol-Vivotex partnership. Garrett's eyes sought hers often, so she did her best to smile for him. But amid the strains of piano music and laughter, she was feeling overwhelmed.

"Ah-ga." Natalie spun at the sound of Grace Song's voice.

"Grandmother. I'm so happy you decided to join the celebration." During their weekly visits, Natalie had begged her to attend. "You must be so proud."

"I expected nothing less from my grandson." The older woman's voice sounded wistful. "His mother should be standing by James's side tonight. I wish she could've seen the man Garrett has become, and the family he's built for himself."

Natalie's chest tightened and hot tears stung her eyes. In her own reserved manner, Grandmother was telling Natalie that Garrett had chosen a good wife…that she accepted her. *Thank you, Grandmother. And I'm sorry for lying to you about our marriage.*

"Well, Grandmother. You should be doubly proud on his mom's behalf then."

A gentle smile lit Grace Song's face and she placed a warm hand on Natalie's cheek. "I am, and you should be, too."

When Grandmother made her way back to her guests, Natalie stared at her husband to memorize every detail about him. With their days numbered, she couldn't hold back. Her hunger and longing saturated her soul and she longed to reach out to him. As though heeding her silent call, Garrett turned to her from across the room, an answering fire flaring in his eyes. She didn't know if it was her nerves playing tricks on her, but he seemed more restless and edgy than he'd been before the contract was signed. She watched him rush through his rounds, tilting back the flutes of champagne offered to him. Despite her insistence that he should go and celebrate, she was desperate to have him by her side and all to herself.

After spending the shortest acceptable time with his guests, Garrett abandoned them and strode toward her with long, impatient strides. "Miss me?" He raised a hand to cup her face.

"Desperately." She placed a lingering kiss on his palm and a tremor ran through him. *Good, because I'm trembling, too.*

"We're leaving," he rasped in her ear, his hot breath caressing her skin.

A thrill of anticipation slid down her spine and gathered mass at its base, where Garrett rested his hand. They stepped out into the night, but instead of heading to his car, he led them toward the garden at the far end of the property.

"Garrett, where are we going?"

"Somewhere private." His voice was low and dangerous.

She quickened her steps to keep up with him, frantic to touch him. To possess him. To mark him as hers.

Soon they were sprinting through a topiary maze with sharp turns and narrow passageways. The maze stood at least two stories tall and the half moon hardly pierced its depth. She'd never be able to find her way out, but Garrett seemed to know it even in near darkness. He stopped at what had to be the heart of the maze, where there was a beautiful but aging pagoda.

"What is this place?" Natalie whispered, not wanting to disturb its eerie peace.

"It used to be my sanctuary." Garrett's voice sounded far away. "No one knew how to find it but me."

"What would you do out here?" She leaned her cheek against his chest as he wrapped his arms tightly around her.

"Nothing exciting. I would just read a book or stare at the clouds." His hand made idle circles on her back. "It's not what I did that made this place special."

"Then what was it?"

"As a kid, you don't have much that you could truly call your own, but this place was mine. It existed only for me."

"I didn't know you could be so possessive," she teased.

"Oh, yes. When I have something rare and special, I want it all to myself." His hands became bolder, dropping to her backside.

"And now? What do you want all to yourself?" She wanted to hear him say it. Even if it wasn't love, she wanted him to claim her as something rare and special, and only his.

"You." His answer didn't sound like a word but a primitive growl. "You're mine and I want you."

Right then, Natalie became a flame, burning wildly for him. She kissed him wherever her lips landed, tearing ineffectively at his clothes. With a suddenness that shocked her into momentary stillness, he picked her up and carried her up the stairs of the pagoda. When he set her on the ground, she slid down his powerful body and felt his unmistakable hardness.

"I need you," he said before crushing her mouth with his. His kiss was erratic and wild; there wasn't a hint of his damn control in sight. He groaned, pushing her against a wooden pillar. "Natalie."

His hand moved under the hem of her dress to her panties. Reaching her center, he growled in satisfaction. "You want this. You want *me*."

"Yes, Garrett. I want you."

He spun her around to face the pillar and pulled her hips back, bending her at the waist. Her arousal was blinding and she didn't know how long she could wait. She heard Garrett unzip his trousers and tear open a condom packet.

Natalie was frantic when he pushed inside her with a moan. His fingers bit into her hips as he withdrew from her and plunged back in, deeper than before. She knew he was trying to slow things down for her but his maddening pace was going to kill her, so she tipped up her rear and pushed against him, setting a pace more to her liking. She felt his control break and she laughed in triumph.

"Natalie."

Too far gone for finesse, he worked frantically to bring them to their climax, his shout coarse and wild in the night.

Garrett made a conscious effort not to grip Natalie's arm too tight as he led her out of the maze. She darted uncertain glances his way, but he didn't trust himself to look back at her. He'd ravished her like a madman in his childhood hideout, but the thought encroaching on his triumph had rattled him to the core. He had no excuses left to hold on to Natalie. She'd held up her part of the bargain, and Sophie's fall had rattled the Davises enough to withdraw their opposition to the adoption. Once the adoption papers were approved by the court, there would be nothing left to prevent Natalie and Sophie from walking out of his life.

But she loves me.

"Garrett—"

"Home." He cut her off more brusquely than he'd intended, and he turned to give her a stiff smile. "We'll talk at home."

He had to eradicate the notion of a temporary marriage from Natalie's mind. He'd put it there in the first place, but things had changed—*he* had changed. Garrett admired and respected her. Burned for her. Couldn't that be enough? There were relationships based on far less.

And she said she loved him. Something warm and aching tore through his heart at the thought. He was afraid his past wouldn't allow him to love her like she deserved, but he could offer her and Sophie everything they could ever need. They would never have to worry about money again. He would move to New York with them, and work out of the office there. He would show his girls the world, promise them a future they never dreamed of.

Would that be enough for Natalie? Would she give up her chance to find someone who truly loved her?

But that was just it. Their relationship was more than sex and companionship. They were incredible together. He had never experienced anything even remotely close to the connection and pleasure he felt making love to Natalie. Their passion. That was rare and special. Not only that, but they could also talk to each other and truly understand what the other person meant…as if they had a distinct wavelength that existed exclusively for them.

What they had might not be the stuff of fairy tales, but they were good together. He might not deserve her, but he would fight to keep her.

Sixteen

Garrett had been traveling often the last several weeks to prepare for Hansol's first joint venture with Vivotex. The trips were short, no more than a night or two at a time, but Natalie felt as though her time with him was being stolen from her.

Natalie took heavy steps to the parking structure, dreading going home to an empty house. Lost in her melancholy, she jumped when her cell phone rang. It was Garrett. She let the phone ring a few more times, trying to work up a cheerful "hello." After a deep breath, she picked up.

"God, I miss you." His words sounded as though they'd been torn from him.

Natalie halted as tears blurred her vision. He'd only been gone for two days, but she missed him with a physical ache. She held back the words on the tip of her tongue. *I love you.* She didn't regret telling him she loved him, but he never acknowledged her confession. And every time she said those words again, he would disappear behind a wall of indifference. At least he missed her. That had to mean something.

"I miss you, too," she said. "Hurry home to me."

"Soon." The single word, a promise filled with longing, stole her breath.

"Garrett."

"I'm headed to my next meeting." A small pause. As though he was waiting for her to say something. Then he sighed softly. "I needed to hear your voice."

"I'm glad you called." She swallowed back her emotion with some difficulty. "Go. Don't be late for your meeting."

Natalie hung up before she said more than she should. She slid into her car clutching the phone to her heart, and jumped when it rang again, thinking for a second it was Garrett calling back. Laughing at her foolishness, she glanced at her screen. It was the family-law attorney Garrett had retained for her.

"This is Natalie."

"Mrs. Song, this is Timothy Duffy. I have some great news."

Natalie's heart dropped to her stomach. "Yes, Timothy. I'm listening."

"Congratulations. You're a mom," he said with a smile in his voice. "The judge signed the adoption papers."

"Oh," she gasped and tears strangled her voice. "I'm a mom. I'm Sophie's mom."

"You certainly are. I've notified the Davises, and as previously agreed, they will have a week to relinquish physical custody of the baby." She could hear the smile in Timothy's voice. "I'll email you the details. You should go celebrate."

"Yes. Thank you."

Her phone fell from her limp fingers and tears streamed down her face as her heart tore into two pieces. One part of her heart was so very happy that Sophie was hers and she was Sophie's. The other half broke and bled. The adoption had been the one last thing that held Garrett to her.

She remembered his words from Ojai only too well. *I want you. But this marriage, it still ends once our objectives are reached. If I make love to you tonight, I'm taking your body and giving you mine, nothing more.*

But they'd come a long way from that night. Hadn't they?

One thing was certain. She couldn't go on like this. She had to tell him she didn't want their marriage to end—she wanted forever with him.

The next evening, Natalie waited in front of the elevator, her heart thumping against her rib cage. The adoption papers were tucked away in her nightstand drawer. She planned on telling Garrett everything—about Sophie, about wanting them to be a real family and about forever. Her ice-cold hands fisted at her sides.

When the elevator opened, Garrett caught her in his arms and spun her around before kissing her senseless. Her fears and worries melted away. He was home and that was all that mattered.

"Did you miss me?" He leaned his forehead against hers.

"Nah." *So much it hurt.* "Not really."

"I'll make sure to remind you what you've been missing."

"Is that a promise?" She looked up at him through her lashes, biting her lower lip.

"Damn it, Natalie," he groaned with a pained expression on his face. "I still have calls to make…"

Natalie laughed and danced out of his reach. "Well, you started it."

"Real mature." He stalked toward her, his eyes shining with intent.

Then his phone rang.

He cursed with gusto and growled when he checked the

caller ID. He pointed at Natalie and mouthed "later" before he answered and stomped toward his office.

Natalie smiled at his back, pleased with his obvious frustration. He really had missed her, and she planned on showing him how much she'd missed him. As she went into the bathroom to take a shower, she pushed aside the thought that they were running out of time.

After putting on a black chemise over her damp skin, she emerged from the bathroom, ready to share the news of Sophie's adoption. But when Garrett strode into their room only to freeze at the sight of her, all rational thoughts fled her mind. His heated gaze was filled with yearning and another emotion she couldn't define. Something akin to desperation...fear. Something primal and possessive filled her veins and she sashayed toward her husband. She had to have him. Show him with her body that they belonged together.

"Now, pay attention," she purred, unbuttoning his shirt and pushing it down his shoulders. "Because I'm going to have you my way."

"Is that so?" He arched an eyebrow and had a ghost of a smile on his lips.

"I didn't say you could talk."

"Natalie..."

He groaned, tilting back his head when she went down on her knees to pull off his slacks. Garrett swayed and planted his feet more firmly as her hand skimmed the outline of his erection on her way up.

"Take off your clothes," he ordered through clenched teeth.

Natalie just smiled and pushed him down onto an armchair. He lunged for her but she fluidly evaded his hands.

"Shh." She placed a finger over her mouth. "You aren't paying attention."

He growled.

With her gaze glued to his face, Natalie stripped off her clothes, standing barely out of reach. She had no idea how to perform a striptease, but judging by the fierce, unblinking attention of her husband, she was doing quite well.

Naked, she strode to the chair and straddled him, then took his hard length in her hands, making him hiss.

She positioned herself over him. "Do I have your full attention?"

"Yes," he rasped.

"Good."

She took him all the way inside her and he groaned against her neck, his hips surging to meet her. Natalie rode him with wild ferocity. Her body knew his intimately and she set a rhythm that would drive him mad. Drive her mad. And like the countless times before, they were caught in a storm neither of them could control.

Afterward, he carried her limp body to bed and they lay down facing each other. She stared at him, feeling too raw and vulnerable to hide the love from her eyes. He stared right back at her with an expression that made her insides melt.

"Wait here."

With that sudden command, he got out of bed and pulled on some pajama pants.

What a shame to cover up such a fantastic ass.

After digging through his suitcase, he strode back to her with a small box in his hands and sat on the edge of the bed.

"What is it?" she said.

He scratched the back of his head and cleared his throat. If she didn't know better, she would've thought he looked nervous.

"I have something for you." He held out the box to her and sat still as a statue as she opened it.

Her hand flew to her mouth and tears filmed her eyes. They were earrings. Emerald with diamond inlays. They looked exactly like his mother's ring, which Natalie wore every day.

"Oh, Garrett. They're beautiful." *But what does this mean?* she wanted to ask him.

"Put them on." His voice was gruff, tense.

"I…" She couldn't put them on. Not when the adoption document sat less than a foot from her. Not before she told him everything. "Garrett, I can't take them…"

"Why?" The absence of emotion in his voice shot fear through her heart.

"It's—it's too much. And you—you might want the ring back soon…" She trailed off, hoping he would correct her. Tell her he wanted to stay married to her. She didn't need a declaration of love. Not yet, anyhow. But she wanted to know this was more than just a business arrangement to him.

Instead, he shrugged and a mask of indifference fell across his features. Did he understand why she couldn't accept the earrings? Did he not care that their time together would soon end? Her heart clenched painfully.

"It's been a long day." He eased down and turned his back to her. "Let's get some sleep."

The distance between them seemed to stretch out endlessly, and Natalie lost the nerve to tell him about Sophie. Because when she told Garrett the adoption was finalized, she was going to bare her soul to him. Tell him that they were already a family. That they belonged together. Forever. But not tonight. Not like this. They didn't have long left, but they still had tomorrow. She would tell him everything tomorrow.

"Okay. Good night."

Out of habit, Garrett's eyes shot open at 4:00 a.m. Then, remembering he'd left his calendar open for the morning, he was about to let his eyelids droop closed when he bolted up, the sheets slipping down to his waist. His wife's side of the bed was empty.

He couldn't believe he'd slept at all. She'd refused the earrings because she intended to return her ring to him. Natalie was planning to leave him. She said soon, but she couldn't be gone already.

Garrett groaned. He'd had the earrings specially designed to match her engagement ring, so he could ask her to never take it off. *Did she understand my intent? How could she when I didn't tell her any of it?* Instead of waiting for her to come back to bed, he strode over to the en suite bathroom.

"Natalie?"

Considering that it was dark inside, he wasn't too surprised when she didn't answer. Maybe she'd gone downstairs for some water. After pulling on the first T-shirt he could grab from the dresser, he jogged down the stairs. The downstairs lights were on and he sighed in relief. He opened his mouth to call her name, but his phone beeped from the room.

Damn it. Who could it be at this hour?

He hesitated before he turned around to get his phone. The timing told him it might be an emergency.

It was a text from Mike. Call me. It's urgent.

"What is it?" Garrett demanded once he had Mike on the phone, impatient to get to Natalie. "Can it wait?"

"We found him." Mike's voice was grim. The spy. His friend was the only person Garrett trusted enough to help with the investigation, but he could deal with that later.

"Good. Is that it?"

"No." The pause on the other end lengthened and Garrett frowned, his gut telling him something was very wrong. "It sounds bad, but I don't want you jumping to any conclusions."

"Spit it out, Mike," he said through clenched teeth. "I'll make my own decisions."

"Starting a few months ago, someone named Peter Klapper was buying up all the Hansol stock he could get his hands on. If he acquired enough shares, he could've swayed some key votes to block your CEO appointment, but the oldest members of the board wouldn't let go of theirs. The board of directors is a curmudgeonly lot, but no one could question their loyalty."

"Who is he?"

"He works for Yami Corporation. He's been climbing up quickly. A clever and ambitious guy, but he's been gambling and amassing quite a sizable debt."

"So he's a puppet for a deep pocket."

"Right. We traced multiple electronic transfers into his bank account. Hundreds of thousands of dollars at a time."

"Did you find the origin of those transfers?"

"Not yet, and Klapper disappeared without a trace."

"Goddamn it. We need to hunt down the mole inside Hansol before he runs, too."

"We're close to finding that link. It's someone in the LA office." Mike sighed. "And the investigator found something out."

"What is it?" Garrett shoved his hand through his hair.

"Peter Klapper and Natalie went to college together. They dated for a few months…" Garrett's heart slammed into his rib cage. "They kept in touch for a while until a couple years ago, and the investigator claims Natalie hasn't been in a relationship since she broke up with Klapper. He thinks she might've been carrying a torch for him…"

"And he approached her to resume their affair and use her as his informant," Garrett said, finishing for him.

"Look, Song. That investigator is playing Sherlock Holmes and failing badly. His theory is so far-fetched and flimsy I was tempted not to tell you, but I refuse to keep information from you." Mike's voice rang with fierce conviction. "I know you've been burned by Samantha, but you need to remember Natalie is nothing like her. I don't know what the story is, but don't shut her out. Talk to her—"

Garrett hung up. He'd heard enough.

The pieces—the nightmarish pieces—started fitting together. The spy. It was Natalie. She'd been feeding Klapper the information. Garrett had been stupid enough to let a woman use him again.

Why, Natalie? What did the bastard offer you?

Garrett could've given her anything that Klapper offered and more. She had to have known that… Then it hit him square between the eyes.

Love. Peter Klapper had offered her love. A real family for her and Sophie. The one thing Garrett made clear he couldn't give her. The room spun at the realization. He shoved away the searing pain and focused on his cold, numbing fury.

He found her in the living room, sitting with her feet tucked under her and staring out at the city lights.

"Natalie."

A sweet smile lit up her face when she saw him. It nearly broke him. *Lies. All lies.*

"What are you doing up?" she said.

"Mike called. We found the spy."

"You caught the spy?" Natalie gasped, her hands rising to her chest. "Thank God for that. Who was it?"

Her feigned relief knocked the wind out of him. He'd never told her about the spy or the investigation. "You knew there was a spy."

"Yes, I found out recently. I wish… I wish you'd told me, Garrett." She sounded both hurt and frustrated. He narrowed his eyes as his fury built. "You didn't have to worry alone."

"I didn't tell you because it's none of your business," he snarled like a wounded beast.

She gasped then looked away. "I—I see."

Oh, she is good.

"Do you, Natalie?"

"What?" Her eyebrows drew together. "What's wrong?"

"Wrong? Well, that depends on one's perspective. I suppose it's for the best I found out sooner than later. Before I made the mistake of my life."

"What are you talking about?" She stood and walked toward him. His gaze flickered to a manila folder that fell from the couch. She cupped his face in her hands. "Garrett, look at me."

"What did he promise you, Natalie? Did he tell you he loves you?"

"Who?"

"Peter Klapper." He watched for her reaction. Guilt? Fear? All he saw was bewilderment.

"How do you know Peter?" She cocked her head.

"I had the misfortune of being the target of his corporate-espionage scheme."

"Peter? Corporate espionage?" Finally, her face reflected the horror he'd been expecting and her hands dropped to her sides. "But how? He used to be a little full of himself, but I can't imagine him doing anything illegal. Besides, he doesn't have any money or connections."

"He doesn't need money. He's just a pawn for someone who has it. As for connections, you supplied those for him, didn't you?"

Natalie stumbled back from him. "What are you saying?"

"Do you love him?" He took a step toward her and she retreated a step. "Is that why you betrayed me?"

"Me?" Her hands flew to her mouth and the blood

drained from her face. "You think I stole information from you to help Peter?"

"Are you trying to tell me it's a coincidence he was your lover?"

"Yes. He *was* my lover for a brief time. It was a long time ago," she said, her voice soft and trembling. "Tell me. Are you playing six degrees of separation or investigating corporate espionage?"

"I am not playing a *game*. I'm confronting my *wife* about being unfaithful to me," he roared, pain searing his heart. "Did he tell you he loves you? Did he promise you forever?"

"Listen, goddamn it." She took a step toward him with her hands outstretched, and this time, he stepped back from her. "I love *you*. Only you."

"Of course. *Love*." A ragged laugh tore from his throat.

Her eyes widened and she swayed slightly on her feet. He fisted his hands to stop himself from steadying her. A part of him shouted for him to stop. To listen. To think. But he couldn't do any of that. The pain and fear he'd run from for so long nipped at his heels, and if he stopped, those feelings would catch him—hurt him.

"I've never said those words to another man."

"Words. Mean. Nothing," he spat.

She hunched forward as though he'd hurt her physically. Her eyelids flickered and her lips parted but no words came out.

Samantha had said she loved him. They were only twenty but he'd asked her to marry him and she'd accepted. All those lonely years after his mom died... He thought she would fill that void. But when she found out his trust fund couldn't be accessed until he was twenty-five, she'd left him for a guy who had immediate cash to burn. Words meant nothing.

"Are there any more secrets you kept from me?"

"Yes." He flinched even though she had whispered the word. "I was going to tell you, but I was too afraid to find out what it would mean for us."

"Find out what? What were you going to tell me?"

"Sophie's adoption was finalized." Her shoulders shook but she held his gaze. "Everything we bargained for—your deal with Vivotex, Sophie's adoption… We did it. We won. Now there is no reason for us to stay married… except I couldn't bear for us to end. I wanted forever with you."

"I don't believe you, and I sure as hell don't believe in love and forever." His head spun and he barely managed to stay on his feet. "It's over."

He wanted to snatch the words back as soon as they left his mouth. It wasn't over. He would beg her to leave Klapper.

But her blood drained from her face and she stood eerily still. Fear gripped his throat. *No. Please, no.*

"You're right." Her voice was steady and strong when she spoke at last. "It really is over."

Natalie walked past him with her chin held high. Every nerve in his body screamed for him to stop her but he couldn't. Time must have passed because the next thing he knew, Natalie was standing in front of him again, fully dressed and holding a suitcase in her hand.

"I'm leaving."

"You can't leave now." *Not ever.* He dragged his hand down his face. "It's not even light out."

"What I do isn't any of your concern. Not anymore," she said, her face drawn but resolute. "If you don't mind, I'll ask my friends to pick up the rest of my things later."

He swayed slightly and widened his stance to steady himself. She seemed to be waiting for him to say something, but he could barely stand, much less speak. *Oh, God. What have I done?*

"Goodbye, Garrett."

It was the final nail in the coffin, and he felt shrouded in darkness. He welcomed the oblivion as he listened to Natalie leave with a quiet click of the door.

Seventeen

Natalie barely made it to Mrs. Kim's apartment before her knees gave out and she crumpled to the ground. Her friend was at Natalie's side within a second.

"What's wrong?" Mrs. Kim supported her by the waist and led her into her living room. "What happened?"

A sob broke from Natalie and sorrow enveloped her. Hot tears streamed ceaselessly down her cheeks until she felt wrung dry. She lay down on Mrs. Kim's couch and closed her eyes. Consciousness was exhausting…

The next time Natalie opened her eyes, it was dark out. She'd barely made a sound, but Mrs. Kim was at her side.

"You need to eat something." The older woman set a bowl of cereal on the coffee table. "I need to go to the market to make you a proper bowl of *jook*, my famous Korean porridge, but I couldn't leave you alone."

Natalie shook her head and flinched. It hurt. It hurt everywhere.

"Fine. Let's start with some water, shall we?"

Mrs. Kim held a cup to her lips and she swallowed. Once. Twice. "No more. I can't."

"Give yourself a few days to grieve, then no more." Mrs. Kim pressed a kiss to Natalie's forehead. "Think of Sophie."

Natalie sat up and looked at the bowl Mrs. Kim had brought her. She never knew Cheerios could expand five times their size by soaking up all the milk in the bowl. Natalie settled in to witness the entire process—without curiosity, without interest. It was food she was meant to eat, but couldn't.

I don't believe you.

She clenched her eyes shut.

It's over.

Her mom had abandoned her and her dad couldn't stand her.

Stupid, lonely girl. You should've known Garrett would never love you back.

The dark, gaping hole in her soul spread—patient in its malice, in its cruelty. Soon it would swallow all that was good and bright in her. She looked forward to it because maybe then she could find some peace. A peace for the dead.

Only the mother in her would survive. She would eat, talk and breathe as long as Sophie needed her.

"What the hell is going on, Garrett?" Adelaide burst into his office and opened the blinds, letting in a shaft of blinding sunlight. "Have you turned into a vampire?"

Garrett hadn't slept in days and it felt like a sledgehammer was pounding inside his head. Sunlight didn't help, so he'd closed all the blinds and shut off the lights.

"Leave. Now."

"I had a feeling he would be a wreck," Mike said, closing the door behind him.

"You told me they might've had a fight, but this is ridiculous," she huffed at his best friend.

Garrett didn't see any reason to talk to them, so he kept abusing the keys of his laptop, even though the document on his screen made no sense. Nothing made sense.

"Where's Natalie?" Adelaide said, stepping deeper into his office. "I've been trying to reach her for over a week, but she hasn't responded to any of my texts except for the first one."

He jerked up his head and met his sister's eyes. "What did she say?"

"All she said was sorry." She leaned toward him, bracing her hands on his desk. "Where is my sister?"

Sorry. Sorry for what? Unbalanced laughter built in his chest.

"*Hal-muh-nee* is worried sick. It isn't like Natalie to ignore her calls." When Garrett didn't respond, Adelaide shook him by the shoulders. "What's wrong, *oppa*?"

Mike gently withdrew her hands from him, and leveled him with disappointed eyes. "I told you not to do anything rash, Song."

"Screw you, Reynolds." His voice was a low croak. He couldn't remember the last time he ate or drank anything other than Scotch.

"Shut up and listen. We found the mole. Peter Klapper seduced a naive new hire in the media department—"

"I know it's not Natalie," Garrett interrupted.

"What? You thought Natalie was the spy? Are you freaking crazy? Please tell me you didn't accuse her of being the spy." His little sister sounded furious and scared at once. Her voice trembled when she said, "She was worried about you, Garrett. She didn't know anything until I told her. Oh, God. You broke her heart, didn't you?"

"Hush. It's going to be all right." Mike wrapped his arm around Adelaide's shoulders and dropped a kiss on the top of her head.

"*Hal-muh-nee* needs to know what happened, but I can't tell her on my own. You'll come with me, right, Michael?"

"Of course," he said in a soothing voice. Then his face turned stoic as he addressed Garrett. "Go find Natalie and fix the mess you've made. I'll deal with the mole and track down the puppet master."

"Look for connections to Rotelle Corporation and Jihae Park." Garrett had suspected Rotelle's involvement for a while.

"Your almost-fiancée Jihae Park?" Adelaide wrinkled her nose. "It was just an informal agreement between the elders. Why would they go through so much trouble to give you grief?"

"Her *jae-bul* family probably hasn't lost a single thing in their life," Garrett said with a humorless laugh. "They felt slighted so they sent her to the States to give me hell."

"If that's true, she played you exceptionally well," Mike said, frustration clipping his words. "You fell right into her trap all because Natalie dated Klapper when she was a college kid."

Garrett gripped his hair in his fists. "Get out."

"You deserve to be happy, Garrett. Both of you do," he said, concern infusing his voice. "Don't throw this away."

"Out!"

"Come on." Mike steered Adelaide toward the door.

"But we can't leave him like this." His sister sounded like she wanted to pummel some sense into Garrett.

"Give him time."

"Time for what?"

"Time to get it through his thick head that he's in love with Natalie."

"He doesn't know he's in love with her? How could...?" The door shut quietly behind them, muting Adelaide's next words.

Garrett tried to inhale. Maybe he needed to exhale. He

couldn't do either because he already knew. He was in love with Natalie and he'd done everything in his power to push her away to protect his sad, scarred heart.

Did I ever believe she betrayed me? No. Natalie was incapable of the duplicity he'd accused her of. It came down to fear. He was afraid she wouldn't stay with him because he couldn't love her. He couldn't admit he loved her because he feared love more than anything. But he couldn't lose her like this.

Now was time to face his fears. All of them.

Garrett had searched everywhere for her, pulling all the strings he had, but she'd disconnected her cell phone, wasn't using any of her credit cards, and there were no flight records. When he hit dead end after dead end, Garrett had hired a private investigator. The idea of a stranger tailing his wife and daughter, observing them unseen and unheard, was distasteful, but they'd been gone for two months and he'd run out of options.

Garrett ran his hand down his face and slammed his laptop closed. The board of directors was convening in a few hours to vote on his appointment as CEO. If he hadn't been a shoo-in as the company's heir apparent, then closing the biggest deal in Hansol's history should secure him the position.

Becoming the head of Hansol had been Garrett's lifelong goal, but it had paled and wilted when Natalie left. He couldn't muster up much concern for his professional future. He had to win back his wife.

Imprisoned in his beautiful and terrifying hope, Garrett arrived close to half an hour late to the board meeting. He was out of his mind with desperation to see his wife, but he wiped his face clean of all emotions as he entered the boardroom.

"Gentlemen. Ladies." Garrett bowed from his waist

to the board members and sat opposite his grandmother. *"Hal-muh-nee."*

She acknowledged him with a nod and studied his face. Her expression betrayed nothing but her eyes clouded with concern. Garrett wanted to place his head on her knees and weep—something he'd never allowed himself to do, even as a child.

The board members continued to go down a list of items on the special agenda. As Garrett waited, the board reached the main agenda, and his grandmother straightened her spine imperceptibly.

"Dear ladies and gentlemen of the board…"

Garrett's cell vibrated in his pocket and his heart picked up speed. Without taking his eyes off the speaker, he took out his phone and unlocked it with his thumb. When it was ready, he lowered his gaze to his lap with the barest shift of his head.

I've located her current residence and workplace.

His private investigator had come through. He stood up so abruptly his chair tipped over and all eyes snapped to him. Garrett had no doubt leaving the meeting at a crucial moment like this could cause a scandal or convince his grandmother to block his CEO appointment. But every minute apart from Natalie was time lost. He made the only choice he could.

"Hal-muh-nee, I found Natalie."

His grandmother's lips trembled for just a second before she nodded with authority. "Go."

Garrett sprinted out of the conference room and the meeting erupted into chaos. He didn't care. All that mattered was finding his wife and fighting for forever.

Eighteen

"Sophie Harper Sobol!"

The eleven-month-old laughed and waddled around the living room buck naked. The rascal had, of course, skipped crawling and gone straight into walking. Natalie just prayed she'd outgrow the streaking phase.

"Look, missy," Natalie said after body tackling her. "Mommy has to go to work and you need to finish getting dressed." If she didn't drop Sophie off with her grandparents soon, she'd be late.

All Natalie got was another evil giggle in response. Raising a natural-born troublemaker was exhausting work, but she was grateful for the all-consuming distraction. Sophie had saved her. Had kept her alive. She shook away the bleak memory of her first days apart from Garrett.

Blowing out a calming breath, she ran to the closet and pulled on her work clothes. She was working as the office manager of a booming chain of diners around Queens and Brooklyn while she looked for a permanent job in New

York. She'd just about given up hope of getting a position in her field after leaving Hansol. If her latest interview didn't pan out, she would start applying for managerial or even entry-level positions and prove herself all over again.

For the time being, she enjoyed her job. There were two employees at the "corporate office." Herself and Debbie, the one-woman accounting department. Debbie was easy-going and kind, but more importantly, she never read tabloids or watched gossip shows, so she didn't know Natalie was Mrs. Garrett Song. Or rather, the soon-to-be ex-wife of Garrett Song.

They'd gotten into a little habit where Natalie brought in pastries and coffee in the morning, and Debbie shared her homemade lunch. Today was supposed to be blueberry-scone day, but after getting Sophie ready and dropping her off at Lily and Steve's, Natalie decided to stop by the nearby doughnut shop so she could make it to work on time.

She started pleading her case as soon as she reached the office. "I know this isn't your favorite, but Sophie was being extra rascally this morning and I was running late." Debbie was standing at the small reception desk with a strange expression on her face. "I'm so sorry. I got us the buttermilk ones that aren't drenched in sugar glaze…"

Natalie trailed off when a tall, dark figure stepped out from her office. His face was impassive, but his eyes were molten onyx, churning with unfathomable emotions.

Garrett.

Debbie took the bag of doughnuts and coffee from her slack hands. "Whoever he is, I'd keep him." With a sly wink, her coworker trotted off to unload their breakfast in the kitchen.

Natalie debated whether to run for it but she wasn't sure which way she would go. She'd missed him so much, and ached to wrap herself around his body. He had to leave before she gave in to her heart.

"How did you find me?" She turned her back because it hurt to look at him.

"You'd disappeared without a trace so I hired a PI to find you for me."

"You did what?" She hugged her arms around her midriff as a shudder ran through her. Her eyes darted around the office, imagining someone watching her.

"I'm so sorry, but I needed to find you." Garrett held out his hand as though to touch her but quickly withdrew it. "I promise you the investigator is discreet and thoroughly professional."

"It doesn't matter," she sighed, waving aside his apology. "I was going to contact you once we were settled in. We need to file our divorce papers. It's uncontested and we have no shared property, so it should be relatively simple."

"Natalie, we aren't finished."

She frowned at the odd tone of his voice. Whatever he'd meant by that, they couldn't talk about it out here. Natalie walked past him into her office and indicated for him to close the door. She sat behind her desk to create some distance between them.

"If you mean the divorce, then no, we aren't finished, but we soon will be. I want all the loose ends tied up, so Sophie and I can move on."

Garrett flinched, and Natalie's frown deepened. He acted as though her words were gutting him.

"How is she?" His voice was a rough whisper.

The suffocating pressure in her heart reached a breaking point and she nearly doubled over in pain. Gripping the arms of her chair, Natalie choked down the lump in her throat.

"She's doing great. She's getting bigger, stronger and faster, which means she can make more trouble in less time."

A sad but genuine smile tilted Garrett's mouth, and Natalie's eyes roamed hungrily over him. When he caught her gaze with fire in his own, yearning blanketed her mind like thick fog blinding a driver. He searched her face and something akin to hope swept across his features. Then, with a suddenness that startled her, he circled her desk and kneeled in front of her.

She pressed back into her seat, not trusting herself to be so close to him. Garrett caught her instinctive retreat and the brief spark that lit his eyes flickered and dimmed. He was quiet for a long moment before he spoke.

"We found the mole who passed the information on to Klapper. A woman in the media department…"

So that's what this is about. He found out she didn't betray him and the guilt was tearing him apart. She clenched her hands to fight her instinct to reach out for him. To hold his head on her lap. She hurt for him but she had nothing left in her to soothe his pain.

"If you're here to apologize, there's no need," she said, sounding as weary as she felt. "I'm sure you had your reasons for suspecting me in the first place."

"My reasons?" His laughter rang with bitter regret. "I had my damn reasons but none of them excuse what I did."

"I already told you. You don't need to apologize." He had to leave. She wouldn't be able to hold on much longer. "If it'll help you sleep better, then I forgive you. I really do, so please leave now. If you care even a little about me, please just leave."

"No." She thought she misheard him. It was a broken rasp. Then determination flared in his eyes and he said with finality, "No."

"How could you—"

"I care more than a little bit about you." He held her arms. "I love you, Natalie."

"Leave." She tugged her arms free and stumbled blindly away from him. "I want you to leave. Now."

"I can't." Garrett rose to his feet, but only his eyes—lost and frightened—followed her. "I'll do anything you want. Everything. Except leave you. I can't do that."

She shut her eyes to the naked need on his face. "Can't or won't?"

"Natalie…"

"How could you say you love me when you don't even trust me?"

"I never believed you betrayed me. I trust you with my life…with my heart." Garrett took a step toward her with his hand outstretched, but stopped short when she backed farther away. "*I* lied to myself because I needed an excuse to push you away. I saw what losing my mother did to my father. I swore never to love like that—to love someone so much that losing them meant losing myself. Then, I met you—beautiful, brave and so kind. I knew there wasn't a wall high enough to keep you out of my heart, and it scared me to death. I was so afraid of being hurt that I broke your heart instead."

"Yes. You did." She breathed in and out through her nose and spoke to a point above his shoulder. "But I understand. It doesn't make it hurt any less, but I think I understand. Maybe it's better this way. You ended whatever was between us. We should move past it and go on with our lives."

"No. I don't think you understand." Anguish drenched his eyes and his Adam's apple worked to swallow. "If you did, you wouldn't tell me to *move on* and *live*, because there is no life for me without you."

"But nothing has changed." Hurt, hope, anger and love screamed in her head and pulled her in opposite directions. "You broke my heart once, and I won't be able to survive a second time."

"Everything has changed." His face was a mask of pain, but his voice was deep and true. "With you gone, everything lost meaning. The company, my family's legacy, the

CEO spot. Those things are nothing more than duty and responsibility. Something I have to do for the benefit of others. Nothing gives me joy or satisfaction. Don't you see? I'm nothing more than a shadow without you."

He put one foot ahead of the other and cautiously approached her as though she was a bird ready to take flight. Natalie shook her head and retreated until she backed into a wall. But this time, Garrett didn't stop until he stood in front of her. He didn't touch her but his gaze roamed her face, desperate, naked and frantic.

No wall or barrier hid him from her, and she saw him. At last, he bared every part of himself, down to his very core. He was exposed and vulnerable, raw and true, and terrified and powerful—the only way a person in love could be.

"You…love me?" she said, body shaking so hard that her teeth were chattering.

"More than life." He lifted a trembling hand and brushed the pad of his thumb across her cheek. Only then did she realize she was crying, and so was he. "But I fought it. God, I fought it. Cancer took my mother, but I pushed you away from me. I know I hurt you and I don't have a right to ask this of you, but if you give me a chance, I'll spend the rest of my life making it up to you."

"The rest of your life?" She was dreaming. She had to be. He didn't want her, or her love, did he?

"The rest of our lives. Forever."

"You didn't want forever. You didn't want *me*." She looked away from him, biting her lip.

"Because I was a coward and a fool. Please, Natalie. Look at me." He cupped her cheek and turned her to face him. "I love you, Natalie. You are my heart."

"Do you…?" But she couldn't hold back the wrenching sobs any longer. Helpless in the face of her sorrow, Garrett gently ran his hands down her arms. "Do you really want to spend the rest of your life with me?"

"I can't live without you." He enveloped her in the warmth of his arms. "I was too afraid to admit to myself that I was in love with you, but I was desperate to hold on to you. I had the earrings made for you because I needed a way to ask you to stay with me. To tell you I didn't want our marriage to end."

"And I wouldn't take them." Her heart cracked and bled. "I didn't know."

"Of course not. How could you?"

"But then, why did you…?" She couldn't finish the sentence, their final encounter too painful to recall.

"When you refused the earrings, I was so terrified of losing you that I pushed you away. That way I could at least control *how* my heart was broken. But now I know. Even if my heart and soul shattered into a thousand pieces tomorrow, I would rather live one day to the fullest, knowing you are mine." Natalie watched in disbelief as Garrett went down on his knee and withdrew a small box from his blazer. He opened it to reveal the engagement ring she'd left behind. "Would you do me the honor of becoming my wife?"

A small sob tore from her and she gave him a watery smile. "I'm already your wife."

"But I need to know, will you be my wife now and forever? To love and to cherish?" His voice broke with the depth of his emotion. "Because I believe in love and marriage and forever. All of it. I believe in us."

Natalie smiled at him, not quite able to believe what was happening. To ensure it was all real—that he was real—she cradled his beautiful face in her hand, and with a shuddering sigh, he turned his head and kissed her palm with aching tenderness. Then, still holding her hand, he rose to his feet.

"I want you to have everything you've ever wanted. As promised, the VP of Human Resources position is yours.

You could transfer to New York at the end of the month as planned."

Confusion drew her eyebrows low and she searched his face. "But you'll be in Los Angeles."

"No, I need to be where you are. If you'd let me, I'd like to come with you."

"But your family, your life, the CEO appointment you worked so hard for... They're all in Los Angeles."

"My life is with you and our daughter," he said with a stubborn set to his jaw. "Besides, I don't even know if I'm the new CEO. I left in the middle of the board meeting when I found out where you were."

"You idiot."

She was angry he'd jeopardized his dream, but if she'd wanted proof of his love, she couldn't ask for anything stronger. Even so, he was an idiot. She grabbed his lapels to shake some sense into him, but changed her mind. Instead, she jerked him close and kissed him senseless until they needed to come up for air.

"That kiss." He sounded as breathless as she felt. "Does it mean what I think it means?"

"Only if you think it means I love you." Her voice shook with joy. She had held those words in check too many times. "I love you so much. I've loved you since you made me sit and watch you sign those damn HR documents. So, yes. I'll be your wife and we can be a real family...from now until forever."

Garrett seemed to stop breathing for a moment. Then a smile radiant with love spread across his face, and he captured her lips in a possessive, savoring kiss. When they at last drew apart, he held her face between his hands as though he couldn't stop touching her.

"I'm not sure if I could let you out of my sight right now, so don't mind me if I follow you around like a shadow," he said in a low, gravelly voice.

"Please do." Her heart filled with joy, and she burst out laughing. "I don't mind at all."

"Good." Garrett gathered her close and bent to kiss her again, but she put a hand on his chest to stop him.

"But if you lost the CEO seat, I'll kill you with my bare hands."

"That's not important right now."

"Like hell it isn't." Natalie crossed her arms over her chest and arched an eyebrow. "But I agree. For now, all that matters is that we'll be together. We'll figure out everything else."

"God, I love you."

"Say it again," she whispered, afraid she might wake up from this dream.

"I love you, Natalie."

"Again." *And again, and again.*

"I love you. More than life."

Smiling up at him with the brilliance of her glowing heart, Natalie kissed her husband, knowing she'd never grow tired of hearing those words.

* * * * *

A REUNION
OF RIVALS

REESE RYAN

To the amazing readers in the Reese Ryan VIP Readers Lounge on Facebook: thank you for your continued support. I appreciate you all so much.

To Jennifer Copeland: thank you for recommending the perfect Robert Frost poem.

To readers Cassandra Hunt, Nalria Wisdom Gaddy, Julie Eichelberger-Ford and Nicole Trudeau Westmoreland: thank you for the peach drink recommendations. I can't wait to try all of them.

One

Max Abbott had a king-size headache and a serious case of jet lag. After spending seven days in Vegas on a business trip that ended with the three-day-long bachelor party of a college friend, he was grateful to be back in Magnolia Lake—his small Tennessee hometown nestled in the Smoky Mountains.

He'd drunk way too much and slept far too little. And this morning, his thirtysomething body was clearly protesting his twentysomething antics over the weekend.

Max was the marketing VP of King's Finest, his family's world-renowned distillery. So he usually made a point of arriving in the office ahead of his team. But today he was so exhausted he could barely see straight. If it hadn't been for his father—Duke Abbott, the company CEO—calling an emergency meeting this morning, he would've stayed home and slept it off.

Instead, he lumbered into the office still wearing his Saint Laurent shades at ten thirty—half an hour before the scheduled meeting. Just enough time to check in with his assistant.

"Good morning, chief." Molly Halloran glanced up from typing furiously on her keyboard.

He removed his shades, squinting at the light pouring in from the nearby windows.

"Sheesh!" she exclaimed in a voice reminiscent of Lucille Ball's in *I Love Lucy.* "Must've been *some* weekend."

"It was." Max parked his butt in the chair in front of Molly's desk, not willing to expend the additional energy to take the dozen or so steps to his office. "And good morning to you, too, sunshine."

"Can I get you some coffee? You're going to need it if you don't want to look like the stiff in *Weekend at Bernie's* the rest of the day." She bounced out of her seat and moved toward the coffeemaker before he'd even grunted his response.

Molly's brutal honesty was one of the reasons he valued her so much. And if it caught him in the chin with a right hook every now and again, so be it.

He pulled out his phone and checked his text messages and email to see if anything pressing required his attention.

There was nothing that couldn't wait until he was fully conscious, which, at this rate, might be in a day or two.

Max thanked Molly when she handed him a black mug engraved with the white King's Finest Distillery logo. He set his phone on her desk and wrapped his hands around the warm cup, inhaled the fragrant black liquid and took his first sip of coffee of the day. He released a small, contented sigh, his eyes drifting closed momentarily.

"We've got twenty minutes to go over everything." She tapped on the fitness wearable on her wrist. "That takes into account the five minutes you'll need to walk to the conference room."

Brutally honest and extremely efficient.

"Fine." He took another swig of coffee, set his mug down and opened the notes app on his phone. "Shoot."

"Your father is being tight-lipped about this meeting." She lowered her voice, her blue-gray eyes shifting away from him. "But last week, while you were gone, he asked me and Emily to compile everything you and Zora had on your proposal to add fruit brandies to the KFD lineup."

That woke him up more than the bulletproof coffee had.

Three years ago, his grandfather, Joseph Abbott, the founder of King's Finest Distillery, had proposed that the company begin making fruit brandy. His father had been opposed. In a compromise, they'd spent a small mint to set up separate stills and bring in a brandy distiller. The company began experimenting with making small batches of fruit brandy, using the excess, overly ripe fruit supplied by his grandfather's best friend, who owned an orchard just outside of Knoxville.

The brandy they'd produced was damn good. So for the past two years, Max and his sister, Zora, the company's VP of sales, had been trying to convince their father to move forward with bringing a KFD brandy to market.

His father agreed that the quality was outstanding. Still, he hadn't been ready to commit to expanding the company's basic product line beyond the limited-edition moonshines they'd rolled out in honor of the company's jubilee three years ago.

He would pick the day I feel like I've been run over by a truck to discuss this.

"Print me a copy of everything you have on—"

Molly shoved a binder with colored tabs in his direction. "That's everything. Oh, and I took the liberty of updating the projected sales numbers. I also created a quick summary of the key selling points. It's on page one."

Note to self: get Molly that limited edition Star Wars electric pressure cooker she's been eyeing for her birthday.

She finished briefing him on the materials, then urged him in the direction of the conference room, armed with a fresh cup of coffee, promptly at five minutes to eleven,.

At least now he more closely resembled a fully functioning human being.

Max entered the room and slid into his usual chair beside Zora.

"Glad you could join us," his sister whispered, elbowing him in the ribs. "I thought we might need to send someone to revive you."

"Ha-ha." He didn't look in his sister's direction. Instead, he focused on the older man seated on the other side of the table whose snow-white hair and beard contrasted his dark brown skin. "Good morning, Mr. Bazemore."

"Morning, Max." A wide smile spread across Dixon Bazemore's face as they both rose to their feet and shook hands. The old man had been the owner of Bazemore Orchards longer than Max had been alive. "Good to see you, young man."

"You, too, Mr. B." Molly's instincts about the reason for the meeting had been right. Why else would Dixon Bazemore be here? Still, he asked, "What brings you to see us today?"

"We'll go over everything during the meeting," Max's father interjected. "We're waiting for one more person."

Max glanced around the table. All of the members of the executive committee were present. His grandfather and father. His brothers Blake and Parker, the operations VP and CFO, respectively. Blake's wife, Savannah—the company's events manager. Zora, him and his father's admin, Lianna, who was there to take notes.

"Who are we—"

"I'm sorry. I got a little turned around finding my way back here from the parking lot. But I've got your portfolio, Grandad."

Max snapped his attention in the direction of the familiar voice. He hadn't heard it in more than a decade, but he would never, *ever* forget it. His mouth went dry, and his heart thudded so loudly he was sure his sister could hear it.

"Peaches?" He scanned the brown eyes that stared back at him through narrowed slits.

"Quinn." She was gorgeous, despite the slightly irritated

flare of her nostrils and the stiff smile that barely revealed her dimples. "Hello, Max."

The *good to see you* was notably absent. But what should he expect? It was his fault they hadn't parted on the best of terms.

Quinn settled into the empty seat beside her grandfather. She handed the old man a worn leather portfolio, then squeezed his arm. The genuine smile that lit her brown eyes and activated those killer dimples was firmly in place again.

Max had been the cause of that magnificent smile nearly every day that summer between his junior and senior years of college when he'd interned at Bazemore Orchards.

"Now that everyone is here, we can discuss the matter at hand." His father nodded toward Lianna, and she handed out bound presentations.

"As you can see, we're here to discuss adding fruit brandies to the King's Finest Distillery lineup—a venture Dad, Max and Zora have been pushing for some time." Duke nodded in their general direction. "I think the company and the market are in a good place now for us to explore the possibility."

"Excellent." His sister beamed. "Would this be a permanent addition to the product lineup?"

"I'll only commit to a limited-edition trial." Duke frowned slightly. He always did what was best for their family-owned distillery. But Zora—the youngest and the only girl in a family of four boys—was still his "princess," and his father hated disappointing her. "But if the numbers support it, as with the special-edition moonshines we introduced a few years ago, I'm willing to discuss making the line permanent."

"Bourbon is what we're known for," Parker, also known as Negative Ned, chimed in. "Won't adding other liquors to the lineup dilute our brand?"

Parker wasn't being argumentative. He was painstakingly methodical and questioned everything. It was the way his intricate mind worked.

Zora rolled her eyes and folded her arms, not bothering to hide her annoyance. "Pepsi sells several types of soda, water, tea, juice and energy drinks. It hasn't damaged their reputation as a top beverage company."

Parker thought about Zora's words for a moment, then nodded sagely. He scribbled on the ever-present pad in front of him and pushed his glasses up the bridge of his nose. "Good point. Go on."

Duke fought back a chuckle, then continued.

Max should have been riveted by the conversation. After all, this project was one he'd been fighting for over the past thirty months. Yet, it took every ounce of self-control he could muster to keep from blatantly staring at the beautiful woman seated directly across the table from him.

Peaches. Or rather, Quinn Bazemore. Dixon Bazemore's granddaughter. She was more gorgeous than he remembered. Her beautiful, deep brown skin looked silky and smooth.

The simple gray shift dress she wore did its best to mask her shape. Still, it was obvious her hips and breasts were fuller now than they'd been the last time he'd held her in his arms. The last time he'd seen every square inch of that shimmering brown skin.

Zora elbowed him again and he held back an audible *oomph*.

"What's with you?" she whispered.

"Nothing," he whispered back.

Maybe he wasn't doing such a good job of masking his fascination with Quinn.

Max opened his booklet to the page his father indicated. He was thrilled that the company was ready to give their brandy initiative a try, even if it was just a test run.

He understood why Mr. Bazemore was there. His farm

had been providing the fruit for the brandy and would continue to do so. But that didn't explain the presence of his ex.

Quinn shifted in her seat beneath Max Abbott's heated stare. She refused to glance in his direction. She wasn't here to flirt with the handsome-as-ever Max Abbott. She'd come to King's Finest Distillery for two reasons: to help save her grandfather's farm and to build a case study for the consultancy she'd launch as soon as the farm was on stable ground again.

It was a venture she'd mused about as an undergrad. But she'd settled into a comfortable public relations career instead. Until six months ago, when she'd found herself out of a job and unable to work in her field within a fifty-mile radius of her home in Atlanta.

With no immediate plans, she'd packed up her condo and accepted her grandfather's invitation to their family farm just outside of Knoxville, where she'd spent her summers as a kid.

Just until she figured out her next move.

The excitement of helping her grandfather establish important strategic partnerships revived her interest in her forgotten venture. So she'd dusted off her business plan, plugged in the holes and improved on it. Now she needed to build her portfolio while she waited out the remaining six months of the non-compete clause in her employment agreement with her former PR firm. Then she'd return to Atlanta and launch her new practice.

This proposed partnership with the world-renowned King's Finest Distillery would be the cornerstone of her growing portfolio. So if that meant pretending not to be affected by the man who'd broken her heart and crushed it into minuscule pieces without so much as a backward glance, she'd suck it up and do just that.

If Max could behave as if that summer between them had never happened, so could she.

Duke was explaining that they would begin the venture with apple-, peach-and cherry-flavored brandies, and that all of the fruit would be sourced from Bazemore Farms.

Quinn's heart swelled when everyone in the room applauded. She was relieved no one had objected to making her grandfather's farm the sole source for the fruit. It was a sweet deal for the farm, which had been struggling in recent years. Partly because of a shift in the market and how difficult it had become to get solid, reliable help at a price the farm could sustainably afford. Partly because of the shady accountant who'd taken over the books after her grandmother's death several years ago.

"This will be a co-branded product, something we've never done before. A partnership that was brokered by Dixon's lovely granddaughter, Quinn." Duke gestured toward her. "She's here in her capacity as an executive of Bazemore Farms, but she's also a collaboration expert. We had a fine chat last week about some of her innovative ideas for quickly getting this venture to market. Quinn."

"Thank you, Mr. Abbott." Quinn stood, pulling a stack of presentations from her bag. She walked around the table, placing one in front of each person as she explained how she'd created lucrative partnerships between clients in the past.

"As a rep at one of Atlanta's most prestigious PR firms for the past eight years, I…" Quinn stammered, unsettled by the jolt of heat that surged through her when Max's eyes met hers as she handed him a copy of the presentation.

It was her nerves, *not* Max Abbott, that had caused her words to come out in a jumble.

Despite the silent outrage in the widened eyes framed by thick, neat brows, the man was still devastatingly handsome. He was a little older and his shoulders were a bit broader.

But he looked essentially like the boy she'd fallen in love with that one passionate summer. The last she'd spent with her grandparents before going off to college. The summer Max had been an intern, living and working on the farm.

That was more than a decade ago. Time had treated him well.

"I've handled sensitive public relations campaigns for some of the biggest names in fintech," she continued.

"We already have a PR person," Parker interrupted, shoving his glasses up the bridge of his nose.

"You have a college student who handles social media, your newsletter, and the occasional press release." Quinn maintained her warm smile. Duke had warned her Parker would be a tough nut to crack, and that Max and Zora might be insulted by the idea of bringing her on to execute the project that had been their baby. "But a project of this magnitude requires a dedicated, experienced professional who'll get vendors and consumers excited about the new product line. Just as Savannah did for the company's jubilee and the associated release of limited-edition moonshines a few years ago."

Savannah smiled approvingly, and Parker nodded in agreement, silenced for the moment.

"If you'll turn to page five, we can quickly review a rundown of how I'm proposing to help King's Finest and Bazemore Farms make the most of this joint venture."

"You're bringing in someone else to execute our proposal?" Max ignored her completely, asking the question of his father instead. "Zora and I are fully capable of—"

"Speak for yourself, big brother." Zora turned her chair toward him before their father could respond. "I have a lot on my plate. We've seen a real uptick in our international sales and domestic market share in regions outside of the South since the jubilee. I'm traveling extensively over the next few months. I can't add another thing to my to-do list right now. Neither can my team. As long as we're consulted regularly, I'm all for bringing someone else on to do the heavy lifting."

Quinn exhaled quietly, and her racing heart slowed in response to Zora's encouraging nod.

"And you've had your hands full with the expansion of our marketing efforts," Duke reminded him. "So it would be better to have someone wholly dedicated to the project."

Max's nostrils flared, and a streak of red bloomed across his forehead and cheeks. He opened his mouth to object further, but his grandfather cut him off.

"Let Quinn finish her presentation, son. Then we can discuss any concerns privately and make our final decision." Joseph Abbott nodded in her direction. "Please continue, Quinn."

She smiled gratefully at the older man she'd always called Grandpa Joe, then inhaled deeply, smiled broadly and put on the presentation of her life.

She'd won over Joseph and Duke Abbott, the company's founder and CEO. Zora and Savannah were also on board. Blake, she couldn't quite read but Parker and Max definitely required convincing. So that was what she would do.

In this room, in this moment, Max Abbott wasn't her first love, her first real kiss, her first…*everything*. He was a skeptical company executive, not unlike the dozens she'd encountered before in her career.

Despite whatever else Max might be feeling toward her—curiosity, animosity, maybe even attraction—he was a sensible individual. And like every other Abbott at the table, she knew he wanted what was best for King's Finest.

She just needed to convince him that she was the best person for the job. And convince herself that working with her ex wasn't her worst idea ever. Her entire future was riding on it.

Two

Max groaned quietly as Quinn finished her presentation. He'd sifted through her proposal and listened carefully, ready to poke holes in it and rip it apart. But the plan was solid, and Quinn had suggested useful partnerships he and Zora hadn't considered.

Still, this project was *his* and Zora's baby. They'd taken their grandfather's request to add flavored brandies to the lineup seriously. Had worked with him to develop it. Worn their father down until he'd agreed to invest in the stills and bring in an expert brandy distiller. Revisited the topic at *every* damn quarterly meeting for the past two years. So for his father to just hand off the project to his ex of all the goddamned people on the face of God's green earth... Yeah, it felt a hell of a lot like a solid knee in the nuts. Even if no one in the room besides him and Quinn were aware of their romantic history.

But his father was right. He and Zora had their hands full with all of the additional business King's Finest was doing. Much of it could be credited to the efforts of his sister-in-law, Savannah, who'd become their de facto PR person since she'd joined the company three years ago. Savannah handled event management for both the distillery and the renovated barn on the edge of his parents' property, which they rented out for weddings and other events.

The company's event and tour business was booming

now. But Savannah was six months pregnant with her and Blake's second child, and their two-year-old son was already a handful. The last thing his sister-in-law needed was another project.

"Well, what do you think?" Grandpa Joseph beamed. Dixon and Quinn had been dispatched on an hour-long tour of the King's Finest Distillery while the Abbotts formally debated the Bazemore Farms proposal. "That one's a sharp cookie, eh?" His grandfather chuckled. "I remember the first time I met Quinn. She was about three years old and she had more questions than any kid that age I'd ever encountered besides Zora." He grinned at his only granddaughter.

"I love the plan she put together for us." Zora thumbed through the document Quinn had prepared. "Having her handle all of this is a godsend. And she's got the right personality for the job. She didn't skip a beat or get frustrated with Parker's myriad questions or Max's pushback." Zora raised an eyebrow at him. "And I love her suggestions for finding new ways to partner with state and local vendors."

"Excellent. Blake, how about you?" Duke asked Max's eldest brother, the heir apparent to the King's Finest CEO-ship.

"I love everything about the plan." Blake tapped the cover of the presentation. "I like Quinn, and I know the distributors will like her, too. If she can do half of what she's presented here, I'm sold."

"Parker?" Duke turned to him, as if prepared for the worst.

Parker scanned the data again. "The numbers look good. If you're sure we can do this without compromising our position in the bourbon market..." He shrugged. "I'm fine with moving forward on a trial basis. Say...six months once it goes to market. If sales are good, we can talk long-term."

"Sounds fair." Duke nodded, then turned to him. "And what say you, Max?"

Max released a quiet breath. Every eye in the room was focused on him. Quinn's plan was flawless; he had no legitimate reason to object to it.

So what was he going to say?

That he didn't want to work with her because it would be a constant reminder that he'd been a complete dick to her thirteen years ago?

"The plan is fine…okay, it's good," he amended in response to everyone's guffaws and raised eyebrows. "It's damn good. I'll give you that. But this is *our* company." He tapped the table with his index finger. "*Our* project. A project we're doing in memory of Savannah's grandfather Martin. Don't you think *we* should be the ones to handle it rather than bringing in an outsider?"

Had that come off as spoiled and elitist as it sounded in his head?

God, I hope not.

"Seriously, dude? *She's not one of us,*" Zora mimicked him in a whiny, low voice. "*That's* the best you can do?"

Everyone at the table laughed.

"You gotta admit, that argument is weak sauce, bruh." Blake chuckled. "Quinn is an experienced professional and she and Mr. B are good people."

"And I know she's not technically family, but I wouldn't exactly call her an *outsider*, either," Grandpa Joe added, sounding a little hurt by the dig. "I've always been quite fond of the girl. Considered her an honorary granddaughter."

"I know, Gramps. And I didn't mean anything by it." Max sighed and scrubbed a hand down his face. "I guess what I'm saying is that I have a lot of time and energy invested in this project. So the idea of relinquishing complete control of it isn't sitting well with me."

"I can respect that, Max." His father nodded sagely as

he rubbed his whiskered chin. He leaned forward on one elbow. "What can we do to make you more comfortable with Quinn running point on the project?"

Translation: This is happening, son. You've been out-voted.

"I want to be the point person on this project internally," Max said definitively. "And it should be clear that Quinn reports to me."

"Done." His father shrugged. "That'll leave me more time to golf. Anything else?"

"I plan to be as involved in the project as my schedule permits." Max folded his hands on the table in front of him. "And I need to have the option to terminate the agreement early should I find just cause."

Duke stroked his chin as he silently contemplated Max's request. He nodded begrudgingly. "Agreed, but I get the final say on such a drastic action."

"Perfect." Grandpa Joe slapped the table and chuckled. "Lianna, order us some lunch. We've got reason to celebrate. And make sure to break out the good mason jars so we can all sample a little of that brandy."

Just peachy.

He'd be working closely with the one ex who had it out for him. The stiff smile she'd given him when he'd used her nickname made it obvious she was still harboring a grudge that would impede their working relationship. This project was too important to his grandfather and their company. He wouldn't permit his past mistake to interfere with family business. He'd handle this the way he handled every other business problem: by facing it head-on.

That meant clearing the air with Quinn the first opportunity he got.

The Bazemores had returned to the conference room where a selection of pastas from a local Italian restaurant awaited them. They'd shared a meal with the Abbotts and sampled the peach, apple and cherry brandies. All of them were remarkably good.

Max's father and grandfather had invited Dixon to join them for a celebratory round of golf and, doubtless, more drinking. Parker had left to walk Cricket—his fiancée Kayleigh Jemison's golden retriever. That left Zora, Quinn, Blake and Savannah, who were seated at the table chatting after the meal.

Quinn was mooning over the adorable photos of Max's nephew, Davis, on Blake's phone.

Max had waited patiently, not actively joining in the conversation, instead staying engaged and nodding or chuckling whenever warranted. He needed a moment alone with Quinn.

He glanced at the text message that flashed on his watch: The league wants to talk sponsorship in an hour. We need to review notes.

For the past several months he'd been working on a sponsorship deal with the Memphis Marauders professional football team. Turning down the call wasn't an option. But he didn't want to put off clearing the air with Quinn, either.

If they were going to work together, they needed to start off with a clean slate.

Max stood abruptly and everyone in the room turned toward him. He cleared his throat. "Hey guys, I need to speak with Quinn for a moment...*privately*," he added, for the benefit of his sister, who'd shrugged.

Blake and Savannah exchanged a puzzled look.

"Yeah, sure." Blake stood, helping his wife up.

Savannah rubbed her growing belly. "It was a pleasure to meet you, Quinn. Lianna will give you my contact information. I'd love to meet for lunch later this week."

Blake and Savannah left, hand in hand. Zora folded her arms.

"Zora." Max gave her his *I'm not bullshitting right now* voice. A voice he'd had to employ often over the years with his little sister.

"Fine." Zora stood, then looked at Quinn. "As long as you're okay with this."

"It's fine, but thank you, Zora." Quinn smiled politely as she stood, gathering her papers. A clear sign that she was leaving, too.

Zora shot Max a warning look and breezed out of the room.

As soon as the door closed behind his sister, Quinn turned to him and scowled. "Why would you give everyone the impression something is going on between us?"

He tried not to take her words personally, but damn if it didn't feel like she'd kicked him in the teeth wearing a pair of steel toe boots.

There was a time when her greatest desire had been for them to go out on a proper date and let the world see them together. Rather than sneaking around and hooking up in his shabby little loft over the barn or in the bed of his truck, parked beneath the stars.

Heat stung his cheeks as he jammed his hands into his pockets. "They probably assume I want to talk about the project or catch up with an old friend."

He pretended not to notice the way she pressed her lips together and furrowed her brows when he referred to them as *friends*.

Damn. Is there a draft in here?

The chilly vibe coming from his ex was all too real.

"And I really would love to catch up at some point. But first, I need to tell you just how sorry I am."

"No." She shook her head, her tousled beach waves swinging gently.

He curled the fingers still shoved into his pockets into tight fists. Max couldn't help remembering how he'd sifted the soft strands through his fingers as she had lain in his arms. And the dreamy way she'd gazed up at him after they'd made love.

There was nothing remotely romantic about the frosty look Quinn cast in his direction from beneath her long, thick eyelashes.

"No, you won't allow me to apologize to you, or no, you're not willing to accept my sincere apology?" He sat on the edge of the conference table.

"Both." Quinn folded her arms, her expression neutral. Despite the iciness that slid over his skin in response to her answer, her tone and expression betrayed no anger. "A—I don't want your apology. B—There's no need for it."

Heat spanned his forehead. Max had imagined having this conversation with Quinn dozens of times. He'd envisioned anger, forgiveness and lots of incredibly hot makeup sex. What he hadn't foreseen was Quinn standing here calm, callous and completely out of fucks to give.

Not that he didn't deserve it.

"I appreciate you saying that, Quinn. But I'd feel better if—"

"No." Her voice vibrated with thinly veiled anger this time and her eyes narrowed. "You don't get to do this."

"I don't get to do what? Apologize?" Max was genuinely stunned by her refusal.

"You don't get to absolve yourself of guilt this way." Quinn raked her fingers through her hair and tucked a few strands behind her ear. "It's been thirteen years. If you didn't see fit to apologize before now, I can't imagine that your apology is sincere. So let's not do this, *please*."

The soft, pleading tone with which she ended her request reminded him of how she'd uttered his name during those sultry summer nights.

Max winced and swallowed hard. His hushed tone matched hers. "You have every right to be angry with me, Quinn."

"I wasn't angry, Max. I was hurt." Her stony expression faltered momentarily. "By the end of that summer you'd proclaimed your undying love for me. Then as soon as you returned to campus you broke up with me via a one-sided, two-minute phone call. For months, I wondered what I'd done wrong. I finally realized that it wasn't anything I'd done." She shrugged, her smile returning. "You were just an ass. A handsome, charming one. But an ass nevertheless."

"On that we can agree." He sighed, folding his arms.

She flashed the triumphant half smile he remembered so well.

"If there's nothing else, I should go." She lifted her bag onto her shoulder. "We can meet in the morning to strategize, if that works for you."

"Are you staying at the farm?" he asked.

"I am," she said in a tone that made it clear she felt the question too personal. "Why?"

"You have nearly an hour drive to get here." He walked her toward the door. "So you name the time."

"Ten o'clock?"

"See you then." His heart thudded as he watched her slip out the door.

He'd screwed up by walking away from Quinn the way he had. Now those chickens had come home to roost.

Max groaned quietly as he sank onto a nearby chair. He and Quinn would only need to work closely together at the outset of the project. After that, they could work together remotely, when necessary. He could certainly keep it together for a few months.

Shit.

It was the same lie he'd told himself when he'd first laid eyes on Quinn that summer.

Just look at how that turned out.

Three

Quinn changed her outfit for the third time this morning. It was unlike her. She was organized and decisive. With her planner on hand, she was always ready for the day ahead. But she hadn't slept well last night. It didn't help that she'd drifted off while reviewing her notes for her upcoming meeting with Max.

He'd seemed disappointed to discover that her proposal was a good one. He'd clearly been expecting her to flop. And if she did, Max would no doubt be ready to pull the plug on their project. So there was no room for failure, fear or hesitance. She had to show up today at Max's office with her game face on. Make it clear that she knew *exactly* what she was doing.

This deal meant too much to her grandfather's farm and to her future. So she wouldn't allow herself to be intimidated by the fact that Max clearly didn't want her there. Nor would she be distracted by Max's good looks, his charm or the fact that when his eyes met hers she still felt…*something* for him.

When she'd seen him yesterday, a jolt of electricity had rocketed up her spine. His dark eyes had seemed to peer straight through her, like armor-piercing rounds shredding her flesh, despite the mental suit of armor she'd donned before she'd stepped into the room.

The truth was that she hadn't gotten lost on her way back

to the conference room that morning. She'd simply needed a moment to compose herself before she came face-to-face with Max again.

It'd been thirteen years since she'd seen Max Abbott, more than a third of her thirty-one years. Enough time to give her distance and perspective. Enough time to realize that Max Abbott hadn't been as important in the overall scheme of her life as her teenage brain had once believed.

Yes, he'd been her first love, and over that long, hot summer she'd allowed herself to believe that Max was the alpha and omega of her romantic life. That there would never be another man for her.

Quinn laughed bitterly. *God, you were naive.*

Unfortunately, she hadn't learned her lesson after Max. She'd still wanted to believe that people were inherently good and could be taken at their word. Her most recent ex had finally cured her of her Pollyanna-ish misconceptions.

The cold, hard fact was that there were a lot more liars in the world than there were people she could count on. But her grandfather was firmly in the latter camp. She wouldn't disappoint him by allowing her inconvenient history with Max to sabotage this deal.

Quinn followed the smell of pancakes, bacon and coffee down the stairs. Her grandfather stood over the sizzling cast-iron pan with a spatula in hand.

The memory of her grandmother—vibrant and beautiful until the day she died—standing there in the kitchen, cooking in that pan, with that spatula, flashed through Quinn's brain. Her mouth curved in a faint smile, though her chest suddenly felt heavy.

"You've got her smile, you know." Her grandfather's voice startled her from the daze she'd fallen into.

"I know." Quinn's smile deepened. She set the heels she was wearing today by the kitchen door. "And I love that I'll always have that connection to her."

She didn't bother to ask how her grandfather knew she'd been thinking of her grandmother. It was hard not to enter what had been Lydia Bazemore's domain and *not* think of her.

"Maybe you'll have a little girl someday with that same smile." Her grandfather winked, chuckling when she rolled her eyes and groaned in response. "Hey, an old man can dream."

"Hate to break it to you, Gramps, but there are zero prospects of a great-granddaughter on the horizon. At least not from me." She kissed her grandfather on his stubbly cheek. "I can't speak for Marcus and Mavis," she said of her younger twin siblings.

"I don't think the world is ready for the progeny of Marcus or Mavis." Her grandfather laughed, and she did, too.

Her younger brother and sister were hyperfocused science geeks who lived in their own little world. A world she never quite fit into. They were just five years younger than she was, but with the emotional distance between her and her younger siblings, it might as well have been five light-years.

The two of them were more like their parents—both scientists working in academia—than Quinn would ever be. At the dinner table with her family, she'd always felt like the answer to one of those *Sesame Street* skits: *Which one of these doesn't belong?*

"One day." He smiled. "Just not today." Her grandfather nodded toward the coffeemaker. "Grab yourself a cup of coffee and have a seat. I know you have to get out of here soon."

Quinn didn't argue. Instead, she poured herself a cup of coffee and added creamer from the fridge. Then she pulled out one of the yellow-vinyl-and-chrome chairs from beneath the chrome and yellow Formica table. Her grandparents had owned the vintage set for years, and, despite its age, it was in excellent shape. She sank onto the chair.

Her grandparents had always been frugal and sensible, saving up for when they'd leave the farm to their children or grandchildren and then travel the world. But none of their children or grandchildren had ever taken an interest in owning the farm. And then her grandmother had died suddenly of a stroke a few years ago, leaving her grandfather devastated.

Since Quinn had come to stay with him a few months ago, he'd been the happiest she'd seen him since the death of her grandmother. Maybe it was because her smile reminded him of his beloved wife's. Or maybe it was because it had given him a new purpose—fussing over her.

Her grandfather brought their plates to the table and they settled into their usual morning rhythm. Only there was nothing usual about this morning. Today she would return to King's Finest, where she and Max would start working together on this project.

"You must've had a good time at the country club yesterday." Quinn put a forkful of the buttery pancakes in her mouth and chewed.

"We did." He nodded. "And I would've told you all about it, but you were knocked out when I got back. I put all of your paperwork on your desk and draped one of your grandmother's quilts over you." He sipped some of his coffee. "You haven't crashed like that since the day you first arrived here from Atlanta. When you were so stressed-out it was like you were all tied in knots."

There was an odd stretch of silence between them as he nibbled on his bacon and she ate her pancakes.

"You seemed tense in the meeting yesterday." He peered at her over his coffee cup. "Particularly with Max." He set his cup down and folded his arms on the table, his dark eyes assessing hers. "Everything okay between you two?"

"Of course." Quinn drank long and deep from her coffee mug before lowering it. She forced a smile much bigger and brighter than the occasion called for. "Why wouldn't it be? I haven't seen him since I was eighteen."

One of her grandfather's wiry eyebrows seemed to levitate. He frowned. "You remember *exactly* how long it's been since you've seen the boy?"

Quinn froze, her smile still in place.

"It was the summer before I went to college." She stuffed more pancakes in her mouth and chewed.

"But there's no bad blood between you two, right? I mean, you got on well enough the summer he interned for me, but if there's something I need to know—"

"There isn't." Quinn placed a hand on her grandfather's forearm. Her voice was firm as she met his gaze. "Everything is fine."

"You're sure? Because I sensed some tension on his side of the table, too. When you walked in that door, it was like the boy had seen a ghost."

It'd felt that way for her, too, though she'd had the advantage of expecting that ghost and bracing for it.

"Well, like I said, we haven't seen each other in… what…?" She made a show of counting in her head. "Thirteen years. That's bound to surprise someone, right?" She laughed nervously. "As for the tension… Look at it from Max's perspective. He's the VP of marketing and I come waltzing in the door with my fancy plan. To him, it must feel like a challenge to his authority. Like I'm saying I can do his job better than he can. But it's not about that. It's about this single joint project and how we can make it amazing by thinking more broadly about opportunities for collaboration."

Her grandfather nodded and sighed—a sure sign he wasn't convinced of her explanation for the tension he'd noticed.

"Well, you don't want to be late on your first day." He stood, collecting his dishes. "Leave everything when you're done. I'll clear the table."

Quinn ate the last of her bacon and finished her coffee. "Thanks, Gramps." She got up, pushed her chair under the table and kissed his cheek again. "I'll keep you posted on how things go today. But don't wait up for me. By the time I drive back from Magnolia Lake, it'll probably be pretty late."

He stopped running the water in the sink and frowned. "You know I believe in doing things face-to-face rather than on the phone or those video calls. But I hate that you'll be on the road so much."

"I know, but it won't be forever. Just until we get everything sorted out and in motion."

"Still, it's an hour each way. Maybe we should rent a place for you in Magnolia Lake for a few months."

"Things are already tight around here." Quinn hated bringing it up. Her grandfather felt bad enough about being so distraught over the death of his wife that he hadn't noticed the accountant he'd hired to manage the books—something her grandmother had handled—was robbing him blind.

It had been Quinn's distinct pleasure to throw the guy out on his ass and report him to the local sheriff.

"I know." He nodded solemnly. "But I'd never forgive myself if something happened to you. So keep an eye out for a room or apartment you can rent short term. I'll ask around at the senior center—"

"Not necessary." Quinn shook her head vehemently. She'd end up staying in some creepy room filled with dolls or cats or hooked up on a blind date with someone's worthless grandson.

No thanks.

"I'll handle it. You just worry about sticking it to them

in the next Scrabble tournament." Quinn grinned at her grandfather.

Her grandfather raised his fists and shuffled his feet as he bobbed and weaved, doing his best Muhammad Ali imitation. "This time, I'm gonna take every last one of those suckers out."

Quinn laughed. Her grandfather was still smarting over his second-place finish in the last tournament. "I know you will, Grandad."

She got into the Honda her younger brother had gifted her when the lease for her expensive import had ended. Here in rural Tennessee, she couldn't get anywhere without a reliable car, and she'd never learned to drive her grandfather's truck—a stick shift.

It was a long drive, and she used the time to review the plan in her head while listening to something soothing and upbeat.

Prepare the plan. Don't worry about the man.

That would be her motto as long as she worked with Max. Still, she couldn't help thinking about how handsome he looked. Or how incredible he smelled. The heat she'd felt standing so close to him when the two of them were alone. His pained expression when she wouldn't accept his apology.

She shut her eyes and sighed. It didn't matter if she was still attracted to him. It didn't matter that her memories of that summer had come roaring back to her in her sleep, as vivid as the day they'd occurred. Her summer fling with Max was a part of her distant past. And that was exactly where it would stay.

Four

Max glided into the office well ahead of his usual start time, but not early enough to beat his assistant.

"Mmm…doughnuts." Molly's eyes danced with excitement when she caught a glimpse of the small box in his hand. "Did you get—"

"A bear claw for you?" He grinned, holding up a separate bag in the same hand as his cup of coffee. "Of course."

She thanked him, accepting the bag. Molly tilted her head as she scanned him for a moment.

"What is it?" He looked down at his shirt. Had he spilled coffee on it?

"You look…nice," she said. Only Molly Halloran could pay someone a compliment and still make it sound like an accusation.

"That's a good thing, right?" He unlocked his office door. "Besides, I'd like to think I look nice every day."

"You do." She trailed him into the office. "But today it feels like you *tried* to look good, and you went a little heavy on the cologne. So I'm guessing this is for the benefit of Ms. Bazemore." Molly stated the facts as if they were the elements of a math equation. Two plus two equals four. She studied his expression, then nodded. "You're definitely into her."

Max wouldn't debate Molly's conclusion, and neither was there reason for him to give it credence. "Remember what we talked about, Mol. Use your deductive powers for good. Not to analyze my romantic interests."

"Right," Molly took a bite of her bear claw as she contemplated his words. "The doughnuts were a nice gesture, since you obviously aren't happy about having to work with her on this project." She put the rest of the bear claw back in the bag and closed it. "I'm going to get one of those cake stands of your mother's from the break room. It'll make a nice display."

"Sounds great. Thanks." He settled behind his desk and took a deep breath, glad for a few minutes alone with his thoughts.

It'd been nearly twenty-four hours since he'd seen Quinn Bazemore again, and his head was still swimming. The memories of their summer fling had kept him up all night, tossing and turning.

He hadn't thought about Quinn in so long. And now he couldn't think about anything else. There had been something so authentically joyful about her. He couldn't ever recall laughing and grinning more than he had during those few months.

Max remembered the first time he'd laid eyes on her that summer. He hadn't seen Quinn since she'd been ten and he'd been thirteen. He'd been stunned that the annoying little chatterbox in pigtails had grown up to be the sexy, long-legged temptress in front of him. And yet, he'd feigned a complete lack of interest and maintained his distance.

Their grandfathers were close friends. Getting involved with her could only mean trouble.

But she'd been flirtatious, persistent, funny and just so damn… Quinn. She'd cut through his resolve to ignore her like a hot knife slicing through whipped butter.

How could he *not* have fallen for her?

Quinn had been gorgeous with her dark brown skin and her thick, black hair pulled back in a single braid. She was bright and amusing. Thoughtful and opinionated. Hopeful yet pragmatic. She'd stimulated his curiosity about the world beyond his privileged purview more than anyone or anything else had. He'd loved seeing the world through her eyes and debating all manner of issues with her.

And there was something mesmerizing about her brown eyes. He still remembered the first time she'd gazed at him like he was everything she'd ever wanted. It was one of those nights she'd snuck up to his loft with leftovers in tow and they'd played video games while debating which male tennis player would win the US Open that year.

She'd been right, as she so often was.

Max sighed softly. He'd felt incredibly lucky to be the object of Quinn's admiring gaze. He'd also felt unworthy of it. But when she'd leaned in and pressed her mouth to his, he'd been an absolute goner. One kiss was all it had taken to get him completely addicted to the sweet taste of her mouth. To the lush feel of her soft curves pressed against him.

The look Quinn had given him when he'd called her *Peaches* at yesterday's meeting was the complete opposite of how she'd regarded him when he used the affectionate moniker back then. Max knifed his fingers through his headful of short curls and groaned quietly. He would never forget the fleeting look of abject disgust in the same brown eyes that had once shone with deep affection.

A knock at the door startled Max.

"Quinn." He stood suddenly, tipping over his cup of coffee. The dark brown liquid spread, soaking the papers on his desk, including the presentation he'd been reviewing.

Not a good look, man.

"Sorry, I didn't mean to startle you." Quinn dropped her bags near the door and quickly scanned the room. She spotted a stack of napkins on the small table in the corner of his office. Quinn grabbed a handful and blotted the mess while he stood there, frozen, staring at her. "I realize I'm a few minutes early, but your assistant was away from her desk, so I just knocked. I didn't mean to—"

"You're fine," he said. He swallowed hard, his cheeks heating as his rogue eyes quickly scanned her deliciously curvy form, highlighted by the fitted skirt and blouse she wore. "I mean…*it's* fine." He finally sprang into action, grabbing a handful of napkins and dabbing at the wet papers. "I shouldn't have been sitting here daydreaming."

"Garbage can?" Quinn asked.

He grabbed the trashcan from beneath his desk and held it up so she could drop the wet napkins into it. "I've got this."

"I don't mind." Her gaze met his momentarily. "After all, I feel partly responsible."

"You shouldn't," he said. *"Really."*

Molly rushed into the room with the sparkling-clean glass-domed cake stand.

"Sorry it took me so long, but I had to wash this. It's been sitting on top of the refrigerator for a few months and—" She stopped short when she noticed Max wasn't alone. "Oh, you must be Ms. Bazemore."

"It's Quinn." She moved toward Molly with her hand extended and a warm smile on her face.

She's even more beautiful than she was that summer. How is that even fucking possible?

"It's a pleasure to meet you…"

"Molly. Molly Halloran." His assistant shook Quinn's hand. "It's a pleasure to meet you, too."

"I'm afraid that I'm to blame for this mess. I startled Max when I came in just now," Quinn said. "Would you have something I can clean it up with? Disinfectant wipes, maybe?"

"No worries. I'll take care of it, Ms.…Quinn." Molly shifted her gaze to Max and gave him a *what happened?* look. "Can I get you some coffee or maybe a doughnut?"

Molly set the cake stand on the small table in the corner and then used the wax paper to carefully arrange each doughnut on the glass stand.

"Is that raspberry jelly–filled?" Quinn pointed to one of the doughnuts.

"It is." Max remembered how much she'd loved them.

Quinn momentarily glanced up from beneath her thick lashes before returning her attention to the assortment. She picked up the raspberry jelly–filled doughnut and took a bite.

"It's delicious. Thank you," she muttered through a mouthful. "That was thoughtful of you."

He exhaled quietly and shoved a hand in his pocket. It was his peace offering since she wouldn't allow him to apologize for how he'd ended things between them.

Molly quickly cleaned up the mess, promised to reprint the ruined documents and left the room.

"Have a seat, please." Max pulled out the closest chair for Quinn, then took his own across from her.

She put down her partially eaten doughnut and wiped the powdered sugar from her hands and mouth with a napkin. She reached into her bag and pulled out two binders: one thick, one thin.

"I thought we could start by going through the plan I laid out yesterday. You can tell me what works for you and if there's anything you object to. Then we can establish an agenda for the next six months."

Six months. He gritted his teeth.

Max had managed to get through more than a decade without running into Quinn even once, despite the friendship that their grandfathers shared. And now he was being forced to work with her for half a year.

Peachy.

"Excellent idea," he said. "Because I'd like to make a few amendments."

He didn't intend to insult her; this was business, not personal. His first obligation was to his family and King's Finest. If Quinn couldn't handle that, he needed to know now.

"Amendments?" Quinn frowned. "Like what?"

Molly brought Max a fresh cup of coffee and the newly printed copies. She was gone as quickly as she'd entered the room.

"You were saying?" Quinn's posture was stiff.

"You've suggested that we have representation at numerous domestic and international distributor conventions."

"Yes?"

"It's a great idea, in theory," he said. "In reality, the plan feels too ambitious. It represents quite an investment of resources for a six-month trial period. And it would spread me and Zora too thin. We already have a lot on our plates."

"Fair point on the budgetary considerations." She opened her planner and made a few notes. "I know you and Zora are busy. That's why I'm here. I didn't expect either of you to attend the listed events."

"Then who would represent...wait... *You'd* be the lone representative of King's Finest at all of these events?" He pressed his back against the chair. "This distillery is my family's legacy. We don't just sell spirits, Quinn. We sell the storied history of this place...of this family. And, no offense, but yesterday was the first day you've ever set foot in this building. I'm not comfortable sending someone who isn't an Abbott out to represent our family and my grandfather's legacy."

"Grandpa Joe didn't seem to have a problem with it." She folded her arms over her ample chest and his heart beat faster in response.

He dragged his eyes back up to meet hers. "I doubt he realized that you intended to fly all over the world as the sole representative of our family." He folded his arms, too.

"I discussed this very idea with him." Quinn pursed

her lips as she put her elbows on the little table—narrowly avoiding squishing her doughnut. "He didn't express any doubts. After all, I'm an experienced public relations professional, and I've represented billion-dollar organizations."

"I don't doubt your abilities, Quinn. But this isn't an impersonal corporation. Here, everything we do, we take it extremely personally." He tapped his index finger on the table. "Because the King's Finest name is on every single bottle we sell. We're all keenly aware that with each transaction, the crack of every single seal, our family's name and reputation is on the line."

"I can appreciate why this is such a sensitive subject for you." Quinn seemed to make a pained effort to keep her voice even and her expression calm. "However, you seem to forget that my family's name will be on those brandy bottles, too. I have just as much invested in the success of this project as you do. Perhaps more. Because if this venture doesn't deliver results, King's Finest will scrap it and move on. My grandfather might never get another high-visibility opportunity like this again."

"Your job is to protect your grandfather's interest. I respect that. But I need someone on hand whose first interest is this distillery."

Her frown deepened. "You don't believe I'm capable of being equally invested in both our interests?"

"I wouldn't know, Quinn." He shrugged. "We knew each other for one summer thirteen years ago."

"And whose fault is that?" she snapped, then shook her head and inhaled deeply. "No, we're not doing this. We agreed not to revisit the past."

"We didn't *agree*, Quinn. You insisted on it." He pointed out, leaning forward with his arms on the table. "But we need to talk about what happened back then."

"Why? It has no bearing on this project."

"Doesn't it?" He searched her face. "We're less than an

hour in and it's already become an issue. Yet, you won't allow me to apologize for my behavior back then."

"Because it isn't—"

"I remember every single word you said yesterday, Quinn, believe me." He held up one hand. "I strongly disagree."

"Is discussing our past a prerequisite for the deal?" she asked.

"Of course not."

"Then I respectfully decline." She looked away, her voice faint. "Sorry I snapped at you—it was a gut reaction, and I apologize." Quinn shifted her gaze back to his. "It's out of my system now. *Really.*"

Was he supposed to believe that all of the pent-up anger she'd apparently been harboring had evaporated in an instant? Did she honestly believe that herself?

"That wasn't fair of me." Quinn stood, leaning against the wall behind her. "But you're not being fair, either."

He cocked a brow. "How so?"

"You're arbitrarily rejecting the key component of my plan. And before you claim that you aren't—" she raised a hand to halt his objections "—we both know that you were the only one in that room yesterday who didn't want me working on this project."

She huffed, taking her seat again. "I realize it must be… disappointing to have an outsider work on your pet project. But Max, I'm *really* good at what I do. I'm not asking you to take my word for it. I'm just asking for a fair shot to prove I can deliver everything I promised."

"I know you probably think I'm being an ass just for the hell of it." Something in his chest tightened. "I'm not, Quinn. My fiduciary responsibilities to King's Finest come before any personal relationship—"

"You think I'm asking you to do me a favor because

we spent one summer together over a decade ago?" She laughed bitterly.

"Aren't you?" He didn't see what was so funny.

"You expect favors of friends," she said. "We aren't… that. And if you'd consider the plan objectively, you'd see the benefits for King's Finest." She tipped her chin defiantly, her eyes meeting his. "I'm not asking for a personal favor here. I'm asking you to do what's in the best interest of King's Finest, *despite* whatever personal feelings you might have about me."

He hated that she believed he harbored ill feelings toward her. Nothing could be further from the truth. True, he hadn't been eager to work with her. But that was because he hadn't wanted a daily reminder of his blunders where Quinn was concerned, not because he had ill will toward her.

He'd be happy to tell her that if she wasn't so insistent on not discussing their past.

Besides, he would've objected to allowing *anyone* outside of their family represent the company's interests. Especially someone he hadn't worked with before.

And if there was any resistance to Quinn specifically, it wasn't because he resented her. It was because he wouldn't blame her for resenting him, and he couldn't allow his past blunder to jeopardize King's Finest. Giving Quinn the power to impact the distillery's reputation left him feeling more vulnerable than he was comfortable with.

Max picked up the document and reviewed all the trade shows that Quinn had suggested the company attend. He took his pen and circled five of the domestic listings. "I'm already attending these." He circled three international events. "Zora is attending these." Max put a question mark by two others. "I'll consider these, based on the results of the first three conferences." Finally, he struck a line through the remaining events. "These are off the table for now." He put his pen down and sat back in the chair. "How's that for compromise?"

"Sounds fair." She took the list and read it over. "But where does that leave me? Your father appointed me to take the lead on the project. How can I do that if I'm not attending any of these?"

Max groaned quietly, already regretting what he was about to suggest. "You can accompany me to the first event."

"So… I get to do what? Play Vanna White? Maybe hold up a bottle of brandy while wearing a sparkly dress?" Quinn folded her arms, her leg bouncing.

Was it crazy that he could see that in his head?

"No, of course not." He cleared his throat. "You'd be there to observe and learn."

"Max, I'm not your summer intern. I'm a public relations *expert*," Quinn reminded him. "I don't claim to know everything, but please don't treat me like some clueless novice."

He sighed. "I need to ensure that these trips will provide an acceptable return on investment and that you can handle representing the distillery."

"Then give me a fair shot at demonstrating that." She leaned forward. "You're making your decision based on the first three domestic conferences. So I should attend all three of them."

Quinn stared at him, as if daring him to reject her reasonable suggestion.

He nodded begrudgingly, extending one hand across the table. "Deal."

Max tried to ignore the electricity that tickled his palm when Quinn placed her much smaller hand in his and shook it. The first time he'd held her hand that summer flashed through his brain.

Quinn yanked her hand from his and stood abruptly. "Thank you for giving the plan an honest chance. And for the doughnut. I won't take up any more of your time this morning. I'll get started on some ideas for marketing collateral. I'll need samples of your past marketing campaigns to ensure the look and message are consistent."

"My team will make sure it is." He stood, too. "Molly will get you anything you need. The first event is in a few weeks. Do you think we can turn everything around by then?"

"Absolutely." Quinn didn't hesitate for a moment. He admired her confidence. She glanced at the small antique watch on her wrist. "I'm meeting with Zora later today, and having lunch with Savannah. They'll help bring me up to speed. And I learned quite a bit on the distillery tour we took while you decided our fate yesterday." She flashed a teasing smile.

"I'll need to review whatever you come up with, and we can bring more of the marketing team in on this to ensure everything is done right and on time," he said as she gathered her things.

"Of course. I'm your partner in this project, Max—not your enemy or rival," she assured him.

"My dad brought you in to head up a project I've been working on for nearly *three years*, Quinn. Maybe it doesn't feel like a competition to you, but it sure as hell feels that way to me," he said gruffly, then quickly changed the topic. "Molly will book your travel, so be sure to give her the necessary info."

"I will. Thank you." Quinn lifted her bag onto her shoulder and raked her fingers through her hair, tugging it over one shoulder.

Max froze for a moment, his eyes drawn to the elegant column of her neck. He'd once trailed kisses down the delicate skin there. Traced a path there with his tongue. He swallowed hard. His pulse quickened, and his throat was suddenly dry.

"I'll have something for you to review by Friday," Quinn said, snapping him out of his brief daze.

"Great. Let's meet first thing Friday morning." His parents' fortieth anniversary party was on Saturday. Savannah was in charge of the arrangements. Still, he expected to get roped into last-minute preparations. "Oh, and Molly will show you the temporary workspace that's been set up for you."

Quinn thanked him, then left to meet with Molly.

Max returned to his desk to work on the football sponsorship deal still in negotiation. But no matter how much he tried to erase all thoughts of Quinn, the vision of her in that fitted skirt and top just wouldn't leave his brain.

Quinn had obviously written off their past as if it had never happened. Why couldn't he do the same?

Five

Quinn gave Molly the information she needed to make her travel arrangements, then settled into her temporary workspace. She appreciated having her own dedicated space to work. Unfortunately, it provided a direct line of sight to Max's office.

She groaned quietly, then made her way toward the executive floor bathrooms. Standing in front of the mirror, she pressed her hands on the cool granite counter and sucked in a deep breath, her eyes drifting closed momentarily.

Quinn should be proud of herself. She'd shown no visible reaction when her hand had touched Max's—despite the bubbling brew of emotions that had come flooding back to her. She'd forgotten how much larger his hands were than hers. And she'd been drawn in by his enticing masculine scent.

After all this time, just being near Max still made her belly flutter and her temperature rise. Had he noticed the beading of her nipples or how her breath caught? The way her hand trembled in his?

How could something as innocent as a handshake evoke such vivid images and visceral sensations?

Quinn couldn't help thinking of the little touches and stolen kisses they had sneaked in whenever they could on the farm.

The secrecy had made the relationship exciting. It was

something for just the two of them. And yet, she'd been bursting to tell someone how giddy and wonderful she felt. Like she was floating in a bubble of contentment. She'd fallen for Max. Hard. And she hadn't been able to imagine going back to a life without him.

Quinn opened her eyes slowly and sifted her fingers through her hair. What she'd felt for Max had been a stupid teenage fantasy. She'd believed him when he professed to love her. When he said he couldn't imagine his life without her, either.

Despite how things had turned out, she couldn't regret being with Max. She regretted her naivete in assigning that chapter in their lives more meaning than it held for him.

Quinn had been the one to pursue Max. She'd barreled right through Max's initial warning that he wasn't looking for a relationship, determined to change his mind. By the end of the summer, it'd seemed as if she'd succeeded.

Until she'd received the call that made it clear she hadn't. She'd stood there stunned long after Max had ended the call. Gutted by a deep, soul-racking pain that had ripped her to shreds.

Eventually, she'd moved on, putting that summer behind her. So why couldn't she look into those dark, brooding eyes without a shiver running down her spine? And why did the timbre of his deep voice still do things to her?

Why didn't matter. She just needed to hold it together for the few months it would take to get this project off the ground. Then they would go their separate ways, and she could put Max Abbott right back where he belonged. In her rearview mirror.

Max sent his last email at the end of what felt like an unbearably long week.

Thankfully, his second meeting with Quinn earlier that morning had gone well. He'd kept their contact during the week minimal and focused on his other projects, allowing Zora and Savannah to bring her up to speed.

The football sponsorship deal was grinding forward, even if it was happening at a snail's pace. And his week had been filled with a series of conference calls. At least he'd gotten a chance to spend some time with his two-year-old nephew, Davis, whom he adored.

Spending time with the precocious little guy was the highlight of any day.

He and Davis had been eating lunch and watching *Bubble Guppies* in the conference room when Savannah had joined them with Quinn in tow.

Quinn had been just as taken with his nephew as he was. Which only made her even more endearing. It'd barely been a week and it seemed that his entire family was enamored with Quinn Bazemore.

Despite being busy with work, he was still preoccupied with thoughts of Quinn.

After all this time, he was as affected by her now as he'd been at twenty-one. When he'd fallen head over heels for her.

Max quietly groaned, thinking of those lush lips and the enticing curve of her hips.

He couldn't pinpoint exactly what it was about Quinn that drove him to distraction. But he was still captivated by her. His heart raced and his pulse quickened when he was around Quinn. And his dreams had been fueled by vivid memories of the intimate moments they'd shared.

"This is more serious than I suspected." Zora startled him when she slid into the chair on the other side of his desk.

"Didn't hear you come in." Max cleared his throat.

"That's because you were in a daze. I called your name twice," she informed him.

"Oh. Well, I was reviewing the day in my head," he stammered.

Zora leaned forward with her elbows on the edge of his desk. "How about we *not* do this thing where you pretend you weren't sitting here thinking about Quinn and let's skip to the part where you tell me what's really going on with you two?"

Max rubbed his jaw and sat back in his chair, narrowing his gaze at the nosiest of his siblings. He'd managed to avoid this conversation all week. Until now. "There's nothing to tell."

"Then why did you freak out when Quinn walked into that conference room?"

"You're being melodramatic. I didn't 'freak out.' I was simply surprised to see—"

"Your ex?" Zora grinned.

"Quinn," he continued, ignoring her accusation. He was prepared to walk the superthin tightrope between lying and just not telling his nosy-ass sister something that clearly wasn't her business. "Because I hadn't seen her in years, and last I heard, she was living in Atlanta."

"So you've been keeping tabs on her since that summer you interned at Bazemore Farms." Zora seemed pleased with herself for extrapolating that bit of information.

"Gramps mentioned it in passing." He shifted his gaze back to his computer and started to shut it down.

"You were floored when you saw Quinn. And you were surprisingly hard on her plan."

"Can you blame me? This project is a big deal. It's Grandpa Joe's way of honoring the last wishes of Savannah's grandfather. Plus, I get the feeling there's a lot riding on this deal for Mr. Bazemore. Maybe you don't feel the pressure of all of those expectations, but I do. So, of course, I'm reluctant to turn the reins for this project over to a virtual stranger."

He shut his laptop and slid it into his bag.

"Quinn isn't a stranger. She's a family friend and an experienced public relations professional. And the way you called her *Peaches*, it felt like you'd had a more intimate relationship." Zora's voice was gentler. "There's no crime in that. But if you still have a thing for her—"

"I don't," he insisted.

Being one of five kids in an outspoken family, it was par for the course that they gave each other a hard time. But Zora's words had definitely struck a nerve, and they both knew it.

Zora stared at him, neither of them speaking.

Finally, Max spoke. "Look, I know you're just looking out for this deal—"

"And you. Because whether you want to talk about it or not, it's obvious you feel *something* for Quinn. Don't let those feelings cloud your judgment." Zora stood. "Let Quinn work her magic."

Damn his nosy little sister and her insightfulness.

"I won't jeopardize this product launch, Brat. Promise." He'd invoked her childhood nickname, which she liked about as much as Quinn liked Peaches.

"You'd better not." She pointed a finger at him, but then her expression softened. "And be careful, Max. You're in deeper than you realize. You both are."

"Everything is just fine with me and Quinn, I assure you." He stood, lifting his bag onto his shoulder. He'd had enough of his little sister's lecture.

"Great." Zora walked him to the door. "Because I invited Quinn to Mom and Dad's anniversary party."

Max turned to his sister, panic flaring in his chest as he locked the door behind them. "Why?"

"I thought it would make Quinn feel welcome." Zora shrugged. "But she seems reluctant to attend. I think she feels like she'd be crashing our family party. Or maybe she's worried she won't know anyone besides us and her grandfather."

"Then maybe it's better if she doesn't come." Max shrugged as they walked toward Zora's office.

"Or maybe you could invite her," Zora prodded. "I put you down for a plus-one, but you never did RSVP with one. So there's an extra space beside you that—"

"If I recall, you and Cole have unused plus-ones, too. No one is bothering either of you about it."

"Dallas is coming as my plus-one."

Dallas Hamilton—Zora's best friend since kindergarten—was a self-made millionaire. He'd started his craft furniture business by fiddling with scrap pieces of wood in his family's run-down barn. Despite his mother's best efforts, Dallas and Zora's relationship was still platonic.

"And I know Cole hasn't RSVP'd." It was one of the many things about his youngest brother that irritated him. "That would be far too considerate."

Zora stopped him just outside of her office. "When are you going to stop being so hard on Cole? He chose not to join the family business. So what? You act like he's committed a crime against humanity."

"Grandad created a legacy for *all* of us." Max waved his hand around the impressive office space that had been expanded and remodeled over the years. "But Cole just blew it off. He's always felt the need to buck the system."

"Yes, Cole is doing his own thing, and he's damn good at it. It's obviously the thing he was meant to do."

"That isn't the point."

"Isn't it? Because what Grandad wants for us more than anything is that we're happy and successful in life. Cole has found that. He's the premier home builder in the area. Why can't you just be happy for him?" Zora poked a sharp finger into his bicep that would likely leave one hell of a bruise.

Maybe he deserved it.

"Ready to shut it down? If so, I'll walk you to your car."

The shift in topic was his clear signal that their discussion about Cole was over.

Max leaned against the door frame while his sister gathered her things. He toyed with her suggestion to invite Quinn to his parents' anniversary party.

A part of him wanted to spend time with Quinn socially. But the part of his brain that was fully functioning when it came to Quinn Bazemore recognized that it was a horrible idea.

"You should reconsider inviting Quinn to the party," Zora said as they left the building and headed into the executive parking lot. "We're working on a really short timeline on this project. You two need to be in sync, and you need to learn to trust each other. This party is the perfect opportunity for you to get reacquainted in a relaxed setting."

"No, Zora," he said firmly as they arrived at his sister's car. "End of discussion." He folded his arms and stared down his scheming little sister, who was clearly amused by his resistance to her not-so-subtle matchmaking.

She squeezed the car door handle and the doors unlocked. "I reserve the right to resume this line of questioning at a later date."

There was that one year of law school Zora had taken, rearing its head again.

"And I reserve the right to ignore it." Max gave his sister a one-armed hug. "Good night, Brat. Drive safe."

Zora laughed as she slung her bags into the back seat and slid in behind the wheel. "You, too."

Max shook his head as he watched his sister drive off. Then he walked toward his SUV.

The only other person as invested in his love life as his sister was their mother. Iris Abbott had been trying to marry her kids off since long before Savannah had arrived in town.

But with Blake married to Savannah, Parker engaged to Kayleigh, and their second grandchild on the way, his mother had eased off on pressuring the rest of them.

Zora was obviously still on mission—as long as she wasn't the person being matched.

Six

Quinn stepped out of her car and handed her keys to the valet. She smoothed down the front of the floor-length, pale blue, one-shoulder Marchesa gown that she'd blown a mint on and had never gotten to wear.

She lifted the hem of the dress so it wouldn't drag on the ground. Quinn felt slightly ridiculous walking into a barn in a floor-length gown with a small train. But Zora had stipulated that the event was black-tie, and this was the only dress she'd brought to Knoxville that seemed dressy enough for it.

"You look beautiful, sweetheart." Her grandfather extended his arm. "If your grandmother could see how much you look like her right now." He chuckled softly. "She'd be pleased as punch."

"Thanks, Gramps." She sucked in a quiet breath and surveyed the large building with its weathered exterior. Bright, festive strings of fairy lights adorned the top of the structure, providing a warm contrast to the cool gray exterior. Strings of hanging white bulbs led up the pathway to the open barn door.

The decor inside was simply breathtaking. Glamorous, but with a nod to the rustic surroundings. Swaths of cream-colored fabric hung from the ceiling, as did several beautiful chandeliers. The tables were draped in rich, sumptuous fabrics. Yet the centerpieces and table decorations evoked the mountains and the nature that surrounded them.

Mason jars of various sizes were adorned with burlap and lace and overflowing with small bouquets of flowers. The table runners were accented with sprawling greenery that ran the length of each table. There were glass bottles in a kaleidoscope of colors and lanterns filled with candles all throughout the space. And the chair backs were topped by chiffon hoods in a dusty rose with ruffled embellishments.

"This place is incredible, Gramps. Did Savannah do all of this?" It was a visual feast.

"She sure did. Before Savannah came along, this was just a run-down barn—a little too rustic." Her grandfather chuckled. "Since the renovation and decor upgrade, they've easily tripled their event income." He nodded in Savannah's direction. "She's a savvy businesswoman, and so are you. You'll show 'em."

"Thanks, Gramps." She squeezed his arm. He always seemed to know when she needed a shot of confidence.

A woman whom Quinn recognized from Savannah's staff took their names and gave them their table assignments.

After they greeted a few of her grandfather's friends, they parted ways. Quinn pressed a fist to the knot in her stomach. Suddenly she wished she'd taken Zora up on her offer to rearrange the seating chart so she could sit with her grandfather.

But the truth was she wouldn't be here if it hadn't been for the series of frantic text messages she'd received last night.

I need a plus-one for my parents' anniversary party.

To which she'd responded, I'm sure you'll have no problem finding someone.

True. LOL. But this is a family event, so I'd rather hang out with someone I have zero interest in.

Your "bedside" manner sucks. No wonder you can't find a date.

Also true. You should take pity on me.

This was followed by the Puss in Boots puppy dog eyes GIF.

Not fair! You know I can't resist a good Shrek GIF!

Besides, there'll be free food and booze plus party favors. And my charming company, of course. Come. PLEASE.

I'm thinking you got in line twice when egos were handed out. But the free food and booze sounds tempting. What kind of party favors are we talking?

Guess you'll have to come to find out.

She hadn't responded, but on the third, increasingly desperate request, she'd given in. The texts had made her laugh, plus she was half-asleep by then, so she'd let her guard down and accepted the invitation. But as she scanned the open space, she didn't see Mr. It's-Definitely-Not-A-Date anywhere.

"Quinn, you look gorgeous." Savannah said as she approached, wearing a long, flowing, wrap gown in a sumptuous red fabric. A sash was tied just above her belly. Her hair was braided in an elaborate updo that completed the goddess look. "I didn't realize you'd changed your mind about coming tonight."

"It was a *really* last-minute decision." Quinn fought back

the urge to touch her hair and make sure her hasty updo was still in place. "I hope it's okay that I'm here."

"Of course, it is." Savannah nodded at someone over Quinn's shoulder and held up her index finger before turning back to her. "I have to take care of a few things before we get started, but I trust that you know where you're seated?"

"I do. Go. We'll catch up later." Quinn's hands trembled slightly as she surveyed the room filled with people. "I could use some of that free booze right about now," she muttered under her breath as she moved toward the bar at the back of the room.

"Quinn, you came after all." Zora gave her a genuine hug that eased some of the tension in her shoulders. "I didn't realize you'd changed your mind."

"Your brother is persuasive and persistent," Quinn said.

Zora's eyes lit up. "Well, good for him. I'm glad he was able to talk you into joining us." She scanned the crowd, then waved at someone on the other side of the room.

Quinn turned to the bartender and ordered a glass of white wine. When she turned around again, she met a familiar stare.

"Hey." Max's gaze drifted down the length of her body before returning to her face.

"Good evening, Max." Beneath his stare, Quinn felt self-conscious in the dress, which exposed her back, one shoulder and a bit of cleavage. "You look…handsome."

"Thanks." He smoothed down his beautiful purple necktie—the perfect complement to his white shirt and charcoal-gray tuxedo, accented by a purple pocket square. "And you look…incredible." Max gestured toward her, then cleared his throat. "But I'm surprised to see you here. Zora said you passed on the invite."

"What do you mean you're surprised to see her here?"

Zora gave Max the strangest look. "Quinn said you invited her."

"No, *I* invited her." As Cole joined them, he signaled for the bartender to give him a refill, then set his empty glass on the bar and leaned in to give Quinn a bear hug. Finally, he released her. "Thanks for rescuing me tonight. I know it was last-minute. I owe you one."

"Cole, *you* invited Quinn?" Zora's eyes went wide.

"Who else would've invited her?" Cole gave Zora a quick hug and acknowledged Max with a slight head nod.

Zora stared at Cole, then shifted her attention to Quinn. "I didn't realize that you two were—"

"Friends," Quinn volunteered quickly, so there would be no misunderstandings. "Cole and I became friends about four years ago. We ran into each other in Atlanta one weekend when Cole was in town visiting friends."

"Wow. I did *not* know that. Did you, Max?" Zora elbowed her brother, who was staring at the two of them as if Quinn had just declared that they'd been abducted by aliens.

"Uh…no," Max said, still staring at her. He turned to his brother. "Cole, how is it that you never mentioned that you and Mr. Bazemore's granddaughter were such good friends?"

So now I've been bumped down to "Mr. Bazemore's granddaughter." Fine.

The more distance between them the easier it would be for them to work together for the next few months.

Cole thanked the bartender for his drink and shoved money in the glass tip jar.

"Just never came up, I guess." He shrugged. "Funny story, though. Quinn and I hooked up at a speed dating event."

Oh, God. He had to tell the story, didn't he?

"You two dated?" Deep grooves formed across Max's forehead.

"No, we did *not*." Quinn paused, allowing that clear statement to sink in before continuing. She shot her friend a warning look and Cole smirked. Quinn turned back to Max and Zora. "*Hooked up* probably isn't the best word choice. Once we started talking, we each recognized who the other was and—"

"She shut me down immediately." Cole chuckled, as if the concept of a woman not being interested in him romantically was remarkable. "What was it that you said exactly?"

Quinn's cheeks stung under the heat of Max's and Zora's stares. She sighed quietly. "I believe I told you that you had a better chance of being hit by a meteorite than you did of getting me into bed."

Cole laughed as hard as he had the night she'd said it. She and Zora couldn't help laughing, too. But Max clearly wasn't amused by their friendship meet-cute.

"I knew right then that we were going to be friends. After the event, we went to this amazing burger joint, then we went out dancing. It was honestly the best time I'd ever had in Atlanta." Cole draped an arm over her shoulder. "Since then, we've kept in touch."

"I'm impressed, Quinn. You're probably my brother's first platonic female friend since middle school," Zora said. "Maybe there's hope for you after all, Cole." She slipped her arm through Max's. "Well, there are a few things we should take care of before the festivities start. Excuse us."

Zora, in her elegant white jumpsuit with a low-cut back, guided Max to the other side of the barn. Quinn couldn't miss the tension in his jaw and shoulders or the narrowing of his gaze as he glanced back at her.

Did Max honestly have the nerve to be angry about her friendship with Cole?

She certainly wasn't trying to make him jealous by being

here with his brother. Cole had blown up her phone with text messages, asking her to be his guest for the event. And they were *just* friends.

Max watched his mother practically float through the room after the big surprise reveal. The presentation had begun with all of the siblings sharing some of their parents' history as a couple. Then they'd shared some of their favorite parenting stories. But then his brother Parker's fiancée came out to deliver the big surprise. King's Finest had purchased Kayleigh Jemison's building as a gift to their mother, Iris.

The building, home to Kayleigh's jewelry design business and consignment shop, was once owned by his mother's family. They'd run a small, family-style restaurant there until it had gone out of business when Max's maternal grandfather had been swindled out of a bundle of cash and he lost the place.

Their mother had mused about opening a family restaurant in memory of her father's legacy. As a surprise to her on her wedding anniversary, the Abbotts had decided to fulfill their mother's dream by buying the building and turning it into a family restaurant associated with the distillery.

The unexpected bonus was that Kayleigh and Parker had resolved a decades-long feud and become engaged during the course of the negotiations.

It had been surreal to see how moved Parker—who rarely exhibited emotion—was over Kayleigh's speech. And how tenderly he'd hugged and kissed his fiancée when she was done.

Max would've bet the house that Parker would end up as that crotchety old uncle who never married and yelled at the neighborhood kids to get off his lawn. But now he and Kayleigh were engaged, and Kayleigh had moved into Parker's house with her golden retriever—whom Parker doted on.

It was a shocking turn of events no one in their family had seen coming.

Cole would clearly be the old player who chose not to marry. He'd still be dating half the women at the nursing home at ninety.

So maybe Max had been demoted to eternal, grouchy bachelor status. Standing alone in the corner, scowling, he was off to a great start.

From where he stood, he could easily see Quinn.

"You okay, big brother?" Zora handed him a glass of punch.

"Why wouldn't I be?" he asked after thanking her for the drink.

"Because you evidently feel something for Quinn and now... Well, she's here with Cole instead. Which wouldn't have happened had you asked her yourself, like I suggested."

Max gritted his teeth, wishing he'd taken his sister's advice. Still, he wouldn't admit as much to Zora. It would only further encourage her to stick her nose where it didn't belong.

"Quinn and I are coworkers, just like we were the summer I interned at the farm," he said. *True.* "And she has every right to be here with her grandfather, Cole, or anyone else on the guest list." Max shrugged. "It's none of my business, *or yours*, who Quinn is seeing."

"Then why are you standing here lightweight stalking her?" Zora shook a finger to head off his objection. "Not up for debate. I saw you watching them just now."

Shit. Had he become *that* guy? The one who didn't know when to let go and move on?

Zora carefully sipped the red punch so she wouldn't get it on her white jumpsuit. "Are you buying this story about Cole and Quinn just being friends?"

Max sucked in a quiet breath, then sighed. "I hope so.

Because if there's more to it and Cole screws up and upsets her, he could throw a wrench into this whole operation. There's a lot at stake here for all of us."

"I know," Zora agreed. "But if they are together, I'm happy for them. I just hate that it'll make you unhappy."

Max draped an arm over his sister's shoulder and sighed. He appreciated her support, even if it would be wiser not to say so. He glanced over to where Cole and Quinn had been sitting, but they were gone. Where they'd gone was none of his business.

"C'mon, Brat. We should check in with Mom and Dad."

"Mom and Dad are fine. They're showing off out on the dance floor. We should join them." She put down her punch and his, then tugged him onto the dance floor without waiting for his response.

Max followed his sister. This was a celebration of his mother and father's forty amazing years of marriage and the incredible family that had resulted from it, for which he was grateful.

Time to stop pouting and at least make a show of having a good time.

Today was about his parents, not him and his regrets.

Seven

Quinn had danced with Cole, her grandfather and his stable of widowed or divorced friends. The sparkly four-inch, open-toe sandals she was wearing were killing her feet and she was pretty sure there would be indentions from the straps across her instep. But it had been an amazing night.

She'd worried that she would feel like an intruder during this momentous occasion. Instead, the Abbotts made everyone in the room feel like they were family. It'd been a lovely evening filled with love. But what had stayed with her most was Kayleigh's speech.

I am so grateful to have my best friend and the love of my life back. I'm thankful that we were able to break down the wall we'd erected between us. That we didn't allow our misguided pride to keep us from the thing we needed most: each other.

When Kayleigh said the words, tears had filled Quinn's eyes and her focus had shifted involuntarily to Max, who met her gaze.

Had Kayleigh's words made him think of her, too?

"Lost in thought?" Cole, her dance partner, leaned in to be heard over the music.

"I was thinking about Kayleigh's speech."

"It was beautiful, huh? I'll admit, she *almost* got me." He chuckled, nodding toward Parker and his fiancée dancing together. "I'm thrilled for them."

"They seem happy and incredibly in love." Quinn stole one more glance at the couple. Kayleigh's curly red hair was twisted up in a bun with a few curls hanging free.

"Switch partners?" Zora asked. She was dancing beside them.

Quinn studied Max's face. He looked as mortified by the prospect as she felt. This obviously wasn't his idea.

"If Quinn doesn't mind." Cole looked to her.

She took a step backward and her heel caught in the hem of her dress. Before she could fall and make a scene, Max was there, his arms encircling her waist.

"I've got it from here." Max's gaze locked with hers.

Quinn nodded to let Cole know she was okay with the switch. She and Max danced together in silence for a few moments before she finally spoke.

"Thank you. My shoe got caught in the back of my dress."

"I noticed." Max's tone was flat and unreadable. "You didn't twist your ankle, did you?"

"No. Just battered my pride." Her face still stung with embarrassment over the near miss.

"Have I told you how amazing you look tonight?" he asked after a beat of silence between them.

"You have." Quinn couldn't help the slow smile that tightened her cheeks. "But it's just as nice hearing it the second time."

Max leaned down and whispered in her ear. "Good. Because it bears repeating. You look sensational."

Quinn's cheeks and chest warmed. She gave silent thanks for the melanin that masked the flush of her skin. Especially in a dimly lit room like this one. But she had no mechanism to disguise the erratic beating of her heart, which Max could no doubt feel through his fingertips pressed to her back.

"Thank you." One of her hands rested on his upper arm.

Even through the fabric of his tailored tux, she could feel the impressive bicep. "But why do I feel like I'm not going to like whatever you're about to say next?"

Max halted momentarily. Tilting his head, he studied her. He lowered their joined hands and resumed their movement. His posture stiffened.

"This thing with you and Cole…"

"You mean my *friendship* with Cole," she corrected him. Now her body tensed. "What of it?"

"Seems odd that neither of you have mentioned it before."

Tension trailed up her shoulders and into her jaw. "And when exactly would I have shared that with you, Max? Before this week, we haven't seen or talked to each other in years."

"I realize that, Quinn, and you may not want to hear it, but I regret that. I regret *how* things ended," he clarified.

"So you don't regret unceremoniously dumping me, just that you were a jerk about it." She met his gaze. "Got it."

"It's not that simple, Quinn." He frowned. After a few moments of uncomfortable silence, he said, "We met twice this week. You didn't mention your friendship with Cole either time."

"I didn't mention any of my other friends, my parents or my siblings, either," she noted calmly. "Because those weren't social meetings. They were business meetings, so we discussed business. Because despite this dance, that's the extent of our relationship."

She stopped, extracting herself from his grip. "Thank you for the dance, but it's been a long night and I have a long drive ahead of me. It's time I say good-night to everyone."

"Quinn, I didn't mean to upset you." He lightly gripped her wrist, pinning her in place. "Wouldn't you be suspicious if I'd showed up at your office in Atlanta and claimed to have a four-year-long friendship with your younger sister?" His pleading tone begged her to be reasonable. "Wouldn't you find that *odd*?"

"Why is it so hard for you to believe that my relationship with Cole is purely platonic? Do you sleep with *every* woman you meet?" She yanked her arm from his grip.

"No, but my brother does." He folded his arms over his broad chest. "Or didn't Cole mention that?"

"Maybe your brother isn't prepared to get involved in a long-term monogamous relationship. But at least he communicates openly and honestly with the women he's involved with. Call me old-fashioned, but I admire that in a man, whether he's a friend or a lover."

Max cringed when she used the word *lover.* It seemed that the very thought of her and Cole together evoked a physical reaction.

If she were a better person, perhaps she wouldn't have taken the slightest bit of delight in the discomfort the thought evidently caused him.

"You don't know my brother the way I do, Quinn. He doesn't do relationships. Whatever this is between you two…he's only going to hurt you."

"Maybe you don't know your brother as well as you think you do." She poked a finger in his chest and did her best not to react to the firm muscles she encountered. Instead, she focused on being indignant on her friend's behalf. "Cole's right. You underestimate him and you don't respect his choices. That's a shame. Because despite everything, he still looks up to his big brothers, including you."

"I'm sure Cole has made me the bad guy in all this, but—"

"Do you honestly think we spend our time together discussing you?" Quinn asked with a humorless laugh. "Spoiler alert—we don't. Get over yourself, Max."

Quinn made her way across the crowded dance floor

and returned to the table where her grandfather and most of the Abbott family were assembled.

She forced a smile and slid into the seat beside her grandfather. Leaning in closer so that only he could hear her, she asked, "Ready to head out? We have a long drive home."

"Actually, there's been a change of plans." He smiled. "The celebration continues tomorrow with brunch at Duke and Iris's place. You and I are invited. Then Joe and I are going fishing tomorrow afternoon with a few friends."

"You're driving all the way back here tomorrow morning?" Looking at her wrist, she checked the thin, delicate antique watch that had once belonged to her grandmother. "It's already so late."

"Which is why I'm staying in one of Joe's spare rooms at the cabin. Don't worry, he's got an extra room for you."

Spend the night with Gramps at his buddy's bachelor pad? Hard pass.

"That's generous of Grandpa Joe," Quinn said. "But I don't want to encroach on your buddy time. I'll just drive back to Knoxville tonight and come back and get you tomorrow afternoon, after you guys have gone fishing. I'll bring the cooler."

"You're not coming to brunch?" Cole slid into the empty seat on the other side of Quinn. He set a small mason jar of peach cobbler and a sculpted glass bowl filled with vanilla ice cream in front of her. "You should definitely come to brunch. The spread is going to be amazing."

Warm peach cobbler and homemade vanilla ice cream?

Cole knew her weakness and was prepared to play dirty. She stared at the cobbler but didn't touch either dish.

"Listen to Cole, sweetheart." Her grandfather got up from his chair and patted Cole on the shoulder before sauntering back onto the dance floor at the invitation of an insistent older woman Quinn didn't recognize.

"Your grandad is right." Cole nudged her with his shoulder. "You should come to brunch tomorrow."

"It sounds nice," Quinn admitted. He handed her a spoon, and she broke down and tried a little of the miniature cobbler with a spoonful of the ice cream. "That's really good."

Not *quite* as good as hers, but still delicious.

"I'm pretty sure there'll be more at brunch tomorrow," he teased in a singsong voice as he dug into a small mason jar of apple crisp.

"By the time I get back to Knoxville tonight, it'll be really late. Then I'll have turn around and come right back here."

"So stay here," he said, as if the solution should be evident.

"I'm not up for a sleepover with our grandfathers at Grandpa Joe's cabin," she muttered through another spoonful of food.

"Don't knock it till you've tried it. Give those two a bottle of top-shelf bourbon and they'll tell you anything you want to know. Actually, way more than you ever wanted to know or can mentally unsee." Cole chuckled.

"That's gross and it proves my point." She nearly choked on her cobbler, laughing. "I'll pass."

Savannah, Blake, Parker and Kayleigh, who'd all evidently tuned into her and Cole's conversation, burst into laughter, too.

"Sounds like Gramps and Mr. B," Blake said.

"So don't stay with the notorious GPs." Cole shrugged, using his and Quinn's shared nickname for their grandfathers. He took another bite of apple crisp. "Stay at my place instead."

There was a collective gasp at the table, which Cole was either oblivious to or chose to ignore.

Maybe she misunderstood him.

"Do you have a rental place in town?" Quinn knew that Cole owned property at the beach in Charleston, but he'd never mentioned having local property aside from his home.

"No. But I do have a guest room, and you're welcome to it." He shoved another spoonful of apple crisp into his mouth, blissfully ignorant that everyone at the table was staring.

"Or you could stay with me. I have a spare guest room, too," Zora offered.

Cole finally seemed to notice he had everyone's attention. He shrugged. "My place is closer."

"She's *not* staying at your place, Cole." The entire table turned toward the source of the gruff voice. Max stood behind them, his hands clenched at his sides.

"As long as she's safe—and she will be—why the hell do you care where Quinn sleeps tonight?" Cole glanced over his shoulder at Max. His expression was neutral, despite the tension evident in his tone. "Who died and made you either of our fathers?"

"No one thinks they're anyone's daddy." Zora glanced cautiously between her brothers. "I think maybe Max just feels Quinn might be more comfortable staying with someone—"

"She barely knows?" Cole raised an eyebrow.

Everyone at the table turned to look at her. Quinn's face was heated as she glanced around. Max was fit to be tied. Cole seemed to straddle the line between being mildly annoyed and gleefully irking his brother. Zora seemed desperate to play peacemaker. Savannah, Blake, Kayleigh and Parker were all riveted by the conversation, as if they were watching a messy reality TV drama.

Quinn stood suddenly, careful not to trip on her dress this time. "Thank you both for the invitation. I don't want to inconvenience either of you. It would probably be best if I just headed home."

"I have a suggestion," Kayleigh spoke up, drawing everyone's attention. "I do have a rental unit in town. Now that the building officially belongs to King's Finest, I won't be renting out the unit anymore. Construction doesn't begin for at least another month, right, Cole?" She looked at her future brother-in-law for confirmation. He nodded begrudgingly. "So why don't you stay there tonight, Quinn?"

"That's a great idea, babe." Parker squeezed her hand. "In fact, the place is just going to be sitting empty for the next month. So you're welcome to use the place rather than commuting back and forth to Knoxville every day."

"That's an excellent idea, Parker," Zora said. Blake and Savannah agreed.

"You're sure?" Quinn was still on the fence about spending the night in Magnolia Lake. However, using the place as a crash pad for the next month would be ideal. The drive back and forth each day was exhausting. "I'd have to pay you, of course."

"No, you don't," Blake insisted. "Like Kayleigh said, it would just be sitting empty."

"But not the entire building," Kayleigh clarified. "My shop is on the first floor, and we won't be moving it for a few weeks." Parker's fiancée pulled a pen out of her crystal-studded Alexander McQueen clutch with its signature skull and knuckle-duster clasp. She scribbled on a napkin, then folded it and passed it to Parker, who handed it to Quinn.

There was an address and two six-number codes.

"The building and the apartment have key code locks. That's all you'll need to get in. I can walk you through the place if you'd like," Kayleigh said.

"No, I'll be fine. Thank you, Kayleigh."

"Will you need clothes? I'm sure I have something you could borrow. We could swing by my place and take a look," Zora offered.

"I have a change of clothing in my workout bag in the trunk, but thank you, Zora," Quinn said absently.

I guess I'm really doing this.

With her overnight arrangements settled, the conversation returned to its normal ebb and flow. But as Max took his seat, there was still a hint of tension between him and Cole.

"You're not upset that I passed on staying with you, are you?" Quinn whispered, nudging Cole.

"No, of course not. I'm just glad you'll be at brunch tomorrow." He flashed that million-dollar smile, the one she could never resist reciprocating. "I have to do something for my dad, but I'll be ready to leave in an hour or so. If you don't mind waiting that long, I'd be happy to do a walk-through with you at Kayleigh's place."

"No need. I'm exhausted, so I'm leaving in a bit. Thanks anyway."

"Then text me once you're settled, so I know you're okay." Cole hugged her, then left the table.

Max peered at her for a moment, then got up and left the table, too.

Quinn sighed softly.

You don't owe him an explanation. Just let it go.

But the hurt look on Max's face tugged at her chest for reasons she couldn't explain. Or maybe she could. But the truth was simply too painful to bear.

Eight

"Cole!" Max hadn't meant to call his brother so loudly, but he was seething with anger as he waited patiently for Cole to finish talking to their parents.

Cole glanced at him and rolled his eyes before stalking over. He folded his arms, his legs planted wide.

"What is it now, Max? Is this our quarterly conversation where you accuse me of being a self-interested ingrate who isn't toeing the family line?"

"Can we talk?" Max refused to acknowledge his brother's flippant remark.

"Isn't that what we're doing?" Cole raised a brow.

"Privately," Max said. He turned and walked toward the back office, near the restrooms. Max used his keys to open the door and they went inside.

"Are you deliberately trying to sabotage this deal with Bazemore Farms?" Max sat on the front edge of the desk.

"Why on earth would you ask a dumbass question like that?" Cole's nostrils flared.

Max forced himself not to react to his brother's raised voice. "Then let me rephrase the question. What the hell is going on with you and Quinn?"

"First, I don't see how that's any of your business. Second, Quinn was pretty clear about it. She and I are friends. We have been for a few years."

"You never mentioned being friends with Dixon Bazemore's granddaughter. Not once." Now Max's voice was slightly elevated.

"I didn't mention it to you," Cole said. "But then our conversations pretty much consist of *this*. You calling me on the carpet like I'm still twelve. I'm not. I'm thirty-three fucking years old, Max. And last I heard, Duke and Iris Abbott are my parents. Not you." He jabbed a finger in his direction.

Max ground his back teeth, his muscles tensing. He and Cole were what his late grandmother referred to as Irish twins, born just under twelve months apart.

Yet, Cole and Zora had always been closer.

"Maybe try not acting like a horny teenager all the time," Max said. "Show a little self-control, as adults do. Like by not taking every single woman you meet to bed. Especially when she's the granddaughter of Grandpa Joe's closest living friend."

Projecting much?

Yep, he was a total hypocrite for that one.

If he got taken out by a lightning strike right this moment, he couldn't even complain. He legit had it coming.

"I am *not* sleeping with Quinn." Cole stabbed his finger angrily at the air in front of Max's face. "Because, as I already told you, she shot me down. I respected her decision then, as I do now. I haven't made a move on her since then."

"Really? Because you two seem *overly* familiar. You keep putting your hands on her. Hugging her. Whispering in her ear. Draping your arm over her shoulder."

"Is that what you've been doing all night? Spying on me and Quinn? Dude, you seriously need to get a life…or get laid. Maybe both." Cole smirked in a way that made Max want to grab him by the collar.

"I have a life. And right now, this joint brandy project with Bazemore Farms is at the center of it. So I need you to back off of Quinn before you blow up the entire deal and cause irreparable damage to Gramps's relationship with Dixon Bazemore," Max said.

"I realize you always think the worst of me," Cole said. A hint of anger and maybe hurt glinted in his brother's dark eyes. "But Quinn told you herself we're just friends. Are you calling her a liar, too?"

"It's not that I think the worst of you, Cole. It's that I expect better. Being an Abbott means something, you know."

"You don't think I know that?" Cole laughed bitterly. "None of you ever let me forget it. But you don't get to define what being an Abbott means for me," he said without a hint of apology. "Now, you want to tell me what this is really about? Because this is extra, even for you."

Cole's voice faded at the end of the sentence and then his eyes widened with realization. He rubbed his chin. "Oh."

"Oh...what?" Max asked casually, despite the subtle quickening of his pulse.

"I've seen this movie before. You're into Quinn. That's why you want me to back off." Cole paced the floor. He stopped, then turned to him abruptly. "No, it's more than that. That summer you worked at Bazemore Farms... The two of you were together, weren't you? *That's* why Quinn shut everything down between us the moment she realized I was your brother."

Max closed his eyes. His cheeks and forehead burned with heat.

Seriously, you had one job, asshole.

He'd promised to keep his relationship with Quinn under wraps. That he'd *never* kiss and tell. Even if she hadn't kept her side of the bargain, it'd been important to him that he kept his promise to her. But watching Cole with Quinn all night... His jealousy had circumvented his better judgment.

What conclusion did he expect Cole to come to after his full-court press about his brother's relationship with Quinn?

Cole was a lot of things. Stupid wasn't one of them.

"You've been spending too much time with Zora," Max said. "I'm just trying to protect our family's interest here. Something you seem to care very little about."

Flames seemed to shoot from Cole's dark eyes as he stepped forward, his hands clenched at his side.

"This isn't about me or this brandy deal. It's about you wanting Quinn. I'm guessing you screwed up with her back then."

Max wouldn't look at Cole, unwilling to confirm or deny his brother's accusation.

"First, Parker thinks I'm making a move on Kayleigh. Now you think I'm screwing Quinn. News flash—I'm *not* that guy. You'd think my own damn brothers would realize that."

Max raised his head and met Cole's intense stare. There was genuine pain in his brother's voice and expression.

Guilt churned in Max's gut. "You're right. Quinn and I were involved back when I worked on the farm. No one else knows."

Max's head spun with all of the complicated emotions he'd felt for Quinn that summer. Emotions he'd buried and thought were long dead until Quinn Bazemore sashayed into that conference room earlier that week and turned his world upside down. It had unearthed a complicated mixture of feelings: affection, admiration, desire, love, guilt and pain.

"But this isn't about how you felt about her back then, is it? You're still into her." There was pity in Cole's voice rather than the resentment that had been there moments earlier. When Max didn't respond, Cole added, "Let me help you out—that wasn't a question."

"I'm not discussing this with you," Max said.

"And I'm tired of you guys projecting your bullshit on me." Cole shoved a finger in his direction again. "If you want another shot with Quinn, man up and tell her. If you're not willing to do that, then leave her the fuck alone. Because you never deserved her anyway."

Max had no argument. Quinn did deserve better.

"Quinn is special, Max. I don't have many friends like her. So make up with her. Don't make up with her. Whatever. But I won't give up my friendship with Quinn just because you're pissed that you screwed things up with her a lifetime ago. So get your head outta your ass and either shoot your shot or get over it. *Period.*"

Cole left the office, slamming the door behind him.

Max closed his eyes and heaved a sigh. God, he hated it when Cole was right.

He sucked in a deep breath, his mind buzzing with all of the things he'd wanted to say to Quinn and all the reasons he shouldn't say them. Starting with the fact that she clearly didn't want to hear them.

Quinn wouldn't even let him apologize. So how could he possibly tell her the truth? That he'd never stopped caring for her. That he'd do anything to hit Rewind and do things differently.

She wasn't ready to hear his truth, and he had no right to impose it on her to assuage his own guilt. He'd screwed up, so he had to take the L.

The words of his high school football coach echoed in his head.

Don't force it, son. Read the field and take whatever the defense gives you.

That was exactly what he needed to do.

Stop behaving like a possessive asshole and accept the small olive branch Quinn has extended.

He needed to find Quinn now.

Nine

Quinn handed her ticket to the valet, and the man left to retrieve her car. Suddenly a familiar voice called her name.

She turned to find Max jogging toward her with an intense look on his face.

Her heart raced. "Is my grandfather okay?"

"Sorry, I didn't mean to alarm you. Mr. B is fine. I just…" He cleared his throat, then shoved his hands into his pants pockets. "You're not familiar with the area, and since half the town is here tonight, downtown will be pretty deserted."

"I don't expect I'll have any problem finding the place," Quinn said.

"Still, I would feel better if someone…" He cleared his throat again. "I would feel better if I saw you home and made sure everything was okay." He straightened out his cuff links.

"Are you concerned about my safety, Max? Or are you worried that I'll meet up with Cole afterward?" Quinn folded her arms, irritated that Max obviously didn't believe there was nothing going on between her and his brother.

"I'm concerned about you, of course." He lightly gripped her elbow and guided her to a spot a few feet away from the valet stand where the two remaining valets had turned their attention toward them. "About earlier, what I said about you and Cole. I'm sorry. I was way out of line. Forgive me?"

She studied the handsome features that had always intrigued her and the dark, piercing eyes that stared back at her. Eyes she'd gotten lost in many a night during that long, hot summer.

Quinn released a quiet sigh and nodded. "Okay."

"Okay, you forgive me for being an ass earlier? Or okay, I can see you to Kayleigh's place tonight?"

"Both." One side of her mouth curved in an involuntary smile. "But I'm leaving now. Don't you need to be here until the end of the party?"

"I'll come back after I see you home." He dug his valet ticket out of his inside jacket pocket and handed it to the valet. "Pull out to the edge of the property and wait. Then you can follow me into town."

"Okay," Quinn agreed.

When the valet returned with her car, she reached into her purse to tip the kid, but Max waved her off and tipped him generously. She thanked him, then drove to the edge of the property and waited.

A small part of her was eager to be alone with Max in that apartment. The same part of her that had relished being in his arms again on that dance floor.

Max was her distant past. That crazy, hot summer they shared was a fantasy they'd both awakened from once they'd returned to the reality of their daily lives.

He'd obviously put it out of his mind. Why couldn't she do the same?

Maybe because what they'd shared had evidently meant more to her than it had to him. Max was her first love, and she'd fallen hard for him.

She'd been so sure they'd shared a deep, unbreakable bond. But Max had forgotten her the moment he'd put her grandfather's farm in the rearview mirror.

She should take notes and do the same.

They could work together. Be friendly. Even share an

occasional dance. But she wasn't a starry-eyed eighteen-year-old anymore. She understood how the world worked. That people didn't always mean what they said...what they promised. Not even the people who'd promised to love you.

Quinn's attention was drawn to the headlights that flashed in her side view mirror. Max pulled beside her in his SUV and indicated she should follow him. She did, though she'd already plugged the address into her phone's GPS app.

They went back past the distillery, then followed the undulating road to a one-lane bridge that led them into downtown Magnolia Lake. Max pulled his black SUV into a parking lot next to an older block of buildings. She parked beside him as he rummaged for something in the back of his truck.

Their cars were the only two in the lot. Suddenly Quinn was grateful Max had insisted on seeing her here. The area did feel deserted. And aside from the dim lighting in the front window of Kayleigh's store, the building looked abandoned.

Quinn grabbed her gym bag from the trunk and slammed it shut, then gathered the bottom of her dress in her other hand, not wanting a repeat of her earlier clumsiness.

Max had what looked like a T-shirt draped over his shoulder. He reached for her bag.

"I've got it," she insisted.

"Your hands are already full." He indicated where she held up the hem of her dress. "And I don't mind. Really."

Quinn handed the bag off to him as they moved toward the side entrance of the building. From her bag she retrieved the napkin with the codes and punched in the six digits for the main door.

Max opened the heavy door and they stepped inside. The sound of her heels clicking against the wooden floor echoed in the narrow stairwell. When they reached the apartment door, Quinn entered the next six-digit code. The decor in the cozy little one-bedroom apartment was absolutely adorable. Nothing extravagant, but the kind of place she could easily imagine spending the next few weeks.

They walked through the space, and Max dropped Quinn's gym bag at the foot of the bed.

"That reminds me," he said. "If you need anything, Zora said give her a call. I assume you have her cell number."

"I do."

Quinn tossed her clutch on the bed and released the bobby pins in her hair that had been killing her all night. She shook her hair loose and raked her fingers through it, sighing with relief. When she looked up, Max was staring at her.

"Is there anything else?" Quinn asked.

"No." Max shook his head and took a step backward. "Actually…yes." He snatched the garment he was carrying off his shoulder. "I had a clean T-shirt in my gym bag. I thought you might need something to sleep in."

He held out a white T-shirt with the words King's Finest Distillery, Magnolia Lake, Tennessee printed on it in black lettering.

"Thank you." She accepted it, noticing how the soft, cotton had already taken on a subtle hint of Max's cologne.

They stood in silence, the air around them heavy with all of the words that neither of them would allow themselves to say.

For the briefest moment, she wished Max would lean down and kiss her. Satisfy her growing curiosity.

Had his kiss really been as amazing as she remembered? Or had she just been a misguided young woman with so little experience that any kiss would've seemed memorable?

Max's phone rang. Heaving a quiet sigh, he pulled the phone from his inside pocket and checked the caller ID before sliding it back into place. His expression was unreadable.

Was it a woman calling him this late in the evening?

After all, if it had been a member of his family, wouldn't he have answered the phone, as he had many times before in her presence?

So what if some woman was calling him at Netflix-and-chill hour? What business was it of hers?

"I have to go," Max said. "Lock up after me."

Quinn followed Max back through the apartment wondering about the identity of his mystery caller.

Was it someone she'd met at the party tonight? Someone who worked at the distillery? Or maybe someone who lived nearby? Maybe that was the real reason he left the party early.

"Good night, Quinn." His intense gaze shot straight through her, sending tingles down her spine and heating her skin. "Guess I'll see you tomorrow."

"At noon, right?" she asked, then added, "Wait, I don't know where we're meeting for brunch."

"At my parents' place. It's at the end of the same road where the barn is. I'll text the address to you." He pulled out his phone and tapped on the screen.

"You have my cell phone number?" She was surprised. They hadn't exchanged numbers.

"I maintain a list of contacts for my entire team," he said casually, without looking up. "While we're collaborating on this project, that includes you and Mr. B." He slid the phone back into his pocket. "The contact list was part of the packet you received during our first meeting."

"Of course." Quinn tucked her hair behind her ear, embarrassed that she'd read more into the fact that Max had saved her number in his phone. "The list is in my portfolio."

"Good. See you tomorrow."

Quinn watched as Max trotted down the stairs. She

locked up behind him and returned to the bedroom where they'd stood together moments ago.

She kicked off her shoes, stripped out of the gorgeous, pricey dress—a reminder of what almost was—and removed her makeup. She slipped on the white T-shirt that smelled faintly of Max. The soft, brushed cotton caressed her naked skin, abrading her already taut nipples and making her fully aware of the throbbing between her thighs.

Max hadn't kissed her, hadn't laid a hand on her there in the apartment. Yet, just being near him, her body ached for his touch.

Squeezing her thighs together, Quinn sucked in a deep breath and released it, trying to ignore the shiver that ran down her spine.

She slid beneath the covers, her body exhausted and ready for sleep. But her anxious mind won the battle. Quinn tossed and turned most of the night, inappropriate thoughts of Max filling her head.

Ten

Max stood by the bar in his parents' outdoor kitchen, quietly surveying the small crowd of friends and family. His mother was still over the moon about her anniversary gift and the prospect of establishing a new restaurant in the same space where her family's diner once stood.

"Mom hasn't been this giddy since Davis was born." Zora sipped her sweet tea.

"She was pretty happy when she learned that Savannah and Blake were pregnant again." Max nodded toward his sister-in-law, who stood on the other side of the space rubbing her protruding belly as she chatted happily with Quinn.

Quinn.

Aside from a cursory greeting when she'd first arrived, he'd tried his best to ignore her. But he couldn't seem to resist stealing glances at her.

She wore a basic, sleeveless minidress. But the cut of the dress gently hugged her full breasts, round bottom and curvy hips. The hem grazed her thighs and highlighted her toned muscles. And the deep turquoise color popped against her dark brown skin.

Her hair was twisted at the nape of her neck. Just a few strands hung loose near her temple, giving him an unobstructed view of her face. Quinn's broad smile was as bright as the midday sun. And something about the sound of her laughter filled his chest with a warmth that reminded him of those nights when she'd snuck to his loft over the barn to hang out with him.

"She's stunning, isn't she?" Zora commented quietly.

"Savannah?" He sipped his tea to cool the heat rising in his neck. "Yes, pregnancy definitely agrees with her."

"You know who I'm talking about." Zora could barely stifle a giggle. "The last time I saw that forlorn a look, it was when Cricket was staring at the pork chop in Davis's hand," she said, referring to Kayleigh's golden retriever.

Note to self: stop staring at Quinn like a lovesick fool.

Max finished his glass of tea and set it down on a nearby table with a thud.

"Actually, I was just keeping an eye on Savannah. She's probably uncomfortable out here in the heat. I'll take her a glass of tea."

He excused himself, retrieved two glasses of sweet tea from the beverage table, then made his way to Savannah and Quinn.

"I thought you ladies might like some refreshments," he said with a smile as he approached them.

"Yes!" Savannah proclaimed, fanning herself with one hand as she reached for the glass with the other. "Thanks, Max. You're a sweetheart." She took a long drink from the glass.

"How about you, Quinn?" Max held up the other glass.

"Sure. Thanks." She flashed an obligatory smile. That brought the total number of words she'd spoken to him so far today to four.

Savannah excused herself to go and check on Davis, who was playing with his cousin Benji's twins, Beau and Bailey. The kids got along well, but occasionally someone didn't want to share. Right now, that was Davis.

Max and Quinn stood in silence as she slowly sipped her tea and looked anywhere but at him.

"How was the apartment?" he asked. "Did you sleep well?"

"The apartment is perfect." She turned to face him. "Grandad is thrilled I won't be making that long drive back and forth every day. We're grateful to your family for providing it. That'll buy me time to find another place before Cole begins demolition."

Why was the mention of his brother's name like a bucket of ice water being poured over his head?

"I'm glad. And I'm sure we can help you find something else between now and then," he said.

"It was nice seeing Benji again." Quinn nodded toward his cousin and his fiancée, Sloane Sutton—the mother of their twins. "He has a beautiful family and he's done well for himself."

Benjamin was a tech genius who'd moved to Seattle, where he'd developed a healthcare tech app that he'd sold for more than two billion dollars a couple of years ago. And he and Sloane—Benji's older sister's best friend and his long-time crush—had hooked up at Blake and Savannah's wedding. Which had resulted in the twins and eventually their engagement.

Benji and Sloane's wedding was in a few weeks. After their honeymoon in Greece, their little family would spend a year in Japan while Benji oversaw a project for the company that had purchased his app. After that, they planned to settle down in Magnolia Lake where Cole was building a custom home for them.

"The marriage bug is hitting your family hard," Quinn teased. "Pretty soon, you and Cole will be the lone bachelors. Unless of course…"

"No, I'm not seeing anyone." He restrained a smile. "If that's what you're asking."

"I wasn't, at least not for the reason you're probably thinking," she said quickly.

He folded his arms, amused. "And just what do you think I'm thinking?"

She pressed a hand to her forehead and groaned. "God, this is awkward, isn't it?"

"It is." Max chuckled. "I was pretty shocked to see you come waltzing into the conference room that day, but the truth is it's good to see you again."

She sank her teeth into her lower lip and nodded. "It's good to see you again, too, Max."

He held her gaze, neither of them speaking. This time, the silence didn't feel uncomfortable.

"Zora," he said finally. "You forgot that Zora is still single, too."

"Is she, though?" They both turned toward where Zora sat on a sofa with Dallas, the two of them laughing. The corners of Quinn's mouth quirked in a soft smile. "I've been watching them for the past two days, and they behave like a couple if ever I've seen one."

Max studied his sister and her best friend. "I've mentioned as much to Zora before. She insists that what they have is a classic bromance. She just happens to be a girl."

"Cute explanation." Quinn laughed. "I'm not buying it, but it's cute just the same. Then again, dating must be tricky when you live in a small town *and* have four older brothers."

"Guess I hadn't really thought about that." Max rubbed the back of his neck as he watched Zora and Dallas. "But my sister is no pushover. She has never had a problem standing up to any of us. That includes my parents and my grandfather."

"I don't doubt that." Quinn smiled. "That doesn't mean she doesn't care what you all think. You're her family, and you're important to her. Of course, she wants your approval. The same goes for Cole."

"I doubt Cole much cares what any of us think." Max glanced over at his younger brother, who was playing with the kids. "Not everyone has that luxury. Some of us have obligations to fulfill."

He looked at Quinn and couldn't help the tinge of jealousy that arose at the sweet smile on her face as she watched Cole with the children.

"Children are an excellent judge of character, and they adore him," Quinn said. "He's a good uncle and a good friend." She turned back to Max. "In fact, he seems to get along well with everyone except you. And if you don't think that bothers him, you don't know your brother very well at all."

"Did Cole ask you to talk to me about—"

"Your dysfunctional relationship?" She laughed bitterly. "You must know Cole's much too proud for that. I doubt he's even willing to admit to himself how much it bothers him that nothing he does is right in your eyes."

"That isn't true." The accusation stabbed at Max's chest and heightened the guilt he already felt.

Yes, he was hard on his brother, but it was because he loved him and wanted the best for him.

"Cole is very good at what he does. Family or no, we wouldn't have engaged his services to renovate the barn or the restaurant if he wasn't the best man for the job," Max said. "And the house he built for our parents—" Max gestured toward it "—I honestly haven't seen finer craftsmanship anywhere."

"Maybe tell him that sometime." Quinn smiled softly, then sighed. "I'd better see if my grandfather needs anything. Thank you again for seeing me home last night."

He nodded. "Anytime, Quinn."

Max couldn't turn his gaze away from Quinn as she walked over to where their grandfathers were gathered with some of the other older folks in town. Sloane's grandfather, Atticus Ames, was among them. He bounced his great granddaughter on his knee, much to Bailey's delight.

Quinn was beautiful and no less opinionated than she'd been that summer when they'd debated everything from sports to politics.

Now, as then, Quinn didn't pull any punches. She had no qualms about calling him out on his bullshit, a trait he admired in business and personal relationships.

Max thought he'd eradicated the feelings he'd once had for Quinn. Instead, they'd clearly burrowed deeper, lying in wait for the opportunity to reemerge.

Every moment he spent with Quinn rekindled those feelings and stoked the fire he'd worked so hard to extinguish.

He'd spent a single summer with Quinn Bazemore. So why was it so damn hard to let go of their past?

Eleven

It was the beginning of a new week and Max found himself in another mandatory, impromptu meeting. This one had been called by his brother Parker—the company's chief financial officer. Max sat at the conference table with his father and grandfather, Parker, Blake and Zora, waiting for Parker to explain why he'd called this meeting when they were already inundated with work and exhausted from the previous weekend's festivities.

Parker pulled a stack of documents out of a manila folder and handed one to each of them.

Max read the title of the document aloud. "'Merit-based Succession vs. Birth-Order Succession in Family-Owned Businesses.' Parker, what the hell is this?"

Everyone else turned toward Parker, but Max glanced at Blake—next in line to become CEO of King's Finest. There was no anger or confusion in Blake's expression. Only keen interest.

"Well, Parker?" Their grandfather frowned. "What exactly is this about?"

Parker pushed his glasses up the bridge of his nose. "If you'd turn to the introduction I've prepared on page one—"

"I don't want to read a prepared statement, son." Their father dropped the document onto the table with a thud without opening it. "If you're proposing what I think you're proposing, you'd damn well better have the balls to explain it yourself."

"All right." Parker set the document down.

He looked at their grandfather, then their father. Finally, his gaze settled on Blake with a hint of apology in his expression. It was a look they'd rarely seen from Parker before he'd started dating Kayleigh. His sister had teased that Kayleigh had sprinkled fairy dust on Parker and made him a real boy with real feelings.

That wasn't exactly true.

Parker had always been keenly aware of his own feelings, and still completely ruled by logic. Emotions didn't factor into his decisions. And he'd been a little too straightforward for his own good. Parker was still that person. His love for Kayleigh had simply shown him the power and usefulness of emotions like love and compassion. And he'd been making an effort to empathize with the people around him. So the pained look on Parker's face was alarming.

"Blake, you are a phenomenal operations manager. The efficiency with which you run the floor and the way you handle the staff... I'd venture that no one else at this table could handle either as well as you do," Parker said.

"Thanks, Park. That means quite a bit coming from you." Blake leaned back in his padded leather chair, his eyebrows lowering as he regarded his brother warily. "But?"

Everyone in the room turned back to Parker, as if they were watching a tennis match.

Parker cleared his throat and shoved his glasses up on his nose again. "You strictly adhere to company standards, and you ensure that your team does, too. It's one of the reasons King's Finest is known for producing some of the best bourbon on the market. But the soft center that makes you a great boss and an exemplary husband and father would be your Achilles' heel as the CEO."

"Seriously, Parker? That's what you're going with?

Blake doesn't have an asshole mode, therefore he isn't tough enough to run the company?" Zora stared daggers at their brother.

"That's bullshit," Max said, taking up Blake's cause. "You just said yourself that no one else could run production the way Blake does. By your own logic, doesn't it follow that if he runs operations so well, he'll also run the entire company well?"

"Not necessarily." Parker shrugged, shoving his hands in his pockets. "How many great players in basketball or football turn out to be substandard coaches or GMs? You're not going to sit there and tell me that you think your all-time favorite basketball player is a good general manager, are you?"

"Point taken," Duke said gruffly. "But it's a hell of a leap to say the same about your brother with no evidence to substantiate your claim."

"And that proof would come at what expense, Dad?" Parker asked. "Should we wait until the company is in decline before we declare that the experiment is a failure?"

Everyone at the table was outraged on Blake's behalf. Yet he just stared intently at Parker with an unreadable expression.

"You act as if King's Finest is struggling. We can afford to absorb a misstep or two," their grandfather said, then turned to Blake. "Not that I'm saying it would be a misstep to appoint you as CEO, son."

"It's okay, Gramps." Blake put a reassuring hand on their grandfather's shoulder.

"That's true," Parker acknowledged. "But we have the potential to achieve even more if we take a more aggressive approach."

"What's the upside of adopting a riskier approach when we're already seeing phenomenal results?" Zora demanded.

"That's the same thing we all thought initially when Savannah came to the company with her ideas about expanding our market share," Blake said quietly. "But she was right and the uptick in sales we've seen in the past three years is directly tied to the fact that we took a risk and adopted her suggestions."

"A project Blake encouraged us to take on," Max reminded Parker.

"True," Parker acknowledged. "But would Blake have had as favorable a view of Savannah's proposal if it hadn't been delivered by a beautiful woman to whom he was attracted?"

Blake stood abruptly and slammed his hand on the table. "If you want to question my leadership ability...fine. Do it. But don't bring my wife into this discussion. This has nothing to do with Savannah."

"That isn't a slight against Savannah." Parker held up a hand. "I hold her in the highest regard, as both my sister-in-law and as the event manager here. We're damn lucky to have Savannah as an employee and part owner of the company."

Parker inhaled deeply, then released a quiet sigh. "You don't have that killer instinct, Blake. Which makes you a great brother and a fine husband and father. But when it comes to our highly competitive industry, it's a fatal flaw."

"The liquor business has always been cutthroat, whether it was legal or not. Running moonshine was dangerous business back in my father's day," their grandfather said, referring to the company's namesake—his father, King Abbott. "And surely you don't think it was easy for me, as a black man, to enter into this business fifty-three years ago."

"Of course not, Grandad," Parker said. "Every single person at this table appreciates the sacrifices you made to start this company and establish a legacy for all of us. But we live in very different times. Everyone and their mother is starting a craft distillery these days. And some of the products are remarkably good. I'm not saying we need to regard the other companies out there as the enemy, but we have to take a focused, straightforward approach if we want to achieve our goal of being the best. That's the goal you established when you started this company fifty-three years ago. I take that seriously. And I've proven my willingness to make hard sacrifices on behalf of the company."

"So now you're trying to leverage the fact that you were willing to play fake fiancée to Kayleigh in order to acquire her building?" Zora asked, her jaw dropping.

During the acrimonious negotiations to convince Kayleigh to sell her building, Parker had agreed to pose as her fiancé at the wedding of her ex's younger sister. Which had led to Parker becoming Kayleigh's actual fiancé.

"Really, Park?" Max laughed. "You're the one who came out ahead in that deal."

Everyone at the table chuckled.

"Definitely," Zora agreed. "Kayleigh is the best thing to ever happen to you, Parker. Plus, she took you on an all-expenses-paid trip to a tropical island. So don't try to spin this like you're some self-sacrificing martyr."

"She *is* the best thing that's ever happened to me, and I'm incredibly grateful to have her in my life," Parker admitted. "But I had no idea things would end up this way. I did something extremely uncomfortable for the greater good of the family and the future of this company."

"This is all a bunch of nonsense, Parker." Their father's face and cheeks were flushed, and his voice was strained. "I'm sorry that you somehow feel wronged because you weren't the firstborn, but that's just the way it is."

"That's not exactly true, either, son." Their grandfather chuckled, rubbing a hand over his thinning gray hair.

"What do you mean, Dad?" Duke asked.

"You were an only child." Joseph shrugged. "Not much competition there. You always knew that I was going to hand the company off to you. But what if you hadn't been an only child? What if you'd been second or third in line? Maybe you'd see Parker's argument differently."

The room grew quiet as they considered his grandfather's words.

They'd simply accepted that as firstborn, Blake was the one who'd be named CEO. Max had no doubt his brother would make a good CEO. But was he the *best* choice? It was a question he'd never considered. None of them had, except Parker, apparently.

"All right, Parker. Maybe you're right." Blake tapped the table, drawing everyone's attention. "This isn't some royal dynasty where birth order determines destiny. Nor do I want there to be any question about whether or not I deserved the position of CEO. I put a hell of a lot of thought into every hire I've ever made for this company. And I've never hired anyone—including Savannah—who I didn't feel was the absolute best candidate for the job. I care enough about Grandad's legacy to insist that the same care and effort be given to deciding who will one day replace Dad at the helm of this organization. So I agree that the decision should be merit based. And whatever choice Dad and Grandad make, I'll stand behind it."

The entire room fell silent. But no one seemed more surprised by Blake's concession than Parker.

"Now, if you'll excuse me, this marshmallow of a man has work to do." Blake stood, pushing his chair beneath the table and leaving the room.

They all sat in stunned silence, staring after him.

Did that mean Parker would be appointed the new company CEO? Max never had any qualms about working for Blake. But working for Parker? He wasn't sure who'd want to strangle his brother first—him or Zora.

Parker's mouth curved in a faint smile, as if he'd already achieved victory.

Zora folded her arms and stared Parker down. "If this is going to be a merit-based decision, that means the CEO–ship is open to any of us. That includes Max and me."

"Max lacks the killer instinct, same as Blake," Parker said flatly. "You have it in spades." He shook a finger in her direction, and she smiled proudly. "But while I struggle to figure emotion into the equation, it's nearly impossible for you to leave emotion out of any decision. With you, *everything* is personal."

"You're playing the emotion card because I'm a girl. How original," she said mockingly.

"No, I'm stating a fact because you're a hothead. The moment someone upsets you, you're ready to key their car." Parker stared at her.

He isn't wrong.

"I might think it, say it, dream about it. Maybe even threaten it. But I haven't keyed anyone's car to date," Zora argued.

They all stared at her and Duke raised an eyebrow.

"Okay, there was that one time. But that mofo totally deserved it."

The room erupted into laughter before it settled into an eerie quietness again.

"This is something your grandfather and I hadn't considered." Duke glanced over at their grandfather. "So we'll need to discuss the matter ad nauseam." He stood, picking up the document Parker had prepared. "Don't expect a decision on this anytime soon." He pointed at Parker, then glanced around the room. "And no matter what, we're a family first. I hope all of you will keep that in mind. Greed and ambition have been the downfall of entire societies. They can easily destroy a family and a company like ours."

"Yes, sir," Max said. "We won't forget that. But if we are making the choice based on merit, Zora and I should be a part of the discussion, too. Regardless of what Parker thinks." He narrowed his gaze at his brother.

"Wouldn't have it any other way, son."

"I do have one question," Zora said to Parker. "This idea that you should be the CEO instead of Blake... Is Kayleigh behind it?"

They all regarded Parker carefully. He and Kayleigh were engaged now, but before then Kayleigh had hated their father, mistakenly believing he'd swindled her mother out of property once owned by her maternal grandfather.

She now knew the truth. Duke had been an anonymous benefactor to Kayleigh and her sister at the request of her now deceased mother. They'd embraced Kayleigh as part of their family. But maybe some residual animosity had prompted her to push Parker into making this power grab.

"No," Parker said adamantly. "This is something I've been thinking about for at least a year. I wanted to do my research first. Then I was looking for the right time to bring it up. Seemed like *after* the anniversary party would be wise."

Max stood. He'd heard all he needed to hear. He said goodbye to everyone and made his way back to his office.

"Ah...there you are, boss. The meeting didn't go too well, huh?" Molly's observation was more of a statement than a question. "Anyway, Quinn dropped by. She wants to know when you two can meet to go over some marketing ideas she has for your first event in two weeks."

Max grunted. Before, he'd been irritated that he had to relinquish control of his pet project to someone else. And now that he had just as much of a shot at becoming CEO as any of his siblings, he resented having to share the spotlight on a project that could sway the decision his way.

He rubbed the back of his neck. "Tell her I'm busy today. Maybe we can meet tomorrow afternoon."

Molly frowned. She knew his schedule better than he

did, so she was well aware that he could spare Quinn an hour or two. But she didn't challenge him on it. She nodded, instead. "Will do. Can I get you anything?"

"No, thanks." He forced a smile and closed the door behind him.

His father had been clear that working with Quinn wasn't an option. But maybe he could change his mind.

Twelve

Quinn drove into town for lunch. Frustrated with Max's sudden lack of communication, she needed fresh air and a change of scenery.

She'd been working on the project furiously and had lots of exciting ideas to pitch to Max. But he'd been nearly impossible to reach all week.

Something is definitely going on with him.

Every time she'd tried to phone him her call rolled over to voice mail. When he was in the office, his door was closed. And Molly, who'd previously known her boss's schedule to the nanosecond, seemed utterly confused about when or if the man would ever have time to meet with her again.

Max was clearly avoiding her, and she intended to find out why.

As she entered the Magnolia Lake Bakery, Quinn inhaled the aroma of the delicious peach tartlets they served. She'd definitely be having one or two of those.

"Quinn!" Savannah grinned. "Kayleigh and I were just leaving. I'm sorry we missed you."

"Me, too." Quinn said. "I would've enjoyed the company."

Quinn studied Savannah's warm smile, her brain churning. She needed help tackling the situation with Max, and she wasn't comfortable going to Duke, Grandpa Joe or her grandfather. It felt too much like tattling. But this deal was important to her family, and she wouldn't allow Max to sabotage it.

"Savannah, if you have a few minutes, I'd love to pick your brain about something," Quinn said.

"Of course." Savannah didn't hesitate. "Let's grab a seat. My back is killing me."

"And that's my cue to leave." Kayleigh smiled. "Besides, I have orders to fill and lots of packing to do."

Kayleigh hugged Savannah and bade them both goodbye before heading to her shop on the other side of Main Street.

"What's going on?" Savannah asked as soon as they'd settled into a booth near the window. "Have you run into a problem planning the marketing materials?"

Quinn explained her dilemma with Max.

"It's like he's become a totally different person in the past few days," Quinn said, wrapping up her concerns. "I'm not sure what I've done to tick the guy off."

"It isn't you, Quinn, so don't take it personally." Savannah's hazel eyes suddenly seemed sad. "There's a lot going on at KFD right now, and everyone is kind of on edge."

That tracked with what she'd noticed over the past few days. It wasn't just Max who seemed distracted. Zora and Blake seemed stressed. Duke and Grandpa Joe hadn't been around that much. Only Parker seemed unaffected by whatever was bothering the rest of the family.

"Max probably just needs time to sort through what's going on. You might actually miss the silence once things are back to normal," Savannah joked.

"Everything is okay with Duke and Grandpa Joe, I hope."

Savannah wasn't going into detail, and she respected that. After all, she had secrets of her own.

Everythang ain't for everybody to know.

Her grandmother's words rang out clear in her head.

"Yes, they're both fine," Savannah assured her.

"Good." Quinn was relieved. She genuinely liked both men. "And I get what you're saying about Max needing time. The problem is we haven't got much of it. Our first trade show is coming up soon."

Savannah frowned. "That is a problem."

She checked her watch, then climbed to her feet. "I have a meeting with a bride and her family at the barn, so I have to run. But I'd give Max until the end of the week. If he hasn't come around by then, do whatever it takes to snap him out of it. If you need reinforcements, I'm prepared to ride shotgun." Her warm smile returned.

Quinn thanked Savannah, hugging her as they parted ways. Then she ordered lunch, including a double order of peach tartlets.

She realized that Savannah's allegiance was to the Abbotts. But Quinn liked her, and trusted that Savannah would keep her word.

So she'd take her advice and give Max a few more days to sort out whatever the hell was going on with his family. Then she'd put her foot down and do what she had to do to get this project back on track.

Because she needed to protect the interest of *her* family. And she wouldn't allow Max Abbott to get in the way of that.

Max was searching the file cabinet beside his desk for a document he needed when his cell phone rang.

Quinn.

He sighed, letting the call roll over to voice mail.

The three voice mails she'd left in the previous days made it clear she was beyond pissed.

Max wasn't exactly avoiding Quinn. He just didn't have anything new to report. Or rather, he didn't have anything he was ready to report to her since their last conversation.

And since he'd been considering campaigns that went in a completely different direction from her idea, he needed to have everything in order before they spoke again.

It was after 5:00 p.m. on a Monday and it was turning out to be another long week.

There was a light tap on his closed office door.

"Come in, Molly," he called without looking up from the file cabinet.

The heavenly floral and citrus scent that wafted into his office indicated it wasn't Molly who'd entered.

Max turned around to see Quinn standing by his desk with one hand propped on a cocked hip and one eyebrow raised.

"Hello, Max." She folded her arms. "I realize that you're busy, but we need to talk."

"Hey, Quinn." Max cleared his throat and smoothed down his tie. "We do. I realize that. But now isn't the best time."

"Now is *never* the right time with you, Max." Quinn inched closer. "It's been over a week since we've had any traction on this project. Our first event is coming up soon, and there's a lot we still need to work out."

"Your concerns are valid, Quinn, and I promise to address them. But right now just isn't the best time."

"Look, Max, blowing me off in our personal lives, that's your prerogative. I accepted it and moved on. Blowing me off on this project is reckless and unprofessional." Her words came flying at him with increased speed and indignation. "This isn't about what happened between us. Or you being mad that Cole and I are friends. Our family legacies are at stake here, and I—"

"Good evening, Quinn." Zora stood up from the little table where she'd been sitting, blocked from Quinn's view.

"Oh, my God." Quinn's eyes widened. She pressed her fingertips to her mouth. "I didn't realize you two were in a meeting. I would never have... I'm sorry." She returned her attention to him. "Max, we can continue this discussion some other time."

"No, stay." Zora's tone was warm and understanding. She placed a gentle hand on Quinn's shoulder. "We were just chatting. Nothing urgent. It sounds like the two of you need to talk. It's been a long day, and I'm ready to head home. Good night, Quinn. Good night, Max."

Zora gave Max a knowing glance, one that urged him to talk to Quinn. Something she'd been vocal about the past few days.

Don't shut her out, Max. Just tell her the truth. She'll understand.

Max clenched his hands in his lap as the door closed behind his sister.

There was a moment of heavy, awkward silence between them. Clearly, Quinn still hadn't recovered from the embarrassment of Zora having heard her entire rant. And he wasn't ready to say what he needed to say. But time was their enemy. He couldn't put off this conversation any longer.

Max shot to his feet and shoved one hand in his pocket. He gestured with the other for Quinn to take Zora's vacated seat and joined her at the table.

"I'm sorry." They both spoke at once, each seemingly surprised by the other's apology.

"I'm sorry I barged in on your meeting with Zora," Quinn said. "I would never have done that intentionally, and I certainly wouldn't have said the things I did about our past and about you and me and Cole. I assume she didn't know about any of it." Quinn tucked her hair behind her ear.

"Zora's part-time job is minding the business of everyone else in the family," Max said, only half-joking. "No, she didn't know, but she did suspect there was something between us."

"Which I just confirmed." Quinn groaned. "God, that was idiotic of me." She shook her head, then suddenly narrowed her gaze at him. "But I wouldn't have felt compelled to take such drastic action if you hadn't been acting like such a—"

"Ass?" He chuckled at her surprised reaction.

"I was going to say *child*." She folded her arms. "But I'll defer to your word choice because it's also accurate."

"I deserve that," Max admitted, dragging a hand down his face. "Which brings me to the fact that I'm sorry, too. I know it seems I've been avoiding you for the past few days…"

"And you're going to tell me you haven't been avoiding me?" She arched her eyebrow and crossed one leg over the other.

His attention was drawn to the smooth brown skin of her toned legs revealed below the fitted, knee-length black skirt. Max was sure his heart was suddenly beating faster.

"Okay, so I have been avoiding you," he admitted. "Mostly because my mood hasn't been conducive to conversation. Nothing against you personally."

"Mostly," she repeated the word. "So tell me about the part that does have to do with me personally."

He walked to the window overlooking King's Lake—the sole source of water for their world-renowned bourbon.

Quinn followed him to the window. "Everything seemed fine between us and then suddenly it wasn't."

He turned toward her. "Everything *is* fine between us. I've been contemplating whether it's the best use of resources for both of us to be working on the project."

Quinn's eyes widened and her mouth fell open. She clutched at her stomach, as if his words had caused her physical pain.

He hated being the cause of more pain for Quinn. But

he hadn't created this situation; Parker had. He was simply trying his best to play the hand he'd been dealt.

"We've been through all of this," she reminded him. "My being here isn't a commentary on how competent you are at you job, and this isn't a competition."

He folded his arms over his chest as he studied her.

Damn, she's beautiful.

His breathing became shallow as he tried to ignore her delicious scent and the electricity that rolled up his spine being this close to her.

He couldn't help remembering how good it had felt to hold her in his arms again on the dance floor at his parents' party.

"Maybe it isn't a competition for you, Quinn. But it is for me."

"I don't understand." She stepped closer, tipping her chin so their eyes met. "Who is it that you feel you're competing with? Certainly not me."

"No." He kneaded the knot at the back of his neck. Zora's words echoed in his ears. *Tell her the truth. She'll understand.* "I find myself in competition with my siblings."

"For?"

"Cone of silence?" he asked.

A slow smile spread across her lovely face, deepening the dimples he'd been obsessed with that summer. It'd given him a thrill to make her smile or to be the source of her unique laugh. "You're invoking *Get Smart* right now?" she asked. "Really?"

"Really, Agent 99." He leaned in closer, one side of his mouth curved in a smirk.

The familiar nickname prompted a giggle from her. The tension in his shoulders eased in response to the infectious sound, which invoked a kaleidoscope of fond memories. His chest ached with both deep want and gut-wrenching regret.

"Okay," she said begrudgingly, her wide brown eyes

filled with curiosity. "Consider the cone of silence invoked." She gestured over her head, as if she was pulling a plastic dome down over it. "Now, tell me why you're being weird all of a sudden."

"Last week, Parker essentially declared that he should be the next KFD CEO." Max's shoulders tensed.

"Who did you expect to succeed your father as CEO? Blake?"

"Yes, because he's the oldest," Max confirmed. "But Parker believes the appointment should be merit based and that it should go to him."

"How did Blake take Parker's proposal?" Quinn asked.

"Better than Zora and I did," he admitted with a shrug.

"Neither of you anticipated being named as your father's successor, so why'd you take Parker's challenge so personally?"

Max ran a hand over his head and sighed. "Parker acts as if the only logical choice is between appointing Blake because he was born first or appointing Parker because he believes that he deserves it. As if Zora and I don't even warrant consideration."

Quinn nodded sympathetically. Her sincere expression was like warm water sluicing over the knotted muscles in his neck and back. A balm that soothed the anger and resentment the entire ordeal had stirred in him.

"I understand why that would be upsetting. After all, you're both an integral part of the organization," she said. "Did you tell Parker how that made you feel? Why you objected to him presenting the situation that way?"

Max turned to look at the placid waters of King's Lake. "We made it clear that if the decision is going to be merit based, it should be open to everyone. Grandad seemed to agree, and my father is considering it."

"That explains why the mood has been tense around here, but it doesn't explain why you seem upset with me."

"I'm not." He turned toward her again. "I'm sorry if I gave you that impression."

"Then why did you suddenly shut me out like I'm the enemy?" Her eyes searched his.

"If the decision is based on who has the biggest impact on the company…" His gaze dropped momentarily from hers and he shrugged. "I've been working on this project for a long time. Long before you got involved. And it's an excellent opportunity for me to demonstrate my value to our organization in an immediate, tangible way."

"You're dismissing me from the project? I thought you liked my proposal. Your entire family approved it."

The hurt in her voice brought back the day he'd called to end their relationship.

Why, Max? Was it something I did? Something I said?

The guilt of that day never seemed to leave him. It retreated to the recesses of his mind and heart, but it was never far-off. Always prepared to rear its ugly head again.

Today that guilt was front and center.

He was disappointing Quinn, again. And now, just as then, she was blaming herself when the culpability was all his.

"I do like your proposal." Max placed a gentle hand on her arm, drawing her gaze back to his again. "You're brilliant, Quinn. There's no doubt about that. Honestly, I've come up with dozens of different takes on this thing, and none of them have surpassed yours."

She sucked in a deep breath and her panicked expression transformed to one of pure bewilderment. "Then I don't understand. Why are you dismissing my proposal? Dismissing me?"

"I never planned to dismiss you from the project. I just hoped to come up with a better plan. A different direction that I would run point on." His thumb absently caressed her arm through the fabric of her sleeve. "It was a mistake, and I'm sorry for being such a jerk."

"Good." Quinn nodded. "Because if your goal is to impress your father and prove you're just as deserving of consideration, I can help you." She stepped closer and tugged on his tie, a teasing lilt in her voice. "I'm not your rival, Max. But I can be a damn good partner. If we work together, we'll impress both our families, and we'll each get what we want."

Her sweet scent filled his nostrils, and he could feel the heat radiating from her flawless brown skin. He couldn't help being mesmerized by this woman. If she asked him right now, he would've given her just about anything.

"Partners?" Quinn's eyes danced and her dimples were in full effect. She extended a hand.

"Partners." He shook her hand.

The sensation of her warm, soft skin against his stunned him, like an unexpected jolt of electricity. Max stood frozen as her eyes searched his.

Quinn slipped her hand from his and stepped backward. She turned toward the speaker mounted high on the wall. Music drifted down quietly from it.

She turned back to him. "'Make It Last Forever.'" A slow smile spread across her face. "Gosh, I remember every word of every song on that Keith Sweat album," she mused.

"I was definitely going through a Keith Sweat phase at the time." Max chuckled at the fond memories. "But c'mon, it's an R & B classic."

"True," she agreed. "And it would be more accurate to say you were going through an eighties and nineties R & B phase." Her eyes gleamed as she listed the artists he'd been obsessed with that summer. "Wow. That feels like forever ago. Come to think of it, you were supposed to make me a mixtape, which I never got."

He stared at her for a moment with his hands shoved in his pockets, debating his next move.

Would she consider him sweet and sentimental? Or would he come off as a pathetic sap?

Max rubbed his stubbled chin and sighed.

Fuck it.

He walked over to his desk, rummaged in the lap drawer and pulled out a plastic case. He handed it to her.

"You've got to be kidding me." She accepted the compact disc—a relic from their past.

"I made the CD, as promised." He sat on the front edge of his desk. "I just never got the chance to give it to you."

"You kept it all this time?" She stood in front of him.

"I probably remember that summer more fondly than you do. But seeing you again after all this time threw me for a loop," he admitted. "I found the disc at my parents' place over the weekend in a box of my things from college. I couldn't bring myself to throw it out." He shrugged. "I brought it here to upload it to my computer."

Quinn stared at him, blinking. She seemed stunned.

"Why are you telling me this?" Her words came out in a rough whisper.

"I don't know." His heart beat rapidly. "I know you don't want to talk about our past." The sound of his own blood rushing filled his ears. "But it's all I've been thinking about lately. I messed up, Quinn. I hurt you, and I am so sorry for that."

"I should go." She turned to leave, but he caught her hand in his.

"I'm sorry if that upsets you. I thought you deserved to know that if I had the chance to go back and do things differently, I would. You have no idea how much I wish that were possible."

Quinn turned back to him, her eyes searching his before she put the jewel case down on his desk.

She was rejecting his gift. Rejecting him.

He should've kept his mouth shut.

"I appreciate your apology. Now, for the sake of this deal, I propose that we let go of the anger and guilt we both seem to feel about what happened that summer." She shrugged. "Maybe we could just hug it out and agree to move on. I hear that's what adults do."

Her sensual lips quirked in a half smile.

"I'd like that." Max grinned. Relief eased the tension in his chest. He opened his arms wide and she stepped forward, looping her arms around his neck as he hugged her waist.

Max allowed Quinn to dictate the physical interaction between them, grateful she'd at least given him the chance to apologize. She held onto him much longer than he'd expected.

Quinn had always given the best hugs. That hadn't changed. He welcomed the heat and the comfort of her embrace, unable to bring himself to be the first to pull away.

Finally, she dropped her arms from his neck. Rather than pulling away, Quinn cradled his face, caressing his stubbled cheek with her thumb as her gaze met his.

There was something so warm and comforting about her soft gaze. Without thought, Max grasped the hand that caressed his cheek and kissed her palm, then her wrist.

Quinn's hand trembled slightly, and she sank her teeth into her lower lip as she leaned in, eyes closed.

Max erased the sliver of space between them, tasting her full, sensual lips. Arms locked around her waist, he tugged her closer. His heart beat wildly in response to the sensation of her luscious curves crushed against his hard chest. He swallowed the sound of her soft sighs with his hungry kiss.

Since Quinn had come back into his life, he'd often found himself wondering what it would feel like to hold her in his arms and kiss her again.

His fantasies hadn't even come close to the reality.

He glided his hands down her back and over the full, round bottom, as firm and plump as the ripe, juicy summer peaches Bazemore Farms was so famous for. Max pulled her tighter against him, reveling in the sensation of her body pressed to his.

Quinn parted her lips on a sigh, and he slid his tongue between them, deepening their kiss. He savored the warm, sweet cinnamon taste of her velvety tongue. Her kiss was hotter and sweeter than he remembered. He honestly didn't think he'd ever get enough of it.

"You know, Max, I was thinking that… Oh, shit. Sorry." Zora had barged into his office unannounced.

Why hadn't he thought to lock that damn door?

Quinn slipped out of his arms and moved toward the window. With her back turned to them, she straightened her blouse and raked her fingers through her hair.

Max heaved a sigh as he glanced down at his lap. *Major hard-on situation.* Standing was not an option.

"What is it, Zora? I'm kind of busy."

"Obviously." She cast an amused glance in Quinn's direction.

"I thought you were leaving." He tried to keep the annoyance with his little sister out of his voice. After all, it wasn't unusual for them to pop into each other's offices. Though the circumstances were clearly different this time.

"I should go," Quinn said suddenly, hurrying past both of them toward the door. "Good night."

"Quinn!" he called after her. She didn't break her stride.

Max groaned, running a hand over his head.

"Sorry, I didn't realize you were entertaining company." Zora's expression was a mixture of contrition and amusement.

"How about knocking next time, Brat?" Max suggested. "And do me a favor—"

"I won't say anything to anyone. I promise," she interrupted. "I'll tell Quinn that myself, if you'd like."

"No, I should talk to her," he said, finally comfortable enough to stand. Nothing killed the mood like your little sister walking in on you. "What did you need?"

"It's nothing urgent. We'll talk tomorrow." She turned to leave. "Good night, Max."

He sighed, his eyes drifting closed at the soft click of the door behind his sister.

That went sideways fast.

Max honestly hadn't intended to kiss Quinn. He'd imagined it, ruminated over it and fantasized about it, without actually planning to do it. But once he held Quinn in his arms again, it was clear he'd never really gotten over her. That he wanted the chance to fix things between them.

Until Quinn had leaned in for a kiss, he hadn't believed that another chance with her was possible. After all, she'd insisted on behaving as if the intense summer they'd shared had never even happened. It had been driving him insane, because he could hardly think of anything else.

Max waited a beat and then followed the carpeted path to Quinn's desk. She wasn't there. She'd evidently fled the building, not just his office.

Hopefully, she hadn't encountered Zora on her way out.

Suddenly the ladies' room bathroom door opened, and Quinn appeared. Her brown eyes went wide, then she glanced around the space as if she expected another of his siblings to pop up.

"Zora's gone. For real this time," he said with a small smile, hoping to inject some humor into the situation and relieve the anxiety she was obviously feeling. "And I'm pretty sure everyone else is already gone. Parker and Blake don't stay late at the office much these days."

Her only response was a sigh of relief as she circumnavigated him and went to her desk. She pulled her purse out of the large bottom drawer and hitched it on her shoulder.

"I'd like to meet tomorrow morning to discuss the upcoming trade show." Her eyes didn't meet his. "If you can make the time."

"Of course, I can," he said, then leaned in closer and lowered his voice. "I realize how awkward that was in there." He jerked a thumb over his shoulder in the general direction of his office. "But you don't need to rush off."

She glared at him with fire in her eyes. As if that was the most ridiculous thing she'd ever heard.

Whatever progress he and Quinn had just made had been erased in an instant.

Thirteen

"You shouldn't have followed me out here." Quinn scanned the space around them. Her heart was still racing. "Isn't it bad enough that your sister just walked in on us kissing?"

Technically, he'd kissed her. But she'd leaned in first. And the hug that precipitated the kiss had been her idea, too.

Quinn cringed. How could she have done something so stupid?

"We need to talk." Max's firm voice shook her from her panicked daze. "We can have the conversation here or in the privacy of my office," he added when she didn't respond.

Quinn huffed, then turned and followed Max back to his office. He closed the door behind them.

"This is a really bad look, Max." Quinn's cheeks flamed, and her pulse raced.

She'd lost it. She'd kissed Max right there in his office. And it hadn't felt like some random, isolated act. She'd felt like that starry-eyed girl falling for Max all over again. Which was crazy. Because she wasn't naive enough to fall for Max again. He'd shredded her heart to pieces once. Wasn't that enough?

Been there and done that. Spoiler alert: it does not end well.

Falling for Max Abbott again would only lead to another

broken heart. And this time, she'd deserve it. Because experience had taught her better.

"No one is here except us," he assured her.

"It doesn't matter, Max." Quinn's head suddenly throbbed and her throat felt dry. "Zora saw us together." Quinn pressed a fist to her belly, her stomach in knots. "By the time we arrive here tomorrow morning, both of our families will know."

Her grandfather would be monumentally disappointed in her. Duke and Iris would never take her seriously again, and they certainly wouldn't refer her to any of their friends and business associates. And she could forget using her work here as a case study, which had been a critical piece of this for her.

Quinn squeezed her eyes shut and took slow, measured breaths. If only she could rewind the clock fifteen minutes. Before she'd gotten dreamy and nostalgic while listening to the unofficial soundtrack of that summer and remembering their first kiss. She opened her eyes and blinked back the tears she refused to let fall.

"I really screwed up." She shook her head.

"Zora won't say anything," Max assured her. "She promised me," he added, in response to her incredulous expression. "And she'd never give Parker that kind of ammunition against either of us. So you don't need to worry, Quinn. This isn't a big deal."

Quinn wished she could believe that. But even if Zora didn't tell anyone else, *she* knew. Even if she never mentioned it, the other woman would be judging her.

"Maybe your sister has walked in on you making out with a business associate before." She could barely contain the bitterness rising in her chest as the old wounds resurfaced. "But it's a first for me, and for me this could have very real consequences."

"What's that supposed to mean?" He frowned but didn't

acknowledge her dig about him making out with other women in his office.

"It means my future is very much at stake here." Quinn smacked a hand to her chest. "I don't have the luxury of being an Abbott. For a moment, I allowed myself to forget that."

"I'd never stand by and let you take the fall for something I was clearly complicit in." Max sat on the edge of his desk again. "That goes for what happened just now and this entire project. Whatever happens, good or bad, we're partners in this. I'd never let you take the blame for me."

An eerie chill ran down Quinn's spine and she clenched her fists at her sides. She'd heard nearly the same promise before. The moment she'd chosen to believe it was the moment her career had begun to unravel.

She wouldn't fall for it again. *She* was the only person she could trust to safeguard her future.

"I kissed you, and I shouldn't have." Quinn didn't acknowledge his insistence that they were partners and that he'd protect her. "I lost my head momentarily. It won't happen again." She forced herself to meet his wounded gaze. "It *can't* happen again."

Deep wrinkles formed above Max's furrowed brows. He folded his arms and sighed. "If that's what you want, Quinn."

"It is." She tipped her chin, hoping she conveyed more conviction than she possessed at the moment. That her tone didn't betray her disappointment at how easily he'd acquiesced. As if she and the kiss really were no big deal for him. Already nearly forgotten.

"All right, Quinn. This is strictly a business relationship. Nothing more. And maybe, if I work really hard at it, I can pretend that summer never happened, too." His tone was biting.

Max had obviously been more perturbed by her refusal

to discuss their past than she realized; nonetheless, it had been a good decision. Just look what had happened the moment she allowed herself the luxury of fondly revisiting their past.

Keeping their relationship strictly professional was in the best interest of her career and her heart—regardless of what her body wanted.

Because, even now, she wanted Max to kiss her again. She wanted to invite Max back to her place and get reacquainted with every inch of his body. To spend the rest of the night making love to him. She longed for the taste of his mouth, and her body ached for the pleasure of his touch.

She sucked in a deep breath, forced an uneasy smile and turned to leave.

"Wait." He held up the CD with *Mixtape for Peaches* scribbled on it in black permanent marker. "You forgot this."

A tiny piece of her heart crumbled, seeing those words and remembering the friendship and intimacy they'd once shared. A part of her wanted all those things with Max again, even knowing that revisiting the past would only lead to more disappointment.

"I appreciate the thought, Max. I really do. But maybe it's better if we leave the past in the past and focus on the future of this project. We both have a lot riding on it." She placed a gentle hand on his forearm and forced another smile, despite the electricity that filtered through her fingertips where her skin touched his. "I'll see you in the morning."

"Good night, Quinn." His voice sounded achingly sad.

She slipped out of his office, closing the door behind her.

It was better this way. Eventually, Max would realize it, too.

Quinn made her way to her car and took the narrow road toward town. She was angry with herself, and her eyes burned with tears. If anyone was aware of the consequences of mixing business and pleasure, it was her.

At the PR firm she'd worked for in Atlanta, she'd fallen for her boss's son. He'd pursued her for more than a year, and she'd finally given in. After a year of dating, he'd asked her to marry him.

She'd accepted Melvin Donaldson's proposal and blown a mint on that Marchesa gown for their engagement party. But the week before the party, she'd walked into his office and discovered him seated at his desk, his pants unzipped and his secretary on her knees in front of him.

Quinn had dumped the lying, cheating bastard and tried to focus on doing the job she loved. Rather than being ashamed of his own behavior, he'd insisted she was making a big deal over nothing. That his encounter with his secretary hadn't meant that he didn't love her. He'd just been stressed and blowing off steam. And he'd been furious that she'd "humiliated" him by calling off their engagement after the party invites had already gone out.

Once it had become clear she wouldn't go back to Melvin, her corporate nightmare began. After being named Employee of the Year two of the previous three years, suddenly Melvin and his father, Oscar Donaldson—the head of the firm—found fault with everything she did. One by one, she'd been taken off the larger, more prestigious accounts. Worse, the Donaldsons had maligned her character to clients who'd complained about her being removed from their accounts. Finally, they'd manufactured cause to fire her. Her only recourse had been to quietly resign.

Embarrassed by the whole ordeal, Quinn hadn't told her grandfather the real reason she'd left the firm. Nor had she admitted the full extent of what had happened to Cole. Only her college roommate, Naomi, knew the truth. She'd called her friend in tears the day she'd been forced to resign.

Naomi had wanted her to hire a lawyer, and her friend was prepared to trash the firm online. She'd even suggested

that Quinn talk to a reporter. Quinn decided she had suffered enough humiliation.

Even now, she hated herself for having been too much
of a coward to stand up for herself. But she had no desire to
become a poster girl for workplace romances gone wrong.
And if she was being honest, she blamed herself for going
against every instinct that had warned her not to get involved with Melvin.

She could still remember her father's words when she'd
told her parents she was dating the boss's son.

Never crap where you eat, sweetheart. It won't end well.

Boy, had her father been right.

Quinn pulled into the parking lot of Kayleigh's building. She walked down the street to Margot's Pizzeria and
ordered the personal-sized Hawaiian pizza Kayleigh and
Parker had recommended so highly. Then she returned to
the apartment with a piping-hot pizza in hand.

She'd agreed to let go of her anger over her and Max's
past and just move on. And that still stood. But she wouldn't
make the same mistake again. Especially not with a man
who'd already let her down in the past.

Max had quickly agreed to her terms. So why had his
easy and immediate acquiescence filled her with a deep
sadness she couldn't quite explain?

It didn't matter. She just needed to get over herself and
let go of the past. Her career and her grandfather's farm
depended on it.

Max spent another hour working in his office with Viv-
aldi's *Four Seasons* playing softly in the background after
Quinn left. He'd needed to switch from the mixtape of old-
school R & B that he'd been playing incessantly for the past
week. Nearly every one of those songs reminded him of
cherished moments with Quinn that summer.

Maybe it's better if we leave the past in the past.

Quinn's words replayed in his head, like an old vinyl record with a deep scratch.

He'd quickly agreed to her request because Quinn was right. Neither of them could afford the distraction of trying to safely navigate the land mines of their past.

So why did a little voice in his head and the knot in his gut call BS on his agreement to let go of the past and move on?

What right did he have to be crushed by Quinn's refusal to explore what their kiss had meant? After all, he'd been the one who'd initially rebuffed her.

Quinn's rejection was a karmic dish of justice served cold.

Yet, he couldn't help the deep ache in his chest. How could Quinn walk away from a second chance for them so easily when he couldn't stop thinking of and wanting her?

He'd been young and stupid. Mostly, he'd been over-whelmed by the intensity of his feelings for Quinn. In her he saw his future set in stone: marriage, a home, kids.

All of the things neither of them had been ready for.

He wasn't the man Quinn deserved then. Maybe he still wasn't, but he wanted to be everything she deserved and more.

All of the things that had frightened him back then— thoughts of marriage and family—still seemed overwhelming. Yet, he found himself wondering if he and Quinn would have had all of those things together if he hadn't broken up with her.

Max dragged a hand down his face and sighed. He'd made his choice back then; now he had to live with it. Despite his growing feelings for Quinn, he'd respect her wishes and keep their relationship strictly professional.

He now regretted his decision to have Quinn accompany him to the trade show in San Francisco.

This trip would put his resolve to the ultimate test.

Fourteen

Quinn sat across from Zora in a booth at the Magnolia Lake Café. She politely waited for the other shoe to drop.

She'd made it all the way to Friday without anyone mentioning the kiss that Zora had walked in on. But when Zora insisted on treating Quinn to lunch today, she knew it was only a matter of time before Max's sister brought it up.

Instead, Zora had shown her photos her best friend, Dallas, had sent from his trip to Sweden. And she'd revealed some of their plans for the family-style restaurant they would be opening across the street.

When Quinn had finally started to relax, Zora pushed aside her empty plate and folded her hands on the table. "So about you and Max…"

Quinn nearly choked on a forkful of chicken potpie. She gulped down some water.

"Sorry, I didn't mean to startle you." Zora looked genuinely concerned. "I just wanted to say that I appreciate how awkward it must be for you and Max to work together. I don't know what happened between you two in the past, but you obviously have feelings for each other."

Quinn poked at the flaky crust and tender chunks of chicken with her fork. She shrugged. "It was a really long time ago, Zora."

"Didn't seem so long ago." Zora could barely contain her grin.

Touché.

"It's a mistake neither of us intends to repeat."

"Or maybe you two have been given a second chance at this."

"I didn't come here to reignite an old flame. I'm working with Max, despite our past. This is a golden opportunity to expand the reach of both of our families' companies."

"No one thinks you came here for Max," Zora assured her. "But if my interruption the other day derailed whatever might be going on with you two, I apologize. I like you, Quinn. And I can see why Max does, too."

"That's kind of you, Zora, and I appreciate it. But I'm sorry to disappoint you. There isn't anything happening between me and Max. That kiss was a one-off. We just got caught up in the moment."

"I respect that." Zora nodded. "But I also realize that a big family like ours can be a lot to deal with. Admittedly, a few of us are a little extra." She raised her hand slowly, and they both laughed, easing the tension. "So if your feelings for Max ever do change, know that I'm rooting for you two." Zora smiled. "Now, unless you decide otherwise, we'll never speak of this again." Zora locked her lips with an imaginary key, then tossed it over her shoulder.

Quinn grinned. Zora was extra, but she couldn't help liking Max's nosy little sister. She was well-meaning and obviously loved her brothers.

"Zora, Quinn." Benji approached the table holding his daughter, Bailey.

Quinn had gotten to know Benji and his fiancée, Sloane, a little at the anniversary party and brunch. They were a sweet couple with adorable one-year-old twins.

"Hi, Zora." Sloane, carrying their son Beau on her hip, leaned down and hugged the other woman. "Hi, Quinn." She surveyed their empty plates. "I wish we'd arrived earlier. We could've eaten together. That is, if you two don't mind eating with two ravenous toddlers who get more food on their bellies than in them." Sloane tickled her son's stomach and the boy doubled over with laughter.

"That would've been fun." Quinn jiggled Bailey's little foot, clad in a sparkly pink ballerina flat that complemented her pink tutu dress. The toddler giggled, burying her face in her father's shoulder.

"We were about to leave, but we can watch the twins while you get your order. And you can have our table." Zora glanced around the packed eatery.

"Thanks." Sloane handed Beau to Zora. The little boy was mesmerized by her dangling earrings.

Benji handed Bailey off to Quinn, and he and Sloane promised to return as quickly as possible.

"The twins are adorable." Quinn tickled Bailey, and the little girl laughed.

Spending time with the twins and Savannah and Blake's son, Davis, made her wish she had nieces and nephews of her own to spoil.

"And they're the sweetest children," Zora said wistfully as she tapped a finger on Beau's nose. "They make me want children of my own."

"The kids all adore you, and you're so patient with them," Quinn said. "You'd be an incredible mom."

"Now, I just need to find the right guy…or not," Zora said with a mischievous grin. "As my gram always used to say, there's more than one way to get a pickle in the jar."

Quinn burst out laughing as she bounced Bailey on her knee. "Wait, are you considering going to a sperm bank?" Quinn covered Bailey's ears and mouthed the last two words.

"Why not?" Zora shrugged. "I want kids now. What if the right guy doesn't come along for another ten years? Or what if I'm not able to have kids anymore when and if he does?"

"You've given this a lot of thought, haven't you?" Quinn moved the salt and pepper shakers beyond Bailey's reach.

"I've been thinking about it for at least six months." Zora kissed the top of Beau's head. "I honestly don't know why I just told you that. Please don't say anything. My family will freak out. I'm prepared to handle the flak, if I decide to go that route. But there's no point in riling them up when I'm still undecided."

"It's not my place to say anything." Quinn smiled reassuringly. "So this stays between us."

"Thank you." Zora seemed relieved. She jingled her car keys, then gave them to Beau so he'd let go of her earring.

Quinn admired Zora's clarity about what she wanted. Max's sister was outspoken and unapologetically direct, but Quinn liked her. And she'd grown increasingly fond of Max and his family.

She smoothed back the little girl's curls, bound by a frilly headband dotted with fabric flowers.

What would her little girl look like? Quinn couldn't help smiling but shook off the thought.

Zora's baby fever was contagious.

"You two are officially relieved of babysitting duty." Benji rolled up highchairs for the twins and helped load the kids in them. "And Quinn, Sloane dropped your invitation to our wedding in the mail yesterday."

"That's generous of you, but I don't want to throw off your seating arrangement." Quinn hated that they'd felt obligated to invite her.

"We want you there," Sloane insisted with a warm smile.

Quinn graciously accepted, then she and Zora said their goodbyes.

On the ride back to the office, they discussed Quinn and Max's upcoming trip to San Francisco. But like a silent movie playing in the background, her kiss with Max played on a loop in Quinn's head.

Maybe she couldn't get her brain to cooperate, but she had full control of her other body parts. This time there would be no reminiscing and she'd keep her hands and lips to herself.

Fifteen

Max sat up and leaned against the headboard, reaching for his cell phone on the nightstand in his darkened San Francisco hotel room. He checked the time and groaned.

Not quite six and he'd gotten very little sleep, despite turning in early.

He and Quinn had arrived the previous afternoon. They'd checked in at the trade show, set up the King's Finest booth, attended a mixer for sponsors, then enjoyed a lovely meal together at the premium steakhouse in the hotel.

Despite their rough start and the unexpected kiss, they'd managed to get back on track. Their collaboration had gone smoothly for the past week. They were finally working in sync toward a common goal, which also served their individual agendas.

With their unique creative styles and different approaches to problem solving, they complemented each other well. Max was proud of the campaign they were building.

By all accounts, he should've slept like a baby.

Instead, he'd been restless, tossing and turning the entire night. Not because he was nervous about the trade show. He simply couldn't stop thinking of Quinn. Wanting her.

She'd looked beautiful in a simple tan suit yesterday. The slim pants were tapered at the ankle, highlighting her strappy, nude-colored, high-heel sandals. The crisp white shirt she wore beneath it provided the perfect contrast to her gleaming brown skin.

He couldn't help wondering if Quinn's hair, worn in glossy beach waves combed to one side, was as smooth and silky as it appeared. And he couldn't stop remembering how luscious her full lips had felt when he'd kissed them or how firm her plump bottom had been when it filled his palms.

The thing that had kept him awake the most was the question that constantly churned in his brain.

What would've happened if Zora hadn't interrupted them?

The only topic that had gotten more rotation in his Quinn-preoccupied brain over the past weeks was how different their lives might be now if they'd stayed together back then.

He and Quinn had agreed to stick to business, and they'd both kept their word. They'd fallen into a relaxed rhythm and gotten comfortable enough with each other to talk about their families and fill each other in on their pasts. They discussed pop culture and current events. They'd even become comfortable enough with each other to joke around a bit.

The easy, familiar relationship they were building wasn't unlike the relationships he'd established with his assistant Molly and other members of his team. Yet, it clearly wasn't the same. No matter how much he tried to convince himself otherwise.

Max groaned and placed his feet on the floor.

No use staring at the ceiling for another hour.

He might as well do something constructive with his time.

Their first meeting today was with a buyer for a nationwide restaurant management company—JRS. They were meeting with the rep before the trade show opened. Getting up this early gave Max a couple of hours to swim—a great way to calm his nerves and get his head on straight.

When he got to the pool downstairs, he tugged his shirt over his head and tossed it onto a lounge chair with his towels and his phone before stepping beneath the poolside shower. But before he could get into the pool, his phone alerted him to a text message.

He picked up the phone.

Quinn.

He obviously wasn't the only one up early this morning.

Can we go over the presentation before we meet with JRS?

He typed in his response: At the pool. About to swim laps. Meet you at the buffet for breakfast at eight?

Three little dots appeared, signaling that she was typing her response: Eight is perfect. Meet you there.

Max slid his phone beneath his T-shirt, put on his waterproof audio player and turned on his old-school hip-hop playlist. He stepped off the deck, plunging into the cool water. Kicking off the tiled wall, he went directly into swimming laps.

Hopefully, an hour of swimming would silence the disquieting chatter in his head and prepare him to spend the next ten hours with Quinn—pretending he didn't want more than just a business relationship with her.

Quinn walked out of the coffee shop on the first floor of the hotel after ending her call with the rep from JRS. He'd rescheduled their appointment. She immediately dialed Max's cell.

No answer.

Not surprising, given that he'd texted her to say he was at the pool swimming laps. The phone rang several times, then rolled over to voice mail. Quinn was about to leave a message when a sign indicating the direction of the pool caught her eye.

She ended the call without leaving a message.

She'd once heard Parker say he didn't believe in coincidences. Maybe he was onto something.

If she left Max a voice mail, he might not get it for another hour. Someone else might have booked the JRS rep's remaining time slots by then. And if they missed their opportunity today, they might not get another.

It had sounded like the rep was hungover and too tired to make their early meeting. The man was evidently a partier. They needed to pin him down before he was either booked or too buzzed for a productive meeting.

JRS was the big fish she'd come here to bag. It was an account King's Finest Distillery didn't already have, and it would be a real coup for her and Max if they could get their new brandy and KFD's other products into the long list of JRS-managed restaurants.

Rather than heading toward the bank of elevators and returning to her room, Quinn followed the signs that directed her to the pool where Max was swimming laps.

She was going to the pool because it would be quicker if she simply strolled down there and nailed down a time with Max. It definitely wasn't because she was hoping to see him emerging from the pool half-dressed.

God, what if he's wearing a Speedo?

She would *never* be able to unsee that.

Quinn followed the signs to a bank of elevators that provided access to the pool and workout room. Hopefully, Max's text about going swimming hadn't been cryptic code for *I hooked up with some chick at the bar last night and I'm busy.*

A knot tightened in her stomach. It pained her to think of Max with someone else. But what right did she have to be jealous?

Quinn shook the thought from her head as she exited the elevator and made her way toward the wall of windows, cloudy with condensation.

She used her key card to enter the pool area. Only a few people were there. A hotel employee who was restocking towels greeted her warmly. There were two lap swimmers; one of them was Max.

Perfect.

Now she wouldn't have to traipse all over the hotel hunting him down in five-inch heels. She'd worn her open-toe Jimmy Choo platform sandals again today partly because they complemented her tan-and-black blazer and black knee-length skirt so well. Partly because Max hadn't been able to take his eyes off them yesterday.

Quinn stood motionless and watched him swim freestyle from her vantage point on the pool deck. She would've been content to sit there with a peachtini and watch him for hours. However, she needed to focus on her reason for coming here, and it wasn't to gawk at Max Abbott.

She walked over to the shallow end and waved to get his attention.

"Quinn?" Max didn't look happy about her intrusion as he tugged the red-and-black waterproof headphones from his ears.

He stood, rising above the shallow water that came up to his hips, and wiped the water from his eyes. Her gaze was drawn to the tattoos on his muscular chest.

Those were new. He hadn't had any ink on his brown skin that summer. She remembered their conversation about it like it was yesterday.

They'd been lying on an old blanket in the middle of a field, staring up at the stars that dotted the darkened sky.

She'd sat up suddenly and turned to him. "When I'm in a serious relationship and I *know* he's the one… I want to get matching tattoos. Maybe instead of rings." She'd only been half-joking.

At the time they'd kissed, had even made out a little, but they hadn't slept together or committed to each other in any way.

Max had chuckled, turned over on his side and traced a finger up her thigh, exposed by her tiny frayed jean shorts. "What tattoo would you get?"

Quinn had thought for a moment, then the perfect idea popped in her head. "I'd get a few lines from one of my favorite poems in a really pretty font."

"Wouldn't it be more significant if the poem was meaningful to the other person?" he'd asked.

She remembered so clearly how something about his answer had warmed her chest. In that moment, she'd truly believed Max Abbott was *the one*. That they'd forever be friends and eventually lovers.

She'd been wrong.

At eighteen, Quinn had been a dreamy teenager with a ridiculous crush while Max had been a man, three years her senior. Only a year away from joining his family's company.

"Quinn, what are you doing here?" Max's question brought her back to the present with all the ease of falling off a soft, dreamy cloud and crashing to the hard, dry earth.

Well, it's good to see you, too, Boo.

Max's chilly reception was a punch to the gut after she'd gotten lost in such a sweet memory. Quinn forced a smile, as if she was completely unfazed by his sour expression and brusque response.

"Martin, the JRS rep, canceled our scheduled meeting this morning. I'm pretty sure he was hungover from last night."

"Okay?" Max folded his arms over his chest, accentuating his toned pecs and triceps. The move prompted her to peer more closely at the tattoo on the left side of his chest that he seemed to be intent on shielding from her.

"We need to reschedule the meeting, hopefully for later today. Marty gave us a few options. I wanted to see which time works best for you so I can get back to him as soon as possible, before someone else books our spot." She spoke quickly, the words tripping from her tongue so she could quickly let him return to his moment of peace. Still she couldn't take her eyes off the black ink etched into his brown skin.

Her eyes widened suddenly, and she sucked in a quiet breath. A chill ran the length of her spine. Quinn pressed her fingertips to her lips, her hand trembling.

She didn't consider herself vain or self-absorbed. And maybe she was making a self-aggrandizing assumption, but...

"Whatever time you pick is fine," he said gruffly. "Just tell me when and where."

"Let's take the one-o'clock spot. We can treat him to a pricey lunch before the show officially kicks off at three," she said absently. "Can I ask you something, Max?"

"Sure." There was apprehension in his voice, as if he anticipated her question. "Give me a sec."

Max climbed out of the pool, then asked the attendant for a couple of towels. He dried himself off before draping the towels over his shoulders. But she'd already seen the tattoos.

The letters QB were tattooed over his heart. Beneath that were a few lines of a poem she'd been obsessed with that summer: Robert Frost's "Stopping by Woods on a Snowy Evening."

The woods are lovely, dark and deep,
But I have promises to keep,
And miles to go before I sleep,
And miles to go before I sleep.

The lines of poetry were bordered by a rendering of woods in black ink.

"Is that…" She pointed at the tattoos. "Did you—"

"Yes." His voice was low.

There was only the sound of little splashes of water as the other swimmer continued his laps. Quinn stared up at Max, waiting for further explanation.

He offered none.

She pressed her fingers to her mouth, ruining her carefully applied lip gloss.

"How long have you had these?" she finally asked.

"Since a few months after we broke up."

Her gaze snapped up to his. She scowled.

"*We* didn't break up. You *dumped* me." She pointed at each of them in turn, underscoring her words. "With no real explanation, no discussion. So I'm having a really hard time understanding—"

"Maybe we should talk over there." Max turned and walked toward the lounge chairs at the far end of the pool.

Quinn followed him and stood with one hip cocked and her arms folded. "Why?" she asked impatiently. "Why would you have my initials and a quote from my favorite poem carved into your body *after* you dumped me? Who does that?" Her voice was unsteady and louder than she'd intended.

"I can only imagine all of the things that must be going through your head right now." He pulled on a white King's Finest T-shirt. "We can talk about this as much as you'd like but preferably not here." He glanced in the direction of the man in the pool and the attendant. Both seemed to be paying close attention to them now.

Quinn lowered her voice but ignored his request to take the conversation elsewhere. "I just need to know why you'd do this *after* it was over. In all these years, you never once tried to contact me."

"That isn't true." There was a pained expression on his face. He sighed and shook his head. "Not that it matters now."

"Of course, it matters. At least, it matters to me. So tell me… When was it that you reached out to me? Because I haven't received so much as a text message from you."

"That's because you changed your phone number." He folded his arms. "Couldn't have been more than a month afterward."

Quinn stood frozen, her heart beating harder.

She'd gotten a new phone a few weeks after Max had broken up with her. She'd decided to remove any temptation to call him and any anxiety about whether or not he'd call her. So she'd requested a new number and made a point of not transferring Max's contact info to her new phone.

But he would only know how quickly she'd changed her number if he'd tried to call her not long afterward.

"Our grandfathers have been best buddies since before either of us was born." She folded her arms defiantly, proud of her comeback. "If you'd really wanted to contact me, you would've found a way to do it."

"We managed to keep our relationship under the radar that summer," he said. "But how long do you think that would've lasted if I'd rung up your grandparents and asked for your new phone number?" Max raked his fingers through his damp hair and sighed. "You didn't want anyone to know about us, and I agreed. The last thing I was going to do was tip off your shotgun-toting grandfather that I'd spent the summer eating at his dinner table and secretly banging his granddaughter."

Now Quinn glanced around to see if anyone else could hear their conversation.

"You knew where I went to school. You could've written to me there."

"Do you *really* not know?" Max narrowed his gaze and stepped in closer.

"Do I really not know *what*? That my ex tagged his chest with my initials and favorite poem *after* he decided he wasn't that into me after all?"

"I *never* said I wasn't into you. If anything, I was too into you and it scared the shit out of me." He huffed. "I loved you, Quinn. But it felt like too much too soon. We were so young." Max rubbed the scruff on his chin. "I panicked and backed away. Within a month I realized I'd made a huge mistake. I tried to call you, but you'd changed your number. I couldn't go to your grandfather without breaking my promise to you. So I decided to go see you in person. I realized how royally I'd fucked up. I needed some grand gesture to prove to you how much I loved you and wanted you back."

He sighed heavily, as if reluctant to continue.

"I remembered what you said about the tattoos. That it was what you'd do once you were sure you'd found the person you wanted to be with for the rest of your life. So that's what I did. Then I hopped into my truck and drove all the way from my campus in Florida to yours in Virginia."

"Then why didn't I see you?" Quinn asked.

"I went to your dorm room and your roommate answered."

"My roommate?" She poked a thumb to her chest. "You must've gone to the wrong room. If you'd come to our dorm room, my roommate—"

"Nora… Natalie…" He frowned, trying to recall the name.

"Naomi." Quinn's heart plummeted to her stomach, then thumped so loudly that the sound filled her ears. Her chest felt heavy, like a tombstone lay on it.

The one she was going to erect after she murdered her college roommate.

"Naomi, right." Max snapped his fingers. "That was her name. Strawberry blonde with grayish blue eyes, about yay high." He leveled his hand just below the earphones hanging around his neck.

Quinn felt dizzy. Her head throbbed and her mouth was dry. "You met Naomi?"

"Fierce little thing." He chuckled bitterly. "Part pretty little coed, part pit bull, and a thousand percent protective of you."

Quinn couldn't have described Naomi better herself.

"She obviously knew exactly who I was and that you never wanted to see or hear from me again. Naomi hated my guts and she had no qualms about telling me *exactly* what she thought of me."

Max had definitely met her friend. She could only imagine how the encounter had gone. Quinn understood why Naomi would've hated Max. But why hadn't her friend told her that Max had driven up from Florida to see her?

"What did Naomi say?"

"I believe her exact words were, 'Fuck off, you fucking fucker, and leave my friend alone. She's finally happy again now and the last thing she needs is for you to pop 'round and fuck with her head, again.'" He said the words in a feigned British accent reminiscent of her friend's.

Naomi always did enjoy a good f-bomb.

"You'd gone to all the trouble of getting my initials tattooed on your skin and you let a five-foot-three-inch sprite run you off." Quinn folded her arms and tipped her chin defiantly.

"No." He sounded incredibly sad. "I told her I needed to hear it from you. That if you told me you didn't want to see me again, I'd walk away and never bother you again."

"And?"

He gathered his things from the lounge chair and shoved

his cell phone into the pocket of his swim trunks. Then he turned to her and sighed.

"Naomi said you were out doing some other guy, and that she didn't expect that you'd be back anytime soon."

"And you believed her?"

Quinn hadn't dated anyone seriously for more than a year and a half after Max. But Quinn could easily imagine her roommate telling him such a lie to bruise his ego. Her overprotective friend would've tried to cut Max deep with her words after spending the previous two months nursing Quinn's broken heart and trying to cheer her up.

At the end of the two months, Quinn had promised herself and her friend that she wouldn't waste another moment of her life mooning over Max Abbott. That she never wanted to hear from or see Max again.

Naomi, evidently, hadn't trusted that Quinn would stick to her resolution when presented with the chance to see Max again. Instead, she'd made the decision for her. Quinn and Naomi had remained best friends, though Quinn had gotten a job in Atlanta and Naomi was now a married mother of two running her own kiddie clothing business in California. In all the years since college, her friend had never once revealed that Max had come to campus to see her.

"No, I didn't believe her." Max rubbed the back of his neck. "I hung around, parked outside of your dorm. If you didn't want to see me again, I would've respected that. But I wanted to hear it from you."

"So why didn't you ask me?"

"I saw the guy bring you home, and I saw him kiss you. I realized Naomi was right. You'd moved on, and you deserved better." Max's mouth twisted and deep wrinkles spanned his forehead.

Quinn thought back to that time in her life. She hadn't been seeing anyone. Maybe Max had mistaken someone else for her. She was about to tell him as much when she remembered the one guy who had kissed her around that time—Naomi's cousin, Rick. The guy her roommate had tried desperately to hook her up with. That explained why Naomi hadn't told her about Max's visit.

She didn't owe Max an explanation, but she had some choice words for her friend.

"Getting those tattoos before you knew if we'd get back together… That was—"

"Dumb?" he volunteered.

"I was going to say risky as hell," Quinn said. "You had no idea how I'd react or if I had, in fact, moved on."

"I realized what a gamble my grand gesture was." He patted his chest where her initials were carved into his skin. "That there was a good chance you still wouldn't forgive me. But I needed to show you how much you meant to me. And even if we never got back together, I guess I wanted to hold on to you in some small way." He rubbed at the tattoo through his shirt.

Quinn frowned, tears burning her eyes. She turned away from Max, abruptly changing the subject. "I should go make sure everything is ready."

"I'll walk you to the elevator." Max gestured toward the door.

Quinn nodded and went with him.

"How did you explain the tattoos to your friends and your family?" she asked after they had stepped into the elevator.

"I'd had them for a few years by the time anyone in my family saw them." Max punched each of their floor numbers. "I played the backup quarterback position for my school's football team. They assumed that was what the QB stood for, and I didn't correct them. As for the poem… Turns out I'm a fan of Robert Frost's poetry, too. More people have those words inked on them than you probably think."

"The way you ended things between us so abruptly without explanation… It seemed like what we'd shared never really meant anything to you. That I meant nothing to you. But—"

"You meant *everything* to me, Quinn." Max swallowed hard, his Adam's apple bobbing. "And it terrified me. I'm sorry I was a dick about it. I should've just been honest with you about how I was feeling, but—"

Quinn planted a hand on Max's chest, lifted onto her toes and pressed her lips to his—salty from the pool. She slipped her hands beneath the damp T-shirt and glided them up the strong muscles of his back.

Max backed her against the elevator wall, his tongue eagerly seeking hers. His hands glided down her body, gripping her bottom and hauling her against him. She could feel him hard against her belly.

The robotic voice alerted them that they were approaching their first stop—Max's floor.

He pulled his mouth from hers, both of them breathless as his dark gaze drank her in. Her mouth curved in a half smile.

She sank her teeth into her lower lip as she dragged her manicured nails over his skin. "Invite me to your room, Max," she breathed.

His eyes danced with excitement momentarily. Then he frowned and heaved a sigh.

"I think you know how much I'd like to take you up on your offer, Quinn." He twirled a strand of her hair around his finger, focusing on it rather than her eyes. "But I don't want you to regret this the way you regretted that kiss in my office. You were adamant about it never happening again."

Shit. She *had* said that, and at the time she'd meant it.

"That was before I knew the whole story." She pressed a palm to where her initials were inscribed on his skin.

The elevator jerked to a stop and the doors slid open, accompanied by the announcement of the floor number.

"I would *love* for you to come to my room, Quinn," he whispered, pressing a fleeting kiss to her lips. "But I never want to see the pain and disappointment in your eyes that I saw there after Zora interrupted us. I hurt you before. I won't do it again. So think about it. Make sure this is what you want. I'm in room 1709."

Max gave her another quick kiss and exited the elevator.

Quinn squeezed her eyes shut, her heart racing and her head still spinning from Max's kiss as the elevator continued its ascent to the twenty-fourth floor. She'd never been more confused about what she wanted than she was right now.

Her heart and body wanted to be with Max. But her brain reminded her that he'd let her down before and warned her that, if given the chance, he'd let her down again.

Sixteen

Max held the razor beneath the running water, then tapped the handle on the side of the sink before returning it to its carrying case. He preferred the look of a five-o'clock shadow, but he'd decided to shave this morning.

There was a knock at his hotel room door. *Good.* After his shower, he'd requested additional towels. He was barefoot and wearing only a pair of pants slung low on his hips. Max pulled on a short-sleeve shirt, quickly buttoned it and opened the door.

"You asked for fresh towels?" Quinn held up the stack of towels as if it was a silver platter. Her sensual mouth curved with an impish smirk that brought out her dimples. She broke into laughter. "Don't worry. I tipped the housekeeper. Is it okay if I come in?"

"Of course, thanks." He accepted the towels from her and stepped aside to let her in, still a bit stunned she was there.

It'd been nearly an hour since he'd left Quinn in that elevator. As much as he'd hoped she'd come to his room, he'd assumed that she'd renewed her resolve not to get romantically involved. He'd even tried to convince himself that it was for the best. But now he hoped like hell that she'd changed her mind. Still, he wouldn't presume that was why she was here.

Max put the towels away. "What's up?"

"I contacted Marty. He's good with meeting us for lunch

at one. He wants to go to the seafood place downstairs. You're not allergic, are you?"

"No." He gestured for her to have a seat in the living room. "The seafood restaurant at one is fine."

Quinn sat in the chair and he sat on the end of the couch nearest her. Neither of them spoke right away.

"It was nice of you to deliver the message," he said. "But you know you could've just called me or sent a text, right?"

Quinn nibbled on her lower lip, looking like a kid who'd gotten busted with a hand in the cookie jar. "I suppose that's true."

"So why'd you really come down here, Quinn?" He wanted to be clear about his intentions. And he needed her to be clear about hers, too.

Quinn set her purse on the small table beside the sofa and stood in front of him. She stripped off her jacket and dropped it on the chair she'd vacated. Her beaded nipples poked through the thin fabric of her camisole.

She slid her skirt up just enough to allow her to straddle him. Her knees dug into the sofa on either side of his hips.

"There is one other reason I wanted to see you." She captured his mouth with a soft, teasing kiss.

"I'm trying *really* hard to respect the boundaries you established, Quinn." His voice was a tortured whisper, which she seemed to relish. Like it fed the ravenous, seductive beast inside her. Something he remembered all too well. "You aren't making this very easy for me."

"Maybe I've changed my mind," she whispered between kisses to his jaw that sent blood rushing below his belt.

Quinn hadn't done anything like this since the summer she'd worn Max down, convincing him to give in to the attraction between them. Mostly because she'd won the battle yet lost the war. In the end, once she'd fallen for Max—heart and soul—he'd walked away.

Just as her mother had warned her.

Men only want fast girls for one reason. They have no intention of ever taking them home to their mothers.

Now here she was, the pull of Max Abbott so strong that she was ignoring her mother's advice again. She'd spent more than a decade being the "good girl." Being pursued rather than going after what she wanted. And what had it gotten her?

She'd ended up alone. Without a job. Her reputation tarnished.

This time she'd get what she wanted: sex with no strings attached. Then they could both just walk away.

"*Maybe* won't cut it, baby." Max held her chin between his finger and thumb, forcing her to meet his gaze. "You need to be sure."

Quinn's heart thudded in her chest as she grabbed her purse from the side table. She stuck a trembling hand inside and produced a small, overpriced box of condoms. "I went to the drugstore and got these." She waved them. "So yes, I'm sure."

Her cheeks and face flamed with heat. She'd never felt more vulnerable.

What if he says no?

The few seconds of silence that elapsed as he studied the box in her hand with furrowed brows were agonizing. Quinn swallowed hard, her pulse racing.

She was about to tell Max that she'd temporarily lost her mind, and he should disregard everything she'd said and done that morning. But then Max slid his arms around her and squeezed her bottom, pulling their bodies closer. His hardened length against her sensitive flesh sent a shiver of pleasure up her spine.

Max pressed his open mouth to hers, his tongue seeking hers in a kiss that was hungry and impatient. Heat spread throughout her body, emanating from every place he touched her—even through their clothing.

He tightened his embrace, his large hands on her back, crushing her breasts and sensitive nipples against his hard chest. She moved her hips, moaning into his mouth at the intense pleasure as she dragged her sensitive clit along the outline of his hardened shaft through the thin material of their clothes.

Max gently bit her lower lip before going in for a deeper kiss.

Her skin tingled, as if tiny licks of fire scampered across her flesh. Max Abbott was an excellent kisser. But now, just as then, he seemed hesitant to take things to the next level.

She'd come this far. *No turning back now.*

Quinn tugged up Max's shirt and skimmed her hands over the dusting of hair on his belly. As they continued the kiss, she slowly unbuttoned his shirt, starting from the bottom. Then she slid it from his shoulders, revealing the tattoos.

She broke their kiss, allowing herself the luxury of admiring the artwork. She traced the letters with her fingertip, applying only the lightest pressure.

QB. Her initials. Followed by her favorite lines from the poem she'd read to him that summer. Both tattoos had been there nearly the entire time they'd been apart.

Quinn pressed a soft kiss to those letters, brushing her lips over the words of poetry inked on his skin. Then she flicked his nipple with her tongue. He sucked in a deep breath, his muscles tensing.

Max speared his fingers into her hair, dragging her mouth to his again. Slipping his hands beneath the hem of the camisole, he tugged it over her head, then dropped it onto the floor. He fumbled with the clasp of her bra, releasing it and gliding it off her arms.

"Fuck," he muttered softly. His appreciative gaze trailed down her exposed torso, and her belly tightened in response.

She gasped in surprise when Max suddenly flipped her onto her back on the sofa and slid down her body. Taking one of the already ultra-sensitive nubs into his warm mouth, he grazed it with his teeth.

Quinn murmured softly in response to the sensation— part pleasure, part pain. She dug her fingers into his soft curls, gripping his hair as she arched her back in a greedy plea for more.

Max's mouth curved in a sensuous smile as his hooded gaze met hers. He shifted his attention to her other nipple, licking and teasing it with his tongue. Pleasure radiated throughout her body, her sex pulsing. Aching for his touch.

Gliding his hand down her side and beneath the short, black skirt, Max cupped the damp space between her thighs. He tugged aside the fabric, plunging a finger inside her as his thumb caressed the slick, hypersensitive bundle of nerves.

She trembled, unable to hold back quiet moans as he circled her clit with his thumb. Max slipped another finger inside her as he continued to lick and suck her sensitive nipple.

The symphony of varying sensations sent Quinn floating higher and higher, the intensity building until she'd reached a crescendo. She cried out in intense pleasure, her body shuddering and spent, yet craving more.

Her chest heaved with rapid, shallow breaths that left her slightly lightheaded.

Max trailed kisses up her chest and neck. Kissed the side of her face. Finally, he pressed a lingering kiss to her mouth. He stood, retrieving the box of condoms. His gaze held hers as he extended his open palm.

"Are you still with me, Quinn?"

Maybe this was a really terrible idea, but being with Max felt amazing. And maybe she shouldn't, but she trusted Max to be discreet.

Standing on unsteady legs, Quinn nodded and placed her hand in his, following him to his bed.

Seventeen

Max hadn't yet mastered the fine art of resisting Quinn. Not when she'd been a smoking-hot college-bound freshman who had her sights set on him. Not now that she was a mature, incredibly beautiful woman who knew exactly what she wanted in the boardroom and was willing to go to the mat for it.

Then again, maybe his inability to resist her was because he wanted the same thing she wanted: to have her in his bed. Which was where she now lay.

He joined her in the bed and kissed her, relishing the sweet taste of her mouth and the feel of her soft lips. The glide of her tongue against his. Their kiss was feverish and hungry. Reminiscent of the desperate need they'd both felt that first time…so long ago.

Max was already on the edge, having watched her fall apart in his arms. He'd always loved the sweet little sounds she made, indicating that she was close or that she wanted more.

What was it about Quinn that had always made him feel a complete loss of control?

He glided his hands along the soft, smooth skin of her back. Inhaled her divine citrus scent and the smell of coconut wafting from her dark hair. Her quiet moans as they kissed ignited a raging fire inside him.

"You are so fucking sexy," he muttered against her lips.

Max trailed kisses down her jaw, down her neck, through the valley between the glorious mounds of her full breasts, then down her belly. His gaze locked with hers. "I haven't stopped thinking about you since the day you waltzed this perfect ass into our conference room."

"Same." A wide smile lit Quinn's brown eyes as she slid her fingers into his hair. There was something so intimate about the gesture. "By the way, the look on your face that day—priceless."

"I'll bet." He pressed another kiss to her stomach as he glided the zipper down the side of the black skirt that had been tempting him all morning. Quinn lifted her hips, helping him slide the garment off. He took a moment to admire the gorgeous brown skin of her full hips and curvy thighs.

Quinn's belly rose and fell with shallow breaths as he laid kisses just above the waistband of her black panties. She gasped softly when he tugged the material down just enough to plant soft kisses on her hip bone.

The scent of her arousal teased him. Made his dick hard as steel. He was desperate to finally be inside her. Yet he wanted to savor every moment with her.

Max dragged the damp fabric down her hips and off her legs. He spread her open with his thumbs and pressed a kiss to the glistening pink flesh between her thighs. He reveled in the salty sweet taste of her desire as his tongue traced the pink slit and lapped at the sensitive, swollen flesh.

Quinn shuddered. In a silent plea for more, she angled her hips, permitting him better access.

Max gladly obliged. He licked and teased her sex, then sucked on the distended bundle of nerves until she cried out. Her legs trembled and the space between her thighs pulsed.

He'd imagined this since the day she'd walked through the door of that conference room and set his world on fire, reminding him of all the things he'd tried so damn hard to forget. That he'd had the most amazing woman in his life, and he'd walked away from her because he'd been a coward. Terrified that one or both of them would regret committing to each other at such a young age. But the only thing he'd ever really regretted was letting Quinn go.

Max stripped off his remaining clothes and tore into the box of condoms, quickly ripping one from its foil packet and rolling it up his shaft. He teased her, pressing the head to her entrance before slowly pushing inside her warm, tight sheath.

He groaned at the searing pleasure of her flesh enveloping his, then slowly glided inside her until he was fully seated.

"God, Quinn, you feel so amazing," he growled, his voice so gruff he barely recognized it.

He leaned down and captured her open mouth in a kiss. Quinn dug her fingers into his back, her hips lifting to meet each stroke. He swallowed her soft murmurs as he moved inside her until she cried out with pleasure again. Until he followed her over the edge.

Max collapsed onto his back beside Quinn, both of them breathing heavily. An awkward silence descended over the room momentarily. When his breathing evened out again, Max rolled onto his side and planted a soft kiss on her lips. He sifted his fingers through her glossy strands of hair.

"No regrets?" It would kill him inside if Quinn regretted, even for a moment, what they'd just shared.

"None." A shy smile animated Quinn's dimples. She grazed the letters on his chest with her thumb and kissed him again.

Max discarded the condom, then crawled into bed. He cradled Quinn in his arms, with her bottom nestled against him, and kissed the shell of her ear. He'd be content to lie with this woman in his arms and not leave this room for the next three days. Until he'd convinced her that this time, things would be different. That he'd never hurt her again.

* * *

Max blinked, looking up at the brown-skinned goddess calling his name.

Quinn, who was fully dressed, shoved his shoulder again. "Max, you have to get up. We're scheduled to meet Marty in forty-five minutes and I still have to go to my room to shower and change." She put on an earring, which he vaguely remembered her losing at some point when they'd made love again.

"Wait...we're still planning on meeting the JRS guy for lunch?" He rubbed an eye as he propped himself up on his elbows. "I thought we were gonna spend a few more hours in bed." He tugged at the hem of her skirt.

She slapped his hand playfully. "There will be plenty of time for that later. Right now, I need to ensure that you're awake and that you'll be there on time. Remember, JRS is the white whale we came here for. Everything else is gravy."

"To be fair, he canceled on us first." Max dragged himself to a seated position, back pressed against the headboard.

"Max." Quinn used the same warning tone his mother had when he was a kid.

"Fine. But shouldn't we at least... I don't know." He rubbed the sleep from his eyes again. "Shouldn't we at least talk about what happened before you run off."

"It's a little late for a conversation about the birds and the bees." She dragged her fingers through her hair.

"I'm not talking about that and you know it."

"Then we're fine. I'm not a virgin this time."

"Which, to be fair, I had no idea about before the fact," he reminded her.

"I know." She smiled. "I'm just saying that while I have no regrets about what happened here, I also have no delusions that this is about anything more than sex for you... for us."

Wait...what?

Had he given her the impression that sex was all he wanted? Or was she making it clear that's all she wanted from him?

Either way, if that's the way you want to play this, sweetheart, fine.

"Good talk, Quinn."

"Look, this was fun, Max. No..." She shook her head, then gazed up dreamily. "This was...intense, and you were amazing. It took me back to that summer when everything between us felt so perfect. Everything was great until I tried to make it more than it was."

"And what was it, Quinn?" It was a sincere question. Because he knew what it had been for him: the best damn summer of his life—until he'd screwed up and lost the perfect girl.

"A summer fling. That's what it was then, and that's what this is now. Two old flames feeling a little nostalgic and reliving the past," she said. "But this time, we keep things simple and be honest with each other about where this is going. That way, no one gets caught up in their feelings or has any false expectations."

She leaned down and kissed him. "You still with me, Max?" She smirked.

Damn. She was using his line on him. But if this was the only way to keep Quinn in his life—in his bed—then he'd accept her terms. *For now.*

"Okay, Quinn." Max sighed. "What are the rules of engagement?"

Quinn sat on the edge of the bed and crossed her legs. She propped her chin on her fist, her foot bouncing, as she contemplated his question.

"The first rule of a secret summer fling is we don't talk

about our secret summer fling—to anyone. Second, we only see each other on our business trips. Third, no overnights. We end the night in our own beds. Fourth, when we complete this project, we walk away. We both get closure and there are no hard feelings."

"Sounds like you've given this a lot of thought." He sifted a few strands of her hair through his fingers. "But things are never quite that simple. What happens if one of us doesn't want to walk away?" he asked.

She frowned, her nose crinkling. "We cross that bridge if we come to it," she said. "But there should be no expectations of anything beyond what I've outlined. Deal?"

"Deal," Max agreed. "But after the trade show today…"

She pressed a lingering kiss to his mouth and smiled. "Meet you back here then."

Max watched as she sashayed from his bedroom and into the main space where she retrieved her purse, then left his suite.

Heaving a sigh, Max got out of bed and hopped in the shower again.

He would play by Quinn's rules. But he looked forward to getting her to break each and every one of them. Because this time he had no intention of walking away so easily from the woman whose initials were branded on his skin.

Eighteen

Quinn sat cross-legged on the sofa in Kayleigh's rental apartment, exhausted after the conference in San Francisco. She hadn't realized how much walking was involved when attending a trade show. Then there were the early-morning meetings and the late nights spent in either her or Max's hotel room.

She and Max had spent nearly every waking hour together. When they weren't working, they'd shared meals, watched movies and spent lots of time discovering new ways to bring each other pleasure. All of it—except for a few meals—had taken place in private. The only thing they hadn't done together was sleep. At the end of the night, she either returned to her room or sent him, begrudgingly, back to his.

Quinn couldn't help smiling as she hugged her knees to her chest. Her week with Max had been incredible.

They'd bagged the deal with JRS and gotten preorders from a slew of other clients, both current and new King's Finest buyers. The trip had been an all-around success.

So why was the time she'd spent with Max the thing she remembered most fondly? Quinn tried not to think too deeply about the reasons. *Why* didn't matter. Her stay in Magnolia Lake was temporary. She wasn't looking for a serious relationship and neither was he.

Her cell phone rang, and she couldn't help hoping it was Max.

She checked the caller ID.

Wrong brother.

"Hey, Cole. What's up?"

"Hey, Q. I know this is really, *really* last-minute…"

"I already don't like where this is going." She put Cole on speakerphone and went to the kitchen to make a snack. "Spit it out, Abbott. What do you need?"

She opened the fridge and took out fruit and cheese.

"I need you to be my plus-one, again," Cole said.

"For Benji and Sloane's wedding this weekend?"

"Yes. Say yes, *please*," he said. "I have three women dropping hints about being my date for this thing. I honestly just want to go, celebrate with my family and have fun."

Quinn put the fruit in a colander and rinsed it, then set it on the counter. "I'm surprised you want a date. I thought wedding receptions were a player's playground."

"I resent the term *player*. I'm up-front with every woman I've ever been with about not wanting anything serious. Plus, weddings might be great for hookups, but they also get women thinking about their own weddings. Like I said, I don't ever lead anyone on. So you'd be doing me a favor. We go as friends. I can enjoy the evening without anyone thinking that I'm going home with them or, worse, that I'd be their best bet for a wedding of their own."

"You're kind of a drama king. Anyone ever tell you that, Cole?" She sliced the apple.

"Only because I'm misunderstood." She could hear the grin in his voice. "Speaking of misunderstandings and drama… Us going to this thing together won't create any static between you and Max, right?"

The knife slipped and she cut herself. Blood oozed from her fingertip and dripped onto the cutting board.

"Shit."

There was a knot in the pit of her stomach.

The first rule of a secret summer fling is we don't talk about our secret summer fling—to anyone.

Had Max broken rule number one already? No, he wouldn't have talked to Cole about them. Had Zora broken her promise and told Cole about the kiss she'd seen? Or was Cole just fishing?

Relax.

"What's wrong?" Cole's voice was laced with concern.

"The knives here in Kayleigh's rental are surprisingly sharp. I sliced my finger." Quinn turned on the water and rinsed the cut beneath the faucet until the bleeding stopped. She cleared her throat. "Why would Max care about me going to Benji's wedding with you?"

Cole didn't respond right away.

"That was the vibe I got between you two at my parents' anniversary party," he said. "Max was... I guess the best word for it would be *territorial.*"

Quinn breathed out a quiet sigh of relief.

They had agreed to keep things casual and not tell anyone. So going to Benji and Sloane's wedding with Max wasn't an option. No doubt, that was why he hadn't asked her to go with him, even though he knew Sloane had invited her.

Besides, Max knew that she and Cole were nothing more than friends.

"Max will be fine," she said. "The real dilemma is what am I going to wear?" Maybe Kayleigh had something in the shop downstairs that would work. "Never mind, I'll figure it out."

"So you'll come?" There was a lilt in Cole's voice whenever he convinced her to do something out of her comfort zone.

"I obviously have zero compunction about crashing your

family's events, so why not?" She shrugged. "This time, I've actually been invited."

She glanced at the open but unanswered invite to Benji and Sloane's wedding on the counter.

"Awesome. That's the good news," he said. "The bad news is we're ahead of schedule on the restaurant project. Construction begins within the next two weeks. Which means—"

"Kayleigh and I both need to be out by then." Quinn sighed.

It looked like she'd be back to making that long daily commute again in a couple of weeks.

She made arrangements to meet Cole at the event on Saturday. He was in the wedding party, so even though she'd be his plus-one, she wouldn't see him until well into the reception.

Hanging out with Cole would be fun, and it would give her an excuse to see Max despite the rule she'd established about not seeing each other while they were in town. The truth was that she missed spending time with him. And she hated seeing Max around the office but pretending there was nothing between them.

Quinn picked up her phone again and typed a text message.

Hey, Max. Just an FYI. Cole asked me to be his plus-one at Sloane and Benji's wedding.

Three little dots showed up on the phone almost immediately. But after five minutes, there was still no message. Quinn put down the phone and went back to preparing her snack.

An hour later Max's single-word response came through.

Okay.

That was all he had to say?

But what exactly did she expect Max to say?

Don't go with my brother. Come with me instead.

Maybe he would've, if she hadn't insisted that they keep the relationship secret and not see each other in town.

You can't have it both ways, babe.

Quinn cursed to herself, grabbed her phone and wallet, and headed down to Kayleigh's shop.

Max watched as Benji and Sloane greeted some of their guests. He couldn't be happier for his cousin and his new bride.

Sloane was beautiful in a simple, strapless, ivory wedding gown. Her short pixie haircut was adorned with a crown made of fresh flowers.

Benji was a tech billionaire who could've easily afforded a huge, lavish destination wedding. But he and Sloane would've been content to get married by the justice of the peace.

Benji and Sloane considered the wedding to be the public formalization of what they already were: a family. The small, elegant ceremony and reception were simply concessions to their families. After their honeymoon, Benji, Sloane and the twins would spend a year in Japan. So it was the last time their entire extended family would be together until Parker and Kayleigh's wedding—scheduled for soon after Benji and Sloane's return.

Max had tried to stay in the moment, celebrating with his family. But he'd been distracted the instant Quinn walked in the door. She was stunning in a pale pink, backless dress with a beaded top. The ethereal, knee-length overlay made it seem as if Quinn floated around the room.

Still soaring after the incredible time they'd had together in San Francisco, Max was completely taken with her.

He could get accustomed to spending time with Quinn.

She was brilliant at her job, and people loved her. She was affable yet persuasive. Fun to be around, and she had the best laugh. And though she was generally thoughtful and careful, there was a side of Quinn that was audacious and slightly uninhibited. He'd enjoyed every moment they'd spent together, and he was eager for their trip to Chicago in a few weeks.

But waiting three whole weeks to spend time with Quinn again didn't sit well with him. Being this close to her now only heightened his hunger for her.

Max had agreed to Quinn's terms, and he understood her hesitance to go public with their relationship while they worked together. But it didn't mean he had to like it.

As he watched Quinn dance with Cole, both of them laughing, he cursed himself for not sending his original text message. Or any of the ten messages he'd composed then deleted before finally sending his lame, one-word response.

Okay.

He definitely was *not* okay with Quinn being here with Cole. Max didn't care if the two of them were just friends. He wanted Quinn to be here with him. And only him.

Max had typed several variations of that message before finally deciding that coming off as jealous, possessive or downright needy would only scare her off.

He went with Option B instead: Just play it cool.

As if Quinn being here with his annoying younger brother was no big deal. Which now felt like the second dumbest idea he'd ever had. The decision his younger self had made to break up with Quinn definitely ranked first.

"Ask her to dance." Zora nudged his shoulder. "It's a wedding reception. There's nothing weird about that."

"Maybe." Max sipped his glass of bourbon neat.

Just the thought of holding Quinn in his arms again brought back vivid memories of their week together. Reminded him of how much he wanted her in his bed.

But sitting there watching Cole and Quinn together was another form of torture. He wasn't sure which was worse.

Max finished the last of his drink, then excused himself from the table before heading onto the dance floor.

He approached Cole and Quinn. "Mind if I cut in?"

"Only if you let me lead," Cole said.

Quinn broke out in her melodic laughter.

Max couldn't help laughing, too. "I meant I'd like to dance with Quinn, smart ass," he said before turning to her. "If you don't mind."

"Not at all." Her brown eyes danced.

Max took her hand and slipped an arm around her waist. They danced in silence for a few moments. "You look gorgeous, Quinn."

"Thank you." Her broad smile revealed the depth of her dimples. "You look pretty dashing in your tux."

He cradled her in his arms as they moved together, his hand pressed to the smooth, soft skin of her bare back. The sensation reminded him of how he'd skimmed his hands over her bare skin as she lay naked in his arms just a few days ago.

Max inhaled the familiar scent of coconut and citrus as he leaned in, whispering into her hair, "God, I've missed you."

She looked up at him. One corner of her mouth curved in an almost shy smile. "Me, too."

It was a small win. The first step toward making his case for breaking rule number two.

"I'm looking forward to Chicago," he said.

"For business or personal reasons?"

"Both," he admitted. "But I've been thinking—"

"Quinn, Benji had a brilliant idea," Cole appeared beside them suddenly with Benji in tow. "The cabin will be empty while he and Sloane are away."

"We'd rather have you stay there than for the place to sit empty," Benji explained.

It was a wonderful offer, though she doubted she could afford to rent the cabin of a tech billionaire.

"That's kind of you and Sloane, Benji. But I don't know if—"

"You'd be doing us a favor." Benji grinned. "You need a place to crash in town, and we could really use a house sitter while we're away." He shrugged. "I consider it a fair tradeoff."

Quinn agreed, thanking Benji for his generosity.

Max was glad Quinn would be staying in town once construction started on Kayleigh's building. But he hadn't finished his conversation with Quinn and couldn't help resenting his brother's awful timing.

Or maybe Cole had timed the situation perfectly.

Max assessed his younger brother coolly, but as usual, Cole was completely unfazed.

He forced a smile through clenched teeth, then put a discreet hand on Quinn's waist and leaned in to whisper in her ear. "Catch up with you later?"

Her brown eyes offered a quiet apology for the interruption. "Of course. Thank you for the dance."

Max nodded and walked away, heaving a quiet sigh. But if his past with Quinn had taught him anything it was not to give up so easily. He'd find another opportunity to make his proposal.

Quinn said goodbye to the bride and groom and to all of the Abbotts.

As she approached the valet stand, Max called her name.

"Leaving already?"

"It's been a long week," she said.

"True," Max agreed. "Mind if I walk you to your car instead?"

Quinn glanced over at the valet, who looked at them expectantly. She returned her gaze to Max. "It's a beautiful night. A short walk would be nice."

Max held out his hand and she gave him her ticket, which he used to retrieve her keys and get the location of her car. He extended his elbow to her and she slipped her arm through his.

It was a common, courteous gesture. But something about it felt warm and intimate, sending a small shiver up her spine.

"So we were talking about how much we enjoyed this past week together in San Francisco and how much we're looking forward to spending time together in Chicago," he repeated.

"All true," she agreed.

"But Chicago isn't for another three weeks, which feels like an eternity," Max said. "So I propose we nix rule number two. Because I'd *really* like to take you back to my place tonight, Quinn. We could spend the rest of this weekend in my bed."

"I'll admit that sounds intriguing, but this is a rather small town, Max." She glanced around the parking lot, suddenly conscious of whether anyone might overhear their conversation. "We agreed to be discreet about this. Hooking up here in town seems imprudent. Like we're asking to get caught."

Max stopped and turned to her. "Fortunately, my place is on the edge of town. Which is why it's the place my family is *least* likely to stop by unannounced. And once you move into the cabin... It's even farther out of town."

Quinn hiked an eyebrow.

"Seems you've given this idea quite a bit of thought."

"I've given *you* a lot of thought, Quinn." His voice was low and gruff as his dark eyes searched hers. "In fact, I haven't been able to think of much else."

His words, uttered so sincerely, filled her chest with warmth and short-circuited her brain.

But then, something about Max Abbott always had.

"It's already late tonight, but maybe I could come by your place sometime tomorrow."

One side of Max's mouth lifted in a crooked half smile. "I'll text you my address."

He saw her to her car. After the intimacy they'd shared over the past week, it seemed odd for him not to hug or kiss her goodnight. A part of her wanted him to—despite the risk.

Quinn released a quiet sigh as she drove away from Max, still standing there in the parking lot.

Do not fall for Max Abbott again.

But even as she repeated the warning in her head, it was clear that her heart had a mind of its own.

Nineteen

Quinn climbed back into Max's bed and cuddled against his broad chest. She traced her initials inscribed over his heart: something she often found herself doing absently as they lay together after making love.

They'd returned from the trade show in Chicago—another successful outing—and she'd moved into Benji and Sloane's cabin. But this Saturday evening, they were at Max's town house on the outskirts of Magnolia Lake. And he was unusually quiet.

Quinn lifted onto her elbow and stroked the whiskered chin that had sensitized her flesh as he'd kissed his way down her body earlier.

"There's obviously something on your mind tonight. Do you want to talk about it? Or would you prefer some space? If so, it's okay. I understand."

Max clamped a hand on her wrist. His dark eyes locked with hers. "What do you want, Quinn?"

Something about the question felt heavy and meaningful. He wasn't asking about her career. He was talking about them.

"You." The immediate, genuine response surprised her. Made her feel exposed. "*This*, I mean," she clarified.

"You've got me." He cradled her jaw, tracing her cheekbone with his thumb. "So now what do you want?"

"I don't know." She shrugged, keeping her tone light. "What do you want?"

"This isn't about me. This is about you being comfortable with asking for whatever you want." He pressed a lingering kiss to her lips. "Demanding whatever it is you need. You deserve that, Quinn. And any man worthy of you would be willing to give that to you."

"You're proposing we play a naughty game of Simon Says?"

He chuckled. "If it's easier to think of it that way."

Tempting. She swallowed hard, her skin on fire with the possibilities. A vision of this beautiful man on his knees worshipping her body flashed through her brain. "You're saying I should take control during sex? What brought this on?"

Max dragged a thumb across her lower lip. "Being with you is incredible, Quinn. But sometimes it feels like you're holding back. I don't want you to feel like you need to do that with me. You should say or do whatever feels good for you. Ask for whatever you need from me."

"Maybe you haven't noticed, but you do a pretty damn good job of anticipating what I want and what I need." She kissed him again. "I assure you—I have no complaints."

"I'm glad to hear it." Max trailed a finger along her collarbone, and she trembled slightly at his touch. "But I want this to be just as amazing for you as it is for me."

"In my experience, men don't take instructions in the bedroom very well. They consider it an attack on their manhood."

"Ah, you've been with one of those guys." He sighed. "The dumb, selfish fucks who never learn to please a woman because they're too concerned about getting off themselves. They don't realize how much better the experience would be if they'd learn to *thoroughly* please their partner."

Max brushed back her hair and tucked a few strands behind her ear. "If a dude gets upset because you're telling him what does or doesn't feel good to you, run. Because he's not just selfish in the bedroom. He's selfish about everything."

"God, that's true." Quinn sat up, scooting back against the headboard. She cleared her throat. "So all of the *skills* you've acquired… Never mind."

Quinn felt her cheeks getting warm as she smoothed the comforter over her lap. It was none of her business what Max had done in the years they'd been apart.

"Yes." He sat up beside her. "I learned by listening and observing, but also by asking." He stroked her cheek.

"What you've done and with whom…is none of my business."

Max's expression was suddenly serious. "Ask me anything you want to know, Quinn."

There was something so sincere in his gaze. Butterfly wings fluttered in her stomach. Her heart felt as if it might burst. She wasn't supposed to be falling for Max Abbott. She wasn't supposed to be feeling any of what she was feeling right now.

Quinn's breath hitched. "Make love to me, Max. Now."

Desire. That was the emotion she should focus on. Not whatever it was that made her feel like her heart might beat right out of her chest.

There was a momentary sadness in his expression. Her tactic wasn't lost on him. He'd wanted to do an emotional deep dive. She wanted sex, plain and simple.

"That's a command, not a question," he said.

"You said I should ask for whatever I want."

He chuckled, a grin spreading across his incredibly handsome face. "I did, didn't I?"

Max retrieved a strip of condoms from the nightstand and reached to turn off the bedside lamp.

"No." She stilled his hand, her heart racing as he met her gaze. "Leave the light on."

Max's eyes widened momentarily. Then a knowing grin curved the edges of his sensual mouth. "Yes, ma'am."

"And Max?" She trailed a hand down his stomach and cupped his growing erection.

"Yes?"

"How sturdy would you say this headboard is?" Quinn asked with a smile.

"Fuck," he whispered. "This is going to be one hell of a night, isn't it?"

It was, and she was going to enjoy every single minute of it. Because as good as things were between them, their little affair had a built-in expiration date. In a few months she'd leave Magnolia Lake, and eventually she'd return to Atlanta. But this time she'd walk away without expectations or regrets.

Max's eyes fluttered opened. An involuntary smile crept across his face. His night with Quinn had been beyond amazing. It was a reel that would replay in his head until the end of time. He reached for Quinn, but she was gone.

Rule number three: no overnights.

Max wasn't sure which he found more exasperating: being kicked out of Quinn's bed or waking to discover that she'd disappeared from his.

He grabbed his phone and checked the time. Apparently, great sex promoted sound sleep. He'd slept right through his alarm. Now he needed to hurry if he didn't want to be late for another Monday morning meeting.

Max climbed out of bed and headed for the shower, hoping the day would end better than it had started.

Twenty

"Nice of you to join us, son," Duke Abbott teased as Max slid into the leather chair beside Zora.

"Sorry, I…overslept." Were his cheeks as bright red as they felt? His sister's knowing grin provided a clear answer.

Max avoided Zora's gaze. "So what's this about?"

"Your grandfather and I have discussed Parker's proposal. We've decided that selecting the next CEO based on merit is a reasonable request," his father said.

"You're naming Parker as the next CEO?" Zora asked.

"We haven't decided who will be the next CEO." Duke gave Zora a pointed look. "We've simply decided the title will be earned, not inherited. I'm sure we can all agree that's fair."

Parker shoved his glasses up the bridge of his nose and grinned. As if the crown had already been placed atop his peanut head.

"You can wipe that self-satisfied smirk off your face, Parker. You're not the only one who has a shot at this." The words left Max's mouth before he could rein them in. He was already cranky about waking up to a cold, empty bed after the night he and Quinn had shared. Now this. "So get over yourself and maybe take the self-righteousness down a notch."

"Maybe use that same energy you're coming at me with to step up your game," Parker suggested smugly.

Something in Max's head snapped. He jumped up and his chair tumbled backward, crashing to the floor. Max made his way toward Parker, who was sitting at the opposite end of the table from their father, like he was already king of the court.

Zora and his grandfather were calling Max's name, and Blake had rounded the table and stepped between him and Parker.

Blake braced his large hands on Max's shoulders. "Park is just trying to get a rise out of you, Max. No one here is questioning your abilities."

Max was still staring down Parker, who seemed oddly confused by the entire ordeal. As always, Parker said whatever popped into his head—the things most people mused about and didn't say aloud. It was difficult for him to know when to let thoughts just simmer in his brain rather than saying them.

Parker was making an admirable effort to do better in that regard when dealing with his fiancée. It would be nice if he tried a little harder where his family was concerned, too.

"Max, what's gotten into you, son? You've never allowed your brother to get to you like this before," his father said.

When Max turned to respond, he noticed his grandfather clutching the back of his head.

"Gramps, are you okay?" Max asked.

"Suddenly got the worse headache of my life." The old man wavered, as if dizzy. "Think I've got a touch of…"

Grandpa Joseph slumped over onto the table, unable to finish his sentence.

Quinn had forgotten how therapeutic cooking could be. She'd loved spending time in the kitchen with her grandmother before a massive stroke had taken her from them.

She'd been cooking for three days straight in Benji and

Sloane's state-of-the-art kitchen. A pot roast was going in the slow cooker. A ham was cooking in one of the ovens. A pot of collard greens cooked on the stove. And the surface of the granite countertop was dusted with flour and covered in strips of pie crust for the peach cobbler she was making.

Three days ago, she'd been floating around the office on a high after an amazing night with Max. Suddenly, an ambulance had come and taken Max's grandfather away. Everyone at the distillery was still stunned.

The indomitable Joseph Abbott had had a stroke caused by a blood clot, and he'd been hospitalized for the past three days, surrounded by his family.

She'd talked to Cole, who'd kept her updated on their grandfather's condition, and Zora, who'd mentioned that first day that they were eating God-awful food from the hospital cafeteria. Since then, Quinn had made it her mission to feed the Abbott family home-cooked meals, which Cole transported to the hospital. She'd probably cooked more in the past three days than she had in the past three years.

Quinn was grateful Joseph Abbott had chosen to work with Bazemore Farms, and she'd grown incredibly fond of the Abbott family. She was glad she could be there for them in some small way during such a stressful time. But more than anything, she wanted to be there for Max.

According to Zora, he blamed himself for his grandfather's stroke, despite the doctor's assurance that it was better that it happened at the office because they'd quickly gotten him medical assistance.

She'd tried calling Max, but he hadn't answered his phone. Nor had he responded to her text messages. He'd sent her a single email authorizing her to make any necessary decisions on his behalf regarding the brandy campaign—including representing King's Finest at the next trade show. And he'd copied his father, Zora and his assistant on it.

Quinn picked up her phone and reread the email for the fifth time. As if the terse business message might reveal something more. Like how Max was doing or if he needed her. Which was ridiculous.

She'd been the one who'd insisted on keeping their relationship a secret and on keeping it casual. What right did she have to be hurt by the fact that Max was clearly shutting her out now?

Quinn checked on the ham and greens, then typed out a text message to Zora.

How is Grandpa Joe?

Same.

How are all of you doing?

We're all holding up as best we can. Cole is trying to lighten everyone's spirits, but we're all on edge. Max is taking it especially hard. Still thinks this is his fault, though we've learned Gramps had a couple of mini strokes before this. Max hasn't slept much. Mom sent him home to get some sleep about an hour ago.

Give my love to Grandpa Joe and to everyone.

Will do. Thanks. We're all a wreck. You've been a godsend. Hugs

Quinn put down the phone, her heart breaking for Max. She could only imagine the guilt he was feeling. Max adored his grandfather. They all did. No wonder he'd taken it so hard.

Maybe Max wasn't ready to let her in or talk about what was bothering him. But hadn't she been the one who'd erected a wall around her heart first?

Max was simply following her lead.

She had laid out the rules. Rules meant to protect her heart and keep her from getting in too deep. But little by little she'd grown attached to Max and his family anyway. He'd been hinting at wanting more and trying to get her to open up to him. He'd even invited her to join him for Sunday night dinner at his parents' home—as a friend. But she'd maintained emotional distance, determined not to be hurt again.

Now it was Max who was keeping his distance. Reminding her of the casual nature of their relationship. They were business associates and fuck buddies. Not the person you turned to in a crisis.

It was what she thought she wanted. So why did she feel such a deep need to be there for Max? And so powerless because he wouldn't let her?

Maybe it was because the wound still felt so fresh from her own grandmother's death and her father's medical emergency just a few years ago. She'd allowed her emotions to cloud her judgment, let down her defenses and gotten involved in ill-advised relationships.

Was that what she was doing again?

Quinn washed her hands at the sink and returned to assembling the peach cobbler. She needed to focus on doing what she could to help the family. Especially since her own grandfather was in Arizona visiting his ill older brother. So she was making sure the Abbotts were well-fed and that their plans for the introduction of the new brandies continued to move forward.

It had been a long, somber day at the office, and she'd been cooking since she'd returned to the cabin. As soon as the ham and the cobbler were done, she'd turn in for the night.

Quinn preheated the second oven then hopped into the shower.

Afterward, she slipped on a short, vintage silk kimono she'd purchased at a little shop in Toronto a few years ago. There was something soothing about the brilliant turquoise hue and luxurious material with its colorful embroidery.

She returned to the kitchen to put the cobbler in the oven. Then she saw headlights approach, flashing through the front windows. She peeked outside.

Max.

He parked his SUV and got out.

Quinn's heart thudded in her chest. Had something happened since Zora's last text message?

She opened the front door, startling Max as he bounded up the stairs.

Lines creased his forehead and shadows hovered beneath dark eyes filled with sadness. He stepped inside, closing the door behind him.

"Max, is everything all—"

He captured her mouth in a hungry kiss that stole her breath and stoked the heat between her thighs.

She leaned into the kiss, parting her lips to give him access as his tongue sought hers. Lost in his kiss, everything faded away except his clean, woodsy scent and the warmth and solidity of his hard body.

Finally, Max pulled his mouth from hers, his chest heaving as he cradled her face in his large hands. His eyes met hers, as if there was something he needed to say, but he couldn't.

Oh no. No, no, no.

Quinn swallowed hard, panic filling her chest. She gripped the back of his T-shirt, terrified of the words Max couldn't bring himself to say.

"Baby, what is it? What's happened?" When he didn't answer, she prodded gently, "Tell me, Max. I'm here. Whatever you need, just—"

"*You*, Quinn," he said in a breathless whisper. "I need you."

He kissed her again, swallowing her gasp of surprise as he glided his hands down her body and lifted her.

Quinn hooked her legs around his waist. Gave into the comfort of his fiery kiss. Pushed aside the nagging questions about what his words meant beyond this moment.

He needed this. Needed her. And whether he was seeking solace in the arms of his lover or the luxury of losing himself to a few hours of passion, tonight she wanted to be that for him. To be a source of shelter from the storm brewing behind those dark eyes. Even if it was only for a little while.

Max carried her to bed. He toed off his shoes and stripped off his shirt, revealing the tattoos she'd kissed more times than she could remember.

The space between her thighs pulsed at the sight of this man's broad chest and toned body. His jeans hung low on his hips and her eyes were instantly drawn to the ridge beneath his zipper and then to the hungry gaze in his dark eyes as he climbed onto the bed, still wearing his jeans.

Max untied the sash of her silk robe. A wicked smile lit his dark eyes upon discovering she wore only panties beneath it. He pressed a sensuous kiss to her lips before trailing slow, tender kisses down her body. He seemed to relish each shudder of anticipation.

Hooking his thumbs in the waistband of her panties. he dragged them down her legs, dropping the scrap of fabric on the floor.

The hunger in his eyes made her belly flutter and something deep in her chest bloomed like a flower welcoming rays of sunlight. What she felt for Max wasn't just desire.

It was need and something more. Something she was afraid to give voice to—even in her own head.

When Max lapped at the sensitive nub between her thighs, all speculation about what tonight meant faded to the recesses of her mind. Her back arched and she clutched at the bedding as the sensation built with each stroke of his tongue.

He slid two fingers inside her, working them until her quiet whimpers ascended to desperate little pleas. Until body trembling, legs quivering and back arched, she tumbled over the edge, his name on her lips. Pleasure exploded in her center and radiated from her core, leaving her on a dreamy wave of indescribable bliss she'd only ever experienced with Max.

He crawled up the bed a little and laid his head on her stomach, his hand bracing her hip. Both of them were silent as she lay there with her eyes closed and her heart rate slowing. She placed a gentle hand on his head.

"Is it okay if I ask about Grandpa Joe now?"

Quinn wasn't being flippant or judgmental. She understood how Max must feel. She'd always appreciated inquiries about her father when he was ill, but there were times when she'd needed the mental reprieve of *not* discussing her father's health. Not being reminded that his life was teetering on the edge.

"Didn't leave much time for talk, did I?" Max's reserved chuckle vibrated against her skin. He kissed her belly. "The old man gave us quite a scare. But he got treatment quickly, and they expect him to make a complete recovery."

"It's okay to be overwhelmed by what happened, Max. I know how terrifying it is to almost lose someone you love." Quinn stroked his hair. "My dad suffered a heart attack a few years ago. He had to have triple bypass surgery. We'd just lost my grandmother a couple years earlier, so it was one of the scariest moments of my life."

Suddenly the timer blared in the other room.

"My peach cobbler." Quinn shot up. "Actually, it's *your* peach cobbler. I promised Zora I'd make one for your family, so I'd better not burn it."

Quinn slipped from beneath him and gave him a quick kiss before making a dash to the adjoining bathroom to freshen up.

"I won't be long." She slipped her robe back on. "But when I return, I don't expect to be the only one naked."

Max grinned. "Yes, ma'am."

Quinn hurried to the kitchen to get the cobbler out of the oven. It wasn't quite brown enough. But if she returned to a naked Max, there was a good chance she wouldn't make it out of the bedroom again. So she spent the extra ten minutes there in the kitchen jotting down her to-do list for the next day in her planner. And she tried not to overanalyze the words Max had uttered when he'd first arrived, the desperation in his eyes when he'd said them or the way they'd seemed to reach into her chest and squeeze her heart.

You, Quinn. I need you.

She shook the thought from her mind as she removed the ham and perfectly golden brown peach cobbler from the ovens and turned them off.

Quinn hurried back to the bedroom.

Max's jeans were on the floor, and he was in bed. His head was buried in the pillow as he snored softly.

She sighed, disappointed they wouldn't get to finish what they'd started.

Don't take it personally. The man has barely slept in three days.

Then there was the sheer mental exhaustion that accompanied anguish and guilt.

Quinn stood there frozen for a moment as she watched him. Max was an incredible man. A man she was definitely falling for. Or maybe she'd just never stopped loving him. Quinn pressed a soft kiss to Max's forehead and pulled the covers up over him. She stared at the empty space beside him.

Rule number three: no overnights.

It had been a hard rule. No exceptions. But wouldn't it be strange if she went to the guest room and left him alone here?

Quinn groaned quietly. Neither solution was perfect. But waking Max up and sending him home would just be plain cruel. Besides, if she was being honest, a part of her had always wondered what it would feel like to wake up with Max in her bed.

It seemed she would find out. Though this wasn't quite the scenario she'd imagined.

Twenty-One

Max woke the next morning, unsure of the time. He definitely wasn't at his own place. And though he was exhausted, he felt as if he'd been asleep for hours.

Rolling onto his back, he threw an arm across his forehead as he stared at the high ceilings with their exposed beams.

Benji and Sloane's cabin.

He glanced at the empty space beside him in bed, and the events of the previous night came rushing back. He'd crashed and burned spectacularly when Quinn had gone to the kitchen.

As desperately as he'd wanted to be with her, his body had won the battle. The sheer exhaustion of being at the hospital around the clock for the past three days had taken its toll, and he'd dozed off, breaking rule number three.

No overnights.

Unlike their decision to start seeing each other while in town, this wasn't something they'd discussed.

Not okay, Max.

He hadn't done it on purpose. But then again, maybe subconsciously he had. Because he'd wanted to spend the night with Quinn since that very first night at the hotel in San Francisco. And now things felt… different between them. Or maybe he was just projecting his own feelings onto Quinn.

Either way, he owed her an apology. First, for falling asleep before they'd actually gotten to the deed. Secondly, for staying over when it wasn't something she'd agreed to. And though he should probably just be content with their arrangement, a growing part of him needed to know where things stood between them. But first, he needed a shower. And he hoped to God there was a spare toothbrush around here somewhere.

After Max showered and got dressed, he followed the heavenly scent of bacon and waffles to the kitchen. Quinn was in that sexy little kimono again, but this time she wore a nightgown beneath it. Her hair was pulled into a messy topknot.

God, she was gorgeous. His mouth tugged into an involuntary grin.

How amazing would it be to wake up to this woman every morning?

Quinn gave him a sheepish smile, her brown eyes glinting in the sunlight. "Morning, sleepyhead."

"Sorry about that." Max dragged a hand down his face. "I don't sleep this late normally, and I know we don't do sleepovers…ever," he added.

Quinn flipped the bacon over on the griddle. "You don't normally spend three days straight awake at the hospital, worrying about your grandfather's health, either. So there's that." She returned her attention to the stove, but there was tension in her voice.

Was Quinn minimizing his breaking of their no sleepover rule because she genuinely felt it wasn't a big deal? Or was it because it was a *huge* deal and she'd rather tiptoe around the subject than address what it might mean for both of them?

Max settled onto a bar stool. "I can't thank you enough for how you've taken care of my family. The food has been amazing and having home-cooked meals has been a source of comfort for us during all of this. I hadn't had your cooking since—"

"Since I helped my grandmother fix meals for the farmhands that summer." Her smile turned sad. "My repertoire has expanded considerably since then. Waffles?"

"Please." He pushed up his sleeves.

She handed him a mug of piping hot coffee and gestured toward the cream and sugar on the counter.

Quinn joined him at the kitchen island where they ate bacon and waffles with peach cobbler flavored syrup in near silence. Neither of them seemed eager to discuss last night.

"Thank you for breakfast. Everything was delicious." Max patted his stuffed belly and stood once they were done eating. "Let me get the dishes."

"I've got it." She stood, too, waving him off.

Max sank back onto his bar stool and cleared his throat. "About last night—"

"Last night was fine." She moved their dishes to the sink. "Fantastic, in fact," she added with an almost shy smile. "I certainly have no complaints."

"Good to hear." He forced a small smile, uneasy about the wall she seemed to be erecting this morning. "Still, it was rude of me to fall asleep."

"Extenuating circumstances and all that."

Max walked over and slipped his arms around her waist. She smelled like summer peaches and sunshine and everything that was good about the summer they spent together. He nuzzled her neck.

Holding Quinn in his arms now didn't feel like revisiting the past. It felt like a glimpse into his future. But rather than dissolving into giggles or climbing him like a tree—her usual responses to him kissing the sensitive spot where her neck and shoulder met—Quinn's shoulders stiffened.

Max turned her in his arms and studied her face.

Was she angry with him?

"Look, Quinn, I know how this must seem… Me showing up at your door so late last night and then taking you straight to bed. But don't think that I—"

"If this is the part where you try to convince me that you didn't come here just for sex—don't. That's the very nature of our little arrangement." She smirked, returning to the dishes. "I'm obviously fine with that."

"True, but last night was about more than that—"

"You're under a lot of stress right now." She shrugged. "Sometimes, we just need the comfort of human connection to get us through those times."

She was minimizing what they'd shared last night. As if it was just a meaningless hookup.

It hadn't been.

And as hard as she was trying to convince herself otherwise, Quinn realized it, too. But then, being with Quinn had never felt inconsequential to Max. And despite the nature of their current arrangement, he doubted that any of their encounters had ever felt insignificant to her, either.

"Admittedly, once I saw you in this little robe," he teased, tugging at the silken material, "all bets were off. But I honestly didn't come here to take you to bed, Quinn. I came here because I really needed to see you." He lightly gripped her wrist to stop her from frantically scrubbing a pan.

The pan fell to the bottom of the sink with a clang.

"*Why* did you need to see me, Max?" She turned to him, nibbling on her lower lip. Despite asking the question, she seemed apprehensive about his answer.

His shoulders tensed and his heart beat double time.

Just tell her.

Max sucked in a deep breath, then slowly released it. "The past few days, I watched Blake and Parker at the hospital with Savannah and Kayleigh. They're both damn lucky to have them in their lives."

He hooked a finger in the sash of her robe and tugged her closer. She braced her hands on his chest to steady herself as she gazed up at him.

"Suddenly, I realized that all the things I've been feeling about us lately… I want that with you, Quinn. You're the only woman I've ever been able to imagine a future with. It scared the shit out of me that summer because neither of us was ready for it. But we're in a different place in our lives now. I'd like to see what the future has in store for us."

Quinn blinked; her lashes were wet. She seemed apprehensive. And the five or ten seconds of silence felt like an eternity to Max.

"That's incredibly sweet, Max." Quinn freed herself from his hold and swiped a finger beneath her teary eyes. "But this is a really emotional time for all of us and—"

"You think this is just some knee-jerk reaction to my grandfather's stroke?" Max asked.

"I'm not discounting your feelings," she said carefully. "But I can't risk mine on something that might only *seem* real to you now."

"If you're not interested in a relationship, I promise to respect that, Quinn. But if this is because—"

"I don't know if I can do this with you again." She blurted out the words suddenly, finally meeting his gaze for a moment before pacing the kitchen floor. "With a no-strings arrangement, there are no expectations, so no one gets hurt. But what you're proposing…that raises the stakes in a way I'm not sure either of us is prepared for."

Max rubbed absently at the ink on his chest. His wounded heart beat furiously beneath the long-healed skin.

Maybe she was right; he'd timed this poorly. But it didn't change how he felt.

Max placed his large hands on her shoulders to halt her

frantic pacing. "You're telling me that this is really just about sex for you—nothing more?"

"I'm saying that I need to be sure of my feelings and yours," she said.

"I *am* sure of what I feel for you." He cupped her cheek, his heart racing as she looked at him expectantly.

Say it. Now. Before you lose your nerve.

Max swallowed hard, his eyes not leaving hers. The corners of his mouth curved in a soft smile.

"I'm in love with you, Quinn, and I don't want to hide that anymore. I want to be with you and only you because you are the most amazing woman, and I am so damn proud of you. My heart belongs to you. It always has. I want everyone to know I'm yours and that you belong to me." He pressed a soft kiss to her lips. "Is that clear enough?"

Her brown eyes were wide and glossy with tears. She searched his face as if trying to determine the answer to a question she had yet to ask.

Quinn stood frozen, her heart swelling with emotion and her eyes brimming with tears. There were so many things she needed to say, but where did she even begin?

"Talk to me, babe. Please." Max rubbed a hand up and down her arm, as if trying to warm her. "Tell me what's going on in that brilliant mind of yours."

Wringing her hands, Quinn walked over to the front windows overlooking the lake. The sunlight filtering through the window warmed her skin. She took a deep breath, then sighed, turning back to face him.

"There's something I need to tell you. Something I should've told you before now."

"Okay." Max kept his voice even, but worry lines spanned his forehead. He extended a hand to her. "Let's sit down and talk."

Quinn put her hand in his and he led her to the sofa in

the great room. He squeezed her hand, as if to encourage her, but waited patiently for her to speak.

She turned toward him and met his gaze.

"Last year, I was engaged to a man I worked with. He was my boss's son," she admitted quietly. "The engagement didn't last very long, but that beautiful Marchesa gown I wore to your parents' anniversary party…it was a splurge for what would've been my engagement party."

"What happened?" Max frowned, gently caressing the back of her hand with his thumb.

"I ended it when I discovered him with his secretary. He felt I was overreacting. His father, who owned the firm, agreed. Neither of them took my rejection well. I stayed on, tried to be professional, like none of it had ever happened. But they held a grudge and eventually pushed me out of the firm. Due to a non-compete clause, I had to wait at least a year before I could work in the industry there again. That's the real reason I left Atlanta."

Quinn's cheeks stung and a knot tightened in her gut from the sheer humiliation of reliving that entire ordeal. One she should've seen coming.

She wiped angrily at the hot tears that leaked from the corners of her eyes. "Just like that, I flushed my career down the drain."

"I'm sorry you had to endure that, Quinn. But you're not to blame for what happened."

"Aren't I?" She tugged her hand from his and smoothed loose strands of hair before securing the knot atop her head. "I should never have gotten involved with my boss's son, and now I…" She sighed, letting her words trail off.

"And now you're afraid you're making the same mistake by getting involved with me." Max rubbed his chin. "So it's not just our history I'm battling. It's your history with him, too."

She shifted her gaze from his without response.

"Quinn, look at me." Max took her hand in his again, meeting her gaze. "I know I hurt you, and I am *really* sorry. I was young and stupid, and I had a lot to learn. I don't blame you for being wary about getting involved with me again. But sweetheart, I'm *not that* guy you were engaged to. I'm not even the guy I was thirteen years ago. Hurting you is the single biggest regret of my life, Quinn. We've been given another chance at our happy ending. There's no way I'm going to screw this up again. I promise you that."

She wanted to believe she could trust Max and that he wouldn't hurt her again. Because she wanted to be with him, too. She'd mused over the idea. Fantasized about what a real, adult relationship between them would be like. But the cautious part of her that had erected a fort around her heart to protect it was still terrified of taking the leap.

Once bitten, twice shy.

"I know you want an answer right now, Max, but—"

"No pressure, beautiful. I understand now. Take whatever time you need." Max stood, giving her a half smile. "Thank you again for breakfast. I'd better get back to the hospital."

"Thank you for last night." Quinn flashed a playful grin, hoping it masked the uneasiness she felt. She lifted onto her toes and pressed a tame kiss to his lips.

Max cradled her face and deepened their kiss, filling her body with heat and making her wish they could pick up where they'd left off last night.

Suddenly, he broke the kiss and released her.

Quinn's body protested. Her nipples throbbed and there was an insistent pulse between her thighs.

He lifted her chin gently, so their eyes met. "I'm sorry for what you went through in Atlanta, Quinn, and I'm glad you felt comfortable enough to share that with me. But that asshole's loss is our gain. I'm grateful you've come back into my life. These past few months have been so special for me, Quinn. I hope they have been for you, too."

Max pulled away, not waiting for a response. He shifted the topic instead. "You mentioned a care package you wanted me to take back to the hospital."

"Yes, right." She pulled the cardboard box neatly packed with all of the food she'd prepared out of the stainless steel refrigerator. Then she watched as Max loaded up his SUV and drove away. She sighed, missing him already.

Quinn checked her phone. She had a conference call soon with one of the vendors they'd met in Chicago.

Her personal life was a complicated mess, but at least the joint brandy project—though still in its infancy—had already hit a homerun. They'd inked a deal with JRS to carry the KFD line, including their brandies, in all of the restaurants they managed nationwide.

After tasting the product, vendors were clamoring for it and preorders already far exceeded even their most ambitious projections. Duke had indicated that they needed to discuss the possibility of expanding the facilities so they could increase production.

In a few more months, she would turn the project over to Max to be handled in-house, so she could go back to concentrating on the farm and on developing her own consultancy. News that should've thrilled her. But the thought of walking away from Max made her chest ache.

This was supposed to be purely physical and just for fun. No hearts involved.

So much for her simple plan.

She hadn't expected Max would spend the night. She certainly hadn't anticipated that he'd declare that he loved her and wanted a future with her. But Quinn had lain awake after nights with Max wondering if things could work out between them this time or if she was just setting herself up for more heartbreak. She'd had more than enough of that.

Fear is a piss-poor decision-maker. Don't ever make a decision strictly out of fear.

More of her grandmother's wisdom, which she'd invariably heeded in her career. But was she brave enough to follow her advice when it came to her heart?

Twenty-Two

Quinn paid the cashier for two caramel vanilla lattes and found an empty table in a secluded area of the hospital cafeteria. She slid into the chair and wrapped her hands around one of the steaming hot paper cups. A group of women in white jackets and colorful scrubs sat a couple of tables away.

Work had kept her preoccupied for the past two days. But not busy enough to prevent her from obsessively reflecting on her conversation with Max at the cabin. In quiet moments, his words echoed in her head. She could recall nearly every word, every gesture, every expression he'd used. She remembered that he'd smelled of her soap. His mouth had tasted like rich caramel-pecan bourbon coffee and there was a hint of the peach cobbler syrup she'd brought from Georgia by the case on his sensuous lips.

I'm in love with you, Quinn.

I want to be with you and only you.

I want everyone to know I'm yours and that you belong to me.

Those phrases had replayed in her head again and again for the past two days as she'd sorted through her jumble of emotions, confronted her immobilizing fears, and contemplated the realities of a future with Max Abbott—the man she'd first fallen in love with in that misty haze of being a wide-eyed college freshman.

"Quinn, hey." Max looked handsome but tired as he approached the table. He wore a button-down shirt and a pair of broken-in jeans.

"How's Grandpa Joe doing?" She resisted the urge to bound out of the chair and wrap her arms and legs around him. It'd only been two days since she'd seen him. Yet she'd missed him desperately, and she had been counting the hours until she would see him again.

"Gramps is good, all things considered. Full of fire and ready to blow this joint. He'll probably outlive us all." Max seemed to debate whether he should hug her. But he sat down in the chair opposite her and folded his hands on the table instead. "Thanks for meeting me here. They're running a battery of tests on Gramps, and I wanted to be here for them."

"I thought maybe you could use some coffee." She slid the paper cup toward him.

"Thanks." He gripped it but didn't take a sip. His attention was focused on her. "You wanted to talk?"

"I do." Quinn widened her nervous smile and tucked her hair behind one ear. She extended her hands across the table, palms open.

Max relaxed his cautious smile. His dark eyes seemed hopeful as he took her hands.

After all of the nights they'd spent together over the past few months, his touch still made her skin tingle and sent chills up and down her spine.

"The other day, when you said that…" Quinn stumbled over the word. She'd repeated Max's declaration in her head again and again, but this was the first time she was saying the words aloud.

"That I'm in love with you?" he offered, a smirk curving one side of his mouth. He was barely able to contain his amusement and seemed to get a kick out of being the one on the offensive this time around.

"Yes." She took a deep breath before meeting his gaze again. "It was a really beautiful moment. But when you compared what you wanted with me to what Blake and Savannah have... I'll admit it freaked me out a little."

"It kind of freaked me out to realize it." He brushed his lips over the back of her hand. "But it's the truth. We've already missed so much time together, Quinn, and I know that's my fault," he added quickly. "But I don't want to miss another minute with you. I want you in my life, in my bed. I want you to be my plus-one. And I want you beside me at those Sunday night family dinners. To quote Roger Troutman, I want to be your man. Plain and simple."

Quinn laughed at his mention of yet another song he'd played for her that summer. Her vision blurred with tears. "Good. Because I love you, too, Max. And I want all of those things with you, too."

"God, I'm glad to hear you say that." He stood, rounding the table and pulling her into a tight hug. Max breathed a sigh of relief that gently rustled her hair. "When I didn't hear anything from you the past couple of days... I'll admit I was a little worried." He chuckled. "But I would've waited for as long as it took to hear those words." He gave her a quick kiss, his gaze lingering on her lips.

"We should get out of here before we're thrown out for making out in the hospital cafeteria." Quinn's cheeks warmed as she glanced around at the people staring at them.

"Good idea. Besides, Gramps is really looking forward to seeing you," Max said. "Walk back with me?"

She nodded and they grabbed their lukewarm coffees and linked hands as he led her toward a bank of elevators. Max pushed the button.

"In case it wasn't already obvious, you're invited back to my place for part two of our sleepover. We have some unfinished business, and I've been thinking of creative uses for that peach cobbler syrup." Quinn smirked.

"Ooh...not fair." He tugged her onto the elevator once the door opened and pushed the button for the fifth floor. "You're not the one who'll have to hide a raging hard-on from his entire family."

He backed her up against the elevator wall and kissed her, both of them trying not to spill their coffee. They got off on the fifth floor and he pulled her aside before they entered a set of secure doors. "Before we walk through those doors, you need to understand what you're getting yourself into," he said ominously.

"Okay," she said apprehensively. "Let's hear it."

He drank most of his cooled coffee then discarded the cup.

"My brothers will tease us mercilessly. My sister will try to push us down the aisle. And my mother will start dropping hints about grandchildren in a month or two, tops."

"You're exaggerating, Max." Quinn laughed, relieved. "Besides, I adore your family, and I'm prepared for whatever they dish out, as long as we're in this together."

"Don't say I didn't warn you." Max kissed her, then pulled away. He stared at her for a moment, a blissful smile animating his face. "By the way, not a proposal, but if I haven't already made it clear, I have every intention of marrying you, Quinn Bazemore."

"You'd better." She grinned. "Otherwise, good luck explaining to some woman why my initials are inked on your chest. *Awkward*."

"Good point, and that reminds me, we need to talk about which of my favorite poems you should incorporate in your tattoo," he teased, barely able to restrain his grin.

The two of them broke into laughter as they walked through the doors and into a private family waiting room, hand in hand.

Iris's brows furrowed with confusion and she whispered loudly to Duke, "I thought Quinn was Cole's girlfriend."

His father responded, "I think Cole did, too."

Cole shot them both a death stare and shook his head. "No one in this family ever listens to me."

He stood and hugged Quinn, then he shook his brother's hand. They'd been making more of an effort to get along since Quinn had been spending time with both of them. "About time you two knuckleheads figured this out. And absolutely no pressure, but it would be nice to have someone else in this family besides Zora who actually gets me."

"I thought you said Zora would be the one pushing us down the aisle," Quinn whispered to Max loudly.

Zora bounded out of her chair and launched herself at Max, hugging him and then Quinn. "We can tag team the whole wedding thing," she said to Cole.

Max and Quinn settled into chairs next to each other amid the questions and excitement of his family. They were all inquisitive and teasing, but also warm and welcoming, making her feel like she was already one of their own.

Maybe she and Max had taken the long route to get here, but she was exactly where she'd always wanted to be.

* * * * *

TERMS OF
ENGAGEMENT

ANN MAJOR

And as always I must thank my editor, Stacy Boyd, and Shana Smith, along with the entire Mills & Boon Desire team for their talented expertise. I thank as well my agent, Karen Solem!

One

No good deed goes unpunished.

When would she ever learn? Kira wondered.

With her luck, never.

So, here she sat, in the office of oil billionaire Quinn Sullivan, too nervous to concentrate on her magazine as she waited to see if he would make time for a woman he probably thought of as just another adversary to be crushed in his quest for revenge.

Dreadful, arrogant man.

If he did grant her an audience, would she have any chance of changing his mind about destroying her family's company, Murray Oil, and forcing her sister Jaycee into marriage?

A man vengeful enough to hold a grudge against her father for twenty years couldn't possibly have a heart that could be swayed.

Kira Murray clenched and unclenched her hands. Then

she sat on them, twisting in her chair. When the man across from her began to stare, she told herself to quit squirming. Lowering her eyes to her magazine, she pretended to read a very boring article on supertankers.

High heels clicked rapidly on marble, causing Kira to look up in panic.

"Miss Murray, I'm so sorry. I was wrong. Mr. Sullivan *is* still here." There was surprise in his secretary's classy, soothing purr.

"In fact, he'll see you now."

"He will?" Kira squeaked. *"Now?"*

The secretary's answering smile was a brilliant white.

Kira's own mouth felt as dry as sandpaper. She actually began to shake. To hide this dreadful reaction, she jumped to her feet so fast she sent the glossy magazine to the floor, causing the man across from her to glare in annoyance.

Obviously, she'd been hoping Quinn would refuse to see her. A ridiculous wish when she'd come here for the express purpose of finally meeting him properly and having her say.

Sure, she'd run into him once, informally. It had been right after he'd announced he wanted to marry one of the Murray daughters to make his takeover of Murray Oil less hostile. Her father had suggested Jaycee, and Kira couldn't help but think he'd done so because Jaycee was his favorite and most biddable daughter. As always, Jaycee had dutifully agreed with their father's wishes, so Quinn had come to the ranch for a celebratory dinner to seal the bargain.

He'd been late. A man as rich and arrogant as he was probably thought himself entitled to run on his own schedule.

Wounded by her mother's less-than-kind assessment of her outfit when she'd first arrived—"Jeans and a torn shirt? How could you think that appropriate for meeting a man so important to this family's welfare?"—Kira had stormed out of the house. She hadn't had time to change after the crisis at her best friend's restaurant, where Kira was temporarily waiting tables while looking for a museum curator position. Since her mother always turned a deaf ear to Kira's excuses, rather than explain, Kira had decided to walk her dad's hunting spaniels while she nursed her injured feelings.

The brilliant, red sun that had been sinking fast had been in her eyes as the spaniels leaped onto the gravel driveway, dragging her in their wake. Blinded, she'd neither seen nor heard Quinn's low-slung, silver Aston Martin screaming around the curve. Slamming on his brakes, he'd veered clear of her with several feet to spare. She'd tripped over the dogs and fallen into a mud puddle.

Yipping wildly, the dogs had raced back to the house, leaving her to face Quinn on her own with cold, dirty water dripping from her chin.

Quinn had gotten out of his fancy car and stomped over in his fancy Italian loafers just as she got to her feet. For a long moment, he'd inspected every inch of her. Then, mindless of her smudged face, chattering teeth and muddy clothes, he'd pulled her against his tall, hard body, making her much too aware of his clean, male smell and hard, muscular body.

"Tell me you're okay."

He was tall and broad-shouldered, so tall he'd towered over her. His angry blue eyes had burned her; his viselike fingers had cut into her elbow. Despite his overcharged emotions, she'd liked being in his arms—liked it too much.

"Damn it, I didn't hit you, did I? Well, say something, why don't you?"

"How can I—with you yelling at me?"

"Are you okay, then?" he asked, his grip loosening, his

voice softening into a husky sound so unexpectedly beautiful she'd shivered. This time, she saw concern in his hard expression.

Had it happened then?

Oh, be honest, Kira, at least with yourself. That was the moment you formed an inappropriate crush on your sister's future fiancé, a man whose main goal in life is to destroy your family.

He'd been wearing faded jeans, a white shirt, his sleeves rolled up to his elbows. On her, jeans looked rumpled, but on him, jeans had made him ruggedly, devastatingly handsome. Over one arm, he carried a cashmere jacket.

She noted his jet-black hair and carved cheekbones with approval. Any woman would have. His skin had been darkly bronzed, and the dangerous aura of sensuality surrounding him had her sizzling.

Shaken by her fall and by the fact that *the enemy* was such an attractive, powerful man who continued to hold her close and stare down at her with blazing eyes, her breath had come in fits and starts.

"I said—*are you okay?*"

"I was fine—until you grabbed me." Her hesitant voice was tremulous…and sounded strangely shy. "You're hurting me, really hurting me!" She'd lied so he would let her go, and yet part of her hadn't wanted to be released.

His eyes narrowed suspiciously. "Sorry," he'd said, his tone harsh again.

"Who the hell are you anyway?" he'd demanded.

"Nobody important," she'd muttered.

His dark brows winged upward. "Wait…I've seen your pictures… You're the older sister. The waitress."

"Only temporarily…until I get a new job as a curator."

"Right. You were fired."

"So, you've heard Father's version. The truth is, my professional opinion wasn't as important to the museum director as I might have liked, but I was let go due to budget constraints."

"Your sister speaks highly of you."

"Sometimes I think she's the only one in this family who does."

Nodding as if he understood, he draped his jacket around her shoulders. "I've wanted to meet you." When she glanced up at him, he said, "You're shivering. The least I can do is offer you my jacket and a ride back to the house."

Her heart pounded much too fast, and she was mortified that she was covered with mud and that she found her family's enemy exciting and the prospect of wearing his jacket a thrill. Not trusting herself to spend another second with such a dangerous man, especially in the close quarters of his glamorous car, she'd shaken her head. "I'm too muddy."

"Do you think I give a damn about that? I could have killed you."

"You didn't. So let's just forget about it."

"Not possible! Now, put my jacket on before you catch your death."

Pulling his jacket around her shoulders, she turned on her heel and left him. Nothing had happened, she'd told herself as she stalked rapidly through the woods toward the house.

Nothing except the enemy she'd feared had held her and made her feel dangerously alive in a way no other man ever had.

When she'd reached the house, she'd been surprised to find him outside waiting for her as he held on to her yapping dogs. Feeling tingly and shyly thrilled as he handed her their tangled leashes, she'd used her muddy clothes again as an excuse to go home and avoid dinner, when her father would formally announce Quinn was to marry her sister.

Yes, he was set on revenge against those she loved most, but that hadn't been the reason she couldn't sit across the table from him. No, it was her crush. How could she have endured such a dinner when just to look at him made her skin heat?

For weeks after that chance meeting, her inappropriate attachment to Quinn had continued to claim her, causing her much guilt-ridden pain. She'd thought of him constantly. And more than once, before she'd returned his jacket to Jaycee, she'd worn it around her apartment, draped over her shoulders, just because his scent lingered on the soft fabric.

Now, retrieving the magazine she'd dropped, she set it carefully on the side table. Then she sucked in a deep breath. Not that it steadied her nerves.

No. Instead, her heart raced when Quinn Sullivan's secretary turned away, saying, "Follow me."

Kira swallowed. She'd put this interview off to the last possible moment—to the end of the business day—because she'd been trying to formulate a plan to confront a man as powerful and dictatorial and, yes, as dangerously sexy, as Quinn Sullivan.

But she hadn't come up with a plan. Did she ever have a plan? She'd be at a disadvantage since Sullivan planned everything down to the last detail, including taking his revenge plot up a notch by marrying Jaycee.

Kira had to sprint to keep up with the sleek, blonde secretary, whose ridiculous, four-inch, ice-pick, gold heels clicked on the polished gray marble. Did *he* make the poor girl wear such gaudy, crippling footwear?

Quinn's waiting room with its butter-soft leather couches and polished wainscoting had reeked of old money. In truth, he was nothing but a brash, bad-tempered upstart. His long hallway, decorated with paintings of vivid mini-malistic splashes of color, led to what would probably prove to be an obscenely opulent office. Still, despite her wish to dislike everything about him, she admired the art and wished she could stop and study several of the pictures. They were elegant, tasteful and interesting. Had he selected them himself?

Probably not. He was an arrogant show-off.

After their one encounter, she'd researched him. It seemed he believed her father had profited excessively when he'd bought Quinn's father out of their mutually owned company. In addition, he blamed her father for his father's suicide—if suicide it had been.

Quinn, who'd known hardship after his father's death, was determined to make up for his early privations, by living rich and large. Craving glamour and the spotlight, he never attended a party without a beauty even more daz-zling than his secretary on his arm.

He was a respected art collector. In various interviews he'd made it clear nobody would ever look down on him again. Not in business; not in his personal life. He was king of his kingdom.

From the internet, she'd gleaned that Quinn's bedroom had a revolving door. Apparently, a few nights' pleasur-ing the same woman were more than enough for him. Just when a woman might believe she meant something to him, he'd drop her and date another gorgeous blonde, who was invariably more beautiful than the one he'd jilted. There had been one woman, also blonde, who'd jilted him a year or so ago, a Cristina somebody. Not that she hadn't been quickly forgotten by the press when he'd resumed chasing more beauties as carelessly as before.

From what Kira had seen, his life was about winning,

not about caring deeply. For that purpose only, he'd surrounded himself with the mansions, the cars, the yachts, the art collections and the fair-haired beauties. She had no illusions about what his marriage to Jaycee would be like. He had no intention of being a faithful husband to Kira's beautiful, blonde sister.

Rich, handsome womanizer that he was, Kira might have pitied him for being cursed with such a dark heart—if only her precious Jaycee wasn't central in his revenge scheme.

Kira was not gifted at planning or at being confrontational, which were two big reasons why she wasn't getting ahead in her career. And Quinn was the last person on earth she wanted to confront. But the need to take care of Jaycee, as she had done since her sister's birth, was paramount.

Naturally, Kira's first step had been to beg her father to change his mind about using her sister to smooth over a business deal, but her father had been adamant about the benefits of the marriage.

Kira didn't understand the financials of Quinn's hostile takeover of Murray Oil, but her father seemed to think Quinn would make a brilliant CEO. Her parents had said that if Jaycee didn't walk down the aisle with Quinn as agreed, Quinn's terms would become far more onerous. Not to mention that the employees would resent him as an outsider. Even though Quinn's father had been a co-owner, Quinn was viewed as a man with a personal vendetta against the Murrays and Murray Oil. Ever since his father's death, rumors about his hostility toward all things Murray had been widely circulated by the press. Only if he married Jaycee would the employees believe that peace between the two families had at last been achieved and that the company would be safe in his hands.

Hence, Kira was here, to face Quinn Sullivan.

She was determined to stop him from marrying Jaycee, but how? Pausing in panic even as his secretary rushed ahead, she reminded herself that she couldn't turn back, plan or not.

Quickening her pace, Kira caught up to the efficient young woman, who was probably moving so quickly because she was as scared of the unfeeling brute as Kira was.

When his secretary pushed open Quinn's door, the deep, rich tones of the man's surprisingly beautiful voice moved through Kira like music. Her knees lost strength, and she stopped in midstep.

Oh, no, it was happening again.

She'd known from meeting him the first time that he was charismatic, but she'd counted on her newly amassed knowledge of his despicable character to protect her. His edgy baritone slid across her nerve endings, causing warm tingles in her secret, feminine places, and she knew she was as vulnerable to him as before.

Fighting not to notice that her nipples ached and that her pulse had sped up, she took a deep breath before daring a glance at the black-headed rogue. Looking very much at ease, he sat sprawled at his desk, the back of his linebacker shoulders to her as he leaned against his chair, a telephone jammed to his ear.

She couldn't, wouldn't, be attracted to this man.

On his desk she noted a silver-framed photograph of his father. With their intense blue eyes, black hair and strongly chiseled, tanned features, father and son closely resembled each other. Both, she knew, had been college athletes. Did Quinn keep the photo so close out of love or to energize him in his quest for revenge?

"I told you to buy, Habib," he ordered brusquely in that

too-beautiful voice. "What's there to talk about? Do it."
He ended the call.

At least he was every bit as rude as she remembered.
Deep baritone or not, it should be easy to hate him.

His secretary coughed to let him know they were at the
door.

Quinn whirled around in his massive, black leather
chair, scowling, but went still the instant he saw Kira.

He lifted that hard, carved chin, which surprisingly
enough had the most darling dimple, and, just like that,
dismissed his secretary.

His piercing, laser-blue gaze slammed into Kira full
force and heated her through—just like before.

Black hair. Bronze skin. Fierce, brilliant eyes… With a
single glance the man bewitched her.

When his mouth lifted at the edges, her world shifted as
it had that first evening—and he hadn't even touched her.

He was as outrageously handsome as ever. Every bit as
dark, tall, lean and hard, as cynical and untamed—even
in his orderly office with his efficient secretary standing
guard.

Still, for an instant, Kira thought she saw turbulent grief
and longing mix with unexpected pleasure at the sight of
her.

He remembered her.

But in a flash the light went out of his eyes, and his
handsome features tightened into those of the tough, heartless man he wanted people to see.

In spite of his attempt at distance, a chord of recognition
had been struck. It was as if they'd seen into each other's
souls, had sensed each other's secret yearnings.

She wanted her family, who deemed her difficult and
frustrating, to love and accept her for herself, as they did
her sister.

He had longings that revenge and outward success had failed to satisfy. What were they? What was lacking in his disciplined, showy, materialistic life?

Was he as drawn to her as she was to him?

Impossible.

So how could he be the only man who'd ever made her feel less alone in the universe?

Hating him even more because he'd exposed needs she preferred to conceal, she tensed. He had no right to open her heart and arouse such longings.

Frowning, he cocked his dark head and studied her. "I owe you an apology for the last time we met," he drawled in that slow, mocking baritone that turned her insides to mush. "I was nervous about the takeover and the engagement and about making a good impression on you and your family. I was too harsh with you. A few inches more…and I could have killed you. I was afraid, and that made me angry."

"You owe me nothing," she said coolly.

"I don't blame you in the least for avoiding me all these weeks. I probably scared the hell out of you."

"I haven't been avoiding you. Not really," she murmured, but a telltale flush heated her neck as she thought of the family dinners she'd opted out of because she'd known he'd be there.

If only she could run now, escape him. But Jaycee needed her, so instead, she hedged. "I've been busy."

"Waitressing?"

"Yes! I'm helping out Betty, my best friend, while I interview for museum jobs. Opening a restaurant on the San Antonio River Walk was a lifetime dream of hers. She got busier faster than she expected, and she offered me a job. Since I waited tables one summer between college semesters, I've got some experience."

He smiled. "I like it that you're helping your friend

realize her dream even though your career is stalled. That's nice."

"We grew up together. Betty was our housekeeper's daughter. When we got older my mother kept hoping I'd outgrow the friendship while Daddy helped Betty get a scholarship."

"I like that you're generous and loyal." He hesitated. "Your pictures don't do you justice. Nor did my memory of you."

His blue eyes gleamed with so much appreciation her cheeks heated. "Maybe because the last time I saw you I was slathered in mud."

He smiled. "Still, being a waitress seems like a strange job for a museum curator, even if it's temporary. You did major in art history at Princeton and completed that internship at the Metropolitan Museum of Art. I believe you graduated with honors."

She had no idea how she'd done so well, but when her grades had thrilled her father, she'd worked even harder.

"Has Daddy, who by the way, has a bad habit of talking too much, told you my life history?"

For a long moment, Quinn didn't confirm her accusation or deny it.

"Well, is that where you learned these details?"

"If he talked about you, it was because I was curious and asked him."

Not good. She frowned as she imagined her parents complaining about her disappointments since Princeton during all those family dinners she'd avoided.

"Did my father tell you that I've had a hard time with a couple of museum directors because they micromanaged me?"

"Not exactly."

"I'll bet. He takes the boss's side because he's every bit

as high-handed and dictatorial. Unfortunately, one night after finishing the setup of a new show, when I was dead tired, the director started second-guessing my judgment about stuff he'd already signed off on. I made the mistake of telling him what I really thought. When there were budget cuts, you can probably guess who he let go."

"I'm sorry about that."

"I'm good at what I do. I'll find another job, but until I do, I don't see why I shouldn't help Betty. Unfortunately, my father disagrees. We frequently disagree."

"It's your life, not his."

Her thoughts exactly. Having him concur was really sort of annoying, since Quinn was supposed to be the enemy.

In the conversational lull, she noticed that his spectacular physique was elegantly clad in a dark gray suit cut to emphasize every hard sinew of his powerful body. Suddenly, she wished she'd dressed up. Then she caught herself. Why should she care about looking her best for a man she should hate, when her appearance was something she rarely thought about?

All she'd done today was scoop her long, dark hair into a ponytail that cascaded down her back. Still, when his eyes hungrily skimmed her figure, she was glad that she'd worn the loosely flowing white shirt and long red scarf over her tight jeans because the swirls of cloth hid her body.

His burning gaze, which had ignited way too many feminine hormones, rose to her face again. When he smiled as he continued to stare, she bit her bottom lip to keep from returning his smile.

Rising, he towered over her, making her feel small and feminine and lovely in ways she'd never felt lovely before. He moved toward her, seized her hand in his much larger one and shook it gently.

"I'm very glad you decided to give me a second chance."

Why did his blunt fingers have to feel so warm and hard, his touch and gaze so deliciously intimate? She snatched her hand away, causing his eyes to flash with that pain he didn't want her to see.

"That's not what this is."

"But you *were* avoiding me, weren't you?"

"I *was*," she admitted and then instantly regretted being so truthful.

"That was a mistake—for both of us."

When he asked her if she wanted coffee or a soda or anything at all to drink, she said no and looked out the windows at the sun sinking low against the San Antonio skyline. She couldn't risk looking at him any more than necessary because her attraction seemed to be building. He would probably sense it and use it against her somehow.

With some difficulty she reminded herself that she disliked him. So, why did she still feel hot and clammy and slightly breathless, as if there were a lack of oxygen in the room?

It's called chemistry. Sexual attraction. It's irrational.

Her awareness only sharpened when he pulled out a chair for her and returned to his own. Sitting down and crossing one long leg over the other, he leaned back again. The pose should have seemed relaxed, but as he concentrated on her she could see he wasn't relaxed—he was intently assessing her.

The elegant office became eerily silent as he stared. Behind the closed doors, she felt trapped. Leaning forward, her posture grew as rigid as his was seemingly careless.

His hard, blue eyes held her motionless.

"So, to what do I owe the pleasure of your visit this afternoon…or should I say this evening?" he asked in that pleasant tone that made her tremble with excitement.

She imagined them on his megayacht, sailing silently across the vast, blue Gulf of Mexico. Her auburn hair would blow in the wind as he pulled her close and suggested they go below.

"You're my last appointment, so I can give you as much time as you want," he said, thankfully interrupting her seduction fantasy.

Her guilty heart sped up. Why had she come at such a late hour when he might not have another appointment afterward?

The sky was rapidly darkening, casting a shadow across his carved face, making him look stark and feral, adding to the danger she felt upon finding herself alone with him.

Even though her fear made her want to flee, she was far too determined to do what she had to do to give in to it.

She blurted out, "I don't want you to marry Jaycee." Oh, dear, she'd meant to lead up to this in some clever way.

He brought his blunt fingertips together in a position of prayer. When he leaned across his desk toward her, she sank lower in her own chair. "Don't you? How very strange."

"It's not strange. You can't marry her. You don't love her. You and she are too different to care for each other as a man and wife should."

His eyes darkened in a way that made him seem more alive than any man she'd ever known. "I wasn't referring to Jacinda. I was talking about you...and me and how strange that I should feel...so much—" He stopped. "When for all practical purposes we just met."

His eyes bored into hers with that piercing intensity that left her breathless. Once again she felt connected to him by some dark, forbidden, primal force.

"I never anticipated this wrinkle when I suggested a marriage with a Murray daughter," he murmured.

When his eyes slid over her body again in that devouring way, her heart raced. Her tall, slim figure wasn't appealing to most men. She'd come to believe there was nothing special about her. Could he possibly be as attracted to her as she was to him?

"You don't love her," she repeated even more shakily.

"Love? No. I don't love her. How could I? I barely know her."

"You see!"

"Your father chose her, and she agreed."

"Because she's always done everything he tells her to."

"You, however, would not have agreed so easily?" He paused. "Love does not matter to me in the least. But now I find myself curious about his choice of brides. And…even more curious about you. I want to get to know you better." His tone remained disturbingly intimate.

She remembered his revolving bedroom door and the parade of voluptuous blondes who'd passed through it. Was he so base he'd think it nothing to seduce his future wife's sister and then discard her, too?

"You've made no secret of how you feel about my father," she whispered with growing wariness. "Why marry his daughter?"

"Business. There are all these rumors in the press that I want to destroy Murray Oil, a company that once belonged to my beloved father."

"It makes perfect sense."

"No, it doesn't. I would never pay an immense amount of money for a valuable property in order to destroy it."

"But you think my father blackened your father's name and then profited after buying your father out. That's why you're so determined to destroy everything he's built, everything he loves...including Jaycee."

His lips thinned. Suddenly, his eyes were arctic. "My father built Murray Oil, not yours. Only back then it was called Sullivan and Murray Oil. Your father seized the opportunity, when my dad was down, to buy him out at five cents on the dollar."

"My father made the company what it is today."

"Well, now I'm going to take it over and improve upon it. Marriage to a Murray daughter will reassure the numerous employees that family, not a vengeful marauder, will be at the helm of the business."

"That would be a lie. You are a marauder, and you're not family."

"Not yet," he amended. "But a few Saturdays hence, if I marry Jaycee, we will be...family."

"Never. Not over my dead body!" She expelled the words in an outraged gasp.

"The thought of anything so awful happening to your delectable body is hateful to me." When he hesitated, his avid, searching expression made her warm again.

"Okay," he said. "Let's say I take you at your word. You're here to save your sister from me. And you'd die before you'd let me marry her. Is that right?"

"Essentially."

"What else would you do to stop me? Surely there is some lesser, more appealing sacrifice you'd be willing to make to inspire me to change my mind."

"I...don't know what you mean."

"Well, what if I were to agree to your proposal and forgo marriage to your lovely sister, a woman you say is so unsuited to my temperament I could never love her—I want to know what I will get in return."

"Do you always have to get something in return? You wouldn't actually be making a sacrifice."

His smile was a triumphant flash of white against his deeply tanned skin. "Always. Most decidedly. My hypothetical marriage to your sister is a business deal, after all. As a businessman, I would require compensation for letting the deal fall through."

Awful man.

His blue eyes stung her, causing the pulse in her throat to hammer frantically.

"Maybe...er...the satisfaction of doing a good deed for once in your life?" she said.

He laughed. "That's a refreshing idea if ever I heard one, and from a very charming woman—but, like most humans, I'm driven by the desire to avoid pain and pursue pleasure."

"And to think—I imagined you to be primarily driven by greed. Well, I don't have any money."

"I don't want your money."

"What do you want, then?"

"I think you know," he said silkily, leaning closer. "*You. You* interest me...quite a lot. I believe we could give each other immense pleasure...under the right circumstances."

The unavoidable heat in his eyes caused an unwanted shock wave of fiery prickles to spread through her body. She'd seriously underestimated the risk of confronting this man.

"In fact, I think we both knew what we wanted the moment we looked at each other today," he said.

He wanted her.

And even though he was promised to Jaycee, he didn't have a qualm about acknowledging his impossible, unsavory need for the skinnier, plainer, older sister. Maybe the thought of bedding his future wife's sister improved upon his original idea of revenge. Or maybe he was simply a man who never denied himself a female who might amuse him, however briefly. If any of those assumptions were true, he was too horrible for words.

"I'm hungry," he continued. "Why don't we discuss your proposition over dinner," he said.

"No. I couldn't possibly. You've said more than enough to convince me of the kind of man you are."

"Who are you kidding? You were prejudiced against me before you showed up here. If I'd played the saint, you would have still thought me the devil…and yet you would have also still…been secretly attracted. And you are attracted to me. Admit it."

Stunned at his boldness, she hissed out a breath. "I'm not."

Then why was she staring at his darling dimple as if she was hypnotized by it?

He laughed. "Do you have a boyfriend?" he asked. "Or dinner plans you need to change?"

"No," she admitted before she thought.

"Good." He smiled at her as if he was genuinely pleased. "Then it's settled."

"What?"

"You and I have a dinner date."

"No!"

"What are you afraid of?" he asked in that deep, velvet tone that let her know he had much more than dinner in mind. And some part of her, God help her, wanted to rush toward him like a moth toward flame, despite her sister, despite the knowledge that he wanted to destroy her family.

Kira was shaking her head vehemently when he said, "You came here today to talk to me, to convince me to do as you ask. I'm making myself available to you."

"But?"

He gave her a slow, insolent grin. "If you want to save your sister from the Big Bad Wolf, well—here's your chance."

Two

When they turned the corner and she saw the gaily lit restaurant, Kira wished with all her heart she'd never agreed to this dinner with Quinn.

Not that he hadn't behaved like a perfect gentleman as they'd walked over together.

When she'd said she wanted to go somewhere within walking distance of his office, she'd foolishly thought she'd be safer with him on foot.

"You're not afraid to get in my car, to be alone with me, are you?" he'd teased.

"It just seems simpler…to go somewhere close," she'd hedged. "Besides, you're a busy man."

"Not too busy for what really matters."

Then he'd suggested they walk along the river. The lovely reflections in the still, brown water where ducks swam and the companionable silences they'd shared as they'd made their way along the flagstones edged by lush vegetation, restaurants and bars had been altogether too enjoyable.

She'd never made a study of predators, but she had a cat, Rudy. When on the hunt, he was purposeful, diligent and very patient. He enjoyed playing with his prey before the kill, just to make the game last longer. She couldn't help but think Quinn was doing something similar with her.

No sooner did Quinn push open the door so she could enter one of the most popular Mexican restaurants in all of San Antonio than warmth, vibrant laughter and the heavy beat of Latin music hit her.

A man, who was hurrying outside after a woman, said, "Oh, excuse us, please, miss."

Quinn reached out and put his strong arm protectively around Kira's waist, shielding her with his powerful body. Pulling her close, he tugged her to one side to let the other couple pass.

When Quinn's body brushed against hers intimately, as if they were a couple, heat washed over her as it had the afternoon when she'd been muddy and he'd pulled her into his arms. She inhaled his clean, male scent. As before, he drew her like a sexual magnet.

When she let out an excited little gasp, he smiled and pulled her even closer. "You feel much too good," he whispered.

She should run, but the March evening was cooler than she'd dressed for, causing her to instinctively cling to his hot, big-boned body and stay nestled against his welcoming warmth.

She felt the red scarf she wore around her neck tighten as if to warn her away. She yanked at it and gulped in a breath before she shoved herself free of him.

He laughed. "You're not the only one who's been stunned by our connection, you know. I like holding you as much as you like being in my arms. In fact, that's all I want to do…hold you. Does that make me evil? Or all too human because I've found a woman I have no will to resist?"

"You are too much! Why did I let you talk me into this dinner?"

"Because it was the logical thing to do, and I insisted. Because I'm very good at getting what I want. Maybe because *you* wanted to. But now I'd be quite happy to skip dinner. We could order takeout and go to my loft apartment, which isn't far, by the way. You're a curator. I'm a collector. I have several pieces that might interest you."

"I'll bet! Not a good idea."

Again he laughed.

She didn't feel any safer once they were inside the crowded, brilliantly lit establishment. The restaurant with its friendly waitstaff, strolling mariachis, delicious aromas and ceiling festooned with tiny lights and colorful banners was too festive, too conducive to lowering one's guard. It would be too easy to succumb to temptation, something she couldn't afford to do.

I'll have a taco, a glass of water. We'll talk about Jaycee, and I'll leave. What could possibly go wrong if I nip this attraction in the bud?

When told there was a thirty-minute wait, Quinn didn't seem to mind. To the contrary, he seemed pleased. "We'll wait in the bar," he said, smiling.

Then he ushered them into a large room with a high-beamed ceiling dominated by a towering carved oak bar, inspired by the baroque elegance of the hotels in nineteenth-century San Antonio.

When a young redheaded waiter bragged on the various imported tequilas available, Quinn ordered them two margaritas made of a particularly costly tequila he said he had a weakness for.

"I'd rather have sparkling water," she said, sitting up straighter, thinking she needed all her wits about her.

"As you wish," Quinn said gallantly, ordering the water as well, but she noted that he didn't cancel the second margarita.

When their drinks arrived, he lifted his margarita to his lips and licked at the salt that edged the rim. And just watching the movement of his tongue across the grit of those glimmering crystals flooded her with ridiculous heat as she imagined him licking her skin.

"I think our first dinner together calls for a toast, don't you?" he said.

Her hand moved toward her glass of sparkling water.

"The tequila really is worth a taste."

She looked into his eyes and hesitated. Almost without her knowing it, her hand moved slowly away from the icy glass of water to her chilled margarita glass.

"You won't be sorry," he promised in that silken baritone.

Toying with the slender green stem of her glass, she lifted it and then tentatively clinked it against his.

"To us," he said. "To new beginnings." He smiled benevolently, but his blue eyes were excessively brilliant.

Her first swallow of the margarita was salty, sweet and very strong. She knew she shouldn't drink any more. Then, almost at once, a pleasant warmth buzzed through her, softening her attitude toward him and weakening her willpower. Somewhere the mariachis began to play "La Paloma," a favorite love song of hers. Was it a sign?

"I'm glad you at least took a sip," he said, his gaze lingering on her lips a second too long. "It would be a pity to miss tasting something so delicious."

"You're right. It's really quite good."

"The best—all the more reason not to miss it. One can't retrace one's journey in this life. We must make the most of every moment…because once lost, those moments are gone forever."

"Indeed." Eyeing him, she sipped again. "Funny, I hadn't thought of you as a philosopher."

"You might be surprised by who I really am, if you took the trouble to get to know me."

"I doubt it."

Every muscle in his handsome face tensed. When his eyes darkened, she wondered if she'd wounded him.

No. Impossible.

Her nerves jingled, urging her to consider just one more sip of the truly delicious margarita. What could it hurt? That second sip led to a third, then another and another, each sliding down her throat more easily than the last. She hardly noticed when Quinn moved from his side of the booth to hers, and yet how could she not notice? He didn't touch her, yet it was thrilling to be so near him, to know that only their clothes separated her thigh from his, to wonder what he would do next.

His gaze never strayed from her. Focusing on her exclusively, he told her stories about his youth, about the time before his father had died. His father had played ball with him, he said, had taken him hunting and fishing, had helped him with his homework. He stayed off the grim subjects of his parents' divorce and his father's death.

"When school was out for any reason, he always took me to his office. He was determined to instill a work ethic in me."

"He sounds like the perfect father," she said wistfully. "I never seemed to be able to please mine. If he read to me, I fidgeted too much, and he would lose his place and his temper. If he took me fishing, I grew bored or hot and squirmed too much, kicking over the minnow bucket or snapping his line. Once I stood up too fast and turned the boat over."

"Maybe I won't take you fishing."

"He always wanted a son, and I didn't please Mother any better. She thought Jaycee, who loved to dress up and go to parties, was perfect. She still does. Neither of them like what I'm doing with my life."

"Well, they're not in control, are they? No one is, really. And just when we think we are, we usually get struck by a lightning bolt that shows us we're not," Quinn said in a silken tone that made her breath quicken. "Like tonight."

"What do you mean?"

"Us."

Her gaze fixed on his dimple. "Are you coming on to me?"

He laid his hand on top of hers. "Would that be so terrible?"

By the time they'd been seated at their dinner table and had ordered their meal, she'd lost all her fear of him. She was actually enjoying herself.

Usually, she dated guys who couldn't afford to take her out to eat very often, so she cooked for them in her apartment. Even though this meal was not a date, it was nice to dine in a pleasant restaurant and be served for a change.

When Quinn said how sorry he was that they hadn't met before that afternoon when he'd nearly run her down, she answered truthfully, "I thought you were marrying my sister solely to hurt all of us. I couldn't condone that."

He frowned. "And you love your sister so much, you came to my office today to try to find a way to stop me from marrying her."

"I was a fool to admit that to you."

"I think you're sweet, and I admire your honesty. You were right to come. You did me one helluva favor. I've been on the wrong course. But I don't want to talk about Jacinda. I want to talk about you."

"But will you think about...not marrying her?"

When he nodded and said, "Definitely," in a very convincing manner, she relaxed and took still another sip of her margarita with no more thoughts of how dangerous it might be for her to continue relaxing around him.

When he reached across the table and wrapped her hand in his warm, blunt fingers, the shock of his touch sent a wave of heat through her whole body. For a second, she entwined her fingers with his and clung as if he were a vital lifeline. Then, when she realized what she was doing, she wrenched her hand free.

"Why are you so afraid of me, Kira?"

"You might still marry Jaycee and ruin her life," she lied.

"Impossible, now that I've met you."

Kira's breath quickened. Dimple or not, he was still the enemy. She had to remember that.

"Do you really think I'm so callous I could marry your sister when I want you so much?"

"But what are you going to do about Jaycee?"

"I told you. She became irrelevant the minute I saw you standing inside my office this afternoon."

"She's beautiful...and *blonde*."

"Yes, but your beauty affects me more. Don't you know that?"

She shook her head. "The truth isn't in you. You only date blondes."

"Then it must be time for a change."

"I'm going to confess a secret wish. All my life I wished I was blonde...so I'd look more like the rest of my family, especially my mother and my sister. I thought maybe then I'd feel like I belonged."

"You *are* beautiful."

"A man like you would say anything…"

"I've never lied to any woman. Don't you know how incredibly lovely you are? With your shining dark eyes that show your sweet, pure soul every time you look at me and defend your sister? I feel your love for her rushing through you like liquid electricity. You're graceful. You move like a ballerina. I love the way you feel so intensely and blush when you think I might touch you."

"Like a child."

"No. Like a responsive, passionate woman. I like that… too much. And your hair…it's long and soft and shines like chestnut satin. Yet there's fire in it. I want to run my hands through it."

"But we hardly know one another. And I've hated you…"

"None of the Murrays have been favorites of mine either…but I'm beginning to see the error of my ways. And I don't think you hate me as much as you pretend."

Kira stared at him, searching his hard face for some sign that he was lying to her, seducing her as he'd seduced all those other women, saying these things because he had some dark agenda. All she saw was warmth and honesty and intense emotion. Nobody had ever looked at her with such hunger or made her feel so beautiful.

All her life she'd wanted someone to make her feel this special. It was ironic that Quinn Sullivan should be the one.

"I thought you were so bad, no…pure evil," she repeated.

His eyebrows arched. "Ouch."

If he'd been twisted in his original motives, maybe it

had been because of the grief he'd felt at losing someone he loved.

"How could I have been so wrong about you?" Even as she said it, some part of her wondered if she weren't being naive. He had dated, and jilted, all those beautiful women. He had intended to take revenge on her father and use her sister in his plan. Maybe when she'd walked into his office she'd become part of his diabolical plan, too.

"I was misguided," he said.

"I need more time to think about all this. Like I said…a mere hour or two ago I heartily disliked you. Or at least I thought I did."

"Because you didn't know me. Hell, maybe I didn't know me either…because everything is different now, since I met you."

She felt the same way. But she knew she should slow it down, reassess.

"I'm not good at picking boyfriends," she whispered.

"Their loss."

His hand closed over hers and he pressed her fingers, causing a melting sensation in her tummy. "My gain."

Her tacos came, looking and smelling delicious, but she hardly touched them. Her every sense was attuned to Quinn's carved features and his beautiful voice.

When a musician came to their table, Quinn hired him to sing several songs, including "La Paloma." While the man serenaded her, Quinn idly stroked her wrist and the length of her fingers, causing fire to shoot down her spine.

She met his eyes and felt that she had known him always, that he was already her lover, her soul mate. She was crazy to feel such things and think such thoughts about a man she barely knew, but when dinner was over, they skipped dessert.

An hour later, she sat across from him in his downtown

loft, sipping coffee while he drank brandy. In vain, she tried to act unimpressed by his art collection and sparkling views of the city. Not easy, since both were impressive.

His entrance was filled with an installation of crimson light by one of her favorite artists. The foyer was a dazzling ruby void that opened into a living room with high, white ceilings. All the rooms of his apartment held an eclectic mix of sculpture, porcelains and paintings.

Although she hadn't yet complimented his stylish home, she couldn't help but compare her small, littered apartment to his spacious one. Who was she to label him an arrogant upstart? He was a success in the international oil business and a man of impeccable taste, while she was still floundering in her career and struggling to find herself.

"I wanted to be alone with you like this the minute I saw you today," he said.

She shifted uneasily on his cream-leather sofa. Yet more evidence that he was a planner. "Well, I didn't."

"I think you did. You just couldn't let yourself believe you did."

"No," she whispered, setting down her cup. With difficulty she tried to focus on her mission. "So, what about Jaycee? You're sure that's over?"

"Finished. From the first moment I saw you."

"Without mud all over my face."

He laughed. "Actually, you got to me that day, too. Every time I dined with Jacinda and your family, I kept hoping I'd meet you again."

Even as she remembered all those dinner invitations her parents had extended and she'd declined, she couldn't believe he was telling the truth.

"I had my team research you," he said.

"Why?"

"I asked myself the same question. I think you intrigued

me…like I said, even with mud on your face. First thing tomorrow, I will break it off with Jacinda formally. Which means you've won. Does that make you happy? You have what you came for."

He was all charm, especially his warm, white smile. Like a child with a new playmate, she was happy just being with him, but she couldn't admit that to him.

He must have sensed her feelings, though, because he got up and moved silently toward her. "I feel like I've lived my whole life since my father's death alone—until you. And that's how I wanted to live—until you."

She knew it was sudden and reckless, but she felt the same way. If she wasn't careful, she would forget all that should divide them.

As if in a dream, she took his hand when he offered it and kissed his fingers with feverish devotion.

"You've made me realize how lonely I've been," he said.

"That's a very good line."

"It's the truth."

"But you are so successful, while I…"

"Look what you're doing in the interim—helping a friend to realize her dream."

"My father says I'm wasting my potential."

"You will find yourself…if you are patient." He cupped her chin and stared into her eyes. Again she felt that uncanny recognition. He was a kindred soul who knew what it was to feel lost.

"Dear God," he muttered. "Don't listen to me. I don't know a damn thing about patience. Like now… I should let you go…but I can't."

He pulled her to him and crushed her close. It wasn't long before holding her wasn't enough. He had to have her lips, her throat, her breasts. She felt the same way. Shedding her shirt, scarf and bra, she burst into flame as he kissed her. Even though she barely knew him, she could not wait another moment to belong to him.

"I'm not feeling so patient right now myself," she admitted huskily.

Do not give yourself to this man, said an inner voice. *Remember all those blondes. Remember his urge for revenge.*

Even as her emotions spiraled out of control, she knew she was no femme fatale, while he was a devastatingly attractive man. Had he said all these same wonderful things to all those other women he'd bedded? Had he done and felt all the same things, too, a thousand times before? Were nights like this routine for him, while he was the first to make her feel so thrillingly alive?

But then his mouth claimed hers again, and again, with a fierce, wild hunger that made her forget her doubts and shake and cling to him. His kisses completed her as she'd never been completed before. He was a wounded soul, and she understood his wounds. How could she feel so much when they hadn't even made love?

Lifting her into his arms, he carried her into his vast bedroom, which was bathed in silver moonlight. Over her shoulder she saw his big, black bed in the middle of an ocean of white marble and Persian carpets.

He was a driven, successful billionaire, and she was a waitress. Feeling out of her depth, her nerves returned. Not knowing what else to do, she pressed a fingertip to his lips. Gently, shyly, she traced his dimple.

Feeling her tension, he set her down. She pushed against his chest and then took a step away from him. Watching her, he said, "You can finish undressing in the bathroom if you'd prefer privacy. Or we can stop. I'll drive you to your car. Your choice."

She should have said, "I don't belong here with you,"

and accepted his gallant offer. Instead, without a word, she scampered toward the door he'd indicated. Alone in his beige marble bathroom with golden fixtures and a lovely, compelling etching by another one of her favorite artists, she barely recognized her own flushed face, tousled hair and sparkling eyes.

The radiant girl in his tall mirror *was* as beautiful as an enchanted princess. She looked expectant, excited. Maybe she did belong here with him. Maybe he was the beginning of her new life, the first correct step toward the bright future that had so long eluded her.

When she tiptoed back into the bedroom, wearing nothing but his white robe, he was in bed. She couldn't help admiring the width of his bronzed shoulders as he leaned back against several plumped pillows. She had never dated anyone half so handsome; she'd never felt anything as powerful as the glorious heady heat that suffused her entire being as his blue eyes studied her hungrily. Still, she was nervy, shaking.

"I'm no good at sex," she said. "You're probably very good... Of course you are. You're good at everything."

"Come here," he whispered.

"But..."

"Just come to me. You could not possibly delight me more. Surely you know that."

Did he really feel as much as she did?

Removing his bathrobe, she flew to him before she lost her nerve, fell into his bed and into his arms, consumed by forces beyond her control. Nothing mattered but sliding against his long body, being held close in his strong arms. Beneath the covers, his heat was delicious and welcoming as she nestled against him.

He gave her a moment to settle before he rolled on top of her. Bracing himself with his elbows against the mattress, so as not to crush her, he kissed her lips, her cheeks, her brows and then her eyelids with urgent yet featherlike strokes. Slowly, gently, each kiss was driving her mad.

"Take me," she whispered, in the grip of a fever such as she'd never experienced before. "I want you inside me. Now."

"I know," he said, laughing. "I'm as ravenous as you are. But have patience, darlin'."

"You have a funny way of showing your hunger."

"If I do what you ask, it would be over in a heartbeat. This moment, our first time together, is too special to me."

Was she special?

"We must savor it, draw it out, make it last," he said.

"Maybe I want it to be over swiftly," she begged. "Maybe this obsessive need is unbearable."

"Exquisite expectation?"

"I can't stand it."

"And I want to heighten it. Which means we're at cross-purposes."

He didn't take her. With infinite care and maddening patience he adored her with his clever mouth and skilled hands. His fevered lips skimmed across her soft skin, raising goose bumps in secret places. As she lay beneath him, he licked each nipple until it grew hard, licked her navel until he had all her nerve endings on fire for him. Then he kissed her belly and dived even lower to explore those hidden, honey-sweet lips between her legs. When she felt his tongue dart inside, she gasped and drew back.

"Relax," he whispered.

With slow, hot kisses, he made her gush. All too soon her embarrassment was gone, and she was melting, shivering, whimpering—all but begging him to give her release.

Until tonight she had been an exile in the world of love. With all other men, not that there had been that many, she had been going through the motions, playing a part, searching always for something meaningful and never finding it.

Until now, tonight, with him.

He couldn't matter this much! She couldn't let this be more than fierce, wild sex. He, the man, couldn't matter. But her building emotions told her that he did matter—in ways she'd never imagined possible before.

He took her breast in his mouth and suckled again. Then his hand entered her heated wetness, making her gasp helplessly and plead. When he stroked her, his fingers sliding against that secret flesh, she arched against his expert touch, while her breath came in hard, tortured pants.

Just when she didn't think she could bear it any longer, he dragged her beneath him and slid inside her. He was huge, massive, wonderful. Crying out, she clung to him and pushed her pelvis against his, aching for him to fill her even more deeply. *"Yes! Yes!"*

When he sank deeper, ever deeper, she moaned. For a long moment he held her and caressed her. Then he began to plunge in and out, slowly at first. Her rising pleasure carried her and shook her in sharp, hot waves, causing her to climax and scream his name.

He went crazy when she dug her nails in his shoulder. Then she came again, and again, sobbing. She had no idea how many climaxes she had before she felt his hard loins bunch as he exploded.

Afterward, sweat dripped off his brow. His whole body was flushed, burning up, and so was hers.

"Darlin' Kira," he whispered in that husky baritone that could still make her shiver even when she was spent. "Darlin' Kira."

For a long time, she lay in his arms, not speaking, feeling too weak to move any part of her body. Then he leaned over and nibbled at her bottom lip.

The second time he made love to her, he did so with a reverent gentleness that made her weep and hold on to him for a long time afterward. He'd used a condom the second time, causing her to realize belatedly that he hadn't the first time.

How could they have been so careless? She had simply been swept away. Maybe he had, too. Well, it was useless to worry about that now. Besides, she was too happy, too relaxed to care about anything except being in his arms. There was no going back.

For a long time they lay together, facing each other while they talked. He told her about his father's financial crisis and how her father had turned on him and made things worse. He spoke of his mother's extravagance and betrayal and his profound hurt that his world had fallen apart so quickly and brutally. She listened as he explained how grief, poverty and helplessness had twisted him and made him hard.

"Love made me too vulnerable, as it did my father. It was a destructive force. My father loved my mother, and it ruined him. She was greedy and extravagant," he said. "Love destroys the men in our family."

"If you don't want to love, why did you date all those women I read about?"

"I wasn't looking for love, and neither were they."

"You were just using them, then?"

"They were using me, too."

"That's so cynical."

"That's how my life has been. I loved my father so much, and I hurt so much when he died, I gave up on love. He loved my mother, and she broke his heart with her unrelenting demands. When he lost the business, she lost interest in him and began searching for a richer man."

"And did she find him?"

"Several."

"Do you ever see her?"

"No. I was an accident she regretted, I believe. She couldn't relate to children, and after I was grown, I had no interest in her. Love, no matter what kind, always costs too much. I do write her a monthly check, however."

"So, my father was only part of your father's problem."

"But a big part. Losing ownership in Sullivan and Murray Oil made my father feel like he was less than nothing. My mother left him because of that loss. She stripped him of what little wealth and self-esteem he had left. Alone, without his company or his wife, he grew depressed. He wouldn't eat. He couldn't sleep. I'd hear the stairs creak as he paced at night.

"Then early one morning I heard a shot. When I called his name, he didn't answer. I found him in the shop attached to our garage. In a pool of blood on the floor, dead. I still don't know if it was an accident or...what I feared it was. He was gone. At first I was frightened. Then I became angry. I wanted to blame someone, to get even, to make his death right. I lived for revenge. But now that I've almost achieved my goal of taking back Murray Oil, it's as if my fever's burned out."

"Oh, I wouldn't say that," she teased, touching his damp brow.

"I mean my fever for revenge, which was what kept me going."

"So," she asked, "what will you live for now?"

"I don't know. I guess a lot of people just wake up in the morning and go to work, then come home at night and drink while they flip channels with their remote."

"Not you."

"Who's to say? Maybe such people are lucky. At least they're not driven by hate, as I was."

"I can't even begin to imagine what that must have felt like for you." She'd always been driven by the need for love.

When he stared into her eyes with fierce longing, she pulled him close and ran her hands through his hair. "You are young yet. You'll find something to give your life meaning," she said.

"Well, it won't be love, because I've experienced love's dark side for too many years. I want you to know that. You are special, but I can't ever love you, no matter how good we are together. I'm no longer capable of that emotion."

"So you keep telling me," she said, pretending his words didn't hurt.

"I just want to be honest."

"Do we always know our own truths?"

"Darlin'," he whispered. "Forgive me if I sounded too harsh. It's just that…I don't want to hurt you by raising your expectations about something I'm incapable of. Other women have become unhappy because of the way I am."

"You're my family's enemy. Why would I ever want to love you?"

Wrapping her legs around him, she held him for hours, trying to comfort the boy who'd lost so much as well as the angry man who'd gained a fortune because he'd been consumed by a fierce, if misplaced, hatred.

"My father had nothing to do with your father's death," she whispered. "He didn't."

"You have your view, and I have mine," he said. "The important thing is that I don't hold you responsible for your father's sins any longer."

"Don't you?"

"No."

After that, he was silent. Soon afterward he let her go and rolled onto his side.

She lay awake for hours. Where would they go from here? He had hated her family for years. Had he really let go of all those harsh feelings? Had she deluded herself into thinking he wasn't her enemy?

What price would she pay for sleeping with a man who probably only saw her as an instrument for revenge?

Three

When Kira woke up naked in bed with Quinn, she felt unsettled and very self-conscious. Propping herself on an elbow, she watched him warily in the dim rosy half light of dawn. All her doubts returned a hundredfold.

How could she have let things go this far? How could she have risked pregnancy?

What if… No, she couldn't be that unlucky.

Besides, it did no good to regret what had happened, she reminded herself again. If she hadn't slept with him she would never have known such ecstasy was possible.

Now, at least, she knew. Even if it wasn't love, it had been so great she felt an immense tenderness well up in her in spite of her renewed doubts.

He was absurdly handsome with his thick, unruly black hair falling across his brow, with his sharp cheekbones and sculpted mouth. She'd been touched when he'd shown her his vulnerability last night. Just looking at him now was enough to make her stomach flutter with fresh desire.

She was about to stroke his hair, when, without warning, his obscenely long lashes snapped open, and he met her gaze with that directness that still startled her. Maybe because there were so many imperfections she wanted to keep hidden. In the next instant, his expression softened, disarming her.

"Good morning, darlin'." His rough, to-die-for, sexy baritone caressed her.

A jolt sizzled through her even before he reached out a bronzed hand to pull her face to his so he could kiss her lightly on the lips. Never had she wanted anyone as much as she wanted him.

"I haven't brushed my teeth," she warned.

"Neither the hell have I. I don't expect you to be perfect. I simply want you. I can't do without you. You should know that after last night."

She was amazed because she felt exactly the same. Still, with those doubts still lingering, she felt she had to protect herself by protesting.

"Last night was probably a mistake," she murmured.

"Maybe. Or maybe it's a complication, a challenge. Or a good thing. In any case, it's too late to worry about it. I want you more now than ever."

"But for how long?"

"Is anything certain?"

He kissed her hard. Before she could protest again, he rolled on top of her and was inside her, claiming her fiercely, his body piercing her to the bed, his massive erection filling her. When he rode her violently, she bucked like a wild thing, too, her doubts dissolving like mist as primal desire swept her past reason.

"I'm sorry," he said afterward. "I wanted you too much."

He had, however, at the last second, remembered to use a condom. This time, he didn't hold her tenderly or make small talk or confide sweet nothings as he had last night. In fact, he seemed hellishly annoyed at himself.

Was he already tired of her? Would there be a new blonde in his bed tonight? At the thought, a sob caught in her throat.

"You can have the master bathroom. I'll make coffee," he said tersely.

Just like that, he wanted her gone. Since she'd researched him and had known his habits, she shouldn't feel shocked or hurt. Hadn't he warned her he was incapable of feeling close to anyone? She should be grateful for the sublime sexual experience and let the rest go.

Well, she had her pride. She wasn't about to cling to him or show that she cared. But she did care. Oh, how she cared. Her family's worst enemy had quickly gained a curious hold on her heart.

Without a word, she rose and walked naked across the vast expanse of thick, white carpet, every female cell vividly aware that, bored with her though he might be, he didn't tear his eyes from her until she reached the bathroom and shut the door. Once inside she turned the lock and leaned heavily against the wall in a state of collapse.

She took a deep breath and stared at her pale, guilt-stricken reflection, so different from the glowing wanton of last night.

She'd known the kind of guy he was, in spite of his seductive words. How could she have opened herself to such a hard man? Her father's implacable enemy?

What had she done?

By the time she'd showered, brushed her hair and dressed, he was in the kitchen, looking no worse for wear.

Indeed, he seemed energized by what they had shared. Freshly showered, he wore a white shirt and crisply pressed dark slacks. He'd shaved, and his glossy black hair was combed. He looked so civilized, she felt the crazy urge to run her hands through his hair, just to muss it up and leave her mark.

The television was on, and he was watching the latest stock market report while he held his cell phone against his ear. Behind him, a freshly made pot of aromatic coffee sat on the gleaming white counter.

She was about to step inside when he flicked the remote, killing the sound of the television. She heard his voice, as sharp and hard as it had been with the caller yesterday in his office.

"Habib, business is business," he snapped. "I know I have to convince the shareholders and the public I'm some shining white knight. That's why I agreed to marry a Murray daughter and why her parents, especially her father, who wants an easy transition of power, suggested Jacinda and persuaded her to accept me. However, if the older Murray sister agrees to marry me instead, why should it matter to you or to anyone else…other than to Jacinda, who will no doubt be delighted to have her life back?"

Habib, whoever he was, must have argued, because Quinn's next response was much angrier. "Yes, I know the family history and why you consider Jacinda the preferable choice, but since nobody else knows, apparently not even Kira, it's of no consequence. So, if I've decided to marry the older sister instead of the younger, and this decision will make the shareholders and employees just as happy, why the hell should you care?"

The man must have countered again, because Quinn's low tone was even more cutting. "No, I haven't asked her yet. It's too soon. But when I do, I'll remind her that I told her yesterday I'd demand a price for freeing her sister. She'll have to pay it, that's all. She'll have no choice but to do what's best for her family and her sister. Hell, she'll do anything for their approval."

One sister or the other—and he didn't care which one. That he could speak of marrying her instead of Jaycee as a cold business deal before he'd even bothered to propose made Kira's tender heart swell with hurt and outrage. That he would use her desire for her family's love and acceptance to his own advantage was too horrible to endure.

Obviously, she was that insignificant to him. But hadn't she known that? So why did it hurt so much?

He'd said she was special. Nobody had ever made her feel so cherished before.

Thinking herself a needy, romantic fool, she shut her eyes. Unready to face him or confess what she'd overheard and how much it bothered her, Kira backed out of the kitchen and returned to the bedroom. In her present state she was incapable of acting rationally and simply demanding an explanation.

He was a planner. Her seduction must have been a calculated move. No longer could she believe he'd been swept off his feet by her as she had by him. She was skinny and plain. He'd known she desired him, and he was using that to manipulate her.

Last night, when he'd promised he'd break it off with her sister, she'd never guessed the devious manner in which he'd planned to honor that promise.

She was still struggling to process everything she'd learned, when Quinn himself strode into the bedroom looking much too arrogant, masterful and self-satisfied for her liking.

"Good, you're dressed," he said in that beautiful voice. "You look gorgeous."

Refusing to meet the warmth of his admiring gaze for fear she might believe his compliment and thereby lose her determination to escape him, she nodded.

"I made coffee."

"Smells good," she whispered, staring out the window.

"Do you have time for breakfast?"

"No!"

"Something wrong?"

If he was dishonest, why should she bother to be straight with him? "I'm fine," she said, but in a softer tone.

"Right. That must be why you seem so cool."

"Indeed?"

"And they say men are the ones who withdraw the morning after."

She bit her lip to keep herself from screaming at him.

"Still, I understand," he said.

"Last night is going to take some getting used to," she said.

"For me, as well."

To that she said nothing.

"Well, the coffee's in the kitchen," he said, turning away.

Preferring to part from him without an argument, she followed him into the kitchen where he poured her a steaming cup and handed it to her.

"Do you take cream? Sugar?"

She shook her head. "We don't know the most basic things about each other, do we?"

"After last night, I'd have to disagree with you, darlin'."

She blushed in confusion. "Don't call me that."

He eyed her thoughtfully. "You really do seem upset."

She sipped from her cup, again choosing silence instead of arguing the point. Was he good at everything? Rich and strong, the coffee was to die for.

"For the record, I take mine black, very black," he said.

"Without sugar. So, we have that in common. And we have what we shared last night."

"Don't…"

"I'd say we're off to a great start."

Until I realized what you were up to, I would have agreed. She longed to claw him. Instead, she clenched her nails into her palms and chewed her lower lip mutinously.

The rosy glow from last night, when he'd made her feel so special, had faded. She felt awkward and unsure…and hurt, which was ridiculous because she'd gone into this knowing who and what he was.

Obviously, last night had been business as usual for him. Why not marry the Murray sister who'd practically thrown herself at him? Did he believe she was so smitten and desperate for affection she'd be more easily controlled?

Why had she let herself be swept away by his looks, his confidences and his suave, expert lovemaking?

Because, your stupid crush on him turned your brain to mush.

And turned her raging hormones to fire. Never had she felt so physically and spiritually in tune with anyone. She'd actually thought, at one point, that they could be soul mates.

Soul mates! It was all an illusion. You were a fool, girl, and not for the first time.

"Look, I'd really better go," she said, her tone so sharp his dark head jerked toward her.

"Right. Then I'll drive you, since you left your car downtown."

"I can call a cab."

"No! I'll drive you."

Silently, she nodded.

He led the way to stairs that went down to the elevator and garage. In silence, they sped along the freeway in his silver Aston Martin until he slowed to take the off-ramp that led to where she'd parked downtown. After that, she *had* to speak to him in order to direct him to her small, dusty Toyota with several dings in its beige body. She let out a little moan when he pulled up behind her car and she saw the parking ticket flapping under her windshield wipers.

He got out and raced around the hood to open her door, but before he could, she'd flung it open.

"You sure there isn't something wrong?" he asked.

She snatched the ticket, but before she could get in her car, he slid his arms around her waist from behind.

He felt so solid and strong and warm, she barely suppressed a sigh. She yearned to stay in his arms even though she knew she needed to get away from him as quickly as possible to regroup.

He turned her to face him and his fingertips traced the length of her cheek in a tender, burning caress, and for a long second he stared into her troubled eyes with a mixture of concern and barely suppressed impatience. He seemed to care.

Liar.

"It's not easy letting you go," he said.

"People are watching us," she said mildly, even as she seethed with outrage.

"So what? Last night was very special to me, Kira. I'm sorry if you're upset about it. I hope it's just that it all happened too fast. I wasn't too rough, was I?"

The concern in his voice shook her. "No." She looked away, too tempted to meet his gaze.

"It's never been like that for me. I...I couldn't control myself, especially this morning. I wanted you again... badly. This is all happening too fast for me, too. I prefer being able to plan."

That's not what he'd said on the phone. Quinn seemed to have damn sure had a plan. Marry a Murray daughter. And he was sticking to it.

"Yes, it is happening…too fast." She bit her lip. "But… I'm okay." She wanted to brush off his words, to pretend she didn't care that he'd apologized and seemed genuinely worried about her physical and emotional state. He seemed all too likable. She almost believed him.

"Do you have a business card?" he asked gently.

She shook her head. "Nope. At least, not on me."

He flipped a card out of his pocket. "Well, here is mine. You can call me anytime. I want to see you again…as soon as possible. There's something very important I want to discuss with you."

The intensity of his gaze made her heart speed up. "You are not going back on your word about marrying Jaycee, are you?"

"How can you even ask? I'll call it off as soon as I leave you. Unfortunately, after that, I have to be away on business for several days, first to New York, then London. Murray Oil is in the middle of negotiating a big deal with the European Union. My meeting tonight in New York ends at eight, so call me after that. On my cell."

Did he intend to propose over the phone? Her throat felt thick as she forced herself to nod. Whipping out a pen and a pad, she wrote down her cell phone number. "Will you text me as soon as you break up with my sister?"

"Can I take that to mean you care about me…a little?" he asked.

"Sure," she whispered, exhaling a pent-up breath. How did he lie so easily? "Take it any way you like."

She had to get away from him, to be alone to think. Everything he said, everything he did, made her want him—even though she knew, after what she'd heard this morning, that she'd never been anything but a pawn in the game he was playing to exact revenge against her father.

She wasn't special to him. And if she didn't stand up for herself now, she never would be.

She would not let her father sell Jaycee *or* her to this man!

Four

"You're her father. I still can't believe you don't have a clue where Kira could be. Hell, she's been gone for nearly three weeks."

Shaking his head, Earl stalked across Quinn's corner office at Murray Oil to look out the window. "I told you, she's probably off somewhere painting. She does that."

Quinn hated himself for having practically ordered the infuriating Murray to his office again today. But he was that desperate to know Kira was safe. Her safety aside, he had a wedding planned and a bride to locate.

"You're sure she's not in any trouble?"

"Are *you* sure she didn't realize you were about to demand that she marry you?"

Other than wanting Kira to take Jaycee's place, he wasn't sure about a damn thing! Well, except that maybe he'd pushed Kira too fast and too far. Hell, she could have overheard him talking to Habib. She'd damn sure gotten quiet and sulky before they parted ways.

"I don't think—"

"I'd bet money she got wise to you and decided to let you stew in your own juices. She may seem sweet and malleable, but she's always had a mind of her own. She's impossible to control. It's why she lost her job. It's why I suggested you choose Jaycee in the first place. Jaycee is biddable."

Quinn felt heat climb his neck. He didn't want Jaycee. He'd never wanted Jaycee. He wanted Kira…sweet, passionate Kira who went wild every time he touched her. Her passion thrilled him as nothing else had in years.

The trouble was, after he'd made love to her that morning, he'd felt completely besotted and then out of sorts as a result. He hadn't wanted to dwell on what feeling such an all-consuming attraction so quickly might mean. Now he knew that if anything had happened to her, he'd never forgive himself.

"I couldn't ask her to marry me after our dinner. It was too soon. Hell, maybe she did figure it all out and run off before I could explain."

"Well, I checked our hunting lodges at the ranch where she goes to paint wildlife, and I've left messages with my caretaker at the island where she paints birds. Nobody's seen her. Sooner or later she'll turn up. She always does. You'll just have to be patient."

"Not my forte."

"Quinn, she's okay. When she's in between museum jobs, she runs around like this. She's always been a free spirit."

"Right." Quinn almost growled. He disliked that the other man could see he was vulnerable and crazed by Kira's disappearance. The need to find her, to find out why she'd vanished, had been building inside him. He couldn't go on if he didn't solve this mystery—and not just because the wedding date loomed.

His one night with Kira had been the closest thing to perfection he'd known since before his dad had died. Never had he experienced with any other woman anything like what he'd shared with Kira. Hell, he hadn't known such closeness was possible. He'd lost himself completely in her, talked to her as he'd never talked to another person.

Even though she'd seemed distant the next morning, he'd thought she'd felt the same wealth of emotion he had and was running scared. But no—something else had made her vanish without a word, even before he'd told her she'd have to marry him if Jaycee didn't. Thinking back, all he could imagine was that she'd felt vulnerable and afraid after their shared night—or that she *had* overheard him talking to Habib.

Then the day after he'd dropped her at her car, Quinn had texted her, as he'd promised, to let her know he'd actually broken it off with Jacinda. She'd never called him back. Nor had she answered her phone since then. She'd never returned to her tiny apartment or her place of employment.

Kira had called her friend Betty to check in, and promised she'd call weekly to keep in touch, but she hadn't given an explanation for her departure or an estimation for when she'd return.

Quinn had to rethink his situation. He'd stopped romancing Jacinda, but he hadn't canceled the wedding because he planned to marry Kira instead. Come Saturday, a thousand people expected him to marry a Murray daughter.

Apparently, his future father-in-law's mind was running along the same worrisome track.

"Quinn, you've got to be reasonable. We've got to call off the wedding," Earl said.

"I'm going to marry Kira."

"You're talking nonsense. Kira's gone. Without a bride, you're going to piss off the very people we want to reassure. Stockholders, clients and employees of Murray Oil. Not to mention—this whole thing is stressing the hell out of Vera, and in her condition that isn't good."

Several months earlier, when Quinn had stalked into Earl's office with enough shares to demand control of Murray Oil, Earl, his eyes blurry and his shoulders slumped, had sat behind his desk already looking defeated.

The older man had wearily confided that his wife was seriously ill. Not only had Earl not cared that Quinn would soon be in charge of Murray Oil, he'd said the takeover was the answer to a prayer. It was time he retired. With Murray Oil in good hands, he could devote himself to his beloved wife, who was sick and maybe dying.

"She's everything to me," he'd whispered. "The way your father was to you and the way your mother was to him before she left him."

"Why tell me—your enemy?" Quinn had asked.

"I don't think of you as my enemy. I never was one to see the world in black or white, the way Kade, your dad, did—the way you've chosen to see it since his death. Whether you believe me or not, I loved your father, and I was sorry about our misunderstanding. You're just like him, you know, so now that I've got my own challenge to face, there's nobody I'd rather turn the company over to than you.

"Vera doesn't want me talking about her illness to friends and family. She can't stand the thought of people, even her daughters, thinking of her as weak and sick. I'm glad I finally have someone I can tell."

Quinn had been stunned. For years, he had hated Earl, had wanted revenge, had looked forward to bringing the man to his knees. But ever since that conversation his feelings had begun to change. The connection he'd found with Kira had hastened that process.

He'd begun to rethink his choices, reconsider his past. Not all his memories of Earl were negative. He could remember some wonderful times hunting and fishing with the blunt-spoken Earl and his dad. As a kid, he'd loved the stories Earl had told around the campfire.

Maybe the bastard had been partially responsible for his father's death. But maybe an equal share of the blame lay with his own father.

Not that Quinn trusted his new attitude. He'd gone too far toward his goal of vengeance not to seize Murray Oil. And he still believed taking a Murray bride would make the acquisition run more smoothly.

"I will get married on Saturday," Quinn said. "All we have to do is convince Kira to come back and marry me."

"Right. But how? We don't even know where she is."

"We don't have to know. All we have to do is motivate her to return," Quinn said softly.

Seabirds raced along the beach, pecking at seaweed. Her jeans rolled to her knees, Kira stood in the shallow surf of Murray Island and wiggled her toes in the cool, damp sand as the wind whipped her hair against her cheeks. Blowing sand stung her bare arms and calves.

Kira needed to make her weekly phone call to Betty after her morning walk—a phone call she dreaded. Each week, it put her back in touch with reality, which was what she wanted to escape from.

Still, she'd known she couldn't stay on the island forever. She'd just thought that solitude would have cleared her head of Quinn by now. But it hadn't. She missed him.

Three weeks of being here alone had changed nothing. None of her confusion or despair about her emotional entanglement with Quinn had lifted.

Maybe if she hadn't been calling Betty to check in, she would be calmer. Betty had told her about Quinn's relentless visits to the restaurant. Thinking about Quinn looking for her had stirred up her emotions and had blocked her artistically. All she could paint was his handsome face.

Well, at least she was painting. When she'd been frustrated while working at the museum, she hadn't even been able to hold a paintbrush.

Since it was past time to call Betty again, she headed for the family beach house. When she climbed the wooden stairs and entered, the wind caught the screen door and banged it behind her.

She turned on her cell phone and climbed to the second floor where the signal and the views of the high surf were better.

Betty answered on the first ring. "You still okay all alone out there?"

"I'm fine. How's Rudy?"

She'd packed her cat and his toys and had taken him to Betty's, much to his dismay.

"Rudy's taken over as usual. Sleeps in my bed. He's right here. He can hear your voice on speakerphone. He's very excited, twitchin' his tail and all." She paused, then, "I worry about you out there alone, Kira."

"Jim's around. He checks on me."

Jim was the island's caretaker. She'd taken him into her confidence and asked him not to tell anyone, not even her father, where she was.

"Well, there's something I need to tell you, something I've been dreadin' tellin' you," Betty began.

"What?"

"That fella of yours, Quinn…"

"He's not my fella."

"Well, he sure acts like he's your guy when he drops by. He's been drillin' the staff, makin' sure you weren't datin' anyone. Said he didn't want to lay claim to a woman who belonged to another."

Lay claim? Kira caught her breath. Just thinking about Quinn in the restaurant looking for her made her breasts swell and her heart throb.

Darn it—would she never forget him?

"Well, today he comes over just as I'm unlocking the door and launches into a tirade about how he's gonna have to break his promise to you and marry your sister, Jaycee! This Saturday!

"I thought it right funny at first, him sayin' that, when he comes by lookin' haunted, askin' after you all the time, so I said up front I didn't buy it. Called him a liar, I did.

"He said maybe he preferred you, but you'd forced his hand. He had to marry a Murray daughter for business reasons, so he would. Everything is set. He told me to read the newspapers, if I didn't believe him. And I did. They're really getting married. It's all over the internet, too."

"What?"

"Tomorrow! Saturday! I know he told you he broke off his wedding plans, but if he did, they're on again. He's every bit as bad as you said. You were right to go away. If I was you, I'd never come back."

So, since he'd never cared which Murray sister he married, he was going to marry Jaycee after all.

Well, she'd stop him. She'd go back—at once—and she'd stop him cold.

Five

A sign in front of the church displayed a calendar that said Murray-Sullivan Wedding: 7:30 p.m.

It was five-thirty as Kira swung into the mostly empty parking lot.

Good. No guests had arrived. She'd made it in time.

The sun was low; the shadows long; the light a rosy gold. Not that she took the time to notice the clarity of the light or the rich green of the grass or the tiny spring leaves budding on the trees. Her heart was pounding. She was perspiring as she hit the brakes and jumped out of her Toyota.

The drive from the coast hadn't taken much more than three hours, but the trip had tired her. Feeling betrayed and yet desperate to find her sister and stop this travesty before it was too late, Kira ran toward the back of the church where the dressing rooms were. Inside, dashing from room to room, she threw open doors, calling her sister's name. Then, suddenly, in the last room, she found Jaycee, wearing a blue cotton dress with a strand of pearls at her throat. With her blond hair cascading down her back, Jaycee sat quietly in front of a long, gilt mirror, applying lipstick. She looked as if she'd been carefully posed by a photographer.

"Jaycee!" Kira cried breathlessly. "At last… Why aren't you wearing…a wedding dress?"

Then she saw the most beautiful silk gown seeded with tiny pearls lying across a sofa and a pair of white satin shoes on the floor.

"Oh, but that's why you're here…to dress… Of course. Where's Mother? Why isn't Mother here to help you?"

"She's not feeling well. I think she's resting. Mother and Quinn told me to wait here."

Odd. Usually when it came to organizing any social affair, their mother had endless reserves of energy that lasted her until the very end of the event.

"Where are your bridesmaids?"

Turning like an actress compelled by her cue, Jaycee pressed her lips together and then put her lipstick inside her blue purse. "I was so worried you wouldn't come," she said. "I was truly afraid you wouldn't show. We all were. Quinn most especially. But me, too. He'll be so happy you're here. I don't know what he would have done if you hadn't gotten here in time. You don't know how important you are to him."

Right. That's why he's marrying you without a qualm.

As always, Jaycee worried about everyone she loved. Kira very much doubted that Quinn would be happy with her once she finished talking to Jaycee.

Guilt flooded Kira. How would she ever find the words to explain to her trusting sister why she couldn't marry Quinn? Jaycee, who'd always been loved by everybody, probably couldn't imagine there was a soul in the world who wouldn't love her if she tried hard enough to win him. After all, Daddy had given his blessing.

"You can't marry Quinn today," Kira stated flatly.

"I know that. He told me all about you two. When Daddy asked me to marry Quinn, I tried to tell myself it was the right thing to do. For the family and all. But…when I found out he wanted to marry you…it was such a relief."

"Why did you show up here today if you knew all this?"

"Quinn will…explain everything." Jaycee's eyes widened as the door opened. Kira whirled to tell their visitor that this was a private conversation, but her words died in a convulsive little growl. Quinn, dressed in a tux that set off his broad shoulders and stunning dark looks to heartstopping perfection, strode masterfully into the room.

Feeling cornered, Kira sank closer to Jaycee. When he saw her, he stopped, his eyes flashing with hurt and anger before he caught her mood and stiffened.

"I was hoping you'd make it in time for the wedding," he said, his deep baritone cutting her to the quick.

"Damn you!" Her throat tightened as she arose. "Liar! How could you do this?"

"I'm thrilled to see you, too, darlin'," he murmured, his gaze devouring her. "You do look lovely."

Kira, who'd driven straight from the island without making a single stop, was wearing a pair of worn, tight jeans and a T-shirt that hugged her curves. She hadn't bothered with makeup or a comb for her tangled hair. She could do nothing but take in a mortified breath at his comment while she stared at his dark face, the face she'd painted so many times even when images of him had blurred through her tears.

"What is the meaning of this?" she screamed.

"There's no need for hysterics, darlin'," he said calmly.

"Don't *darlin'* me! You have no right to call me that!"

she shrieked. "I haven't even begun to show you hysterics! I'm going to tear you limb from limb. Pound you into this tile floor... Skin you alive—"

"Kira, Quinn's been so worried about you. Frantic that you wouldn't show up in time," Jaycee began. "Talk about wedding jitters. He's had a full-blown case..."

"I'll just bet he has!"

"I see we misunderstand each other, Kira. I was afraid of this. Jacinda," he said in a silky tone that maddened Kira further because it made her feel jealous of her innocent sister, "could you give us a minute? I need to talk to Kira alone."

With a quick, nervous glance in Kira's direction, Jaycee said, "Kira, are you sure you'll be okay? You don't look so good."

Kira nodded mutely, wanting to spare Jaycee any necessary embarrassment. So Jaycee slipped out of the room and closed the door quietly.

Her hand raised, Kira bounded toward him like a charging lioness ready to claw her prey, but he caught her wrist and used it to lever her closer.

"Let me go!" she cried.

"Not while you're in such a violent mood, darlin'. You'd only scratch me or do something worse that you'd regret."

"I don't think so."

"This storm will pass, as all storms do. You'll see. Because it's due to a misunderstanding."

"A misunderstanding? I don't think so! You promised you'd break up with my sister, and I, being a fool, believed you. Then you slept with me. How could you go back on a promise like that after what we—"

"I wouldn't. I didn't." His voice was calm, dangerously soft. "I've kept my promise."

"Liar. If I hadn't shown up, you would have married my sister."

"The hell I would have! It was a bluff. How else could I get you to come back to San Antonio? I was going mad not knowing where you were or if you were all right. If you hadn't shown up, I would have looked like a fool, but I wouldn't have married your sister."

"But the newspapers all say you're going to marry her. Here. Today."

"I know what they say because my people wrote the press releases. That was all part of the bluff—to get you here. We'll have to write a correction now, won't we? The only Murray sister I plan to marry today is you, darlin'. If it'll help to convince you, I'll repeat myself on bended knee."

When he began to kneel, she shrieked at him, "Don't you dare…or I'll kick you. This is not a proposal. This is a farce."

"I'm asking you to marry me, darlin'."

He didn't love her. He never would. His was a damaged soul. He'd told her that in plain, hurtful terms right after he'd made love to her.

The details of the conversation she'd overheard came back to her.

"Let me get this straight," she said. "You always intended to marry a Murray daughter."

"And your father suggested Jaycee because he thought she would agree more easily."

"Then I came to your office and asked you not to marry her, and after dinner and sex, you decided one sister was as good as the other. So, why not marry the *easy* sister? Is that about it?"

"Easy?" He snorted. "I wish to hell you were easy, but no, you disappeared for weeks."

"Back to the basics. Marrying one of the Murray daughters is about business and nothing more to you?"

"In the beginning…maybe that was true…"

"I repeat—I heard you talking to Habib, whoever the hell he is, the morning after we made love. And your conversation made it seem that your relationship with me, with any Murray daughter, was still about business. Your voice was cold, matter-of-fact and all too believable."

"Habib works for me. Why would I tell him how I felt when I'd only known you a day and was still reeling, trying to figure it out for myself?"

"Oh, so now you're Mr. Sensitive. Well, I don't believe you, and I won't marry you. I've always dreamed of marrying for love. I know that is an emotion you despise and are incapable of feeling. Maybe that's why you can be so high-handed about forcing me to take my sister's place and marry you. I think you…are despicable…and cold. This whole situation is too cynical for words."

"It's true that our marriage will make Murray Oil employees see this change of leadership in a less hostile way, as for the rest—"

"So, for you, it's business. I will not be bought and sold like so many shares of stock. I am a human being. An educated, Western woman with a woman's dreams and feelings."

"I know that. It's what makes you so enchanting."

"Bull. You've chosen to ride roughshod over me and my family. You don't care what any of us want or feel."

"I do care what you feel. I care too damn much. It's driven me mad these last few weeks, worrying about you. I wished you'd never walked into my office, never made me feel… Hell! You've made me crazy, woman."

Before she had any idea of what he was about to do, he

took a long step toward her. Seizing her, he crushed her against his tall, hard body.

His hands gripping her close, his mouth slanted across hers with enough force to leave her breathless and have her moaning…and then, dear God, as his masterful kiss went on and on and on, she wanted nothing except more of him. Melting, she opened her mouth and her heart. How could she need him so much? She'd missed him terribly—every day they'd been apart.

Needle-sharp thrills raced down her spine. His tongue plunged inside her lips, and soon she was so drunk on his taste and passion, her nails dug into his back. She wanted to be somewhere else, somewhere more private.

She'd missed him. She'd wanted this. She hadn't been able to admit it. His clean, male scent intoxicated her. The length of his all-too-familiar body pressing against hers felt necessary. Every second, asleep and awake, she had thought of him, craved him—craved this. Being held by him only made the need more bittersweet. How could she want such a cold man so desperately?

"We can't feel this, do this," she whispered in a tortured breath even as she clung to him.

"Says who?"

"We're in a church."

His arms tightened their hold. "Marry me, and we can do all we want to each other—tonight…and forever," he said huskily. "It will become a sacred marital right."

How could he say that when he didn't care which Murray sister walked down the aisle as long as it saved him a few million dollars?

The thought hissed through her like cold water splashed onto a fire.

Her parents' love had carried them through many difficulties. Her dad was a workaholic. Her mother was a perfectionist, a status-seeking socialite. But they had always been madly in love.

Kira had grown up believing in the sanctity of marriage. How could she even consider a marriage that would be nothing more than a business deal to her husband?

A potential husband who had lapped up women the way she might attack a box of chocolates. Maybe he temporarily lusted after her, but he didn't love her and never could, as he'd told her. No doubt some other woman would soon catch his fancy.

Even wanting him as she did, she wasn't ready to settle for a marriage based on poor judgment, a momentary sexual connection, shallow lust, revenge and business.

She sucked in a breath and pushed against his massive chest. His grip eased slightly, maybe because the handsome rat thought he'd bent her to his will with his heated words and kisses.

"Listen to me," she said softly. "Are *you* listening?"

"Yes, darlin'."

"I won't marry you. Or any man who could dream up such a cold, cynical scheme."

"How can you call this cold when we're both burning up with desire?" He traced a fingertip along her cheek that made her jump and shiver before she jerked her head away.

"Cheap tricks like that won't induce me to change my mind. There's nothing you can say or do that will convince me. No masterful seduction technique that you honed in other women's bedrooms will do the job, either."

"I wish I had the time to woo you properly and make you believe how special you are."

Special. Now, *there* was a word that hit a nerve. She'd always wanted to feel beloved to those she cared about. How did he know that? It infuriated her that he could guess her sensibilities and so easily use them to manipulate her.

"What you want is revenge and money. If you had all of eternity, it wouldn't be long enough. I won't have you or your loveless deal. That's final."

"We'll see."

His silky baritone was so blatantly confident it sent an icy chill shivering down her spine.

Six

"You told him—the enemy—that Mother might be dying, and you didn't tell me or Jaycee! And you did this behind my back—weeks and weeks ago!"

Kira fisted and unfisted her hands as she sat beside her father in the preacher's library. Rage and hurt shot through her.

"How could you be so disloyal? I've never felt so completely betrayed. Sometimes I feel like a stray you picked up on the side of the road. You didn't really want me—only you have to keep me because it's the right thing to do."

"Nonsense! You're our daughter."

He blanched at her harsh condemnation, and she hung her head in guilt. "I'm sorry," she muttered.

She wanted to weep and scream, but she wouldn't be able to think if she lost all control.

"You know your mother and how she always wants to protect you. I thought only of her when I confided in him."

"First, you sell Jaycee to him because, as always, she's your first choice."

"Kira…"

"Now, it's me."

"Don't blame me. He wants *you!*"

"As if that makes you blameless. Why didn't either of my parents think about protecting their daughters from Quinn?"

"It's complicated. Even if your mother weren't sick, we need someone younger at the top, someone with a clearer vision of the future. Quinn's not what you think. Not what the press thinks. I knew him as a boy. This can be a win-win situation for you both."

"He grew into a vengeful man who hates us."

"You're wrong. He doesn't hate you. You'll never make me believe that. You should have seen how he acted when you disappeared. I think he'll make you a good husband."

"You don't care about that. You don't care about me. You only care about Murray Oil's bottom line, about retiring and being with Mother."

"How can you say that? I care about you, and I care about this family as much as you do. Yes, I need to take care of your mother now, but like I said—I know Quinn. I've watched him. He's good, smart, solid. And he's a brilliant businessman who will be the best possible CEO for Murray Oil during these tumultuous economic times. He's done great things already. If I had time, I'd fill you in on how he helped organize a deal with the EU while you were gone. He's still in the middle of it at the moment."

"For years he's worked to destroy you."

"Hell, maybe he believed that's what he was doing, maybe others bought it, too, but I never did. I don't think *he* knew what was driving him. This company is his heritage, too. And I saw how he was when you were gone.

The man was beside himself. He was afraid you were in trouble. I don't know what happened between the two of you before you ran away, but I know caring when I see it. Quinn cares for you. He's just like his father. You should have seen how Kade loved his wife, Esther. Then you'd know the love Quinn is capable of."

"You think Quinn will come to love me? Are you crazy? Quinn doesn't believe he can love again. The man has lived his life fueled by hate. Hatred for all of us. How many times do I have to repeat it?"

"Maybe so, but the only reason his hatred was so strong was that the love that drove it was just as strong. You're equally passionate. You just haven't found your calling yet." Her father took her hands in his as he continued, "You should have seen him the day he came to tell me he had me by the balls and was set to take over Murray Oil. He could have broken me that day. Instead, he choked when I told him about Vera because he's more decent than he knows. He's ten times the man that his father ever was, that's for sure. Maybe you two didn't meet under ideal circumstances, but he'll make you a good husband."

"You believe that only because you want to believe it. You're as cold and calculating as he is."

"I want what's best for all of us."

"This is a deal to you—just like it is to him. Neither of you care which daughter marries Quinn today, as long as the deal is completed for Murray Oil."

"I suggested Jaycee primarily to avoid a scene like the one we're having, but Quinn wants you. He won't even consider Jaycee now, even though he was willing to marry her before you meddled."

"Oh, so this fiasco is my fault."

"Someday you'll thank me."

"I'm not marrying him. I won't be sacrificed."

"Before you make your decision, your mother wants to talk to you." He pressed a couple of buttons on his phone, and the door behind him opened as if by magic. Her mother's perfectly coiffed blonde head caught the light of the overhead lamp. She was gripping her cell phone with clawlike hands.

She looked so tiny. Why hadn't Kira noticed how thin and colorless her once-vital mother had become? How frail and tired she looked?

"Dear God," Kira whispered as she got up and folded her precious mother into her arms. She felt her mother's ribs and spine as she pressed her body closer. Her mother was fading away right before her eyes.

"Please," her mother whispered. "I'm not asking you to do this for me, but for your father. I need all my strength to fight this illness. He can't be worried about Murray Oil. Or you. Or Jaycee. I've always been the strong one, you know. I can't fight this if I have to worry about him. And I can't leave him alone. He'd be lost without me."

"I—I…"

"I'm sure your father's told you there's a very important international deal with the EU on the table right now. It can make or break our company."

"*His* company."

"Your father and I and the employees of Murray Oil need your help, Kira. Your marriage to Quinn would endorse his leadership both here and abroad. Have I ever asked you for anything before?"

Of course she had. She'd been an ambitious and very demanding mother. Kira had always hoped that when she married and had children, she'd finally be part of a family where she felt as if she belonged, where she was accepted, flaws and all. How ironic that when her parents finally needed her to play a role they saw as vital to their survival, their need trampled on her heartfelt dream to be at the core of her own happy family.

Would she ever matter to her husband the way her mother mattered to her father? Not if the man who was forcing her to marry him valued her only as a business prize. Once Quinn had Murray Oil under his control, how long would she be of any importance to him?

Still, what choice did she have? For the first time ever, her family really needed her. And she'd always wanted that above all things.

"I don't want to marry you! But yes!" she spat at Quinn after he had ushered her into one of the private dressing rooms. She'd spun around to face him in the deadly quiet. "*Yes!* I will marry you, since you insist on having your answer today."

"Since I insist we marry today!"

Never had she seemed lovelier than with her dark, heavily lashed eyes glittering with anger and her slender hands fisted defiantly on her hips. He was so glad to have found her. So glad she was all right. So glad she'd agreed without wasting any more precious time. Once she was his, they'd get past this.

"Then I'll probably hate you forever for forcing me to make such a terrible bargain."

Her words stabbed him with pain, but he steeled himself not to show it. She looked mad enough to spit fire and stood at least ten feet from him so he couldn't touch her.

Looking down, staring anywhere but at her, he fought to hide the hurt and relief he felt at her answer, as well as the regret he felt for having bullied her.

Bottom line—she would be his. Today. The thought of any man touching her as Quinn had touched her their one night together seemed a sacrilege worthy of vengeful murder.

"Good. I'm glad that's finally settled and we can move on," he said in a cool tone that masked his own seething passions. "I've hired people to help you get ready. Beauticians. Designers. I selected a wedding gown that I hope you'll like, and I have a fitter here in case I misjudged your size."

"You did all that?" Her narrow brows arched with icy contempt. "You were that sure I'd say yes? You thought I was some doll you could dress up in white satin…"

"Silk, actually, and no, I don't think you're some doll—" He stopped. He wasn't about to admit how desperate he'd felt during the dark days of her absence, or how out of control, even though his silence only seemed to make her angrier.

"Look, just because you bullied me into saying yes doesn't mean I like the way you manipulated my family into taking your side. And, since this is strictly a business deal to all of you, I want you to know it's nothing but a business deal to me, too. So, I'm here by agreeing to a marriage in name only. The only reasons I'm marrying you are to help my father and mother and Murray Oil and to save Jaycee from you."

His lips thinned. "There's too much heat in you. You won't be satisfied with that kind of marriage…any more than I will."

"Well, I won't marry you unless you agree to it."

He would have agreed to sell his soul to the devil to have her. "Fine," he said. "Suit yourself, but when you change your mind, I won't hold you to your promise."

"I won't change my mind."

He didn't argue the point or try to seduce her. He'd

make the necessary concessions to get her to the altar. He'd pushed her way too far already.

He was willing to wait, to give her the time she needed. He didn't expect it would be long before he'd have her in his bed once more. And perhaps it was for the best that they take a break from the unexpected passion they'd found.

Maybe he wanted her to believe his motive for marrying her was business related, but it was far from the truth. Need—pure, raw, unadulterated need—was what drove him. If they didn't make love for a while, perhaps he could get control over all his emotions.

After they'd made love the last time, he'd felt too much, had felt too bound to her. Her power over him scared the hell out of him. She'd left him just as carelessly as his own mother had left his father, hadn't she?

He needed her like the air he breathed. Kira had simply become essential.

But he wasn't about to tell her that. No way could he trust this overwhelming need for any woman. Hadn't his father's love for Quinn's own mother played the largest part in his father's downfall? And then his own love for his father had crushed him when his father died.

Grief was too big a price to pay for love. He never wanted to be weak and needy like that again.

Seven

"You look...absolutely amazing," her mother said, sounding almost as pleased as she usually did when she complimented Jaycee. "Don't frown! You know you do!"

In a trancelike daze, Kira stared at the vision in the gilt mirror. How had Quinn's beauty experts made her look like herself and yet so much better? They'd tugged and pulled, clipped and sprayed unmercifully, and now here she was, a sexy, glowing beauty in a diaphanous silk gown that clung much too revealingly. The dress flattered her slim figure perfectly. How had he known her exact size and what would most become her?

All those blondes, she told herself. He understood glamour and women, not her. The dress wasn't about her. He wanted her to be like them.

Still, until this moment, she'd never realized how thoroughly into the Cinderella fantasy she'd been. Not that she would ever admit that, on some deep level, he'd pleased her.

"How can I walk down the aisle in a dress you can see straight through?"

"You're stunning. The man has flawless taste."

"Another reason to hate him," Kira mumbled, brushing aside her mother's hard-won approval and pleasure for fear of having it soften her attitude toward Quinn.

"Haven't I always told you, you should have been playing up your assets all along," her mother said.

"Straight guys aren't supposed to know how to do stuff like this."

"Count yourself lucky your man has such a rare talent. You'll have to start letting him dress you. Maybe he knows how to bring out your best self in other areas, as well. If he does, you'll amaze yourself."

The way he had during their one night together. A shiver traced through her. "May I remind you that this is not a real marriage?"

"If you'd quit saying that in such a sulky, stubborn tone, maybe it would become one, and very soon. He's very handsome. I'll bet there isn't a single woman in this church who wouldn't trade places with you."

"He doesn't love me."

"Well, why don't you start talking to him in a sweet voice? More like the one that you always use with that impossible cat of yours?"

"Maybe because he's not my loyal, beloved pet. Maybe because being bullied into a relationship with him does not make me feel sweet and tender."

"Well, if you ask me, the men you've chosen freely weren't much to brag about. Quinn is so well educated and well respected."

A few minutes later, when the wedding march started, Kira glided down the aisle in white satin slippers holding on to her father's arm. When she heard awed gasps from the guests, she lifted her eyes from the carpet, but in the sea of faces it was Quinn's proud smile alone that made her heart leap and brought a quick, happy blush to her cheeks.

Then her tummy flipped as their souls connected in that uncanny way that made her feel stripped bare. Fortunately, her father angled himself between them, and she got a brief reprieve from Quinn's mesmerizing spell.

Not that it was long before her father had handed her over to her bridegroom where she became her awkward, uncertain self again. As she stood beside Quinn at the altar, she fidgeted while they exchanged rings and vows. With a smile, he clasped her hand in his. Threading her fingers through his, he held them still. Somehow, his warm touch reassured her, and she was able to pledge herself to him forever in a strong, clear voice.

This isn't a real marriage, she reminded herself, even as that bitter truth tore at her heart.

But the tall man beside her, the music, the church and the incredibly beautiful dress, combined with the memory of her own radiance in the mirror, made her doubt what she knew to be true. Was she a simple-minded romantic after all, or just a normal girl who wanted to marry a man she loved?

After the preacher told Quinn he could kiss his bride, Quinn's arms encased her slim body with infinite gentleness. His eyes went dark in that final moment before he lowered his beautifully sculpted mouth to hers. Despite her intention not to react to his lips, to feel nothing when he kissed her, her blood pulsed. Gripping his arms, she leaned into him.

"We'd better make this count because if you have your way, it will probably be a while before I convince you to let me kiss you again," he teased huskily.

She threw her arms around his warm, bronzed neck, her

fingers stroking his thick hair, and drew his head down. Fool that she was, it felt glorious to be in his arms as he claimed her before a thousand witnesses.

Such a ceremonial kiss shouldn't mean anything, she told herself. He was just going through the motions. As was she.

"Darlin'," he murmured. "Sweet darlin' Kira. You are incredibly beautiful, incredibly dear. I want you so much. No bridegroom has ever felt prouder of his bride."

The compliment brought her startled eyes up to his, and his tender expression fulfilled her long-felt secret desire to be special to someone. For one shining instant, she believed the dream. If a man as sophisticated as he was could really be proud of her and want her...

He didn't, of course... Oh, but if only he could...

Then his mouth was on hers. His tongue inside the moist recesses of her lips had her blood heating and her breath shuddering in her lungs. Her limbs went as limp as a rag doll's. When she felt his heart hammering against her shoulder blade, she let him pull her even closer.

The last thing she wanted was to feel this swift rush of warm pleasure, but she couldn't stop herself. How could a single, staged kiss affect her so powerfully?

He was the first to pull away. His smile was slow and sweet. "Don't forget—the last thing I want is for our marriage to be business-only," he whispered against her ravaged lips. "You can change your mind anytime, darlin'. Anytime. Nothing would please me more than to take you to my bed again."

"Well, I won't change my mind! Not ever!" she snapped much too vehemently.

He laughed and hugged her close. "You will. I should warn you that nothing appeals to me more than a challenge."

After a lengthy photography session—she was surprised that he wanted photos of a wedding that couldn't possibly mean anything to him—they were driven by limousine to the reception, held at his opulent club in an older section of San Antonio.

Once again he'd planned everything—decorations in the lavish ballroom, the menu, the band—with enough attention to detail that her critical mother was thoroughly impressed and radiantly aglow with pride. Vera sailed through the glittering throng like a bejeweled queen among awed subjects as she admired the banks of flowers, frozen sculptures and the sumptuous food and arrangements. Kira was secretly pleased Quinn had at least married her under circumstances that gave her mother, who loved to impress, so much pleasure.

With a few exceptions, the majority of the guests were employees and clients of Murray Oil. The few personal friends and family attending included Quinn's uncle Jerry, who'd been his best man, and her friend Betty. The guest list also included a few important people from the Texas art world, mostly museum directors, including Gary Whitehall, the former boss who'd let her go…for daring to have an opinion of her own.

Since the wedding was a business affair, Kira was surprised that Quinn had allowed his employees to bring their children, but he had. And no one was enjoying themselves more than the kids. They danced wildly and chased each other around the edges of the dance floor, and when a father spoke harshly to the little flower girl for doing cartwheels in her long velvet gown, Quinn soothed the child.

Watching the way the little girl brightened under his tender ministrations, Kira's heart softened.

"He's very good with children," Betty whispered into her ear. "He'll make a wonderful father."

"This is not a real marriage."

"You could have fooled me. I get all mushy inside every time he looks at you. He's *so* good-looking."

"He's taken over my life."

"Well, I'd be glad to take him off your hands. I think he's hunky. And so polite. Did I tell you how nice he was to Rudy after he found out the reason the beast wouldn't stop meowing was because he missed you? He sat down with that cat and commiserated. Made me give the beast some tuna."

"I'll bet he got you to feed him, too."

"Well, every time Quinn came to the restaurant he did sit down with me and whoever was waiting tables, like he was one of us. He bragged on my pies."

"Which got him free pies I bet."

"His favorite is the same as yours."

"Your gooey lemon meringue?"

"I thought he was sweet to remember to invite me to the wedding. He called this evening after you showed up."

Betty hushed when Quinn appeared at his bride's side and stayed, playing the attentive groom long after his duties in the receiving line ended. Even when several beauties— one a flashy blonde he'd once dated named Cristina, whom he'd apparently hired as a junior executive—came up and flirted boldly, he'd threaded his fingers through Kira's and tucked her closer.

For more than an hour, ignoring all others, he danced only with Kira. He was such a strong partner, she found herself enjoying the reception immensely as he whirled her around the room. She could see the admiring glances following them. He smiled down at her often, no doubt to give the appearance that she delighted him. The women who'd flirted with him watched him with intense interest, especially Cristina, whose lovely mouth began to pout.

"I've never been much of a dancer," Kira confessed during a slow number.

"You could've fooled me. Just goes to show that all you need is a little self-confidence."

Had his attentiveness given her that, at least briefly? When Gary Whitehall's gaze met hers over Quinn's broad shoulder, he smiled tightly. As Quinn's wife, she'd taken a huge step up in the art world. Was Gary wishing he'd let someone else go other than her when the budget had been tight? Why had Quinn included him on the guest list?

After a fast number, when Kira admitted she was thirsty, Quinn left her to get champagne. Seeing his chance, Gary rushed up to her.

"You look lovely," he said, smiling in the way he used to smile at major artists and important donors. How rare had been the smiles and compliments he'd bestowed on his lowly curator for her hard work. "I'm very happy for you," he said.

She nodded, embarrassed to be so pleased that her marriage had won his respect.

"If I can do anything for you, anything at all, just call me. I am rewriting your letter of recommendation. Not that you'll need to work now."

"I intend to work again. I loved my job."

"Your husband has been most generous to the museum. We value his friendship and expertise almost as much as we will value yours—as his wife," he gushed. "I have a feeling we may have a position for a curator opening up soon. If so, I'll give you a call."

She thought about what Gary had said about a position possibly being available and was surprised she was so pleased. Maybe…she would consider working for him again…if he made her the right offer. She would, however, demand to have more power.

Stunned, she stared at him. Then Quinn returned with her champagne. The two men shook hands and exchanged pleasantries. When Quinn made it clear he preferred his bride's conversation to art talk, Gary quickly eased himself back into the crowd. But every time after that conversation, when their eyes met, Gary smiled at her.

For a man who supposedly hated her family, Quinn was excessively attentive to her mother and father and Jaycee. He talked to them, ordered them wine and appetizers, acted as if he actually wished to please them. He was especially solicitous of her mother, who positively glowed.

Kira watched him during dinner, and his warm smiles and polite comments rang with sincerity. If she hadn't known better, she wouldn't have believed he was simply acting a part in order to reassure oil company clients and executives that Murray Oil was in good hands.

Never had a bridegroom appeared more enthusiastic, even when his uncle Jerry congratulated him on his marriage.

"Kira, he's had his nose to the grindstone so long, we were beginning to think that's all he'd ever do," Jerry said. "We'd given up on you, son. Now I see you just hadn't met the right girl. Sooner or later, if we're lucky, love comes our way. The trick is to know it and appreciate it. When you fall in love, wanting to spend the rest of your life with the same woman doesn't seem that hard to imagine."

Quinn stared at her as if he agreed. The two men shook hands again and laughed. But since Quinn's heart wasn't really in their marriage, she wondered how soon he'd give up trying to pretend to people like his uncle. After that, when she felt herself too charmed by one of Quinn's thoughtful smiles or gestures, she reminded herself that she'd be a fool if she fell for his act. Their marriage was a business deal. She didn't matter to him. She never would.

All too soon the dinner and dancing came to an end, and she and Quinn had changed into street clothes and were dashing out to his limo while cheering guests showered them with birdseed. When someone threw seeds straight at her eyes, and a tear streamed down her cheek, Quinn took out his monogrammed handkerchief and dabbed her face while everybody cheered.

She expected to be driven to his loft. Instead, the limo whisked them to his sleek private jet, which had been prepared for flight and was waiting outside a hangar at the San Antonio International Airport.

"Where are we going?" she asked as he helped her out into the blinding glare of dozens of flashes.

"Honeymoon," he whispered, his mouth so close to her ear she felt the heat of his breath. Her heart raced until she reminded herself he was only staging a romantic shot for the press.

Putting his arm around her, he faced the reporters, who asked him questions about his pending international oil deal as well as his marriage.

With abundant charm and smiles, he answered a few and then, grabbing her by the elbow, propelled her into his jet.

"Surely a honeymoon isn't necessary," she said when they were safely on board.

He smiled down at her. "A man only marries once."

"Like that reporter asked—how can you afford the time when you're working on that important EU deal?"

"You have to make time…for what's important."

"So, why did you notify the press about our honeymoon? Was it only so the EU people would know you married into the Murray family?"

"Why don't you relax? Step one, quit asking so many questions. Step two, just enjoy."

"You're thorough. I'll have to give you that. Even so,

how can I leave town when I haven't even packed for a trip," she said. "Besides, I have a cat—Rudy. I promised Betty I'd relieve her... He's been crying for me."

"I know. Rudy's all taken care of. Jacinda's going to look after him at your apartment. So, he'll be on his own turf. I bought him a case of tuna."

"You shopped for Rudy?"

"Okay—so I sent my assistant. And your mother helped me shop and pack for you."

"I'll bet she loved that."

"She did—although I did make certain key choices."

"Such as?"

"The lingerie and bikinis."

"Lingerie? I'm not much for lingerie! Or bikinis!"

"Good. Then you'll be exquisite in nothing. You slept in my arms like that all night, remember."

Hot color flooded her face. "Don't!"

"With your legs wrapped silkily around me," he added. "You were so warm and sweet, I can't believe you really intend to sleep alone tonight."

The images he aroused in her, coupled with his warm gaze and sexy grin, made her blood hum.

"I meant I feel bad about going away again so soon without telling Betty."

"Already done. Betty's fine with the idea."

"You *are* thorough."

When her temples began to throb, Kira squeezed her eyes shut. "Did everyone, absolutely everyone, know I was getting married to you today before I did?"

"Not me, darlin'. I was scared sick you wouldn't turn up or that you'd order me straight to hell after I proposed."

Had he really felt that way? Did he care a little?

No! She couldn't let herself ask such questions.

Or care at all what the answers might be.

Eight

An hour later, after a flight to the coast and a brief but exciting helicopter ride over Galveston Island, they dropped out of the night sky onto the sleek, upper deck of the white floating palace he kept moored at the Galveston marina. She took his arm when the rotors stopped and sucked in a breath as he helped her onto his yacht. Gusts of thick, humid air that smelled of the sea whipped her clothes and hair.

Promising to give her a tour of the megayacht the next day, the captain led them down a flight of steep, white stairs and through a wood-lined corridor to Quinn's master stateroom. Clearly the captain hadn't been told that they would not be sharing a room. Crewmen followed at a brisk pace to deliver their bags.

Once alone with Quinn in his palatial, brass-studded cabin, her brows knitted in concern as she stared at the mountain of bags.

"Don't worry. If you really insist on sleeping alone, I'll move mine."

Shooting a nervous glance toward his big bed, she felt her body heat.

Above the headboard hung a magnificent painting of a nude blonde by an artist she admired. The subject was lying on her tummy across a tumble of satin sheets, her slender back arched to reveal ample breasts. Long-lashed, come-hither eyes compelled the viewer not to look away. Surely such a wanton creature would never send her husband away on their wedding night.

"Last chance to change your mind," he said.

Feeling strangely shy, Kira crossed her arms over her own breasts and shook her head. "So, where will you sleep?"

"Next door." There was a mesmerizing intensity in his eyes. "Would you like to see my room?"

She twisted her hands. "I'll be just fine right here. So, if that's settled, I guess we'll see each other in the morning."

"Right." He hesitated. "If you need anything, all you have to do is punch this button on your bedside table and one of the staff will answer. If you want me, I'll leave my door unlocked. Or, if you prefer me to come to you, you could ring through on that phone over there."

"Thanks."

He turned, opened the door, shoved his bags into the passageway and stepped outside. When the door slammed behind him, and she was alone with his come-hither blonde, a heavy emotion that felt too much like disappointment gripped her.

To distract herself, she studied the painting for another moment, noting that the artist had used linseed oil most effectively to capture the effect of satin.

Feeling a vague disquiet as she considered the nude,

she decided the best thing to do was shower and get ready for bed. As she rummaged in her suitcase, she found all sorts of beautiful clothes that she never would have picked out. Still, as she touched the soft fabrics and imagined her mother shopping for such things without her there to discourage such absurd purchases, she couldn't help smiling. Her mother had always wanted to dress Kira in beautiful things, but being a tomboy, Kira had preferred jeans and T-shirts.

What was the point of fancy clothes for someone who lived as she had, spending time in art vaults, or painting, or waiting tables? But now, she supposed, for however long she was married to a billionaire with his own jet and megayacht, she would run in different circles and have fundraisers and parties to attend. Maybe she did need to upgrade her wardrobe.

Usually, she slept in an overlarge, faded T-shirt. In her suitcase all she found for pajamas were thin satin gowns and sheer robes, the kind that would cling so seductively she almost regretted she wouldn't be wearing them for Quinn.

Instead of the satin gown, which reminded her too much of the blonde above the bed, she chose black lace. Had he touched the gown, imagining her in it, when he'd picked it out? As the gossamer garment slipped through her fingers she shivered.

Go to bed. Don't dwell on what might have been. He's ruined enough of your day and night as it is.

But how not to think of him as she stripped and stepped into her shower? What was he doing next door? Was his tall, bronzed body naked, too? Her heart hammered much too fast.

Lathering her body underneath a flow of warm water, she imagined him doing the same in his own shower. Leaning against the wet tile wall, she grew hotter and hotter as the water streamed over her. She stood beneath the spray until her fingers grew too numb to hold the slippery bar of soap. When it fell, she snapped out of her spell.

Drying off and then slipping into the black gown, she slid into his big bed with a magazine. Unable to do more than flip pages and stare unseeingly at the pictures because she couldn't stop thinking about Quinn, she eventually drifted to sleep. But once asleep, she didn't dream of him.

Instead, she dreamed she was a small child in her pink bedroom with its wall-to-wall white carpet. All her books were lined up just perfectly, the way her mother liked them to be, in her small white bookcase beneath the window.

Somewhere in the house she heard laughter and hushed endearments, the sort of affection she'd never been able to get enough of. Then her door opened and her parents rushed inside her bedroom. Only they didn't take her into their arms as they usually did. Her mother was cooing over a bundle she held against her heart, and her father was staring down at what her mother held as if it were the most precious thing in the world.

She wanted them to look at her like that.

"Kira, we've brought your new baby sister, Jaycee, for a visit."

A baby sister? "Where did she come from?"

"The hospital."

"Is that where you got me?"

Her mother paled. Her father looked as uneasy as her mother, but he nodded.

What was going on?

"Do you love me, too?" Kira whispered.

"Yes, of course," her father said. "You're our big girl now, so your job will be to help us take care of Jaycee.

She's *our* special baby. We're all going to work hard to take very good care of Jaycee."

Suddenly, the bundle in her mother's arms began to shriek frantically.

"What can I do?" Kira had said, terrified as she ran toward them. "How can I help? Tell me what to do!"

But they'd turned away from her. "Why don't you just play," her father suggested absently.

Feeling lonely and left out as she eyed her dolls and books, she slowly backed away from them and walked out of her room, down the tall stairs to the front door, all the while hoping their concerned voices would call her back as they usually did. She wasn't supposed to be downstairs at night.

But this time, they didn't call her. Instead, her parents carried the new baby into a bedroom down the hall and stayed with her.

They had a new baby. They didn't need her anymore.

Kira opened the big front door. They didn't notice when she stepped outside. Why should they? They had Jaycee, who was special. They didn't care about Kira anymore. Maybe they'd never really cared.

Suddenly, everything grew black and cold, and a fierce wind began to blow, sweeping away everything familiar. The house vanished, and she was all alone in a strange, dark wood with nobody to hear her cries. Terrified, she ran deeper into the woods.

If her family didn't love her anymore, if nobody loved her, she didn't know what she would do.

Hysterical, she began sobbing their names. "Mother! Daddy! Somebody! Please…love me. I want to be special, too…"

Quinn opened her door and hurled himself into her stateroom.

"Kira!" He switched on a light. She blinked against the blinding glare of gold with heavy-lidded eyes.

"Are you okay?" he demanded. "Wake up!"

"Quinn?" Focusing on his broad shoulders, she blinked away the last remnants of that terrifying forest. He was huge and shirtless and so starkly handsome in the half shadows she hissed in a breath.

Her husband. What a fool she'd been to send him away when that was the last thing she really wanted.

When he sat down on the bed, she flung herself against his massive bare chest and clung. He felt so hard and strong and hot.

Snugging her close against his muscular body, he rocked her gently and spoke in soothing tones. "There...there..."

Wrapped in his warmth, she almost felt safe...and loved.

"I was a little girl again. Only I ran away and got lost. In a forest."

He petted her hair as his voice soothed her. "You were only dreaming."

She stared up at his shadowed face. In the aftermath of her dream, she was too open to her need of him. Her grip on him tightened. She felt his breath hitch and his heart thud faster. If only *he* loved her...maybe the importance of her childhood fears would recede.

"Darlin', it was just a dream. You're okay."

Slowly, because he held her, the horror of feeling lost and alone diminished and reality returned.

She was on his megayacht. In Galveston. He'd forced her to marry him and come on a honeymoon. She was in his bed where she'd been sleeping alone. This was supposed to be their wedding night, but she'd sent him away.

Yet somehow *she* was the one who felt lonely and rejected.

She liked being cradled in his strong arms, against his

virile body. Too much. She grew conscious of the danger of letting him linger in her bedroom.

"You want me to go?" he whispered roughly.

No. She wanted to cling to him…to be adored by him…. Another impossible dream.

When she hesitated, he said, "If you don't send me packing, I will take this as an invitation."

"It's no invitation," she finally murmured, but sulkily. Her heart wasn't in her statement.

"How come you don't sound sure?" He ran a rough palm across her cheek. Did she only imagine the intimate plea in his voice? Was he as lonely as she was?

Even as she felt herself softening under his affectionate touch and gentle tone, she forced herself to remember all the reasons she'd be a fool to trust him. Squeezing her eyes shut, she took a deep breath. "Thanks for coming, but go! Please—just go."

She felt his body tighten as he stared into her eyes. Time ticked for an endless moment before he released her.

Without a word he got up and left.

Alone again, she felt she might burst with sheer longing. When she didn't sleep until dawn, she blamed him for not going farther than the room next to hers. He was too close. Knowing that all she had to do was go to him increased her frustration. Because he'd made it clear he would not send her away.

Twisting and turning, she fought to settle into slumber, but could not. First, she was too hot for the covers. Then she was so cold she'd burrowed under them.

It was nearly dawn when she finally did sleep. Then, after less than an hour, loud voices in the passageway startled her into grouchy wakefulness. As she buried her head in her pillow, her first thought was of Quinn. He'd probably slept like a baby.

When the sun climbed high and his crewmen began shouting to one another on deck, she strained to hear Quinn's voice among theirs shouts, but didn't.

Sitting up, alone, she pulled the covers to her throat. Surely he couldn't still be sleeping. Where was he?

A dark thought hit her. Last night he'd left her so easily, when what she'd craved was for him to stay. Had she already served her purpose by marrying him? Was he finished with her?

Feeling the need for a strong cup of coffee, Kira slipped into a pair of tight, white shorts and a skimpy, beige knit top. Outside, the sky was blue, the sun brilliant. Normally, when she wasn't bleary from lack of sleep, Kira loved water, boats and beaches. Had Quinn been in love with her, a honeymoon on his luxurious yacht would have been exceedingly romantic. Instead, she felt strange and alone and much too needily self-conscious.

Was his crew spying on her? Did they know Quinn hadn't slept with her? Did they pity her?

Anxious to find Quinn, Kira grabbed a white sweater and left the stateroom. When he didn't answer her knock, she cracked open his door. A glance at the perfectly made spread and his unopened luggage told her he'd spent the night elsewhere. Pivoting, she stepped back into the corridor so fast she nearly slammed headlong into a crewman.

"May I help you, Mrs. Sullivan?"

"Just taking a private tour," she lied. On the off chance he'd think she knew where she was going, she strode purposefully past him down the wood-lined passageway.

Outside, the gulf stretched in endless sapphire sparkle toward a shimmering horizon. Not that she paid much attention to the dazzling view. Intent on finding Quinn, she was too busy opening every door on the sumptuously appointed decks. Too proud to ask the numerous crew members she passed for help, she averted her eyes when she chanced to meet one of them for fear they'd quiz her.

The yacht seemed even bigger on close inspection. So far she'd found six luxury staterooms, a cinema, multiple decks, a helipad and a grand salon.

Just when she was about to give up her search for Quinn, she opened a door on the uppermost deck and found him slumped over a desk in a cluttered office. Noting the numerous documents scattered on chairs, desks, tables and even the floor, she crossed the room to his side. Unfinished cups of coffee sat atop the jumbled stacks. Obviously, he'd worked through the night on a caffeine high.

At the sight of his exhausted face, her heart constricted. Even as she smoothed her hand lightly through his rumpled hair, she chastised herself for feeling sympathy for him. Hadn't he bullied her into their forced, loveless marriage?

Now that she knew where he was, she should go, order herself coffee and breakfast, read her magazine in some pristine chaise lounge, sunbathe—in short, ignore him. Thinking she would do just that, she stepped away from him. Then, driven by warring emotions she refused to analyze, she quickly scampered back to his side.

Foolishly, she felt tempted to neaten his office, but since she didn't know what went where, she sank into the chair opposite his. Bringing her knees against her chest, she hugged them tightly and was pleased when he slept another hour under her benevolent guardianship. Then, without warning, his beautiful eyes snapped open and seared her.

"What the hell are you doing here?" he demanded.

She nearly jumped out of her chair. "He awakens—like a grumpy old bear," she teased.

Managing a lopsided grin, he ran a hand through his

spiked, rumpled hair. "You were a bit grumpy...the morning after...you slept with me in San Antonio, as I recall."

"Don't remind me of that disastrous night, please."

"It's one of my fondest memories," he said softly.

"I said don't!"

"I love it when you blush like that. It makes you look so...cute. You should have awakened me the minute you came in."

"How could I be so heartlessly cruel when you came to my rescue in the middle of the night? If you couldn't sleep, it was my fault."

When his beautiful white teeth flashed in a teasing grin, she couldn't help smiling back at him.

"I could bring you some coffee. Frankly, I could use a cup myself," she said.

He sat up straighter and stretched. "Sorry this place is such a mess, but as I'm not through here, I don't want anybody straightening it up yet."

She nodded. "I sort of thought that might be the case."

"What about breakfast...on deck, then? I have a crew ready to wait on us hand and foot. They're well trained in all things—food service...emergencies at sea..."

"They didn't come when I screamed last night," she said softly. "You did."

"Only because you didn't call for their help on the proper phone."

"So, it's my fault, is it?" Where had the lilt in her light tone come from?

Remembering how safe she'd felt in his arms last night, a fierce tenderness toward him welled up in her heart. He must have sensed what she felt, because his eyes flared darkly before he looked away.

Again, she wished this were a real honeymoon, wished that he loved her rather than only lusted for her, wished that she was allowed to love him back. If only she hadn't demanded separate bedrooms, then she would be lying in his arms looking forward to making love with him again this morning.

At the thought, her neck grew warm. She'd been wishing for the wrong stuff her whole life. It was time she grew up and figured out what her life was to be about. The sooner she got started on that serious journey, one that could never include him, the better.

Nine

Breakfast on deck with his long-limbed bride in her sexy short shorts was proving to be an unbearable torture. She squirmed when his gaze strayed to her lips or her breasts or when it ran down those long, lovely legs.

If only he could forget how she'd clung to him last night or how her big eyes had adored him when he'd first woken up this morning.

"I wish you wouldn't stare so," she said as she licked chocolate off a fingertip. "It makes me feel self-conscious about eating this and making such a mess."

"Sorry," he muttered.

He tried to look away, but found he could not. What else was there to look at besides endless sapphire dazzle? Why shouldn't he enjoy watching her greedily devour her fresh-baked croissants and *pain du chocolat?* The way she licked chocolate off her fingers made him remember her mouth and tongue on him that night in his loft. *Torture.*

Even though he was sitting in the shade and the gulf breeze was cool, his skin heated. His bride was too sexy for words.

If he were to survive the morning without grabbing her like a besotted teenager and making a fool of himself, he needed to quickly get back to his office and the EU deal.

But he knew he wouldn't be able to concentrate on the deal while his forbidden bride was aboard. No. He'd go to the gym and follow his workout with a long, cold shower. Only then would he attempt another try at the office.

Dear God, why was it that ever since she'd said no sex, bedding her was all he could think about?

With the fortitude that was so much a part of his character, he steeled himself to endure her beauty and her provocative sensuality, at least until breakfast was over and they parted ways.

"So, are we heading somewhere in particular?" she asked playfully.

"Do you like to snorkel?"

"I do, but I've only snorkeled in lakes and shallow coves in the Caribbean."

"Once we get into really deep water, the gulf will be clear. I thought we'd snorkel off one of my oil rigs. It's always struck me as ironic the way marine life flourishes around a rig. You're in for a treat."

Her brief smile charmed him. "I read somewhere that rigs act like artificial reefs." She stopped eating her orange. "But you don't need to interrupt your precious work to entertain me."

"I'll set my own work schedule, if you don't mind."

"You're the boss, my lord and master. Sorry I keep forgetting that all-important fact." Again her playful tone teased him.

"Right." He smiled grimly. What could he say?

They lapsed into an uncomfortable silence. Focusing on his eggs and bacon, he fought to ignore her. Not that he didn't want to talk to her, because he did. Very much. But small talk with his bride was not proving to be an easy matter.

"I'd best get busy," he said when he'd finished his eggs and she her orange.

"Okay. Don't worry about me. Like I said, I can entertain myself. I love the water. As you know, I spent the past few weeks on Murray Island. I don't know where we are, but we probably aren't that far from it."

Scanning the horizon, he frowned. He didn't like remembering how much her stay at her family's isolated island had worried him.

How had he become so attached—or whatever the hell he was—to her so fast? They'd only had one night together!

Biting out a terse goodbye that made her pretty smile falter, he stood abruptly. Pivoting, he headed to his gym and that icy shower while she set off to her stateroom.

The gym and shower didn't do any good. No sooner did he return to his office on the upper deck than who should he find sunbathing right outside his door practically naked but his delectable bride.

She lay on a vivid splash of red terry cloth atop one of his chaise lounges, wearing the white thong bikini he'd picked out for her while under the influence of a lurid male fantasy.

He'd imagined her in it. Hell, yes, he had. But not like this—not with her body forbidden to him by her decree and his unwillingness to become any more attached to her. He would never have bought those three tiny triangles if he'd had any idea what torture watching her would give him.

Clenching his fists, he told himself to snap the blinds shut and forget her. Instead, mesmerized, he crossed his office with the long strides of a large, predatory cat and stood at a porthole, staring at her hungrily, ravenous for whatever scraps of tenderness the sexy witch might bestow. He willed her to look at him.

She flipped a magazine page carelessly and continued to read with the most maddening intensity. Not once did she so much as glance his way.

Damn her.

She was on her tummy in the exact position of the girl in the painting over his bed. He watched her long, dark hair glint with fiery highlights and blow about her slim, bare shoulders. He watched her long, graceful fingers flip more pages and occasionally smooth back flying strands of her hair. Every movement of her slim wrist had her dainty silver bracelet flashing.

Was she really as cool and collected as she appeared?

How could she be, when she'd given herself to him so quickly and completely that first night? Her eyes had shone with desire, and she'd trembled and quivered at his touch. She hadn't faked her response. He'd bet his life on it. He would never have forced her to marry him if he'd thought her cold and indifferent.

And last night he'd definitely felt her holding on to him as if she didn't want to let go.

So, she must be clinging to her position of abstinence out of principle. Wasn't she turning those pages much too fast? Was she even reading that magazine? Or was she as distracted as he was? Did she sense him watching her and take perverse delight in her power over him?

Damn the fates that had sent her to him!

Always, before Kira, he'd gone for voluptuous blondes with modern morals, curvy women who knew how to dress, women who thought their main purpose was to please a man. Women with whom he'd felt safe because they'd wanted his money and position more than they'd valued his heart.

This slim, coltishly long-limbed girl hadn't yet learned what she was about or even how to please herself, much less how to seduce a man. But her innocence in these matters appealed to him.

Why?

Again, he told himself to forget her, but when he went to his desk, he just sat there for a full half hour unable to concentrate. Her image had burned itself into his brain. She had his loins hard and aching. The woman lured him from his work like the Sirens had lured Ulysses after Troy.

He began to worry that she hadn't put on enough sunblock. Weren't there places on that long, slim body she couldn't reach?

Hardly knowing what he was about, he slammed out of his office and found himself outside, towering grimly over her. Not that she so much as bothered to glance away from her damn magazine, even though she must have heard his heavy footsteps, even though he cast a shadow over the pages.

He felt like a fool.

"You're going to burn," he growled with some annoyance.

"Do you think so? I've got lotion on, and my hat. But maybe you're right. I need to turn over for a while." She lowered her sunglasses to the tip of her nose and peered up at him saucily with bright, dark eyes.

Was she flirting with him? Damn her to hell and back if she was.

"Since you're out here, would you mind being a dear and rubbing some lotion on my back for me?"

He sank to his haunches, his excitement so profound at the thought of touching her that he didn't worry about her request for lotion on her back being illogical. Hadn't she forbidden his touch? And didn't she just say she intended to turn over onto her back?

He didn't care.

The lotion was warm from the sun, and her silky skin was even warmer as he rubbed the cream into it.

A moan of pure pleasure escaped her lips as his large palm made circular motions in the center of her back, and his heart raced at her response. He felt a visceral connection to her deep in his groin.

"You have strong hands. The lotion smells so deliciously sweet. Feels good, too," she whispered silkily, stretching like a cat as he stroked her.

"Thanks," he growled.

She rolled over and lay on her towel. Throwing him a dismissive glance, she lifted her magazine to shut him out.

"You can go now," she whispered.

Feeling stubborn and moody, he didn't budge. Only when he saw his oil rig looming off the starboard side did he arise and ask his crew to assemble their diving gear: fins, wet suits, marker floats and masks.

So much for working on the EU deal...

Later, when he and she stood on the teak diving platform at the stern of the yacht in their wet suits, she noticed nobody had thrown out an anchor.

"What if your yacht drifts while we're in the water?"

"She won't," he replied. "*Pegasus* is equipped with a sophisticated navigational system called dynamic positioning. On a day this calm she'll stay exactly where we position her. Believe me, it's much better than an anchor, which would allow her to swing back and forth."

"You plan so much that you think of everything. Does your planning and your fortune allow you to have everything you want?"

"Not quite everything," he murmured as he stared hungrily at her trim body.

Didn't she know she had changed everything?

For years, he'd been driven to avenge himself against her father, but no sooner had he been poised to seize his prize than he'd learned of Vera's illness. From that moment, his victory had begun to feel hollow.

Just when he'd wondered what new challenge could ever drive him as passionately as revenge once did, Kira had walked into his office to fight for her sister. He'd known he had to have her.

Trouble was, he was beginning to want more than he'd ever allowed himself to dream of wanting before. He wanted a life with her, a future, everything he'd told himself he could never risk having.

Kira stood on the platform watching Quinn in the water as he adjusted his mask.

"Come on in," he yelled.

She was removing her silver jewelry because he'd told her the flash of it might attract sharks.

"You know how I told you I've mainly confined my snorkeling to lakes or shallow lagoons," she began. "Well, the gulf's beginning to seem too big and too deep."

"I'll be right beside you, and Skip and Chuck are in the tender."

"I've seen all the *Jaws* movies."

"Not a good time to think about them."

She squinted, searching the vast expanse of the gulf for fins.

"Are you coming in or not?" he demanded.

Despite her doubts, she sucked in a deep breath and jumped in.

As she swam out to him, the water felt refreshingly cool.

After she got her mask on she and Quinn were soon surrounded by red snapper and amberjack. She was enjoying their cool, blue world so much that when he pointed out a giant grouper gliding by, she stared in awe instead of fear. Quinn's sure presence beside her in the water instilled in her a confidence she wouldn't have believed possible.

Snorkeling soon had her feeling weightless. It was as if she were flying in an alien world that dissolved into endless deep blue nothingness. As he'd promised, Quinn stayed beside her for nearly an hour. Enjoying herself, she forgot the vast blue darkness beneath them and what it concealed.

Just when she was starting to relax, a tiger shark zoomed out of the depths straight at Quinn. In her panic, she did exactly what she shouldn't have done. Kicking and thrashing wildly, she gulped in too much water. Choking, she yanked off her mask. As the fin vanished, Quinn ordered her to swim to the yacht.

In seconds, the fin was back, circling Quinn before diving again. Then the shark returned, dashing right at Quinn, who rammed it in the nose and made a motion with his arm for her to quit watching and start swimming. Staying behind her so he could keep his body between hers and the shark, he headed for the yacht, as well.

A tense knot of crewmen on the platform were shouting to them when she finally reached the yacht.

"Quinn," she yelled even as strong arms yanked her on board. "Quinn!" She barely heard his men shouting to him as she stood on the teak platform panting for breath. Then the dorsal fin slashed viciously right beside Quinn, and her fear mushroomed.

"Get him out! Somebody do something! Quinn! *Darling!*" she screamed.

Quinn swam in smooth, rapid strokes toward the stern. When he made it to the ladder, his crewmen sprang forward and hauled him roughly aboard, slamming him onto the teak platform.

Quinn tore off his mask. When he stood up, he turned to Kira, who took the desperate glint in his eyes as an invitation to hurl herself into his arms.

"You're as white as bleached bone," he said, gripping her tightly. "You're sure you're okay?"

The blaze of concern in his eyes and his tone mirrored her own wild fears for him.

"If you're okay, I'm okay," she whispered shakily, snuggling closer. She was so happy he was alive and unhurt.

"You're overreacting. It would take more than one little shark—"

"Don't joke! He could have torn off your arm!"

"He was probably just curious."

"Curious! I saw the movies, remember?"

He stared down at her in a way that made her skin heat. "In a funny way I feel indebted to the shark. Because of him, you called me darling."

"Did not!"

"Did, too," he drawled in that low tone that mesmerized her.

When she wrenched free of him, he laughed. "Okay. It must have been wishful thinking on a doomed man's part. Guess it was Chuck who let out the *d*-word."

She bit her lip to keep from smiling.

After they dressed, they met on the upper deck where they'd had breakfast earlier. Quinn wore jeans and a blue Hawaiian shirt that made his eyes seem as brilliant as the dazzling sky.

He ordered pineapple and mangoes and coffee. She was still so glad he was alive and had all his body parts she couldn't take her eyes off him.

"I have an idea," she said. "I mean…if we're looking for a less exciting adventure."

"What?"

"I could show you Murray Island."

"Where is it?"

"South of Galveston. Since I don't know where we are, I can't tell you how to get there. But it's on all the charts."

He picked up a phone and talked to his captain. When he hung up, he said, "Apparently, we're about forty nautical miles from your island. The captain says we could run into some weather, but if you want to go there, we will."

"What's a raindrop or two compared to being lunch for Jaws?"

"I love your vivid imagination."

In little over an hour, *Pegasus* was positioned off the shore of Murray Island, and Kira and Quinn were climbing down into the tender together. After Quinn revved the outboard, they sped toward the breaking surf, making for the pass between the barrier islands and the tiny harbor on the island's leeward side.

The bouncy ride beneath thickening gray storm clouds was wet and choppy. Heedless of the iffy weather, she stared ahead, laughing as the spray hit them. Quinn's eyes never strayed from his course—except when they veered to her face, which secretly thrilled her. She knew she shouldn't crave his attention so much, but ever since the shark incident, her emotions refused to behave sensibly.

He's alive. I have this moment with him. It's our honeymoon. Why not enjoy it? Why not share this island sanctuary I love with him?

Ten

Quinn watched his beachcombing bride much too avidly for his liking. He hated feeling so powerfully attracted to her. It was incomprehensible. She was Earl's daughter, a woman he barely knew, a wife who wouldn't even share his bed.

She'd slept with him once and then she'd left him, causing a pain too similar to what he'd felt after his father's death. The tenderness he continued to feel for her put him on dangerous ground, but still she possessed him in a way no other woman ever had.

It was the shark. Before they'd snorkeled, he'd been able to tell himself that he was under a temporary spell, that he could vanquish his burning need for her simply by staying out of her bed.

But he'd been afraid for her when she'd been swimming for the boat, more afraid than he'd ever been in his life.

Then he'd seen her bone-white face and the wild terror in her eyes when she'd imagined him in danger.

Once he'd been safely on board, her slim face had become luminous with joy. She'd hurled herself into his arms so violently she'd all but knocked them both back into the water again.

Nobody had ever looked at him like that.

Surely his father had loved him more, but she was here, and so beautiful, and so alive, and his—if only he could win her.

The prevailing southeasterly wind, cooler now because of the dark gray clouds, licked the crests of the waves into a foaming fury and sent her dark chestnut hair streaming back from her face as she scampered at the surf's edge. Every few steps, she knelt, not caring if a wave splashed her toes. Crouching, she examined the beach debris: tangles of seaweed, driftwood and shells.

Her long slim feet were bare, her toenails unpolished. Flip-flops dangled from her left hand.

For twenty years, his determination to succeed and get revenge had made time seem too valuable for him to waste on a beach with a woman. Most nights he'd worked, and most mornings, he'd left for his office before dawn. Driven by his dark goals, he'd often worked through entire weekends and holidays. His main sources of relaxation had been the gym or a willing woman and a glass of scotch before he hit his bed or desk again. He'd been more machine than human.

But that was before Kira.

Memories, long suppressed, stirred. As a child, he'd looked forward to the hour when his father's key would turn in the lock and he'd holler Quinn's name.

Quinn would race into his father's arms. After hugging him close, his father would lift him so high in the air

Quinn could touch the ceiling. So high, he'd felt as if he was flying. Then his dad would set him down and ruffle his hair and ask him about his day.

Never had his father been too tired to pass a football around the yard or take him to the park to chase geese. His father had helped with Quinn's homework, helped him build models, played endless games with him. His mother, on the other hand, had always been too busy to play. Then his father had died, and Quinn had known grief and lone-liness.

For the first time, while indulging in this simple walk on the beach with Kira, Quinn felt a glimmer of the warmth that had lit his life before his father's death.

His father would want him to stop grieving, he realized. He'd want him to choose life, to choose the future.

Kira didn't realize she was beautiful, or that her lack of pretention and artifice made her even more attractive. Her every movement was graceful and natural. On the beach, she seemed a lovely wild thing running free.

This island was her refuge. For however long they were together, he would have to accept her world if he wanted her to accept his. No doubt, she would need to come here again from time to time.

He frowned, not liking the thought of her leaving him to stay out here all alone. Anyone could beach a small boat or tie up at her dock. Jim, the island's caretaker, had the far-away look of a man who'd checked out of life a long time ago. Quinn wasn't about to trust a dropout like him as her protector. No, he would have to get his security team to figure out how to make her safe here without intruding on her privacy. She was a free spirit, and Quinn wanted her to be happy, the way she was now, but safe, as well.

The sky was rapidly darkening from gray to black. Not that Kira seemed concerned about the gathering storm as she leaned down and picked up a shell. When she twisted, their gazes met. At her enchanting smile, his heart brimmed with way too much emotion. Then she ran over to show him her newfound treasure. When she held it up, her eyes shone, and the tiny window that had opened into his soul widened even further.

"Look, it's a lightning whelk," she cried.

"It's huge," he said, turning the cone-shaped shell over in his hand to properly admire it.

"At least a foot long. I've never seen one so big. And it's in perfect condition. Did you know it's the state shell of Texas?"

Shaking his head, he shot a glance at the darkening sky before he handed it back to her. "Do you collect shells?"

"Not really, but I'd like to give you this one. So you can remember Murray Island."

And *her,* he thought. "As if I could ever forget," he said. "I'll cherish it."

"I'm sure." She attempted a laugh and failed. "A new gem for your art collection."

"It's already my favorite thing."

Stronger now, the wind whipped her hair, and the sand bit into his legs.

"We should take cover," he said. "Storm's coming in. Fast. I think we'd better make a run for the house!"

"I'll race you!" Giggling as she danced on her toes, she sprinted toward the house, and because he liked watching her cute butt when she ran, he held back and let her win.

Darting from room to room as the wind howled and the frame structure shuddered, she gave him a quick tour of the house. A shady front porch looked out onto the raging gulf. Two bedrooms, a bath and a kitchen were connected by screened breezeways to each other and to the porch.

The southern bedroom had a wall of windows. "This is my favorite room," she said. "There's always a breeze, so I usually sleep here."

When she cracked a window, the room cooled instantly as storm gusts swept through it.

Deliberately, he stared outside at the rain instead of at her narrow bed. Since it was much too easy to imagine her long, lithe body on that mattress beneath him, he concentrated on the fat raindrops splatting on sand.

"With all the doors and windows open, the prevailing breezes cool the house on the hottest summer days," she said.

"If you open everything up, doesn't that make you vulnerable to a break-in?"

"No one usually comes here except me and Jim."

All anybody had to do was slit a screen to get inside. She would be defenseless. If Quinn had known how vulnerable she was while she'd been gone, he would have been even crazier with worry.

"Would you like some tea?" she said. "While we wait out the weather?"

"Sure."

When he nodded, she disappeared into the kitchen, leaving him to explore the room. A violent gust hit the house as the storm broke with full force. Somewhere, a breezeway door slammed so hard the entire house shook. Then papers fluttered under her bed. Curious, he knelt and pulled them out.

To his amazement, he discovered dozens of watercolors, all of himself, all ripped in two. He was trying to shove the entire collection back under the bed, when he heard her light footsteps at the doorway.

"Oh, my God," she said. "I forgot about those. Don't think... I mean... They don't mean anything!"

"Right."

You just painted picture after picture of me with violent, vivid brushstrokes. Then you shredded them all. For no reason.

"You obviously weren't too happy with me," he muttered.

"I really don't want to talk about it."

"Did you paint anything else...besides me?"

"A few birds."

"How many?"

"Not so many. One actually." She turned away as if uncomfortable with that admission.

Obviously, she was just as uneasy about her feelings for him as he was about his obsession with her.

"Why don't we drink our tea and go back to the yacht," he said brusquely.

"Fine with me."

"I shouldn't have pulled those pictures out," he said.

"We said we were going to forget about them."

"Right. We did." So, while he'd been obsessing about her absence, maybe she'd done a bit of obsessing herself. He took a long breath.

They sat on the porch drinking tea as the gray fury of the storm lashed the island. Now that he wanted to leave, the weather wasn't cooperating. To the contrary. Monstrous black waves thundered against the beach while rain drummed endlessly against the metal roof. No way could he trust his small tender in such high seas.

"Looks like we're stuck here for the duration," he said. So much for distracting himself from his bride anytime soon.

She nodded, her expression equally grim. "Sorry I suggested coming here."

The squalls continued into the night, so for supper she

heated a can of beans and opened cans of peaches and tomatoes. Happily, she produced a bottle of scotch that she said she kept hidden.

"We have to hide liquor from the pirates," she told him with a shy smile.

"Pirates?" he asked.

"We call anyone who lands on the island pirates. We leave the house open so they don't have to break in. Because they will if we don't."

"So, you're not entirely unaware of the dangers of being here all alone?"

"Jim's here."

"Right. Jim."

Quinn poured himself a drink and toasted good old Jim. Then he poured another. When he'd drained the second, she began to glow. Her smile and eyes looked so fresh and sparkly, he saw the danger of more liquor and suggested they go to bed.

"Separate bedrooms, of course," he said, "since that's what you want."

Nodding primly, she arose and led him to the guest bedroom. When she left him, he stripped off his shirt and lay down. She wouldn't leave his thoughts. He remembered her brilliant eyes lighting up when she saw him hauled safely onto *Pegasus.* He remembered how shyly she'd blushed every time she'd looked at him in his office, when she'd faced him down to ask him not to marry her sister. He remembered her breasts in the skimpy T-shirt she'd worn today and her cute butt and long legs in her white shorts as she'd raced him across the deep sand back to the house.

With the scotch still causing visions of her to warm his blood, he couldn't sleep for thinking of her on her narrow bed in the next room. Would she sleep curled in a ball like a child or stretched out like a woman? Was she naked? Or in her bra and panties? Did she desire him, too?

Remembering all the things she'd done to him in his loft in San Antonio, he began to fantasize that she was in the bed with him, her long legs tangled with his. That got him even hotter.

If only they were on board the yacht so he could hide out in his office on the upper deck and bury himself in paperwork. Here, there was nothing to think about but her lying in the bed next door.

At some point, he managed to fall asleep only to dream of her. In his dream, she slipped as lightly as a shadow into his bedroom. Slim, teasing fingers pulled back his sheet. Then, calling his name in husky, velvet tones, she slid into bed beside him. Her eyes blazed with the same fierce passion he'd seen when she'd realized he was safely back on board the yacht, away from the shark's teeth.

His heart constricted. Was this love? If it wasn't, it felt too dangerously close to the emotion for comfort. Even in his dream he recoiled from that dark emotion. Love had ruined his life and the life of his father. Hadn't it?

Then, in the dream, she kissed him, her sensual mouth and tongue running wildly over his lips and body while her hands moved between his legs and began to stroke. Soon he forgot about the danger of love and lost all power to resist her.

Lightning crashed, startling him. When his eyes flew open he heard the roar of the surf. He was alone in a strange, dark bedroom with sweat dripping from his long, lean body onto damp sheets, aching all over because he wanted to make love to his forbidden wife.

She was driving him crazy. On a low, frustrated groan, he hurled himself out of bed and stalked onto the breezeway in the hope that the chill, damp wind whipping

through the screens would cool his feverish body and re-
store his sanity.

"Quinn!" came Kira's soft, startled cry, the sexy sound
setting his testosterone-charged nerves on high alert.

He whirled to face her just as a bolt of lightning flashed.
Her hair streaming in the wind, she leaned against a post
some ten feet away, in the shadows. Momentarily blinded
from the lightning, he couldn't make her out in the darkness. Imagining the rest of her, his blood notched a degree
hotter.

"You'd better get back to your room," he rasped.

"What's the use when I couldn't sleep even if I did?
Storms like this are exciting, aren't they?"

"Just do as I said and go."

"This is my house. Why should I do what you say, if I
prefer watching the storm...and you?" she said in a low,
breathless tone.

"Because if you plan to keep me in a separate bedroom,
it's the smart thing to do."

"Used to giving orders, aren't you? Well, I'm not used to
taking them. Since I'm your wife, maybe it's time I taught
you that. I could teach you a lot..."

Thunder rolled, and rain slashed through the breezeway furiously, sending rivulets of water across the concrete
floor.

"Go," he muttered.

"Maybe I will." But her husky laughter defied him.
"Then, maybe not."

When she turned, instead of heading across the breezeway toward her bedroom, she unlatched a screen door
behind her and ran onto the beach. As she did, a blaze of
white fire screamed from the wet black sky to the beach.

Hell! She was going to get herself fried if he didn't bring
her back.

"Kira!" he yelled after her.

When she kept running, he heaved himself after her, his bare feet sinking deeply into the soft, wet sand and crushed shells as he sprinted. Sheets of rain soaked him through within seconds.

She didn't get more than twenty feet before he caught her by the waist and pulled her roughly into his arms. She was wet and breathless, her long hair glued to her face, her T-shirt clinging to her erect nipples.

Quinn closed his eyes and willed himself to think of something besides her breasts and the light in her eyes. But as the cold rain pounded him, her soft warmth and beauty and the sweetness of her scent drew him. He opened his eyes and stared down at her. Slowly, she put her arms around him and looked at him as she had in his dreams, with her heart shining in her eyes.

Laughing, she said, "Have you ever seen anything so wild? Don't you love it?"

He hadn't deliberately stood in the rain or stomped in a puddle since he'd been a kid, when his dad had encouraged him to be a boy, as he'd put it. Hell, maybe that was his loss. Maybe it wasn't right for him to control himself so tightly.

As the torrents washed them, he picked her up and spun her crazily, high above his head. Then he lowered her, slowly, oh, so slowly. He let her breasts and tummy and thighs slide against his body, which became even harder in response to hers.

If only she'd stop looking at him with such fire in her eyes… She made him crave a different kind of life.… One of brightness, warmth and love.

"Kiss me," she whispered, pressing herself into his rock-hard thighs, smiling wantonly up at him when she felt his impressive erection.

So—she wanted him, too.

Kissing her so hard she gasped, he plunged his tongue into her mouth. The rain streamed over their fused bodies and the lightning flashed and the thunder rolled. He knew he should take her inside, but she tasted so good that, for the life of him, he couldn't let her go.

He would regret this, he was sure. But later. Not now, when she smelled of rain. Not when the wild surf roared on all sides of them. Not when his blood roared even louder.

Tonight, he had to have her.

Eleven

When he stripped her and laid her on the bed, she closed her eyes. With her face softly lit by an expectant smile and her damp hair fanning darkly across her pillow, she looked too lovely and precious for words.

"I wanted you to come to me… Even before…you appeared in the breezeway," she admitted, blushing shyly. "I know I shouldn't have…but I just lay on my bed craving you."

"Imagine that. We're on the same page for once."

"I don't want to want you…"

"I know exactly how you feel."

Thank God, he'd thought to stuff some condoms into his wallet before they'd left the yacht—just in case. Thinking about them now made him remember the first time— the one time he'd failed to protect her—and the little clock ticking in the back of his mind ticked a little louder.

She could be pregnant.

Part of him hoped she *was* pregnant...with a son. His son... No, *their* son. A little boy with dark hair who he could play ball with as his father had played with him. They would call him Kade. Quinn would come home, call his name, and the boy would come running.

Foolish dream.

Stripping off his wet jeans and Jockey shorts, he pulled the condoms out of his wallet and laid them on the bed-side table. Still thinking she could very well be pregnant and that he wouldn't mind nearly as much as he should, he stroked the creaminess of her cheek with his thumb. When her eyes sparked with anticipation, he kissed each eyelid and then her smiling mouth.

"Such tiny wrists," he said as he lifted them to his lips. He let his warm breath whisper across her soft skin. "Your heart is beating faster than a rabbit's. So, you did want me...my darlin'. Feed my bruised ego—admit it."

She laughed helplessly. "Okay—I'm tingling in so many places, I feel weak enough to faint."

He touched her breasts, her slender waist, the thatch of silken curls where her thighs were joined. He pressed his lips to all those secret places so reverently that his kisses transcended the physical.

"Better." He smiled. "I told you that you'd change your mind about sex." Triumphantly, he skimmed his mouth along her jawline. With each kiss that he bestowed, she claimed another piece of his heart.

"That you did. Are you always right? Is that how you became so rich?"

He kissed her earlobe, chuckling when she shivered in response.

"Focus is the key in so many endeavors. It only took a day, and I didn't once try to seduce you, now, did I?"

"Stop crowing like a rooster who's conquered a henhouse! I see you brought plenty of protection...which means you intended this to happen."

"I was hopeful. I usually feel optimistic about achieving my goals." He trailed the tip of his tongue along her collarbone.

She moved restlessly beneath him. "You're rubbing it in, and I said don't gloat." When he licked her earlobe again, she shuddered, causing a blazing rush of fire to sizzle through him. "Just do it," she begged.

"Why are you always in such a hurry, sweet Kira?"

Because she was unable to take her eyes from his face, she blew out a breath. Except for clenching her fingers and pressing her lips together, she lay still, as if fighting for patience.

"After all," he continued, "for all practical purposes, this is our wedding night."

Her quick scowl made him wonder why the hell he'd reminded them both of the marriage he'd forced her into.

Before she could protest, he kissed her lips. Soon her breathing was deep and ragged, and it wasn't long until she was quivering beneath his lips and begging him for more.

Her hands moved over his chest and then lower, down his torso and dipping lower still. When her fingers finally curled firmly around the swollen length of his shaft, he shuddered. Soon she had him as hot and eager to hurry as she was. He was out of control, completely in her thrall.

"I bet we're on the same page now," she said huskily, a triumphant lilt in her husky tone.

"Sexy, wanton witch." Unwrapping a condom, he sheathed himself.

Compelled to claim her as his, he plunged into tight, satiny warmth. Stomach to stomach. Thigh to thigh. The moment he was inside her, she wrapped her legs around his waist and urged him even deeper.

"Yes," she whispered as a tortured moan was torn from her lips.

"Yes," he growled, holding her even closer.

Then, some force began to build as he stroked in and out of her, his rhythm growing as hard and steady as the surf dancing rhythmically against the shore. His blood heated; his heart drummed faster. When he fought to slow down, she clung tighter, writhing, begging, urging him not to stop—shattering what was left of his fragile control.

With a savage cry, he climaxed. She felt so good, so soft, so delectable. Grabbing her bottom, he ground himself into her, plunging deeper. As she arched against him, he spilled himself inside her.

She went wild, trembling, screaming his name, and her excitement sent him over the fatal edge he'd vowed never to cross. Walls inside him tumbled. He didn't want to feel like this—not toward her, not toward any woman.

But he did.

Long minutes after he rolled off her, he lay beside her, fighting for breath and control.

"Wow," she said.

Even though sex had never felt so intense before, he didn't trust his feelings. Why give her any more power than she already had by admitting them? But though he confessed nothing, her sweet warmth invaded him, soothing all the broken parts of his soul.

She sidled closer and touched his lips with feverish fingertips, her eyes alight with sensual invitation. As she stroked his mouth and cheek teasingly, desire sizzled through him. He was rock-hard in another instant.

No way in hell would one time suffice. For either of them. With one sure, swift movement, he slid nearer so that his sex touched hers. When she stared up at him hungrily, he kissed her brow, her eyelids and then the tip of her pert nose. Then he edged lower, kissing her breasts and navel. Spreading her legs, he went all the way down, laving those sweet forbidden lips that opened to him like the silken petals of a warm flower. The tip of his tongue flicked inside, causing her to moan.

"Darlin'," he said softly. "You're perfect."

"I want you inside me. So much."

He wanted that, too, so he eased into her, gently this time, and held her tight against him. How could she feel so wonderful in his arms? So right? Like she belonged there, always, till the end of time? How could this be? She was Earl's daughter, a woman he'd coerced into marriage.

"How can this be?" she asked, her words mirroring his dark thoughts.

He took his time, and when it ended in violent, bittersweet waves of mutual passion, he felt again the inexplicable peace that left no space for hate or thoughts of revenge. He simply wanted her, wanted to be with her. He didn't want to hurt anything or anybody she loved.

"You're dangerously addictive," he whispered against her earlobe.

Her sweet face was flushed; her lips bruised and swollen from his kisses.

"So are you," she said with a tremulous smile even as her wary eyes reminded him that she hadn't married him for this. "This wasn't supposed to happen, was it? You didn't want this connection any more than I did."

"No…" His mood darkened as he remembered she didn't believe this was a real marriage.

His old doubts hit him with sweeping force. Tomorrow… if it would make her happy, he'd swear to her he'd never touch her again. But not tonight. Tonight, he had to hold her close, breathe in her scent, lose himself in her…dream of a different kind of life with her.

Just for tonight she was completely his.

Hugging him close, she sighed and fell asleep. Beside her, he lay awake for hours watching her beautiful face in the dark, longing and...wishing for the impossible.

When Kira awoke, her arms and legs were tangled around Quinn's. She'd slept so well. For a fleeting instant she felt happy just to be with him.

Last night he'd made her feel precious and adored. Until...the end. With a frown, she remembered how tense and uncertain he'd seemed right before he'd crushed her close and she'd fallen asleep in his arms.

How could she have thrown herself at him? Begged him? He was determined never to love again. Sex, even great sex, would not change his mind.

Despite regrets and misgivings, the gray morning was beautiful. Rain was falling softly, scenting the island with its freshness. A gentle breeze whirred in the eaves while dazzling sunlight splashed the far wall with vivid white.

Had she been sure of Quinn's love, it would have felt romantic to be nestled so warmly in his strong arms. She would have reveled in the sensual heat created by his breath stirring her hair.

But wrapped in cocoonlike warmth with him when she knew he couldn't ever care for her only aroused longings for forbidden things like friendship and affection.

He was going to break her heart. She knew it.

Slowly, she shifted to her side of the bed. Careful not to wake him, she eased herself to her feet. When he smiled in his sleep, she couldn't help thinking him the most stunningly handsome man she'd ever seen.

He looked so relaxed. So peaceful. Last night, he'd taken great care to make her happy in bed. Longing to brush his thick hair away from his brow filled her. Because of what they'd shared, she simply wanted to touch him.

No… She had to remember his experience. He was probably just a great lover and had taken no special pains with her.

Fearing she'd accidentally awaken him if she didn't stop gaping at his virile, male beauty, she tiptoed onto the breezeway where salty air assaulted her. When her tummy flipped violently, causing a brief dizzy spell, she sank against the doorjamb.

After a deep breath, the dizziness loosened its hold. She wasn't sick exactly, but her face felt clammy and she was queasy in a way she'd never been before.

Alarmed, she swallowed. Shakily, she smoothed her damp hair back from her face.

Again, she remembered that Quinn hadn't used a condom their first time in bed. In her head, she began to count the days since her last period, which she already knew was a little late. It was time…past time…for her period to start…and under the circumstances, her odd light-headedness made her anxious.

What if she were pregnant? How would Quinn react? He had not married her because he loved her or wanted a family. Quite the opposite. He'd used protection every single time since that first lapse. She'd never want to force him to stay married to her because of a baby. She wanted love, acceptance. Making their marriage of convenience a permanent situation was the best way to guarantee she'd never find it.

Quickly, she said a little prayer and decided not to borrow trouble just yet. Why upset him until she knew for sure? Still, no matter how she denied it, a seed of worry had taken root.

By the time Quinn had awakened, yanked on his jeans

and called for her, Kira had had her first cup of coffee and felt almost calm enough to face him. As she sat on the front porch, she watched the last gusts of the storm whip the high waves into a frenzy and hurl them against the shore.

At the sound of his approaching footsteps her belly tightened. Then she reminded herself there had only been one lapse...so there really wasn't much danger of pregnancy, was there?

"Kira?"

Concentrating on the angry seas, she wondered how soon the waves would calm down enough for them to leave. When she heard Quinn turning away from the porch, maybe because she hadn't answered, and stomping around somewhere inside the kitchen calling her name, she sensed he was out of sorts, too.

The door behind her creaked.

"Why didn't you answer when I called you?" His low voice was harsh, uncertain. "Avoiding me, are you?"

She didn't turn around to look at him. "Maybe I didn't hear you."

"Maybe you did."

"The seas are still so high, it may be a while before we can leave," she said.

"I see. After last night, you're too embarrassed to talk about anything but the weather. Are you blaming me because I didn't stick to our no-sex deal?"

Hot color climbed her cheeks. "No. I know that what happened was as much my fault as yours."

"But you don't like it."

"Look, what I don't like is being bullied into this marriage in the first place."

"Right."

"If you hadn't forced me to marry you, we wouldn't be

trapped on this island together. Then last night wouldn't have happened."

"Okay, then. So, am I to assume from your mutinous expression that you want to go back to our no-sex deal?"

Why were men always so maddeningly literal? All she wanted was a little reassurance. Instead, he'd launched into the blame game.

Well, she wasn't about to admit she'd craved him last night or that she'd enjoyed everything they'd done together. Nor would she admit that despite everything, she still wanted him. That the last thing she wanted was their no-sex deal. To admit any of that would prove her irrational and give him too much power over her.

When she sat staring at the stormy gulf in silence, he squared his shoulders. "It's too bad the waters are so rough and you're stuck with me, but if we've waited it out this long, I don't intend to push our luck by trying to take the tender out when we could capsize. I'm hungry. Do you want to share that last can of pork and beans with me for breakfast or not?"

The mere thought of canned pork and beans made her mouth go dry and her tummy flip. Within seconds, she began to perspire.

"Or not," she whispered, shaking her head fiercely as she inhaled a deep breath to settle her stomach.

"Are you all right? You look a little pale," he said, stepping closer. "Sick almost."

"I'm fine," she snapped, turning away so he couldn't read her face.

"I wasn't too rough last night, was I?" he asked, the genuine concern in his low tone touching her.

"The less said about what happened the better!"

With a weary look, he nodded. "I talked to my captain via satellite phone. *Pegasus* held up well under the rough seas and squalls. The crew had a bit of a bad night, but other than a case or two of seasickness, all is well."

"I'm glad."

"Look, for what it's worth, I'm sorry I reneged on our bargain and made love to you."

She knotted her hands and unknotted them.

"I took advantage."

"No, you didn't! I was the one who ran out in the storm and lured you after me!" She jumped up. Hugging herself, she walked over to the window. "I'm sure any man would have done the same."

"Look, I'm not just some guy you picked up off the street who is out to get what he can get."

She whirled on him. "Whatever you may think because of that night we shared in San Antonio, I don't do one-night stands, either!"

"I know that. I believe that. I wouldn't have married you otherwise."

"I wonder. Did anything besides my last name really matter to you?"

His face went cold. "I'm your husband. Last night I knew what you wanted and what you didn't want. But in the end, it didn't matter."

"You told me you'd have me in your bed in no time, and you did. So why don't you chalk up another win for your side in your little plan to get revenge against my father."

"Damn it. Because that's not how I feel about it! Or about you!"

"Don't romanticize what happened! We were bored and trapped. Big deal. It's over."

"The hell it is."

"Ours is only a marriage of convenience."

"Do you have to constantly remind me of that?"

"Why not, if it's the truth?"

"Is it? Does it have to be?"

"Yes! Yes!"

He was silent for a long moment. "If that's really how you feel, I won't sleep with you again. You can have your marriage of convenience—permanently. I hope it makes you happy!"

His cold announcement chilled her. Not that she was about to let him see how hurt she felt.

"Great! Now that that's settled, go! Eat your beans and leave me alone!"

"All right. And after I eat them, I'm going out. For a walk. To check on the tender. And I won't be back till the storm's over."

"Great! Perfect!"

When he slammed out of the porch and stalked toward the kitchen, her stomach twisted sharply. She felt ill, really ill. Clutching her stomach, she ran out the back door so he wouldn't see, knelt on the damp sand in the lightly falling rain, and was sick.

She *was* pregnant. She just knew she was.

His strides long and quick because he was anxious to get as far from the house—and from her—as fast as he could, Quinn stalked down the beach toward the dock. As his heels thudded into the deep sand, his head pounded viciously. Their quarrel had given him the headache from hell.

How different he felt now than he had when he'd first woken up. The air had smelled so fresh. He'd lain in bed, his eyes closed, drinking in a contentment he hadn't known in years. Then, he'd reached for her and discovered cool sheets instead of her warm, silky body, and some part of him had gone cold.

He didn't regret his harsh words because she'd smashed

his heart. He didn't regret the sex, either. She'd been sweet, and she'd felt too good—so good that just thinking of her naked and writhing in his arms, her shining eyes big as she'd begged for more had him brick-hard all over again.

When he saw the dock up ahead and the tender riding the waves, he felt intense relief.

He wasn't used to second-guessing himself or feeling the slightest guilt or confusion after sex. In his whole life he'd never awakened beside a woman who hadn't wanted him. Quite the opposite. They always clung, wanting more than he could give. Then he'd be the one to pull away. With her, he felt different. That's probably why he'd been fool enough to marry her.

From the moment Kira had shown up in his office to beg him not to marry her sister, he'd changed all the rules he'd lived by for so long. She'd tangled his emotions into a painful knot.

For some insane, ridiculous reason, he wanted to please her. He'd actually hoped she'd be happier with him after last night, so her obvious misery this morning ate at him all the more.

In his frustration, he broke into a jog. His marriage be damned. The sooner he ended this farce of a honeymoon and got back to business the better.

From now on, their marriage would be as she wished— all for show. He'd ignore the hell out of her except when there were in public.

When he reached the dock, he grabbed the stern line. After snugging the tender closer, he sprang on board.

Crafted of teak for the turbulent waters of the North Sea, she was an efficient, self-bailing craft. Maybe that was why she hadn't sunk. Also, the dock was on the leeward side of the island and in a well-protected cove.

He started the engine and smiled grimly when it purred

to life. Once he made sure the tender was sound, he shut it off, sat down and let the wind buffet him.

In no mood to return to the house or to his wife, he kept an eye on the distant horizon. As soon as the seas calmed, he'd take his bride home and get back to work. He'd lose himself in negotiations with the European Union and forget all about Kira.

His marriage was turning out to be the last thing from convenient, whatever Kira might say to the contrary.

Twelve

Quinn spoke to her as little as possible now.

If Kira had wondered how long Quinn would pretend to be interested in her, she had her answer and was miserable as a result.

No sooner had they returned to San Antonio than he'd made it clear he intended to live as he had before his marriage—working nearly every waking hour.

"The EU deal is going to command my full attention, so I won't be around much for a while," he'd said.

"Fine. I understand."

"Jason will come promptly at ten every morning to take care of you and the house."

"Jason?"

"My houseman. He's at your command. You'll find him highly competent."

Quinn had ensconced her in his fabulous loft apartment, and yes, he'd given her the master bedroom. Now she slept alone in the vast bed they'd shared that first night. As for himself, their first evening home, he'd packed a suitcase and moved his things into a second bedroom. Then he'd politely bid her a terse good-night, gone to bed early and left for work the next morning hours before she'd woken up.

That first morning Jason, a much older man, who was thin-lipped and skeletal, had greeted her so haughtily in the kitchen, she'd felt she was invading his territory.

"I'm Jason," he'd said with a vague sneer in his upper-class tone. "I'm here for whatever you need, cleaning, shopping, cooking—anything. It is my duty and privilege to please you, madam."

Madam?

"Wow! I'm really not used to being waited on. I can't think of a thing for you to do. I mean, I can pour my own cereal out of a box, can't I?"

"Cereal?" He scowled briefly. "Would you prefer an omelet?" he'd suggested with a contemptuous lift of his brows.

"Well, why not," she'd whispered, sensing they were getting off to a bad start. She wanted to be agreeable, yet she despised herself for giving in to him when he was supposed to be serving her. The man made her feel more out of place in Quinn's home than she'd felt before.

Jason had cooked a very good ham-and-vegetable omelet, and she'd dutifully eaten it. Then she'd rushed off to Betty's restaurant to help out while one of the waitresses was away, and the kitchen smells had bothered her way more than usual.

The rest of the week followed the same pattern with Quinn leaving early and returning late. Jason cooked her breakfast and made her dinner, and she began to feel grateful for his presence since it meant she wasn't totally alone.

Since Quinn was gone all the time, she might hardly have noticed she was married if she hadn't missed him so much. She was on her own, as she had been before her marriage, but because her husband was a man she found exceedingly attractive, she felt rejected and constantly unsettled. If he was home behind his shut door, she thought of him every minute.

When he was gone, she felt lost. With every passing day she grew more acutely sensitive to odors, which made her increasingly worried that he'd made her pregnant. She wanted to talk to Quinn about the situation, but she dreaded the conversation, especially now that he was so intent on avoiding her.

On the eighth day of their return, when her period still hadn't started and she was queasier than ever, she called her doctor and made an appointment for the next morning. She'd agreed to take her mother to a routine chemo treatment the same afternoon.

Jaycee had called her earlier in the week, begging her to pick up their mother for her appointment as a favor because escorting her mother for treatment made Jaycee so sad.

"So, how's it going with Quinn?" Jaycee had asked after Kira agreed.

"Fine."

"Fine? Hmm? Well, they do say the first few months are an adjustment."

"I said we're fine."

"I know you don't believe this, but he cares about you. He wanted to marry you."

"Right."

"He bought you that beautiful wedding dress, and you should have seen him when you were gone and nobody knew where you were."

"Well, he's ignoring me now," Kira confided.

"Did you two have a fight?"

She didn't answer.

"If you did, and I think you did, you need to find a way to kiss and make up."

"Why bother to make up, if we have no future?"

Kira changed the subject to her cat, Rudy, and asked if Jaycee minded keeping him a while longer. "I don't want him attaching himself to Quinn...if we're just going to break up."

"He's only a cat."

"Rudy's sensitive."

"And Quinn's not? If I were you, I'd worry more about your husband."

She was; she just wasn't going to admit it.

When Jaycee hung up, Kira had marked her mother's appointment on her calendar. She was glad to have something other than Quinn and her possible pregnancy to concentrate on.

Hours later, she was in bed that night with her light out when she heard Quinn at the door. Throwing off her covers, she started to go out and greet him. Then, pride made her stay where she was.

Wishing he'd knock on her door, she counted his approaching footsteps as he walked across the great room before he made his way down the hall.

When he paused at her door her heart beat very fast. But after a minute, he resumed walking to his own bedroom.

When his door slammed, a strangled sob rose in her throat. With a little cry, she got out of bed and ran to her window. Staring out at the brilliant city, she imagined other married couples, happier couples, slipping into bed together, snuggling close, talking about their day or their children, taking such blissful marital pleasures for granted.

Suddenly, Kira felt as lonely as a butterfly trapped in a child's glass jar.

Pulling on her robe, she wandered out into the great room. Baby or not, she could not live like this, with a husband who didn't want her.

Behind her, she heard a floorboard creak. Whirling, she caught her breath at the sight of Quinn standing bare-chested in the dark. His shadowed eyes looked haunted.

"You okay?" His low, harsh voice made her shiver. She wanted to be held, loved and crushed against him.

"I'm fine. And you?"

"A little tired, but the deal with the EU seems to be coming together. I'll be going to London for a few days."

"Oh."

"A car's coming for me at 5:00 a.m. Don't worry. I'll be careful so as not to wake you."

How could he be so obtuse? Was he just indifferent? Or was he still angry with her for their harsh exchange on the island?

She wanted to scream at him that he should kiss her goodbye properly. She wanted to drive him to the airport herself. But she kept such foolish thoughts to herself, and he only stared at her from the dark with his intense, burning gaze. She thought he was watching her, waiting—but for what?

Jaycee had advised her to kiss and make up. But how? To what purpose, when he so clearly had his mind on more important things?

After a few minutes of staring at each other in stony silence, he said good-night.

The next morning, when she heard the front door close behind him, she got up. Throwing away all pride, she rushed from her room into the foyer that was filled with crimson light, managing to catch up to him as he waited for the elevator.

"Sorry to wake you," he murmured, concern in his eyes.

"Don't be. I had to say goodbye and wish you a safe journey, didn't I," she whispered, surprised that she could sound so calm, so normal when she felt so incredibly depressed. "I'll miss you."

His dark brows arched warily. "Will you now?"

"I will," she said.

After another long moment spent considering her, he sighed and drew her close against his long, hard body. "I'll miss you, too." He paused. "Sorry about the last week or so."

"I'm sorry, too."

"Habib will call you later and give you all the numbers where I can be reached. I'll think of you in London. I really will miss you. You know that, don't you?" he murmured.

Would he really?

Wrapping her closer, he kissed her hard. She clung to him, probably revealing more of her real feelings than was wise. Then the elevator pinged, and he was forced to let her go or be late. Holding her gaze, he picked up his suitcase and strode through the doors.

She couldn't turn away or stop looking at him or take even one step toward the loft until the door shut.

Pregnant! Needing a moment to take in that news, Kira clenched the steering wheel of her Toyota as she sat in the parking lot of the medical complex and kneaded her forehead with her knuckles.

After a brief exam, the doctor had ripped off his latex gloves and confirmed she was pregnant.

"How do you know? You haven't even tested me."

"When you've been doing this as long as I have, young lady, you just know."

Within minutes, a pregnancy test administered in his office confirmed his opinion.

After the office visit, she felt both numb and tingly as she sat in her car. Biting her lip, she pulled out the slip of paper where she'd written all the numbers Habib had given her earlier. After calculating the time difference between the U.K. and Texas, she grabbed her cell phone and started dialing. Then she stopped. Quinn was probably extremely busy or in an important meeting. Her news would distract him from what was all-important to him—the deal. Better to share the news with him in person when she was sure she had his full attention and could gauge his reaction.

Still, her heart felt as if it was brimming over. She was bursting to tell someone…who would be every bit as excited as she was.

Mother. Suddenly, she was very glad she would be taking her mother to treatment today. Who better to confide in than her precious baby's grandmother? Nobody adored babies, anybody's babies, more than her mother did. Her mother would be happier about this news than anyone, and goodness knew, with all she was going through, she needed a cheerful future to contemplate.

"Oh, my dear," her mother gushed, setting her flowered china teacup aside and seizing Kira's hand in both of her thin ones. Kira had waited until after her mother's treatment, when they could sit down together at Betty's, to share the news.

How weak her mother's grasp felt, even if her eyes were alight with joy.

"Such wonderful news! The best ever! Unbelievable! And it was so easy for you two! And so soon!"

A fierce rush of pride swamped Kira. Never had her mother been so pleased with her. Such rapture had always been reserved for Jaycee's accomplishments.

"Have you told Quinn yet?" her mother asked.

"I started to call him. Then I thought I'd wait…until he comes home, until he's not so distracted."

"So, I'm the first!" Her mother beamed so brightly she almost looked as she had before the illness. Her grip strengthened. "I'm going to beat this thing and live for a very long time. I have to…if I'm to see my darling grand-baby grow up."

Kira's gaze blurred, and she had to turn away to hide her emotion. She felt exhilarated and proud, and a big part of her pleasure had to do with the fact that for once she'd trumped Jaycee.

Oh, why hadn't she ever felt sure of her parents' love?

The river sparkled beside their table outside Betty's. Kira was thrilled her mother's fighting spirit was intact and that she felt reasonably strong. But most of all, she couldn't help being glad that she'd been the one to make her mother so happy.

"Your father will be just as excited as I am. He's very up on Quinn's successes in London, too. So this will be a doubly great day for him."

"Oh, so he's already heard from Quinn?" Kira whispered, feeling more than a little hurt that Quinn had called her father and not her.

"Yes, and it sounds like things are going very well," her mother replied. "Am I to assume by the way you're biting your lip that *you* haven't spoken to him?"

"He texted me, saying he'd arrived in London safely. I'm not hurt. Not in the least."

After studying her for a long moment, her mother looked

dubious. "Well, I'm sure he'll be so happy to hear your exciting news."

Would he be? Oh, how she hoped so, but her doubts soon had her biting her lower lip again.

"Don't do that, dear. How many times have I told you that biting your lip like that chaps your beautiful mouth?"

"When I was a child, Mother!"

"Well, just the same, I know you want to be beautiful for Quinn when he comes home, now, don't you?"

"Right. I do." She glanced at the muddy green river and tried to focus on a white duck. "Frankly, I'm a little worried about telling him. You know…we didn't marry under the best of circumstances."

"I wish you wouldn't make so much of that. I really think it means something when a couple gets pregnant so easily," her mother said almost enviously.

"What are you saying?"

"Sometimes it doesn't work that way… Earl and I had a terrible time getting pregnant with…with you. But let's not go there."

Did she only imagine the shadow that passed over her mother's thin face?

"Is anything wrong, Mother?"

"No, dear."

But her mother looked away and something in her manner and stiff posture rang alarm bells inside Kira. When the silence between them lengthened and grew more strained, she was sure her mother was worrying about something.

"What's wrong? Have I upset you?"

Her mother stared at her, hesitating. "I guess…it's only natural that your news would stir up the past."

"When you were pregnant with me?"

A single tear traced down her mother's cheek. "No…" She clenched her napkin.

"Did the doctor tell you something when you were alone with her that has you upset? Bad news of some kind?"

"Dear God, no!" Her mother took her hand. "No. It's not that. It's nothing like that. It's about you…" Her mother's eyes filled with some unfathomable emotion. "I was never pregnant with you."

"What?"

"I…*we* tried so hard, your father and I, to have a baby. So dreadfully hard. You know how I am. I took my temperature all the time. Ten times a day. But I didn't…I couldn't get pregnant…no matter what I did. We went to so many specialists, and they told us that it was my fault, not your father's. Some hormone imbalance. And then…we never told anyone, not even you, the truth."

"What truth?" Under the table Kira's hands fisted so tightly her nails dug bloody crescents into her palms.

"I couldn't conceive, so, in the end, we adopted."

"What?"

"You're adopted. Please don't look so upset! I could never have had a daughter of my own as wonderful as you. You've always been so sweet. Like now. Coming with me for my treatment when poor Jaycee couldn't bear it. She hates thinking of me being sick. She's too much like me, you see. I'm strong in some ways, but weak in others. Until now, I could never admit, not to anyone, that you weren't my biological child. It represented my biggest imperfection as a woman."

"Oh, my God." Kira felt overwhelmed, hollow. Suddenly she remembered all the little things that had never added up in her life. The rest of her family members were blond and blue-eyed, while she had dark eyes and hair. She was tall and slim, while her mother and Jaycee were more petite and curvy.

She'd never been as interested in style or fashion as they were. She'd been wired more emotionally and hadn't thought as logically as they did. Maybe this was why she'd always felt as if she hadn't belonged in her family. Maybe she'd always sensed this huge falsehood in her life.

"I felt like such a failure," her mother continued. "As a woman. For not being able to conceive a child. And then suddenly, inexplicably, when you were two years old, I became pregnant with Jaycee…without even trying. When she was so perfect, so gorgeous, I felt I'd achieved something grand by giving birth. But really, having you was always just as big an achievement. Only I never appreciated it until now. Illness like this can change you, make you wiser somehow.

"I was silly and so unsure when I was young. I know I haven't always understood you, but you are very precious to me."

Kira could say nothing. She was as overwhelmed as a stage actress in a drama who'd forgotten all her lines. Her mind had gone blank.

"I'm so glad you have Quinn. We all suffered so much when Kade died right after selling the company to us. Your father loved Kade like a brother. And then, all these years later, to have Quinn take over the company at the best possible moment for us was a fortunate irony. And now this baby. This wonderful baby will make everything right again. I just know it will.

"I'll get well, and you'll be happy with Quinn. You'll quit…doubting you belong together because you'll have this baby to love together. Nothing can bring a couple closer than a child."

"If only life were that simple."

"Sometimes it is."

Kira couldn't think about her adoption and what it meant right now. So she focused on finding out more about Quinn's past.

Squeezing her eyes shut, she reopened them. "Mother, why did Quinn blame Daddy for his father's death?"

"Your father and Kade Sullivan created Murray Oil. Well, back then it was Sullivan and Murray Oil. Esther Sullivan was extravagant, but Kade adored her. Of course, he was always borrowing from Earl, always needing more… because of her, you see. Esther's needs were insatiable. In time, Kade began to gamble on the side and play the market. For years he was lucky, but then one day his luck ran out.

"When money went missing at the company, from accounts he was responsible for, your father asked him some pointed questions. Kade got angry. The money was found eventually, but the misunderstanding had caused a rift between them.

"Kade said he wanted out, so Earl bought him out. But when times got better and the stock price took off, Kade got hard feelings and started drinking and bad-mouthing your father, especially to Quinn, I think. Around that time, Esther divorced Kade and took whatever he had left.

"Not too long afterward, Earl made a deal that tripled the worth of Murray Oil. Kade claimed the deal had been his idea and wanted compensation, so he sued. He lost the suit, and Quinn discovered his father's body in his shop off the garage. Supposedly Kade had been cleaning his shotgun and it went off. Accidentally. But who knows? Not that Kade ever seemed like the kind of man who'd kill himself. In fact, your father definitely believes it was an accident.

"Oh, my darling, let's not talk of such depressing things.

I much prefer to think about my future grandbaby. Do you want a boy or a girl?"

"A little boy," she whispered. "A little boy with blue eyes who looks just like Quinn and Kade."

"So, you're beginning to love him a little."

With all her heart. Yet she wasn't ready to admit that, not even to her mother.

But her mother saw the truth. "I told you so," she said triumphantly. "And no wonder. He's everything any woman with half a brain would want in a husband."

Not quite everything. He could never return her love, Kira thought.

Thirteen

Quinn remained in London for a week, during which time Kira ached for him. She didn't know how she could miss a man who'd worked so hard to ignore her before he'd left, but she did.

Then, suddenly he sent her a brief text informing her of his flight information for the next day. He said he'd hired a driver to pick him up. Then, right before he boarded his plane, he called her cell while she was still asleep. When she didn't answer, he left a message saying he'd called to remind her of a company party they were attending that evening an hour after his flight was scheduled to land.

So, there would be no private time together his first night home.

"You can call my secretary to find out what to wear," he'd said over the phone. Then his voice had lowered. "Missed you…worse than I thought I would," he'd whispered before ending the call.

Damn. Damn. Damn. What rotten luck that she'd missed his call. What else might he have said if they'd actually talked? She replayed his message several times just to hear his mesmerizing voice say he'd missed her.

A lump formed in her throat. Why had she muted her phone before laying it on her bedside table?

Dialing his secretary, she asked what she should wear to the party.

"It's formal, but Mr. Sullivan did tell me to suggest you wear something red."

"Why red?"

"He didn't say. The deal he pulled off with the EU will have far-reaching consequences for Murray Oil, hopefully positive. Since he's returning in triumph, the party's important to him. I'd suggest you go with his color choice, in case it fits with a bigger plan."

Her heart thumping wildly, Kira took off early from Betty's to indulge in a shopping spree with her mother in search of the perfect sexy red dress. Then she rushed home, with her low-cut scarlet gown and a pair of new heels, so she could take special pains getting dressed.

After the party, if Quinn was in a good mood, she would tell him she was pregnant.

At six, while she was combing her hair, his driver called to tell her Quinn's plane had just landed. "I'll have him home soon."

"Can I please talk to him?"

"He's on the phone. Business. But I'll tell him to call you as soon as he finishes."

When Quinn's key turned in the lock, Kira hurried to the door to greet him. His luggage thumped heavily on the floor. Then he strode through the foyer with his phone still pressed to his ear.

His voice rang with authority as he stepped into the living room. When she met his hard, dark eyes, she saw the shadows of weariness under them. Even if he hadn't bothered to call her from the car, she was so thrilled he was home, her heart leaped with pure joy.

"Gotta go," he said abruptly. "We'll wrap this up in the morning." He flipped his phone shut and stared at her. "Sorry about the phone call. Business."

"Of course. I understand." She smiled tremulously.

His mouth curved, but his smile played out before it reached his eyes.

She wanted to rush into his arms, and it was only with great effort that she remained where she was. No matter how eager she felt, she would not throw herself at him.

"You look pale," he said. "Thinner. Are you okay?"

She hadn't been eating as regularly due to her morning sickness, but she couldn't tell him that. At least, not now.

"I'm fine," she whispered.

"Right. Why is that answer always your first line of defense?"

She didn't know what to say to him. If only he would take her in his arms and kiss her, maybe that would break down the barriers between them.

His eyes burned her, and his hands were clenched. Was being married to her so difficult for him?

"I like the dress. It becomes you," he murmured.

She blushed, pleased.

"I bought you something." He tossed a box onto the sofa carelessly. "Open it and see if you like it." He spoke casually, as if the gift was a token and nothing more.

When he turned sharply and walked down the hall to his bedroom, she felt a sickening sensation of loss. How foolish she'd been to dream they might have a new beginning.

Sinking onto the sofa, she opened the black box and let

out a pleased cry when a necklace and earrings of rubies and diamonds exploded in fiery brilliance. He'd tucked his business card inside the box. On the back of it, scrawled in bold black ink, she read, "For my beautiful wife."

Tears filled her eyes as she hesitantly touched the necklace. She quickly brushed the dampness away. The necklace was exquisite. Nobody had ever given her anything half so lovely.

In the next breath, she told herself the gift meant nothing. He was wealthy. It was for show. He'd bought the jewels to impress Murray Oil's clients, stockholders and employees. He'd probably had someone pick them up for her. The gift wasn't personal.

"Do you like it?" Tall and dark, he stood in the doorway looking gravely handsome in his elegant black suit.

"It's too beautiful," she whispered. "You shouldn't have, but thank you."

"Then stand up, and I'll help you put it on. You have no idea how many necklaces I looked at. Nothing seemed right until I found this one."

"You shopped for it yourself?"

"Indeed. Who could I possibly trust to select the right gift for my bride? The wrong necklace could overpower you."

He let her secure the earrings to her ears before he lifted the necklace from the black velvet box and fastened it around her neck.

At the warmth of his fingertips against her nape, her skin tingled and her heart beat wildly. Was it possible to have an orgasm from sheer longing?

"With your dark hair, I thought rubies would become you, and they do," he said, staring so long at the sparkle on her slim neck his gaze made her skin burn. "I imagined you wearing them and nothing else."

In spite of herself, she giggled. *This was more like the homecoming she'd fantasized about.* In another moment, he would kiss her.

He stepped back to admire her and shot her an answering grin. Why, oh, why hadn't he kissed her?

She pursed her lips, touched her hand to her throat.

His face grew guarded again; his lips set in that firm line she'd come to dread. Instead of taking her in his arms, he backed away almost violently. "Shall we go?" he said, his tone rough and deliberately impersonal.

Cut to the quick, she didn't dare look at him as she nodded. During the short drive, he didn't speak to her again.

As soon as they arrived at the party, he put his arm around her as executives and clients rushed up and surrounded him, all clamoring to congratulate Quinn on his successes in London.

Black silk rustling, Cristina was among the first who hurried to his side. Barely managing a cool smile for Kira, she placed a bejeweled, exquisitely manicured hand on Quinn's cheek with practiced ease and kissed him lightly.

"I'm *so* proud of you," she gushed in a low, intimate tone. "I knew you'd pull it off. See—everybody loves you now. Worries over."

Clearly, he'd taken the time to inform *her* personally of his successes.

"So the deal went well?" Kira whispered into his ear when the lovely Cristina glided away.

He nodded absently as he continued shaking everybody's hand.

"Why didn't you tell me?"

"You know now, don't you?"

"But I'm your wife…"

"Unwillingly, as you keep reminding me. Which is why

I've been working hard not to burden you with too much attention."

Stung, her eyes burning and her heart heavy, she turned away. Why did it hurt that he saw no need to share the things that mattered to him when she'd known all along their marriage was for show?

She was sure he had a duty to mingle, so she was surprised when Quinn stayed by her side. When she noticed a dark-skinned man talking animatedly to her family, she asked Quinn who he was.

"Habib."

"The man you were talking to after we made love that first time?"

He nodded. "I thought you two had met...at the wedding."

"No, but we've talked on the phone this past week. Why did he think you should marry Jaycee instead of me?"

"Whatever he thought, he was wrong. What difference does it make now?"

"My mother told me today that I was adopted."

When Quinn's blue eyes darkened, she sensed that he knew more than he wanted to let on.

"Something you said that morning made me wonder if you and he somehow knew that," she persisted.

He stiffened warily.

"I thought that if you had known, maybe you assumed my family cared more about her...and maybe that was why Habib concurred with my father that she was the better choice...?"

"Habib's research did indicate a partiality on your father's part for Jacinda."

Her chest constricted. That truth was one of the reasons being loved in her own right by her husband was something that was beginning to matter to Kira more than anything.

"I preferred you from the first," he countered.

He kept saying that. Could she dare to believe him?

"Doesn't that count for something?" he asked.

"Our marriage was a business deal."

"So you keep reminding me."

"You only married me to make taking over Murray Oil go more smoothly, and now that you've made a place for yourself, your need for me is at an end."

"I'll decide when my need for you is at end. What do you say we end this depressing conversation and dance?" He took her hand. "Shall we?"

"You don't really want to dance with me— I'm just—"

"Don't put yourself down," he growled as he pulled her into his hard arms. "You're my wife."

"So, dancing with me at the company party is expected?" she said.

"I suppose." His grip strengthening, he smiled grimly down at her. "Did it ever occur to you that I might want to dance with you even if it wasn't expected?"

She was aware of people watching them and reminded herself that he was only dancing with her to make the guests believe their marriage was real.

From a corner, her laughing parents and a smiling Jaycee watched them, too. Looking at them, so happy together, Kira felt left out, as usual. Even being in Quinn's arms, knowing she was pregnant with his child, gave her no joy. How could it? Had he touched her other than for public viewing, or shown her any affection since he'd returned? Their marriage was a business deal to him, and one that wasn't nearly as important as the one he'd just concluded in London.

"Quit thinking dark, mutinous thoughts, and just dance," he whispered against her ear. "Relax. Enjoy. You're very beautiful, you know, and I'd seize any excuse to hold you in my arms."

Despite her determination to resist his appeal, his words, his nearness and his warm breath against her earlobe had her blood beating wildly.

She knew it was illogical, but being held in his arms reassured her. Soon she almost forgot dancing with him was just for show. Everyone in the gilded room blurred except her handsome husband.

They didn't speak again, but his eyes lingered on her lips as the music washed through her. Did he want to kiss her? She wanted it so much, she felt sick with longing. Surely he knew it. If so, he gave no indication, and, after a while, all the spinning about began to make her feel dizzy and much too hot.

She didn't want to be sick. Not now…not when he was finally holding her, when he seemed almost happy to be with her. Still, she couldn't take another step or she'd faint.

"I need some air," she whispered.

"All right." He led her round along the shadowy edges of the room until they came to a pair of tall French doors that opened onto a balcony overlooking the sparkling city. Gallantly, he pulled her outside. The night was mild, pleasant even. Once they were alone, his grip around her tightened in concern and he pressed her close.

"You look so strained and pale. Are you sure you're okay?"

She gulped in a breath of air. And then another. "I'm perfectly fine," she lied, believing that surely in a minute or two she would be.

"Obviously, even being in my arms is an ordeal."

"No!"

"You don't have to lie. I know well enough that I've given you ample reason to dislike me."

"I don't dislike you."

"But you don't like me. How could you? I was your father's enemy."

"Quinn—"

"No, hear me out. Since the island, I've kept my distance in order to make our marriage less onerous to you. I know I pushed you into this situation too hard and too fast, and I took advantage of you the night of the storm. I'm not proud of that. But do you have any idea how difficult it's been to stay away from you ever since?

"I wanted to give you your precious space and time to get used to our arrangement. I prayed that a week's separation would give me the strength to resist you when I returned," he muttered. "So, I didn't call you from London, and when I came home, I tried to be the cold husband you desire. But after our days apart, when you looked so ethereal and beautiful in your flashy red dress, my vow not to touch you drove me crazy. God help me, ever since the first day I saw you at your parents' ranch, you've obsessed me."

"But I don't desire a cold husband. I've wanted you, too," she whispered, wishing her feet felt a little steadier beneath her. Despite the fresh air, she was beginning to feel light-headed again.

"You have?"

Whatever encouragement he sought in her eyes, he found. Instantly, his lips were on hers, but when he crushed her closer, holding her tightly and kissing her, her dizziness returned in a sickening rush.

"I've wanted you so much," he murmured. "Missed you so much. You have no idea. Darlin', tell me you missed me, at least a little?"

Her heart beat violently even as she gulped in another breath. "Of course I did," she managed to say even as his dear face blurred and the walls of the building and the twinkling lights beneath them whirled dizzyingly like bright colors dancing in a kaleidoscope.

She willed herself to be strong, to fight the dizziness. "I did... But there's something I have to tell you, Quinn. Something...wonderful."

Little blue stars whirred. *Not good.* On the next beat the bottom dropped out of her tummy, and try as she might to save herself by gulping in mouthfuls of air, she couldn't get her breath.

"Quinn—"

Her hands, which had been pushing frantically against his hard chest, lost their strength. She was falling into a heavy darkness that was hot and swirling and all-enveloping.

The last thing she saw was Quinn's anxious face as his arms closed around her.

Fourteen

When Kira regained consciousness, Quinn was leaning over her in a small room, pressing a cool rag to her brow. To his right, a tall blond man with an air of grave authority had a finger pressed to her wrist while he studied his watch.

"Dennis is a doctor, and he wants me to ask you if…if you could possibly be pregnant," Quinn said.

"I wanted to tell…you. First thing… I really did."

"What?"

"Yes!" She blushed guiltily as Quinn stared down at her. "Yes. I'm pregnant. "I…I think that's why I got too hot while we were dancing. I've been having morning sickness while you were gone."

"That's why you were so pale. Why didn't you call me? Or tell me when I got home?" Quinn's hand tightened on her arm, and his expression grew grim. "Because you were unhappy about the baby? Were you planning to end the pregnancy without telling me?"

"No!" she exclaimed, horrified.

Quinn turned to the doctor and grilled him about her condition. The man quickly reassured him that her pulse and blood pressure were just fine. Still, he advised that she see her own doctor the next day, just to make sure.

"We're going home," Quinn said. "You're going to bed. No wonder I thought you looked thin. You should have told me."

"I was going to…"

"When?" he demanded so coldly she couldn't answer him.

That was the last word either of them said until they reached his loft. In the car, he gripped the steering wheel with clenched fists, while his profile seemed fashioned of unyielding granite. Never once did he look her way. Deliberately, he shut her out. The walls between them thickened and grew taller. Would she ever be able to reach him again?

Once inside the loft, he lingered in the crimson shower of light by the door while she fled to the master bedroom.

Alone in the vast room, she stared at the bed they'd shared. Silently, she kicked off her heels and pulled off the red dress and then slipped into a frothy white nightgown.

This wasn't the way she'd imagined telling him about the baby.

The rubies on her neck felt heavy, unbearable, but when she went to undo the clasp, her fingers shook too badly for her to manage it. The weight on her heart was even heavier. How could he have thought, even for one second, she might want to end her pregnancy? How could she go to bed when heartbreak was suffocating her?

She had to talk to him, to at least try to make things

right. Without remembering to grab a robe, she raced to the huge living room. It was empty, so she tiptoed back down the hall to his bedroom door, which he'd shut against her. She called his name, softly at first. When he didn't answer, she knocked.

His door swung open and he stood before her, his powerful, bare-chested body backlit by the lamp on his nightstand. He looked so glorious, she caught her breath. For a long moment, she could only stare at his bronzed muscles with bemused fascination. He was so fit and hard. If only she could throw herself into his arms and tell him she loved him and his baby.

But she knew he didn't want her love.

"I want this baby, and I was going to tell you," she whispered.

She watched his magnificent muscles cord as he pushed the door wider. "When?" he muttered roughly, disbelieving her.

"Just before I passed out at the party. I wanted to tell you in person, and… It was just that I was scared," she continued breathlessly. "I—I…couldn't believe you'd want my baby, too."

"Our baby," he corrected in a tight tone. "Couldn't the baby give us something more positive to build on?"

"How? If you regret marrying me. And blame our child for trapping you into a permanent involvement with a woman you don't want.

"Quinn, if you'd planned to dissolve our marriage after your takeover of Murray Oil, you don't have to stay with me because of this. I hope you know that. This doesn't have to change the businesslike nature of our arrangement."

He sucked in a breath. "Damn it. Are you ever going to quit telling me what I feel?"

"But isn't that…how you feel?"

For a long moment he was silent. "Would you listen to me for once, instead of being so sure you've got me pegged?"

"Yes. All right."

After another lengthy interval, his expression softened. "I guess I'm a little scared by your news," he said simply.

"Because you know our marriage isn't real?"

His mouth tensed. "No! Because babies are a lifetime commitment. Because they are so little…and so helpless. Because they know how to turn their parents into doting sots—and they do it with charm, in no time flat. Anything could happen to a baby." He caught her hand, and when she didn't struggle, he pulled her into his arms. "Or to you… while you're pregnant. I couldn't bear it." He kissed her brow.

It was bliss to be in his arms.

So he didn't love her, couldn't love anybody. But he cared. She was sure he cared, at least a little. He was holding her as if he did.

"But nothing will happen because we'll take good care of the baby…and me," she said reassuringly.

"My father was strong, and he died. We're all only a heartbeat away from death." There was so much grief and passion in his voice she felt hot tears sting the back of her eyelids.

"Which is why we have to live each moment to the fullest," she whispered. In a burst of tenderness, she raised her fingertips to stroke his temples in consolation. "We don't have a second to waste. We might as well be dead if we're afraid to live." To love, she wanted to add.

Quinn's arms tightened around her. He lowered his face and this time it was her mouth he sought. When he found it, he kissed her long and deeply. She opened her lips and sighed. She'd wanted him to kiss her like this for hours, days. Maybe that was why she couldn't help shivering in delight and giving him everything—all her love, even her soul—when she kissed him back.

"Oh, Kira…" For an endless time, he couldn't seem to stop kissing her. Then, suddenly, he let her go and jerked free of her embrace.

"Forgive me. I forgot—you don't want me pawing you. That's what made you sick, earlier." His dark face was flushed and his breathing ragged.

"No… I told you… I've had morning sickness. Only sometimes it's not just in the morning."

"Go to your own room. We can talk tomorrow." Even as his harsh rejection wounded, his eyes continued to hungrily devour her.

He wanted her. He was pushing her away *because* he desired her so much. And because she'd made him promise not to sleep with her.

She'd been wrong, impossible from the first. She'd missed him while he was away. She was carrying his child.

Everything had changed for them.

If she had to beg, she would.

"Don't make me sleep alone tonight," she pleaded. "Because I won't sleep. I'll just lie there…wanting you."

"I won't sleep, either. Still, in the morning you'll regret it if you don't go." His expression darkened. "Like you did before…on the island."

But she hadn't regretted it. He had.

"I don't think so," she said. "You did say we should focus on the positive…for the baby's sake. Am I right?"

His sensual mouth quirked ever so charmingly, and the heat in his gaze soon had her bones melting.

"How do you make me break every rule that allowed me to survive during my long, dark years of grief?"

"I get that you don't want to love anybody ever again.

Especially not me," she whispered. "But I'm not asking for your love tonight."

When he would have protested, she sealed his lips with a fingertip. "I'm not asking for anything you can't give. I just want to be with you."

"My father loved my mother too much, and…she destroyed him…when she left. I can't help thinking you're just waiting for the right moment to walk out."

Don't you know how much I love you? Don't you know that if only you loved me, I would never leave you?

Her knees were so weak with desire, she could barely stand. No way did she possess the courage to voice her true thoughts. She was afraid they would only drive him further away.

Her hold on him was tenuous, and only sexual. She had to accept that, use it and hope that someday she could build on that foundation.

Reaching toward him, she splayed her fingertips against his massive chest. Flesh and bone and sinew felt solid and warm beneath her open palm. When she ran her fingers over his nipples and through the dark hair that matted his torso, he groaned, which pleased her.

"Kira. Darlin'." On a shuddering sigh, he pulled her close and teased her lips and jawline with his mouth and tongue.

Lifting her, he carried her to the bed. There, he slid off his belt and slacks and pushed her nightgown down her shoulders. As it pooled onto the floor, he pulled her against him and pushed inside her slick satin warmth. Riding their mutual passion, they let it carry them like a charging black steed, faster and faster, until they soared together in torrid surrender. Afterward, as she held on to him, her sated body melted into his.

"You've ruined me," he whispered.

"Whiner," she teased.

"Seriously. I'll never be able to move again," he said.

She laughed. "Sure you will. And it better be sooner than you think. Because I'm going to be wanting more... very soon. You've neglected me...you know."

"Have I now? And whose fault was that, darlin' Kira?"

For an entire hour, he held her against his body as if she was precious to him. When she kissed his rough cheek, his throat, his nipples, he muttered huskily, "You weren't kidding, were you?"

"I've missed you."

"Slave driver."

But he smiled and ran his hands through her hair as he pulled her close.

This time his love was sweeter, and slower, and afterward, when he kissed her belly gently, he showed her that his intense passion included their precious child.

"So, you want my baby, do you?" he whispered.

"So much, too much," she admitted in a breathless whisper as she pressed his dark head against her flat stomach. "More than anything. In fact, I hope the baby's a boy and that he looks just like you."

He laughed in husky delight and nuzzled her tummy with his feverish lips. "Be careful what you wish for. He'll be a handful, I assure you."

"I can't wait."

When he held her close like this and was so teasingly affectionate, she could almost forget he didn't love her, that he never could. She could almost forget how inadequate and uncertain she'd always felt.

Almost...

He was a handsome billionaire, who could have any woman he wanted. What could she do to hold him?

Nestled in his arms, she fell into a restless sleep and

dreamed. She was a child again, standing beside her parents as they cheered Jaycee and her basketball team to victory. Then she was sitting in her room alone. The house was empty because her mother and father had driven Jaycee to a slumber party.

Older now, Kira was walking across the stage at Princeton where she'd graduated with honors. As she posed for photographs, she smiled brightly through her disappointment. None of her family was in the audience because Jaycee had a conflicting high school event. The picture was all they'd have to remember this huge milestone in Kira's life.

"Remember to smile," her mother had commanded over the phone. "You never smile." A pause. "Oh, how I wish I could be there to see you graduate!"

"Couldn't Daddy stay with Jaycee?"

"You know your father. He's no good at those high school functions without me."

The dream darkened into a nightmare. Quinn was standing in a shower of crimson light, holding Cristina against his long, lean body. "I have to marry *her,* don't you understand? I don't want to. You're the one who's special to me. Don't ever forget that my marriage to her is strictly business. You're the woman who really matters. Who will always matter. Nothing will change between us. You'll see."

Then he kissed Cristina as those awful words repeated themselves in her mind. "Strictly business…"

Kira woke up crying that phrase even as Quinn wrapped his arms around her and held her close.

"Hush. It's okay, baby. You were only dreaming."

Was she? Or were her dreams where she faced the harsh truths she denied when awake?

"I'm fine," she murmured, pushing him away. "You

don't have to comfort me. I can take care of myself—just like I always have. I didn't ask you to love me—did I?"

"No, you damn sure didn't."

Strictly business.

God, if only Quinn could feel that way, too, maybe then he'd survive this nightmare.

As soon as Kira's breathing had become regular again and Quinn was sure she was asleep, he'd tossed his own covers aside and shot out of bed.

Groping clumsily for his slacks on the dark floor, he yanked them on and stalked out of the bedroom in bare feet. When he got to the bar, he splashed a shot of vodka into a glass.

Strictly business.

Damn her! Not that he didn't feel sorry for her, because he did. Even now, her stricken cries echoed in his mind. She was no happier than he was.

He'd been right to think she'd regret the sex. So, why the hell had she slept with him when he'd given her an out?

He'd never figure her out. She might regret what had happened, but he couldn't. She'd been too sweet, and he'd craved her too desperately. Hell, it embarrassed him to think of how needy he'd felt all week without her in London.

Frowning as he stared into his glass, he remembered how he'd grabbed his cell phone at least a dozen times in his eagerness to call her, only to shove it back in his pocket. All he'd wanted was to hear her soft voice. Without her, he'd felt cut off, alone, alienated in a city he usually enjoyed.

Once in San Antonio, he'd rushed home. And when he'd seen her, he'd wanted nothing except to sweep her into his arms and kiss her endlessly. But she'd been pale and with-drawn.

Every day his obsession for her increased. If she could not reciprocate, they were shackled together on the same fatal course his own parents had traveled. He would not endure that kind of marriage.

His father had given his mother everything, and it hadn't been enough.

He would not make the same mistake.

Fifteen

Quinn's side of the bed was ice-cold.

Nothing had changed.

He was gone.

It wasn't the first time Kira had woken up alone in Quinn's bed, but this morning, she felt needier than usual. Maybe because of what they'd shared the night before, or maybe because of her bad dreams, she wanted a good-morning kiss. And maybe breakfast together punctuated with a lot more kisses.

But he'd left her for work, which was all-important to him. Hadn't business been the sole reason he'd married her?

To him, last night must have been about sex and nothing more. She'd known that, hadn't she? Still, as she lay in bed, her body sore from making love, she felt lonely. Would it always be like this?

Stretching, she rolled onto his side of the bed where his

scent lingered and hugged his pillow. Then, realizing what an idiot she was, she hurled his pillow at the wall. It struck an etching, which crashed to the floor.

Footsteps in the corridor brought a quick blush to her face.

"Mrs. Sullivan? Is that you? Do you need my assistance?" Jason sounded so stiff and formal, she cringed. She wanted her husband, not some uptight houseman with high-class British airs.

"I'm fine," she cried.

How was she going to get from Quinn's room to hers in her sheer nightie without Jason seeing her wrapped in a blanket? Such an encounter would be embarrassing for both of them.

When five minutes passed without another sound, she cracked the door. There was no sign of him, so she ripped a blanket off the bed, covered herself and shot down the hall on flying tiptoes. Once inside her bedroom, she bolted the door.

As she dressed, taking her time because it was hours before she needed to be at Betty's, she turned on the television. Murray Oil and the EU deal were all over the news.

Both the local news channels and the national ones were full of stories about Quinn's heady successes. In too many shots, a beaming Cristina stood so close to Quinn the pair seemed joined at the hip. Why hadn't Quinn told her that Cristina had gone to London with him?

Cristina worked for him. Surely he'd taken other executives. It was no big deal.

But in her fragile mood, and after her dream last night, it felt like a big deal to her.

You can't blame a man for something you dreamed!

Maybe not, but she still had to ask him about Cristina and his reasons for taking the woman to London. So, when the phone rang, she rushed to pick it up, hoping it was Quinn.

"Hello!" she said a little too brightly.

"Kira? You don't sound like yourself."

The critical male tone was very familiar. Still, because she was focused on Quinn, it took her a second to place the voice. Then it came to her: Gary Whitehall, her former boss.

"Hi, Gary."

"Are you still looking for a job?"

"I am," she said.

"Even though you're Quinn Sullivan's wife?"

"Yes, even though. He's a very busy man, and I love doing what I'm trained to do."

"Well, Maria is retiring because she needs more time to help her daughter. The minute she told me she wanted to play grandmother, well, naturally, we all thought of you."

She lifted a brow. *And Quinn.*

"You could have your old job back… Although, like I said, I wasn't at all sure you'd be interested now that you're *the* Mrs. Sullivan."

"Well, I am, so…this is wonderful news."

"Then you'll make yourself available for a meeting? No hurry, though. Don't want to pressure you."

"I'm available. In fact, I'm free for an hour or two this afternoon."

They agreed upon a time and hung up.

The call boosted her mood until she remembered how Quinn had rushed off to work this morning without even a goodbye. Until she remembered what a gorgeous couple he and Cristina had made on television. They were both so stylish and good-looking. They had business concerns in common, too.

With an effort, she quit thinking about Cristina and refocused on Gary's offer. She was glad Gary had called, even if it was her marriage to Quinn that had made her more attractive as a job applicant.

On a whim, she decided to call Quinn and run the job idea by him just to see what he'd say.

Oh, be honest, Kira, you just want to hear his sexy voice and distract him from Cristina.

Kira made the call, only to be deflated when his secretary told her, "I'll have him return your call. He's in a meeting."

"With whom?"

"Cristina Gold. They're taking a last look at the contracts for the EU deal before everything is finalized."

Don't ask a question if you don't want the answer.

"Would you please tell him...that I'll be on my cell."

"Are you all right, Mrs. Sullivan?"

"I'm fine," she whispered as she hung up.

Perfectly fine.

Clutching the phone to her breast, she sank onto her bed. She didn't feel fine. She felt more uncertain than ever.

Leave it alone. Cristina works for him. That's all there is to it. Go to Betty's. Do the interview with Gary. Forget your stupid nightmare.

But being pregnant had her feeling highly emotional. She couldn't leave it alone. She had to see him. After last night, she had to know how he felt.

Dressing hurriedly, she was in his office in less than an hour. The same beautiful blonde secretary who'd greeted her on her first visit greeted her again, more warmly this time.

"Mr. Sullivan told me you two are expecting a baby. He sounded so happy about it. Congratulations."

"Thank you."

"Would you like coffee? Or a soda?"

"I just want to talk to my husband. He didn't call me back, and since I was in the neighborhood…"

"I'm afraid he's still going over those contracts."

"With Miss Gold?"

The young woman nodded. "I'm afraid the documents are long and very complicated. A mistake could cost millions. Miss Gold is one of our attorneys, you see. She had several concerns."

"Please tell him I'm here."

After the young woman buzzed him, she looked up almost immediately. "He says he'll see you. Now."

Intending to lead her down the hall, she arose, but Kira held up a hand. "I remember the way."

When Kira reached his office, Cristina was just exiting with a thick sheaf of documents. She tossed Kira a tight smile. Behind Cristina, Quinn leaned negligently against the doorjamb.

When he opened the door, Kira said, "I hope I'm not interrupting."

"Glad that meeting's over. And doubly glad to see you." He shut the door. "I needed a break."

Despite the welcoming words, when their eyes met, she felt a sudden unbearable tension coming from him.

"Sorry I left so early this morning, but I had a couple of urgent texts."

"From Cristina?"

"One was. Unfortunately, I still have a lot of balls in the air related to the EU deal," he said.

"No problem."

"You look upset." His voice was flat.

"I didn't realize Cristina went to London with you… until I saw some of the news coverage on television."

A cynical black brow lifted. "I took a team of ten. She

was part of the team. She's very talented at what she does, or I never would have hired her."

"Not only is she talented, but she's beautiful, too."

He stood very still. "I imagine her looks are part of why she made it into so many of the TV shots. Look, there's no need for you to be jealous of her...if that's what this is."

"I'm not."

"I'm married to you, and whether you believe it or not, that means something to me."

What did it really mean if he could never love her?

"Since you obviously want to know more about Cristina and me," he began in the maddening, matter-of-fact tone of a lawyer presenting his case, "I'll clarify our relationship. We dated briefly. The press gave our romance more attention than it deserved.

"Then she broke up with me—for another man with whom she's still seriously involved. At the time, she complained I never had time for her. He did. Naturally, I was angry, but since then I've realized she was right."

"A vengeful man might have held what she did against her," she said coolly. "Why did you hire her?"

"We worked together on several projects before we dated. She will do a lot for Murray Oil."

"So, as always, business is all-important to you? Does nothing else ever matter? Not even your own injured feelings?"

He shrugged. "They weren't that injured. I got over her pretty quickly."

Would he get over Kira and be this matter-of-fact about it? At the thought, Kira cringed.

"Business will always be an important part of my life. I don't deny that. It's part of who I am. I hired her...before I met you." He paused. "What is it you want from me this morning, Kira?"

"Right. I'm interrupting you. You're a busy man. You probably have many more important meetings to get through today. All those balls in the air. And here I am, your pregnant, overly emotional wife needing reassurance."

He studied her warily. "What do you want, Kira?"

Why couldn't she be as cool and logical as he was? Because everything in her life was out of balance. She was pregnant and feeling needy. There were too many unanswered questions in their relationship, and she was still reeling from the discovery that she'd been adopted.

She wanted to belong somewhere, to someone. She wanted to matter to *Quinn*. If she'd been more important to him, wouldn't he have kept her in the loop while he was gone? Wouldn't he have shared more details concerning his oil deal?

"I guess I want the impossible," she blurted out. "I want a real marriage."

"Now you want a real marriage, when all along you've said that's the last thing you want? Last night you woke up crying from some dream, apparently about me, demanding 'strictly business.' You pushed me away as if you wanted nothing to do with me. If I give you space it's wrong. If I push myself on you it's wrong."

"I know I'm not making sense," she said. "Our marriage was never based on love, mutual understanding or anything that makes up a true partnership. I guess I'm upset because…because I don't know… I just know I can't go on like this!"

"As soon as I complete this deal, I'll have more time…"

"How will that matter if you don't want the same kind of marriage I do? Now, maybe because of the baby and finding out I was adopted, I have this huge need for things to be right between us. I want more. I've wanted more my whole life. I don't want to feel left out anymore. Most of all, I want to count to my husband."

"If you wanted to belong in this marriage, then why did you tell me from the first that you didn't want to sleep with me?"

"I guess to protect myself…from ever feeling like I feel now—needy…confused. I knew this marriage was only a business deal for you. I didn't want to get my heart broken," she whispered.

"What are you saying?"

"What we have isn't enough. Not for me…or for you."

"You're pregnant. We can't just walk away from each other. It's not about you and me anymore, or even Murray Oil. We have a child to think about now."

"That's all the more reason I don't want us trapped in a loveless marriage. I want a husband who can love me. I want my child to grow up in a loving home. After the deal you just made, the executives at Murray Oil trust you. You don't need to be married to me anymore. You can divorce me and date somebody who understands you, someone who can make you happy…someone like Cristina."

"Damn it. I don't want a divorce. Or Cristina. Like I said—if you'd ever once listen to me—she's practically engaged."

"But you don't love me…"

"Well, I damn sure don't love anyone else. And I'm not lusting after anybody else. I'm focused solely on you! You're very important to me, Kira. Vital. Still, it's true that I'm not sure I'll ever be capable of loving anyone—even you. Maybe I've been hard and dark and driven for too long."

"Well, I want a man who will commit his heart to me, or I want out."

"Okay," he said in a tone that was cold, infuriatingly

logical and final. "Now that our marriage has served its purpose, you want out. Well, I don't want out, and I'm not ready to let you go. But if that's what you want, I won't hold you against your will any longer."

"What?"

"I'll give you what you say you want. You're free to leave. But understand this—I intend to take an active role in raising our child."

"Of course," she whispered, feeling shattered.

"Then so be it," he said.

He stared at her, waiting for her to walk out the door, and, for a brief moment, his guard fell. She saw longing and pain flash in his eyes.

Suddenly, she realized just how much she'd wanted him to fight for her, for them.

After stumbling blindly out of his office, she sat behind the wheel of her car, clenching her keys in her hand. All her life she'd wanted someone to fight for her, someone to put her first. She'd had a right to push for more from her marriage.

He wasn't willing to fight for her as he'd fought for his oil deal in London, so she would do the fighting.

She would fight for her self-respect, and she would teach their child to fight for his, too.

Kira had been in no condition to be interviewed by Gary the afternoon she'd parted from Quinn, so she'd rescheduled.

Two miserable days later, she still didn't feel strong enough, but here she sat, facing Gary across his wide, cluttered desk in his flashy corner office that overlooked the museum grounds and the busy street that fronted the modern building.

If only she could stop thinking about Quinn and how

bereft she'd felt ever since he'd agreed to end their marriage.

Concentrating on Gary, who wasn't the most fascinating man, was difficult. Lately, everything had been difficult. Returning to Quinn's gorgeous loft, packing the beautiful clothes that she would no longer need and then moving back into her cramped apartment with her dead plants and resentful cat had been full of emotional hurdles.

Rudy wouldn't sit on her lap or use his scratching post. Only this morning he'd peed on her pillow just to show her how much he resented being abandoned.

"Quit feeling sorry for yourself! I'm the one who got married and pregnant…and separated," she'd yelled at him.

Swishing his tail, he'd flattened his ears and stalked indifferently to his bowl where he'd howled for more tuna.

She tried to pay attention to Gary, she really did, but her mind constantly wandered to her miserable new separated state and to Quinn and how cold he'd been right before he'd watched her walk away.

Suddenly, she found Gary's droning insufferable and longed to be anywhere else, even home alone with her sullen cat. If she didn't interrupt Gary, he might easily rant on for another half an hour.

"Gary, this is all very fascinating, but I need to ask a question."

He frowned.

"Is this job offer contingent on me remaining married to Quinn?"

"What?"

"Let me be blunt."

His mouth tightened. "You do that so well."

"Quinn and I have separated. Do you still want me for this job? "

His face fell. "Separated?" Flushing, he pushed himself

back from his desk. "Well, that does change things." Recovering quickly, he ran a nervous hand through his hair. "Still, I want you to work here, of course."

Her voice was equally silky as she leaned toward him. "*Of course.* I'm so glad we understand each other."

A few minutes later he hastily concluded the interview. "I'll call you," he said.

She left, wondering if he would.

As she stood on the curb outside the museum, about to cross the street, Jaycee called her on her cell.

"How are things going?"

"I've been better," Kira replied. "The interview with Gary went okay, I guess."

"And Rudy?"

"He peed on my pillow this morning."

"Well, you abandoned him. He's still mad at you."

"I guess. Hold on—"

Pressing the phone against her ear, she looked both ways to cross the street. But just as she jumped into the crosswalk a motorcycle made a left turn, going too fast.

She felt a surge of panic, but it was too late. In the next moment, she was hurled into the air.

It was true what they said about your life flashing before your eyes.

She saw Quinn's darkly handsome face and knew suddenly, without a doubt, that she loved him.

It didn't matter that he could never love her. Or maybe she knew, on some deep level, that he must love her, too—at least a little.

She remembered all the times he'd looked at her and she'd felt her soul join to his.

She'd been an idiot to walk out on the man she loved, to

abandon a man so afraid of love that he denied what was in his own heart. He needed her.

She wanted to get up and run back to his office. She wanted to beg him for another chance. But when she tried to sit up, her body felt as if it were made of concrete.

Someone knelt over her, but she couldn't see his face.

"Quinn," she cried. "I want Quinn."

The man spoke, but she couldn't hear what he said.

Then everything went black.

"A Jerry Sullivan is here to see you," Quinn's secretary informed him crisply. "Says he's family."

"Show him in," Quinn ordered in a dull voice as he set the lightning whelk Kira had given him back on the shelf. "He's my uncle. He'll want coffee with cream and sugar."

Uncle Jerry didn't wait for Quinn's secretary to return with his coffee before he pounced.

"Sorry to interrupt you, but I just heard you separated from your beautiful wife. I'd ask you to tell me it isn't true, but since you look like something my dog dragged in from the gutter, I won't bother."

"Good to see you, too, Uncle J."

"What the hell did you do to drive her away?"

"I never should have married her in the first place."

"If you let her go, you'll be making the biggest mistake of your life. You've already wasted too many years of your life alone."

"Let me be, why don't you?"

"You're still in love with her. I can see it!"

"The hell I am. Did anybody ever tell you to mind your own business?"

"Sure. You. Plenty of times. Good thing I've got better sense than to listen to the likes of an upstart nephew who doesn't have a clue about what's good for him."

"I think some men are better off single. And I'm probably one of them."

"Bull. I saw the way you were with her. You're like your father. He was the most loving man I ever knew."

"And what did it get him—other than a broken heart and an early grave?"

"You're not your father. Kira's not Esther. Kira's the real thing. Esther was a beautiful woman who knew how to play your dad. And, yes, your dad foolishly loved her with all his heart—just like he loved you. But when you get down to it, even when you're wrong about the people you love, loving is still the best way to live. That's why we still miss Kade. He loved us all so much!"

"My father killed himself because my mother left him."

"You'll never make me believe that! Kade wouldn't ever deliberately walk out on you. You were everything to him. His death was an accident."

"Uncle Jerry, thanks for coming by."

"Great. Now you're giving me the brush-off."

"I know you mean well…but I'm a grown man—"

"Who has the right to screw up his life royally and who's doing a damn good job of it."

"If you've said your piece, I've got work to do."

"You've always got work to do! Maybe it's time you got a life." Uncle Jerry smiled grimly. "Okay, I'll leave you to it, not that it's any fun watching my favorite nephew walk out on the best thing that ever happened to him."

"I didn't walk out on her! Damn it! She left me!"

"So, quit sulking, and go after her!"

"If only it were that easy!"

"Trust me—it is. The only thing stopping you is your damn arrogance."

"Get the hell out of here!"

Holding a silver tray with a coffee cup, Quinn's secretary pushed the door open and would have entered except Quinn held up a hand. "Uncle Jerry won't be having coffee after all. He's leaving."

For some time after his uncle had gone, Quinn sat in his office and seethed. Slowly, as he cooled down, everything the older man had said began replaying in his mind. Since his father's death, Uncle Jerry was the one person Quinn had been able to count on.

Quinn walked over to the shelf where he'd placed the lightning whelk. How full of hope he'd felt when she'd given it to him. He remembered her shining eyes, her glowing beauty.

Turning away, he grabbed his cell phone. For a long moment he just held it.

Quinn didn't just want to call Kira for his own selfish reasons. He was genuinely worried about her and the baby. The longer he went without talking to her, the more worried he grew. Would it be so wrong to call just to make sure she and the baby were all right? Would it? Even if they never got back together, she was the mother of his future child.

Swallowing his pride, he lifted his phone and punched in her number. As he waited for her to answer, his gut clenched.

Then, on the third ring, a man answered.

"I want Kira," Quinn thundered. "I need to speak to my wife."

"Sir, I'm so sorry. I'm terribly afraid there's been an accident…"

The man introduced himself as someone working at the local hospital. He said something about a motorcycle hitting Kira and that Kira had been taken to his emergency room by ambulance. After getting the specifics, Quinn hung up and was grabbing his jacket and on his way to the door, when Earl Murray rang his cell phone.

Quinn picked up on the first ring. "I just heard Kira's been hurt."

"Apparently, Jaycee was talking to her when the motor-cycle hit her... I don't know anything else."

"Then I'll meet you at the hospital," Quinn said. His heart was in his throat as he bolted out of his office in a dead run, praying he wouldn't be too late.

Sixteen

Quinn had never been as scared in his life as he was when he stood over Kira watching the IV drip clear liquid into her veins. Her narrow face had the awful grayish tint Quinn had seen only one time before—on his father's face as he'd lain in a pool of his own blood.

"Tell me she's going to be all right. Tell me the baby's all right."

"I've told you," the doctor repeated patiently. "Apparently, she was thrown onto the pavement, but seems to have suffered only a concussion and a few bruises. After a night or two of rest, she and the baby will be fine. She's one lucky young lady."

"You're sure?" For some reason, the facts weren't sticking in Quinn's head as they usually did.

"As sure as I can be under the circumstances."

"When will she wake up?"

"Like I told you before—soon. You just have to be patient."

An hour later, the longest hour of Quinn's life, her long lashes fluttered. Sensing that she was struggling to focus on him, Quinn gripped her hand and leaned forward.

"Kira… Darlin'…"

"Quinn… I wanted you to come. I wanted it so much."

"Kira, you're in a hospital. You're going to be okay. The baby, too."

"I love you," she said softly. "I was such a fool."

Rather than terrifying him, those three words brought a rush of joy.

"I love you, too. More than anything." He squeezed her hand tightly. "So much it scares the hell out of me."

It had only taken her admission to make him brave enough to admit his own feelings for her.

With glistening eyes, she laughed softly. "You really love me?"

"Yes. Maybe even from the first moment I saw you. I just didn't know what had hit me." He paused. "Jaycee's here, along with your parents. We've all been so scared for you and the baby. Half out of our minds."

"They're all here, too?"

"Of course we're here," her father roared.

Kira smiled radiantly up at them. "It's almost worth getting hit by a motorcycle to have all of you all here… together, knowing…knowing that you love me."

They moved closer, circling her bed. Holding hands, they smiled down at her. "Of course we love you," her father said. "You're our girl."

"You gave us a terrible scare," her mother said. "You're very important to all of us."

"I'm so happy," Kira whispered. "I've never been happier."

"By the way," her father said, "your old boss called and said you'd better get well soon because you've got a big job at the museum waiting for you. So, no more waitressing…'

Kira smiled weakly. "I guess that's good news…but not nearly as good as all of you being here." Her grip on Quinn's hand tightened as she looked up at him. "I never, ever want to let go of you again."

"You won't have to."

Quinn needed no further encouragement to lean forward and kiss her. Very carefully, so as not to hurt her, he pressed his mouth to her lips.

As always, she gave her entire being to him, causing warmth and happiness to flow from her soul into his.

She was everything to him. He would love her and cherish her always, or at least until the last breath left his body.

"Darlin'," he whispered. "Promise me you'll never leave me again."

She nodded. "Never. I swear it. Like I said, I was a fool."

Circling his neck with her hands, she brought his face down to hers and kissed him again.

Epilogue

One Year Later
July the Fourth
Wimberley, Texas

Kira looked across the green lawns that sloped down to cypress trees shading the sparkling river. The air stirring through the leaves was warm, while the water was clear and icy.

Kira couldn't believe her happiness. Ever since that afternoon in the hospital, when she'd awakened to Quinn and her family gathered around her bed, her happiness had grown a little every day.

Despite the pain in her shoulder and back, she'd seen the love shining in all their eyes.

Love for her.

Had it always been there? Whether it had or not, all her doubts about herself, about Quinn, about her adoption, had vanished. She'd simply known that she mattered—to all of them.

She belonged.

Knowing she was truly loved, her confidence had grown in every aspect of her life, including in her career as a curator. Naturally, Gary had been thrilled that she was to remain Mrs. Sullivan. Quinn had thrilled him even more by being most generous to the museum, stipulating with every donation that his wife be in charge of the funds.

This lazy summer afternoon on the grounds of the Sullivans' new weekend home on the Blanco was perfect for a July Fourth celebration that included friends, family and business associates. The star of the show was only a few months old.

Thomas Kade Sullivan fulfilled his mother's most fervent hopes as he sat on his red-and-blue quilt by the water, holding court. He shook his rattle while Aunt Jaycee laughed and held up a stuffed bunny rabbit. With his brilliant blue eyes, Tommy Kade was every bit as handsome as his father.

Off to one side, a band played as their guests took turns swimming in the cool waters or serving themselves barbecue.

Quinn left the men he'd been talking to and walked up to her. Grinning down at her, he circled her with his arms. Contentment made her feel soft and warm as he held her close. Never had she dreamed she'd feel this complete with anyone.

She smiled at the sight of her mother ordering the caterers about. With her illness in remission, her mother was her old formidable self. When Vera had been well enough for Kira's dad to leave her at home, Quinn had made a place for him at Murray Oil.

"Murray Oil's too big for one man to run," Quinn had said when Kira had tried to thank him.

Life was good, she thought as her husband brushed his lips against her cheek. Very good.

"Happy July Fourth," Quinn said.

"The happiest ever."

"For me, too. Because you're in my life," he murmured huskily. "You're the best thing that ever happened to me... besides Tommy Kade. And you're responsible for him, too."

"Stop. We're at a party. We have to behave."

"Maybe I don't want to behave."

He drew her away from the crowd into the shade of the towering cypress trees. Once they were hidden from their guests, he wrapped her in his arms and kissed her long and deeply.

"I love you," he whispered. "I love you, and I always will. We have a real marriage, now—wouldn't you agree?"

The most wonderful thing of all was that she knew it and accepted it—down to her bones—because she felt exactly the same way. "I would! And I love you, too," she murmured. "Oh, how I love you."

* * * * *

LET'S TALK
Romance

For exclusive extracts, competitions
and special offers, find us online:

 facebook.com/millsandboon

 @MillsandBoon

 @MillsandBoonUK

Get in touch on 01413 063232

For all the latest titles coming soon, visit
millsandboon.co.uk/nextmonth

MILLS & BOON
A ROMANCE FOR EVERY READER

FREE delivery direct to your door

EXCLUSIVE offers every month

SAVE up to 25% on pre-paid subscriptions

SUBSCRIBE AND SAVE

millsandboon.co.uk/Subscribe

WANT EVEN MORE

ROMANCE?

SUBSCRIBE AND SAVE TODAY!

'Mills & Boon books, the perfect way to escape for an hour or so.'

MISS W. DYER

'Excellent service, promptly delivered and very good subscription choices.'

MISS A. PEARSON

'You get fantastic special offers and the chance to get books before they hit the shops.'

MRS V. HALL

Visit millsandboon.co.uk/Subscribe and save on brand new books.

JOIN THE
MILLS & BOON
BOOKCLUB

* **FREE** delivery direct to your door

* **EXCLUSIVE** offers every month

* **EXCITING** rewards programme

50% OFF
YOUR FIRST
PARCEL

Join today at
Millsandboon.co.uk/Bookclub

MILLS & BOON

THE HEART OF ROMANCE

A ROMANCE FOR EVERY READER

MODERN

Prepare to be swept off your feet by sophisticated, sexy and seductive heroes, in some of the world's most glamourous and roma locations, where power and passion collide.

HISTORICAL

Escape with historical heroes from time gone by. Whether your passi for wicked Regency Rakes, muscled Vikings or rugged Highlanders, the romance of the past.

MEDICAL

Set your pulse racing with dedicated, delectable doctors in the high-p sure world of medicine, where emotions run high and passion, comfo love are the best medicine.

True Love

Celebrate true love with tender stories of heartfelt romance, from th rush of falling in love to the joy a new baby can bring, and a focus on emotional heart of a relationship.

Desire

Indulge in secrets and scandal, intense drama and plenty of sizzling action with powerful and passionate heroes who have it all: wealth, st good looks…everything but the right woman.

HEROES

Experience all the excitement of a gripping thriller, with an intense r mance at its heart. Resourceful, true-to-life women and strong, fearle face danger and desire - a killer combination!

To see which titles are coming soon, please visit

millsandboon.co.uk/nextmonth